SHROUD of
PROPHECY
BOOK ONE

FATE
OF THE
FALLEN

KEL KADE

TOR

**A TOM DOHERTY
ASSOCIATES BOOK**

NEW YORK

FATE OF THE FALLEN

Copyright © 2019 by Dark Rover Publishing LLC

A Tor Book
Published by Tom Doherty Associates
120 Broadway
New York, NY 10271

www.tor-forge.com

Tor® is a registered trademark of Macmillan Publishing Group, LLC.

The Library of Congress Cataloging-in-Publication Data is available upon request.

ISBN 978-1-250-29379-4 (hardcover)
ISBN 978-1-250-29380-0 (ebook)

Our books may be purchased in bulk for promotional, educational, or business use. Please contact your local bookseller or the Macmillan Corporate and Premium Sales Department at 1-800-221-7945, extension 5442, or by email at MacmillanSpecialMarkets@macmillan.com.

First Edition: November 2019

Printed in the United States of America

0 9 8 7 6 5 4 3 2 1

CONTENTS

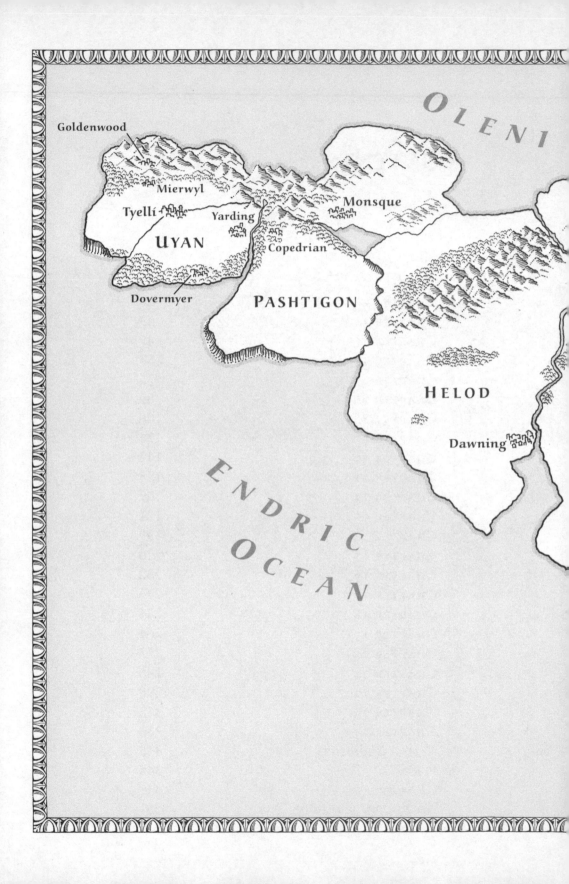

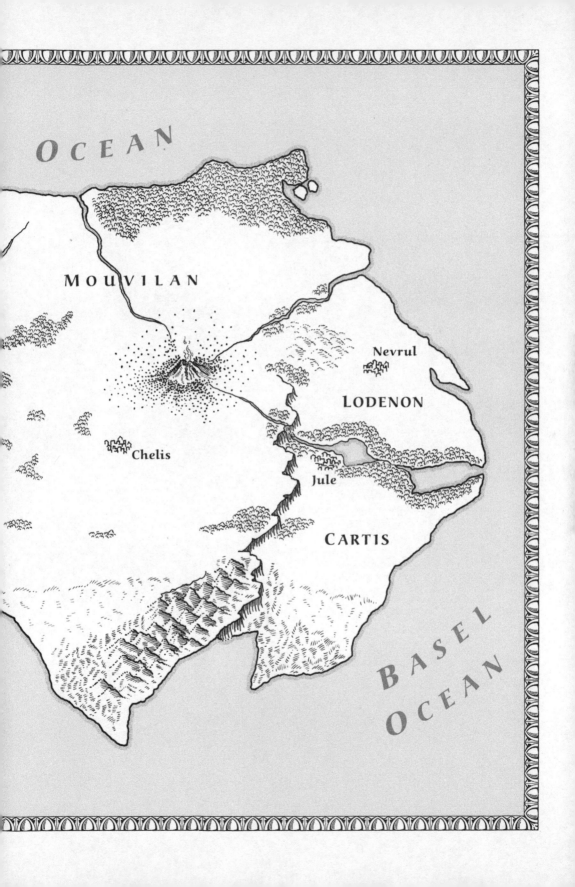

FATE
OF THE
FALLEN

PROLOGUE

"You have all heard of the time when the dead didn't tread upon the land?"

The sea of youthful faces shone with the golden light of the hearth. The children nodded, expressions flooded with concern or fear. Even so, they were spellbound, as they were every night at this time, when they huddled on the floor surrounded by adults who gathered in chairs or leaned against the walls.

I turned to gaze out the window. The children's curiosity prompted them to follow my lead. By the silvery light of the moon, we could see the wanderers ambling in the dark. Their cloudy gazes appeared distant as they searched. Their pale flesh was frigid blue in the moonlight, cold as the late autumn night. The front door rattled, and everyone jumped. It failed to open, and the wanderer moved on, passing by the window without a glance.

Beside me, young Corin gripped his older brother's hand. "I don't like to think about it," he said.

I mussed the boy's hair and replied, "We cannot ignore the truth just because we don't like it. It's important to understand how the world became the way it is so that we can learn and grow. Survival is never guaranteed. In fact, it's quite the opposite."

Corin glanced up at his brother, then back to me with a nod.

I leaned back in my chair and recalled the words of my mother, the same words spoken by her father and his before him. "The living once walked this world alone. They worked the land, growing sustenance for themselves and their children. They built homes and palaces. They sailed the seas, explored distant lands, and shared their dreams in artwork and mesmerizing enactments. Wizards and witches, mages and sorcerers, and all sorts of other magi performed feats great and small with their wondrous magic. For seculars like ourselves, life was made easier.

"Back then, when a person's time was finished, his or her soul passed into the next realm, and the body was laid to rest—to rot—beneath the ground." I met their pensive stares and leaned forward. "That was before the dead rose, before the Grave War—before the King of the Dead stole the power of a god."

A few of the younger children gasped, while the older ones, having already heard the story, grinned with excitement. Waving my hand over their heads, I said, "Look around the room, and listen well, for one day, you may be the one to tell the story. For countless ages, men have been ruled by prophecy, but what happens when the path of good and right, the triumph of light over darkness, the only path to salvation . . . *fails*?

"It begins in a forest . . ."

CHAPTER 1

"Why?" Mathias said as he stared down at the back of his best friend's head.

Aaslo patted the rich soil around the base of the sapling, then stood. "Why what?"

Wind surged through the trees, rustling their green and gold leaves and nearly whipping the dirty rag from Mathias's fingers as he held it out for Aaslo. "Why won't you go with Elanee to the dance? She wants to go with you."

Aaslo took the proffered rag and dragged it across his soiled hands, but Mathias wondered if they weren't becoming dirtier for the effort. Aaslo probably didn't notice, and if he did, he likely didn't care. The forester seemed the most content when he was covered in dirt and leaves. Aaslo didn't immediately answer the question, either. He never did. Mathias waited, knowing that Aaslo would mull over every conceivable reply before settling on one. While others might consider it irritating, Mathias found comfort in knowing that whatever Aaslo finally said had been well considered. He had long since lost any frustration with his friend's oddities. The foresters had their own strange way of looking at things.

Aaslo's mouth twisted in consternation before he met Mathias's gaze. His eyes were the dark, rich green of an ancient forest hiding epic mysteries. His fingers scratched his scruffy jawline, leaving a smear of dirt in their wake. Finally, Aaslo grumbled, "You know I'm going with Reyla."

"You asked her?" Mathias said, already knowing the answer.

Aaslo's lips turned down a well-worn path to a frown. "Why would I need to ask her? We always go together."

Mathias shrugged and tossed a golden lock from his eyes. "I'm just saying, if you don't ask her, how do you know she plans to go with you? Just because you went together to the last dance—"

"And the one before—and each of the six before that," said Aaslo.

"Right," Mathias replied, "but it doesn't mean she's planning to go with you to *this* one."

Aaslo huffed as he scraped the mud from his boot on one of the many stumps that dotted the dense forest that had been recently visited by the loggers. "That's ridiculous. She knows I'm making progress on the house. Pa and I set the beams yesterday. It'll be ready to move into in a few months, and Reyla and I'll be married. There's no reason for her to go to the dance with anyone else."

Mathias's gaze was drawn to the tops of the tall pines where they bent under the force of the wind. He looked back to Aaslo and said, "True, but I still think you should ask her. Women like that kind of thing, you know."

Aaslo checked his tools, then slung the bag containing all his forestry supplies over his shoulder. Glad he wasn't carrying the bulky monstrosity that looked to weigh as much as his friend, Mathias picked up his much smaller pack, containing their water and lunch, and followed Aaslo through the trees. He never worried about getting lost. He was quite certain Aaslo could navigate the forest blindfolded in a blizzard.

After walking in silence for several minutes, Aaslo said, "Who are you going to ask?"

Mathias grinned to himself as he pictured how Neasey would react when he asked her—or maybe Arielle. Then he remembered a promise he had made at the previous dance.

"I guess I'll have to take Jessi. She was pretty upset when I went with Laney to the last one. She said I should have taken her first since *J* comes before *L*."

Aaslo glanced over his shoulder. "You're taking them in alphabetical order?"

Mathias's laughter was swallowed by the crackling of limbs and leaves as another gust tore through the timbers. "No, that hadn't been my plan, but I guess it's as good as any." He groaned when Aaslo stopped and pointed to a clump of mushrooms growing from the side of a tree.

"That one," said the forester.

"I don't see why I have to know that, Aaslo. I'm not a forester."

Aaslo rounded on him, his jaw tightening as the wind touseled his shaggy brown hair. He crossed his meaty arms and stared at Mathias. Although Aaslo was a few inches shorter than he, the forester was strong—a condition bred by a lifetime of lugging equipment and planting and maintaining the trees of the Efestrian Forest. Still, Mathias knew he could take Aaslo down if needed, since he won every two out of three sparring matches. He waited for Aaslo to say something, and eventually he did.

"If I have to learn the letters and numbers, and histories and sciences—"

Mathias threw up his hands. "Come on, Aaslo, that's different."

"—and maps and cultures, and languages and fighting—"

"*Aas*—"

"—then *you* can learn the forest."

With a heavy sigh, Mathias said, "All right, I get that, but I have no use for mushrooms. I don't even like the taste. What you're learning with Grams is useful."

Aaslo grunted. "How is knowing that Akyelek is the official language in Mouvilan useful? It's on the other side of the world. I'll never go there, and I'll probably never meet a Mouvilanian, either."

Mathias hopped onto one of the many fresh stumps and spread his arms. "The world is huge and full of mysteries! Where's your sense of adventure, Aaslo?"

Aaslo's gaze bore into him as if he were staring down an enemy. "Words shouldn't be wasted on telling you things you already know."

With a chuckle, Mathias said, "That sounds like something your father would say."

Aaslo nodded. "It is."

Mathias crossed his arms. "It's not like you get a limited number of words to use in your lifetime. You're not going to run out."

"That's what I always say," Aaslo said with a smile. It was more of a smirk, but it was the closest to a smile that Mathias had ever seen. Aaslo's expression soured again, and he said, "Still, it applies. You know I have no desire to leave this forest or Goldenwood—*ever*. There's nothing but trouble out *there*, and everything important can be found right here."

Mathias raised his brow. "Important like the mushroom?"

"Yes," Aaslo said with a curt nod, "because the mushroom is right here in front of us, and if not for your grandmother, we wouldn't even know Mouvilan existed."

As usual, Mathias was both humbled and amused by Aaslo's artless mind-set. His gaze dropped to the bright orange mushroom, and he sighed. "*Laetiporus*?"

Aaslo nodded once. "Good enough. Couldn't have been any easier."

Mathias grinned as Aaslo turned back to the path that only he and other foresters could see. He was glad the foresters kept the underbrush to a minimum; otherwise the hike would have been much more strenuous and Aaslo would have had a plethora of foliage over which to quiz him. Although his friend would never admit it, Mathias knew that Aaslo enjoyed teaching him about the forest. A bud of mischief began to unravel inside him, and Mathias said, "You can lose the pride, Aaslo. You know I'll be ripping it *and* your hide in the practice yard this afternoon."

Aaslo didn't turn as he answered. "Probably, but I'll be sure to make you a bit prettier for Jessi. A black eye and split lip should go well with whatever absurd poetry you spout."

"Did I say Jessi? Maybe I meant Reyla."

Aaslo's machete sliced the air, lopping the top off a toadstool. "You even joke about that, and I'll remove your head."

Satisfaction bloomed as he successfully penetrated the forester's thick skin, and Mathias said, "You can try, but I got Cromley to teach me a new form. I was going to make it a surprise, but it's more fun to watch you sweat."

Aaslo whacked a tangle of vines in their path and groused, "If that old captain is going to give anyone an advantage, it should be me. I come away more bruised than you even when I win."

"You do," Mathias conceded, "but that's not the point."

"And what *is* the point?" Aaslo said with a glance.

Mathias grinned broadly. "To beat you, of course."

Aaslo shook his head, then continued with his survey of the third sector, planting, transplanting, fertilizing, trimming, and treating trees and other plants important to the forest ecosystem for their ailments. Mathias didn't care for the work, but going to the forest was the most adventure his grams had ever allowed and only in the company of Aaslo or Ielo. He had never even been to Mierwyl, where the villagers of Goldenwood traded for most of their food. It would have been only a three-day ride if he'd had a horse, which he didn't. Grams had a horse, but she would have rained fire and devastation down on his head if he had taken it without asking, not that she would approve if he did. Thus, he was stuck tromping through damp leaves as more showered his hair and clothes with each gust. Aaslo had finished his inspection of the youngest saplings by the time the sun began its descent. The hike back to the village was more direct but steeper. To Aaslo's amusement, Mathias had managed to don almost as much dirt as the forester.

After an unplanned slide halfway down a slope of loose soil and scree, Mathias picked himself up on shaky legs and said, "I don't know why I came with you." He swept damp dirt and leaves from his rear while Aaslo waited patiently at the base with crossed arms.

"You secretly like being in the forest," Aaslo replied.

Mathias scowled down at him. "No, I like being out of the house. It's not the same thing. You know I don't get out much when Grams is home—except for practice and work, anyway."

Aaslo frowned. "This *is* work."

Mathias was grateful when he successfully made it to level ground without another messy incident. "This is *your* work," he said. "That's different. Besides, I'd only be stuck with my nose in those musty old books at home. Don't get me wrong. I like to learn. It's just that it seems like she wants me to learn all of the knowledge of the world, and for what? She won't even take me with her on her travels. I *could* be helping the merchant master take the goods to Mierwyl, or I *could* be going with you over the mountain, but no. *Stay home, Mathias.* When am *I* going to see the world? Never."

"Well," Aaslo said, pausing to rub his scruffy chin, "everyone says you'll be town mayor someday. I guess the mayor needs to be pretty smart, and you'll get the chance to travel to regional meetings."

They turned down the path toward Mathias's home, which lay on the outskirts of the village that was nestled a hundred yards ahead in an open expanse where once resided a small meadow. A rocky perimeter surrounding the entire town had been cleared of trees and undergrowth to prevent Goldenwood from burning down in the event of a forest fire. Mathias mulled over Aaslo's observation as they tromped through talus that had been painstakingly spread over the area to deter new growth.

Eventually, he said, "I don't know, Aaslo. Mayor Toca doesn't seem to be the most learned man. He didn't even know who Parshia was."

"Nobody knows who Parshia was," Aaslo said, "except you and me and Grams."

"The people of Lodenon know."

"And nobody around here knows Lodenon exists, therefore Parshia didn't exist. Mayor Toca doesn't need to know anything about Parshia."

"Exactly, so why do I need to know about her?"

Neither spoke for a few minutes as the crunch of gravel underfoot took them farther from the rustling of the forest and closer to the clangs and shouts of the town. When they were within a few yards of the first building, Aaslo said, "I see your point."

Mathias glanced at his friend, who was still frowning in contemplation. "About what you said this morning—you know you don't have to take the lessons with me."

Aaslo's head jerked up, and he spun, forcing Mathias to draw up short. The forester looked at him as if he had just lost his mind. "Of course I do," Aaslo snapped. His face had darkened, and his eyes sparked with anger. Mathias immediately regretted bringing it up when his friend said, "It's like you always say—brothers in all things." Aaslo nodded toward the mountain. "It's why you come to the forest with me when you don't have to. Now stop saying stupid things." Without waiting for a response, Aaslo turned toward town.

Goldenwood was busy in the afternoon, but the incessant wind prevented many from straying beyond their porches. There, in that man-made hole in the forest, the unfettered breeze tossed hats from heads, snagged curls from coifs, and tore linens from lines. Still, the townsfolk smiled and hollered greetings as Mathias and Aaslo trod through the village center. Most of the paths were made of dirt, hard-packed by years of foot traffic, with wagon ruts carved down the centers of the wider lanes. In the more prominent areas, wooden boardwalks prevented the tragic loss of footwear during the wet months, and these were kept in good repair by the town's loggers and carpenters, which was most everyone. The wooden buildings faced the village center, and most were painted in bright colors, in stark contrast to the dark forest that surrounded them.

Mathias glanced back at his friend, who now trailed behind him. As usual, the moment they'd set foot in town, Aaslo had allowed Mathias to take the lead. The forester's shoulders slumped forward, his chin brushed his chest, and he barely raised his eyes to meet the appreciative stares of the onlookers. Aaslo was one of the few foresters who ventured into town more than a few times per year, but most of the townsfolk knew by now not to pester him. Mathias turned his gaze back to the path in front of him and abruptly stopped.

"Hello, Mathias!" called Mr. Greenly as he stepped from his office to greet them. The man pushed his spectacles onto the bridge of his nose, leaving a smudge of ink on the tip. "You boys been out in the woods today? Seems a mite gusty for outdoor work, if you ask me."

In a barely audible grumble, Aaslo said, "I'm surprised he knows the outdoors exists."

Mathias knew that the aged Mr. Greenly couldn't have heard, but he gave his friend a reproachful scowl anyway. Aaslo only shrugged and went back to tracing the planks with the toe of his boot.

Mathias turned and smiled at the elderly bookkeeper. "Hello, Mr. Greenly. The breeze wasn't so terrible in the forest. I'd say we had the better luck."

"Wasn't luck," Aaslo mumbled. "Trees are good for more than chopping to pieces."

Mr. Greenly turned his azure gaze toward Aaslo. "What's that? I didn't quite catch it."

Aaslo glanced at Mathias with a frown, perturbed by having been heard. He raised his voice. "I said the forest takes care of those who care for it."

Mr. Greenly nodded and smiled. "Quite so and said like a true forester. This town would have died long ago if not for you kind wood folk. My grandpappy told me of a time before the foresters. The trees disappeared, and whole villages died out. People had to pick up and leave their homes, their friends—all because they'd go and chop the whole forest down without thinking it through." The man squinted, his gaze turning toward the treetops. "Seems like there's so many. Couldn't imagine they'd run out, you know." The bookkeeper turned back to the forester. "You know we all appreciate your sacrifice, we do. It can't be easy spending your life away from everyone, planting trees and caring for them—just so we can chop them down again."

Aaslo shifted his pack and ducked his head noncommittally, but Mr. Greenly seemed satisfied with the acknowledgment. Mathias knew that Aaslo felt it was a greater sacrifice each time he *left* the forest.

Mathias cleared his throat to get Mr. Greenly's attention. And then cleared it again. The older man continued to stare at the forester, and Mathias could tell that Aaslo wasn't enjoying the scrutiny. Mathias raised his voice and said, "Sorry, Mr. Greenly, but we need to get going. Captain Cromley is expecting us. It was good see you."

Mr. Greenly blinked several times, as if awakening from a daze. "What's that? Oh, yes, of course, Mathias. Please tell your grandmother that Eleanor and I would love to have you two over for dinner soon." He turned to Aaslo and said, "You and your father are welcome, too, of course, Sir Forester."

Aaslo nodded and with practiced civility said, "Thank you for the invitation, Mr. Greenly, but I must respectfully decline."

Mr. Greenly nodded knowingly, then stepped back into his office, clearing the way for them to finish the short walk to Mathias's home.

"How many times do we have to hear about the *time before the foresters*?" Aaslo grumbled.

Mathias glanced back at his friend with a grin as he stepped from the boardwalk to cut across the square. "*Every* time."

When they reached the paving stones that surrounded the fountain, Mathias paused. The wind brushed across his ears, muffling the sound, but he was nearly certain that it carried his name. He caught a flash of color from the corner of his eye just as Aaslo groaned.

"Mathias!"

This time, the voice was clear and feminine. Mathias's grin returned as he slapped Aaslo on the back. "Now's your chance, brother. Your fair lady approaches."

Reyla, Jessi, and Mirana advanced in their direction with a gaggle of girls in their wake. Mathias imagined that, had they been in a larger town, the women wouldn't have accepted the younger girls into their company; but companions were scarce in Goldenwood, especially when so many of their peers were already with child or busy caring for infants of their own.

"Hello, Reyla," said Aaslo.

Reyla glanced at Aaslo and smiled sweetly as she pulled a lock of wind-whipped hair from her face. "Hi, Aaslo. How was the forest?"

"Would have been better with you there. I visited our tree. It's already grown to nearly twice my height—a good sign."

Mathias noticed Reyla's smile tighten and the light in her eyes retreat. It wasn't the first time he had seen the reaction, but Aaslo never seemed to notice.

She said, "That's nice." Then she turned to Mathias. She tilted her head as she twisted an errant lock around one finger. "So, Mathias, have you decided who you'll ask to the dance?"

Mathias glanced at Jessi and Mirana and feigned confusion. Opening his palms to the sky, he said, "What dance? I, ah, have to get home. Grams'll be roiling if I'm late." He turned to Aaslo, pointed to where the path reentered the forest on the other side of the square, and said, "I'll wait for you there while you speak with Reyla."

Jessi and Mirana exchanged a mischievous glance.

"We'll come with you," said Jessi.

Mirana added, "We should give Reyla and Forester Aaslo some privacy."

Both women grinned at Reyla, who seemed less than pleased when she returned the courtesy, saying, "Thank you. You're both such dears."

Mathias returned Aaslo's smirk with a proud nod as Jessi and Mirana pulled him across the square, each clinging to an arm.

AASLO GAZED AT REYLA WHILE SHE STARED AFTER HER FRIENDS. HER long, slender neck and alabaster skin were reminiscent of the aspens that peacefully dotted the mountain. The mahogany mane that draped over her shoulders had the soft appearance of a willow swaying in the breeze. She turned to him, her eyes grey like the sky after a storm, and her pert lips pink as the petals of the cherry blossom. She smiled and looked at him expectantly, although it seemed she already knew what would be said. As she *should*, he thought. Mathias was being an idiot for suggesting this.

Aaslo cleared his throat and forced himself to say the words that needn't be said. "Reyla, will you go to the dance with me?"

Her smile fell. "I—um—thought you weren't going to ask me this time."

"I wasn't," Aaslo grumbled. "Needless words for an obvious out-come. We always go together—but Mathias thought you might want me to ask anyway. He says it's romantic."

Pleasure teased at her lips, but she didn't smile. "Well, as you say, we always go together. I was thinking of going with someone else this time."

Aaslo's stomach sank like a rock. "Someone else? *Why?*"

Reyla reached up to gather her hair and twisted it into a rope over one shoulder. When it was under control, she said, "It's fun. Everyone else goes with different people—except the married couples, of course."

"Exactly," Aaslo said, glad to hear some sense at last. "Our house will be finished soon. If we are to be married, there's no point in going with anyone else."

"Um . . . about that," Reyla said with a glance toward her friends.

Aaslo looked as well. Mirana and Jessi were shamelessly compet-ing for Mathias's attention while the younger girls gawked and giggled. As a forester, Aaslo had received his fair share of attention, but he had made it clear that he only wanted Reyla. He turned back to her and said, "About what?"

She looked at him, but her gaze did not venture above his chest. She said, "You've been talking about marriage for a while, I know, but we've never really agreed on anything—"

"What are you talking about?" Aaslo said as his heart attempted to tear its way out of his chest, and his blood heated beyond comfort. He looked around to see if the world was staring. They received no more than a passing glance as people ducked into shops and homes to es-cape the howling wind. He knew that even if the whole town had gath-ered to watch his world crumble, the words would not have reached their ears. Turning back to her, he said, "You approved of the house plans. You said you like the location."

She nodded slowly. "Yes, but you only asked for my opinion. I do like it—for *you.*"

"You knew what we were talking about," he said.

Shaking her head, she said, "No, I couldn't have known what you were thinking."

Aaslo gave her a disparaging look filled with the protests he wouldn't voice. He knew by her expression that she understood.

"Okay, that's not true," she conceded, "but you never *asked.* I thought you would ask, and then I could tell you how I really felt."

"Tell me what? You don't want to marry me?" A gust rushed past, and it felt as though the words had been snatched from his lips only to smack him in the face.

She laid her fingers on his chest and finally met his gaze. "It's not that, Aaslo. You're great—wonderful even. It's just that—I want to marry someone else."

"But I can give you everything you need," he said. "You're special, Reyla. You deserve to be given the respect of a forester's wife. It's an honor."

Reyla shook her head vigorously. "You and the other foresters are worthy of that honor, but I'm not prepared to make the sacrifice."

Collecting her shaking hands, he caught her gaze. "It's not a sacrifice, Reyla. The forest is a blessing, and we foresters are honored to live in her embrace and contribute to her glory."

She pulled her hands away and occupied them with reclaiming her hair from the relentless currents. "I don't want to live in the forest. I'm afraid of the wild, and I don't want to be so far from my friends and family."

"You were never afraid before—during all those walks and picnics."

"That's because you were with me. I trust you. I knew you would keep me safe."

"As I would my wife."

"If I were your wife, you would not always be there. You would be off in the forest, and I would be trapped in the house too afraid to leave."

Aaslo pulled his hood over his head. Feelings he hadn't considered since his youth welled within him, threatening to drip from his eyes. "You know my mother felt the same. At least you realized it before we married." He swallowed the lump in his throat. "You've waited this long. Most of our peers are already married or betrothed. If not me, then who?"

Reyla glanced toward her friends, but Aaslo knew what truly held her attention. His overheated blood froze, as though all the life within his body had been extinguished in an instant. She looked back to him with tears in her eyes.

"I'm sorry, Aaslo. I've already asked my father to approach Ms. Brelle with a proposal. Don't look at me like that. I know what you're thinking. Of all people, why him? I swear, if not for him, it would be you." She said it as if to make him feel better and then went on to make it worse. "But he's *Mathias*. He's handsome and smart and romantic. He'll be mayor someday. Everyone knows it. Mayor's wife is a position better suited to my tastes. I might even get to travel with him to see Fernvalle or Dempsy. Can you imagine?"

"I'd rather not imagine it," Aaslo muttered. "I'd rather not imagine any of it. My best friend—my *brother*—with the woman I was to marry. Are you so cruel as to wish that upon my imagination?"

"Oh, Aaslo, I didn't mean—"

"No," Aaslo said, "I apologize. I said too much." His was an echo of his father's voice battering against his heart. "Words erupted of emotional turmoil will be tumultuous at best. Tremulous gales break boughs and topple timbers, but peace and serenity encourage growth."

Reyla blinked at him, then wiped the moisture from her eyes. "I don't understand."

"Don't worry about it," he said. "It's a forester's wisdom—one that I've too often failed to appreciate. I'll heed it now for both our sakes."

Reyla started to speak, but he held up a hand. He had heard something. Beneath the howling gale, beyond the thump of loose shutters and cracking of distant limbs, a pulse thundered through the ground. He reached for Reyla just as Mathias crashed into him. Drawing her tight against his chest, Aaslo pulled Reyla to the ground with him, bracing himself so as not to crush her in the fall. He stared at her as she blinked up at him in startlement; then he was yanked from the ground by his collar. Aaslo stumbled over his feet as Mathias practically dragged him across the square yelling something unintelligible. He gained his footing and was finally able to focus.

"Come on, Aaslo!" Mathias called. "We have to stop them!"

Aaslo finally saw what had caused the stir as Mathias released his shirt. A rampaging horse had streaked into town, nearly trampling Reyla and the oblivious forester. They came to an abrupt halt, causing him to collide with Mathias. When the horse reached the fountain at the center of the square, it reared and rounded on them, flinging the unconscious rider around its legs to be trampled beneath it. The man's foot was trapped in the stirrup, and by the look of him, he had been dragged for some time.

Mathias pushed Aaslo to one side. "You come in from the left, I'll go to the right. Slowly now. We don't want to spook her."

The furious mare stomped and huffed deep, wheezing breaths as blood sprayed from her nose with every exhale. Her eyes rolled wildly, and she turned and trampled the rider with every step.

"Easy now," Aaslo calmly said as he took a few careful steps closer. "Easy. We're not going to hurt you."

He could see now that the mare had arrows sticking from her neck and haunch, and the rider bore what remained of at least two through his back. Aaslo reached out as he got close enough to grab one of the dangling reins, snagging it just as Mathias grabbed the other. The horse shrieked and tried to back away, but Aaslo and Mathias stayed with her, offering pats and coos until she calmed. Mathias held the horse's bridle while Aaslo worked to free the rider's leg from the stirrup.

"What's going on here?" called a husky voice.

The townspeople, overcome with curiosity, had begun gathering in the square. They parted to admit Captain Cromley of the village militia.

"They've been shot," said Mathias, "and the rider's been trampled."

Aaslo pulled the mangled leg free but noted that the boot was far too small. As Mathias led the horse away, Aaslo turned the rider over, and his suspicions were confirmed.

"It's a woman," he said, kneeling beside her.

Captain Cromley stood over him as Aaslo wiped blood-soaked hair and dirt from her face. The woman suddenly gasped, and her eyes popped open. Blood burbled from her lips as she struggled for air, and she grabbed Aaslo's shirt with broken hands. Her teeth were chipped and her face smashed to barely human. Beyond the gore, she stared at him with a brilliant mossy-green gaze. Then her eyes began to glaze, and just before she lost consciousness, two words escaped.

"The light—"

CHAPTER 2

"WHAT DID SHE SAY?" MATHIAS SAID AS THE TOWN DOCTOR SHOOED Aaslo away.

"I'm not sure," Aaslo said. "It was hard to understand. I think she said, 'the light,' but I don't think that was the whole message."

Captain Cromley pointed their way. "Mathias, you take the horse to your stable. I need to look into this. There won't be any practice this afternoon."

"Yes, sir," Mathias said. "Do you think we need to be worried? Someone shot her. What if they're coming here?"

"Probably highwaymen. They're more likely to prey on lone riders, and they don't usually come out this way."

"How do you know she was alone?" Mathias said. "It's unusual for a young woman to be traveling by herself."

Cromley nodded. "Yes, and that's one thing I'll be looking into. We'll have to send out a search party to see if anyone's left behind on the road."

Mathias's muscles twitched in anticipation. With a thrill, he said, "Can we go?"

"I've got people to do that," said Cromley. "You get home to your grandmother. You know she'll be furious if I send you out there without her permission."

"I'm twenty-six," exclaimed Mathias. "I don't need Grams's permission."

Cromley gave him a knowing look. "You settle that with your grandmother. Now, you two get on with yourselves." He pointed to Reyla and the other young women, waving them toward the crowd. "You all get home and stay there until we find out what's happened. Go on! Clear out!"

With the horse's reins in hand, Mathias yanked Aaslo toward the path but only got a few steps before he was forced to a halt. Aaslo stepped forward to intercept Reyla, but she took no notice and slipped around him.

"Thank you, Mathias," she said, wrapping her arms around his neck. "You saved me. That horse would've run me over."

Mathias gently pulled her arms away, easing a distance between them. "Of course I did," he said with a wink. "That's why they call me the Hero of Goldenwood."

"No one calls you that," Aaslo muttered as he grabbed his pack and tromped toward the path out of town.

Mathias nodded toward Reyla, then stooped to collect his bag. With the reins in hand, he led the injured mare toward his grandmother's home. After a few minutes, when the town was behind them, he caught up with the forester. "Hey, Aaslo. What's wrong? Is it because we couldn't go with Cromley? That would have been exciting. I hate that he still treats me like a child, but I do understand his reticence toward inciting Grams's wrath."

Aaslo said nothing, and this time, Mathias wasn't sure if the forester was brooding or being his usual quiet self.

"Maybe we can convince Grams to let us go. I guess you could go *without* me. No one is stopping *you*—"

"You saved me," Aaslo said.

Mathias paused. "Yeah, I guess I did. You should be showering me with praise."

"No," Aaslo said. "You saved *me. I* saved Reyla."

Mathias glanced up at the trees tossing about overhead but wasn't really seeing them. He grinned with satisfaction and said, "Well, if I hadn't saved *you*, then you couldn't have saved Reyla, so technically I saved you both."

"You didn't even come close to her. If I hadn't reached for her, she would've been trampled."

Realizing that Aaslo was taking things too seriously, Mathias dropped the humor and said, "You're upset. I know you love her, and I realize you probably would have preferred that I save her instead of you—but, it wasn't that I didn't *want* to save her. It's just that, well, you were closer, and I didn't really think about it. The horse was rushing right toward you. Truthfully, there wasn't anything to consider. You're my brother, Aaslo."

"That's not the point," Aaslo grumbled.

"What *is* the point?" Mathias said in exasperation.

Aaslo huffed but said nothing. Mathias knew better than to press him for more before he was ready to talk. Once the forester had gathered his thoughts and reconsidered them a hundred times, he *might* broach the subject again.

The quaint country cottage came into view as they emerged from the patch of woods that loomed between it and the town. The home was nestled within the shade of the trees. A garden lent color and life to the front yard, which was delimited by a short, crumbling wall of stones. The familiar scent of herbs mingled with the sweet aroma of wildflowers, and flecks of white and yellow pollen danced on the breeze like fabled pixies.

Mathias had not even unlatched the gate when his grandmother slipped from the shadows into the waning afternoon sunlight that cut across the front porch. The older woman's jet-black hair was tied back tightly and wound atop her head so that the white streaks swirled in the dark like river eddies in winter. Her arms were crossed over her black riding jacket, from which spilled white lacy frills that climbed up her neck to frame a face bearing red-painted lips pursed in disapproval. She glared at them over the rim of her spectacles, the toe of her knee-high boot slapping the planks in a slow, methodical cadence—a sure sign they were in for a berating. Magdelay Brelle was not a patient woman.

Mathias didn't bother to check if Aaslo still followed him toward his doom. Aaslo would weather any storm beside him. As Aaslo had pointed out earlier, they were brothers in all things, and misery was best when shared.

With the most cheerful smile he could muster, Mathias said, "Greetings, Grams! I'm glad to see you made it back in one piece—and quite swiftly, I might add."

Magdelay's eye twitched. "Whose horse is that? No, never mind that. You can tell me later." Her gaze slid to Aaslo. "Did he learn anything useful?"

Mathias glanced at Aaslo hopefully but saw only the signs of his usual obstinacy.

"Everything I do is useful," Aaslo grumped.

"Don't take that tone with me, boy. You know what I'm asking," said Magdelay.

"I'm not a boy, and neither is he," Aaslo huffed. "Most of the villagers our ages are already married or betrothed. Half of them have children of their own."

"You'll always be a boy to me," Magdelay said, her eyes softening briefly before she apparently remembered she was in the middle of a rebuke. "You two were off wasting time in the forest while you should have been studying. Cromley will be waiting in the clearing by now. When you're finished with him, you can work on the list I left for you."

"Cromley isn't coming," Mathias said. "A rider came into town nearly trampled to death and shot full of arrows. The captain told us to bring the horse here." Mathias stroked the mare's muzzle and said, "She needs your help. She's stuck with two arrows of her own."

Magdelay frowned. "A rider? Did he have any insignia? A uniform?"

"I didn't see anything that might identify her," Mathias said.

"She? Was she a very large woman?" Magdelay said suspiciously.

Mathias glanced at Aaslo.

"No, ma'am," Aaslo said. "She was small, young." He glanced at the horse. "I see what you mean."

"What am I missing?" said Mathias.

His grandmother's pointed stare nearly bored straight through him. She said, "*Think*, Mathias. What *are* you missing?"

Mathias looked back at Aaslo, who scowled at him. He had no idea why his friend was angry, but he knew he would be receiving no help. He studied the horse, and it dawned on him. "The horse is too big. A woman that small probably would have needed a smaller horse for the long journey between here and—well, anywhere—*if* she'd had a choice."

"Precisely. I'll see to the horse's injuries then speak with Cromley." Magdelay strode over to take the reins and looked up at him. Even with her high-heeled riding boots, the top of her head reached just above his shoulders. "You stay in the house tonight. If I find out you've been out looking for bandits, you'll regret it. Get busy with that list you neglected to notice this morning."

"But what about dinner?" said Mathias.

Magdelay smiled ruefully. "You may have dinner after you've finished your studies." She glanced at Aaslo again and shrugged. "Of course, Aaslo is free to return to his father's house for dinner whenever he wishes. I'm sure there will be plenty. Ielo killed a boar today. He left a haunch for us in the smokehouse."

Mathias's stomach grumbled its approval, and without thinking, he frowned at Aaslo in envy.

Aaslo caught the look and shoved past him to stomp up the front steps, grumbling all the way. "Don't look at me like that. You know I'll help you with your studies—for all the good it'll do. You're weeks ahead of me."

Mathias wrapped his grandmother in a hug, then bounded up the steps in Aaslo's wake. "You shouldn't have taken all that time off," he said.

"*Time off?* You call traveling over the mountain to help clear debris and replant everything destroyed by a fire caused by both molten rock spewing from a volcano and lightning from an ash cloud *time off?*"

"You didn't do anything the forest wouldn't have done naturally," Mathias said, turning away to hide his grin.

"Yes, yes," Aaslo muttered. "The forest *might* have grown back by itself—in a couple of generations. A good portion, though, would have been lost for good. We had to dig runoff channels and secure several steep slopes so all the topsoil didn't wash away in the storms last week. If we hadn't, the town of Jabois would have been destroyed by a lahar after the first good rain."

"I see!" Mathias said. "The Mighty Aaslo has saved the town and brought life back to the forest. We should have held a celebration—a parade! We'll build a statue in your honor. It can stand right next to, but shorter than, the one of the Hero of Goldenwood."

Aaslo slammed down his pack in the middle of the floor and spun around with a raised fist. "I never said it was *me*. It was all of us—the foresters—as it's supposed to be. And none of us are needing or wanting of parades and statues."

Mathias tucked his hands under his arms and rocked back on his heels with a grin. "But you want credit for saving Reyla."

"No! I told you, that's not the point." Aaslo pulled off his jacket and tossed it on top of his pack. With frustration, he mussed his hair, causing leaves to litter the floor. Then he looked up at Mathias and said, "You didn't put her first. You don't love her."

"Who? *Reyla?*" Mathias said. "Why would I—"

"If she is to be your wife, you must put her first," Aaslo snapped.

Mathias was suddenly at a loss. He leaned back against the wall, and his breath left him in a rush. "*What?*"

"It's not right," Aaslo said, and he began pacing in circles. Mathias had never seen Aaslo agitated in such a way. Sure, his friend would grouse and protest their studies or the necessity to leave the forest for *any* reason, but never had Aaslo seemed so—*unhinged.* "You don't love her. She deserves to be loved." Aaslo abruptly stopped to look at him, his fathomless green gaze filled with pain. "Did you know?"

"Did I know *what?*" Mathias said.

Aaslo swallowed and glanced out the window before looking back again. "Reyla is arranging a proposal—a proposal to marry *you.*"

"*Me?*" Mathias exclaimed. "Why would she do that? She's *your* girl."

"She doesn't want me. She wants you."

Mathias sighed. "No, Aaslo, she doesn't want *me.* She wants the next mayor of Goldenwood. Grams has received at least a dozen proposals for me over the years, and maybe a few of the girls even thought they were in love with me. Aaslo, Reyla is beautiful, and she's nice—but, she's a bit shallow—"

"Don't speak of her like that!"

"She *is.* I'm sure she cares for you, but I always suspected she mostly liked to brag that she was seeing a forester. She doesn't seem like the kind of girl who wants to live the way you do."

"She doesn't," Aaslo conceded as he dropped onto the stool by the hearth. He turned his back to arrange the kindling and said, "You'll take care of her, though."

Mathias struggled to maintain only the slightest indignation as he said, "Aaslo, I'm not going to marry Reyla."

Aaslo paused. "You're not?"

"No, I'm not going to marry the woman that captured my best friend's heart."

Aaslo exhaled heavily, and his shoulders dropped. "All right," he said. "She might come back—"

"No," Mathias said. He threw his hands down and dragged a chair over to sit across from Aaslo. "Reyla *will* come back. You can be sure of it. She wants to marry for recognition. She might have been willing to give up a forester's honor for the convenience of marrying the mayor, but anything less won't do."

Aaslo looked up. "You think? That's good—"

Mathias shook his head and met his friend's gaze. "No, it's not good. You're going to say no. You'll turn down her proposal."

Aaslo frowned. "Why would I do that?"

"You deserve better. You're a *forester.* You hold the highest honor in this town, and despite the ribbing I give you about it, you *deserve* that honor. What you do is *hard*, and it's lonely, and even though the economy of this town—of *every* logging town, and in no small part, the *kingdom*—depends on you, you will never see wealth. Whatever riches you have, you find in the forest you personally nurture. You, Aaslo, will never settle for being second." Sitting back, Mathias said, "Surely someone else has caught your eye at some point."

"I had Reyla," Aaslo replied. "There was no point in considering anyone else. What does it matter if she wanted you? That doesn't mean she cares for me any less."

Mathias sighed, resigned to the fact that Aaslo would marry Reyla despite her flaws.

Aaslo grabbed a small box from the mantel and crouched in front of the hearth. Sparks jumped from the flint and steel, and eventually the kindling began to smoke. As Aaslo coaxed the flame, Mathias began rummaging through the books on the center table. The only task on his grandmother's list that he had been looking forward to was the practice with Cromley, but that wouldn't be happening. An hour later, Aaslo tossed a book in front of him. He flipped it open to the page Aaslo had marked and grinned.

"How did you know I was looking for that?"

"I read the list," Aaslo mumbled as he dug through the pile in front of him to find the worn map of Aldrea.

Mathias's gaze lingered on the map, as it did each time he saw it. Every country known to the scholars of Uyan, the entirety of the explored world, was painted in detail upon its parchment. The brilliant landscape was filled with distant mountains, forests, seas, and rivers—and still, parts were blank. Mathias thought that if *he* had drawn the map, his kingdom of Uyan would be in the center, but the cartographer who had created it was not from Uyan. Like most maps, Mouvilan was at its center. The much smaller kingdom of Uyan occupied the northwest corner of the map, and Goldenwood was marked with a tiny point in the northwest corner of Uyan. The only reason the insignificant village graced the map at all was because his grandmother had added it on the day he had first laid eyes upon the masterpiece.

A sound echoed in his mind, and he realized Aaslo was speaking to him. Mathias pulled his gaze away from the beauty of Aldrea and said, "What?"

Aaslo scowled at him, obviously unhappy to repeat himself. "I asked why you haven't married."

Mathias laughed, his usual mechanism for stalling the conversation until he could come up with an excuse to change the subject. "You first."

Aaslo sat back in his chair. "Why?"

Mathias grinned. Pleasantries were supposed to be disarming, and he wanted Aaslo to drop the subject. Then again, mockery also worked. "Brothers in all things, right? You're a year older. The oldest has to marry first."

Aaslo narrowed his eyes. "That tradition applies to sisters. We are men and not actually related. Besides, I've been planning to marry Reyla. We were supposedly waiting until the house was finished. *You* aren't even betrothed."

"Come now, Aaslo," Mathias said as he stood from the table to pour drinks at the sideboard. "Why choose just one when there are so many? There is plenty of time to settle down." He kept his back to the room as he spoke so that Aaslo would not see his struggle. He refused to lie to his friend, even if he couldn't tell him the truth.

"There are not so many left," Aaslo said. "Were you waiting on her?"

Mathias paused and looked at Aaslo with genuine confusion. "*Who?*"

"Reyla. Were you hoping I would change my mind so that you could have her?"

Mathias's shoulders relaxed; he was glad this was an issue he could address honestly. "No, I told you that I will reject the proposal."

"Only because you feel that you'll be stealing her from me. If I had chosen another, you would be free to accept her without guilt."

"Honestly, Aaslo, it wouldn't matter who did the rejecting. My decision would be the same."

"Why then?"

With a roll of his eyes, Mathias said, "Because I don't want to marry Reyla."

"No, I mean why haven't you married."

Mathias met Aaslo's accusatory stare, hoping it would appear as if he had nothing to hide, and immediately realized it wasn't working. Aaslo was suspicious.

"I knew it," Aaslo snapped. "How long have you been keeping this from me? *Why* would you keep it from me?"

"Keeping what? I don't know what you're talking about," Mathias replied. "I didn't say anything."

Aaslo slapped the table and said, "You're leaving."

Magdelay lashed at him from the doorway like an angry wasp. *"You told him!"*

Mathias glanced up to see his grandmother standing there with a disapproving glare, not unlike the one he was getting from Aaslo.

"No! I haven't said anything. He's only guessing. You know how he is."

Magdelay looked at Aaslo. "Stubborn foresters."

"Determined," said Aaslo.

"Obstinate," said Mathias. He wished he'd kept his mouth shut when Aaslo turned back to him. He said, "I would've told you, but Grams—"

"It doesn't matter now," Magdelay said as she came into the room and began shuffling through the papers and books on the table. "It will be dark in an hour. We will leave then." She took the map of Aldrea from the table, stacked it with a few more maps and scrolls, then rolled up the bunch before shoving them into a leather map case. She glanced over at Mathias and said, "Get packed. One bag of traveling gear only. We travel light."

Mathias said, "You're kidding, right? We're not leaving *right now*."

Magdelay continued sorting through items in the study, shoving them into a bag that she had somehow procured during his shocked mental absence.

"Well, how long do we expect to be gone?" Mathias said.

"Forever," she said. "We're not coming back."

Aaslo lurched from his seat at the table. "You're leaving *now*? You weren't even going to tell me?"

Mathias shook his head. "No, I don't know what's going on. She told me we would be leaving *someday*. That was fifteen years ago!" Turning to his grandmother, Mathias said, "Is this because he knows? We have to leave because he figured it out?"

Magdelay didn't cease her preparations to answer. She muttered, "No, that was coincidence." Then she paused and gave Aaslo a sidelong look.

Aaslo crossed his arms over his chest and said, "Don't look at me like that. You're the one who's been keeping secrets."

"How did you know?" Magdelay said, taking a step toward the forester.

Mathias was suddenly uncomfortable with his grandmother's hostile demeanor. Aaslo must have picked up on the change as well, because he abandoned his mulishness to answer.

"It was because of Reyla."

"Reyla told you?"

"No, Reyla said she had given you a proposal, but he says he won't marry her."

"So?"

"So, the only reason I can think of that he wouldn't want to marry Reyla is because he's leaving."

A smile threatened Magdelay's lips, and she relaxed her stance. "You place too much value in that silly girl. Mathias is meant for endeavors greater than she, greater than us all. Aaslo, I have helped raise you since you were barely a year old. You have been a second grandson to me. I hope you marry that silly girl and live the rest of your days in the shade of the trees." She looked to Mathias. "You've been friends for a long time, and this parting is abrupt, but you must say your farewells quickly."

She then swept from the room, dropped her pack in the foyer, and jogged up the stairs.

Aaslo looked at him in dismay. "What's going on?"

Mathias held up his hands. "Truly, Aaslo, I don't know. She told me a long time ago that I shouldn't get too attached to anyone. I wasn't supposed to make any long-term plans because someday we would be leaving. I couldn't tell anyone—including you. She swore me to secrecy on my honor." He leaned forward and whispered, "I tried to drop hints—like today on the way home. I tried to get you thinking about it." His eyes landed on the pack on the floor of the foyer. "I think she's serious, though. I—I guess I need to pack."

Aaslo crossed his arms. "You're not going anywhere until I get an explanation."

Mathias said, "I don't have one. I'm sorry."

Magdelay reappeared in the doorway looking none too pleased. Despite the matriarch's demanding gaze, neither Mathias nor Aaslo moved. Magdelay scoffed and said, "Fine. I'll explain, but only for *you*, Aaslo." Her gaze softened. "I suppose I owe you that much. Did you know your mother left the day I came to Goldenwood with Mathias? You were only one and he a newborn. You've been a good friend to Mathias, practically a brother. We have no time for questions, though."

Perching upon the arm of a high-backed chair, Grams held her hands before her and began moving them as if she were knitting with imaginary needles and yarn. She muttered under her breath, and an image suddenly appeared, floating in front of her. It was bright and translucent. Mathias and Aaslo both jumped at the sudden intrusion of light. Mathias had never seen anything like it.

"What is that?" he blurted. "What are you?"

"I am a sorceress—the high sorceress, to be more precise."

"The high sorceress?" Aaslo mumbled. "Like from the stories you told us? The one in charge of the magi?"

"Yes, and the stories are true, not just fantasies I made up to put you to sleep. Now listen. For all of human existence, certain members of the magic community, collectively called the magi, have been foretelling the future—"

"You mean prophecies," said Mathias.

"Yes. *You* are part of one such prophecy."

Mathias's heart lurched, and his blood rushed with a thrill. He leaned forward in his seat. "Which prophecy?"

"The only prophecy that really matters. For hundreds of years, prophets from every country have been following the lines of the *same* prophecy." Small red lights popped up all over the spinning globe, showing each of the places the prophecy had emerged, until the entire spectacle was red. "It is the only prophecy known to have visited magi in every corner of Aldrea, and it is the prophecy that foretells the future of us all. For this reason, it is called the Aldrea Prophecy."

One of the fine tendrils that had been restraining Mathias's excitement snapped. *"I'm* in this prophecy?" he said. Somehow, he knew it to be true. He had felt like he was waiting for something his entire life, waiting in anticipation for something big, bigger than Goldenwood could ever offer.

Magdelay said, "More accurately, you *are* the prophecy—at least as much of it as anyone cares to consider. Prophecies have many branches or *lines.* For every decision and every event, the lines of destiny and vertices of fate can change the outcome."

"I don't understand," said Mathias. "What's the difference between destiny and fate?"

Magdelay closed her hand, and the image disappeared. She glared at him. "I told you we don't have time for questions."

"But you're so good at answering them."

"Don't try that on me, boy. I know you too well." After another glance, she sighed and said, "Fine."

Mathias grinned. She might know him, but that didn't mean it wouldn't work.

She said, *"Destiny* is your life path—your soul's plan. It is the map of events and experiences your soul decided to endure during this life-time. It has many branches because you have many decisions to make. If you are true to yourself, the branches will eventually lead back to your path of destiny. Every soul has a destiny, and we are all interacting, so sometimes our destinies cross. At times, the crossing is intentional and remains part of your destiny. The point where they unintentionally cross is *fate.* Fate is unplanned, at least by *us,* but still part of the over-all tapestry. These points of fate are most often where people diverge from their destinies. Sometimes people never make it back, and some-times a person goes so far that the only way back is to return to the point where he or she stepped off the path."

Mathias was crestfallen. "So, my whole life is planned?"

"Were you not listening? Your destiny is planned. The decisions you make determine whether or not you reach it. Think about this. In life, for every action you take, you have a goal. If you cook a meal, your goal is to feed yourself. If you practice the sword, your goal is to de-fend yourself. Life without a goal would be pointless."

"That makes sense," Aaslo said.

Mathias looked at him, surprised the forester would accept the no-tion so readily.

"So, where do I fit into this prophecy?" Mathias said.

"In short, the Aldrea Prophecy is nothing but darkness. It is the death of everything—all life, all souls—gone from the face of Aldrea. A great enemy will desiccate the land, subjugating and destroying its people until those few survivors will be met with nothing but despair before they finally succumb. For more than two hundred years, the Prophets of Aldrea have followed the branches of the prophecy—millions of them—seeking hope. Every single branch leads to terror—except one. One, and only one, branch leads to our salvation. It is *your* branch, Mathias."

Excitement twisted in his stomach until he felt sick. "The entire world, all of *life,* depends on *me*? You're not serious. Are you doing this to punish me for slacking in my studies?" He looked to Aaslo. "Was this Aldrea Prophecy in the material I was supposed to read today? It's a test, right?"

Aaslo didn't look at him. The forester's infernal gaze might have succeeded in burning Magdelay to the ground had she not been a sorceress. Aaslo said, "I don't think she's kidding."

Mathias looked back to his grandmother. "You're saying I'm *the one*. In the stories, there's always the unwitting hero—the *chosen one*—"

"Someone who gets all the world's problems dumped on him," Aaslo muttered.

Mathias's voice cracked when he said, "—and *I'm* it?"

"Yes," Magdelay said.

Mathias could sit no longer under the rising internal tension. He stood from his seat and paced the room. "But, what about Aaslo? The chosen one always has a friend, a comrade, a sidekick."

Magdelay eyed Aaslo sideways. "He does not appear in your prophecy."

"What do you mean? He's my best friend. My whole life he's been my brother. He has to be in it somewhere."

"He is not, and believe me, I've checked. We do not believe him to be a part of your destiny, but rather fate. The council and I decided to permit the friendship because he was not seen as being responsible for your demise in any of the prophecies. I, personally, hoped that this point of fate was a gift of the gods."

"How do you know it's him?" Aaslo said. The forester still had not taken his gaze from the woman, even for a second.

"It is part of the prophecy: *He who bears the mark of the world will*

*call upon the light, and within that light, shadows will swarm the
enemy. Death to the god-bearers, he will stay the righteous hand, and
bless this land with life reclaimed from their destruction."*

"He who bears the mark of the world," said Mathias. "You mean
my birthmark." He reached up to stroke the tiniest smudge at his
temple that was usually covered by his hair. "The one that looks like
the map of Aldrea?"

Magdelay said, "Isn't it obvious?"

Aaslo finally looked at Mathias. He said, "Everyone chooses *you.*
The whole world wants Mathias." The forester rose from his seat,
grabbed his pack from the floor, and left without another word. Mathias's mind swirled in every direction. He didn't know what he might
have said, but he felt he should have said *something.* He knew Aaslo,
though. He would say what needed to be said and assume everything
else to be understood.

THE DISTANCE SEEMED MUCH FARTHER THAN ON ANY OTHER RETURN
to his home. The shuffle of dirt under Aaslo's feet and the rustling of
his pack against his back were louder to his ears than the wailing
wind. He glanced toward the southwest to see the sun disappear
behind the trees. It would sink beneath the distant mountains soon.
He was glad it was not yet winter, when the village would be cast into
night much earlier by the mountain on which he lived. Time was
short. It was never a good idea to travel through the woods at night.
Grams was a smart woman. They had always believed her to be a uni-
versity professor who had retired upon taking custody of Mathias
after his mother died in childbirth. Now, they knew her to be much
more. She knew better than to travel at night. Something serious had
to have occurred if she felt the need to risk it—something worth en-
dangering their lives. He thought it must have to do with the rider.

Someone stepped in front of him, and he drew up short. He took a
moment to pull himself from his thoughts and realize who it was.

"Reyla."

"Hi, Aaslo," she said softly.

He waited, his impatience mounting, while she stood there looking at him. Her brow was furrowed and her eyes were entreating.

"What is it, Reyla? I'm in a hurry."

"I—I ran into Ms. Brelle a little while ago."

"And?"

"She said no—to my proposal. Just like that. *No.* She said I couldn't marry Mathias and was kind of rude about it. She acted like she didn't even have time to think about it."

"What's your point?"

"Well, it's just that I thought he liked me. He and I have spent so much time together—"

"You and I spend time together," said Aaslo. "Mathias and I spend time together. Sometimes you both spend time with *me* at the same time. You and Mathias don't spend time together."

She dropped her gaze to the ground, and he wondered if she truly felt the shame she bared. She looked up again and said, "I realize that now. It was you. It was always you. I'm sorry for doubting that."

"I have to go, Reyla. It's getting dark."

Stepping into him, she put her hands on his chest and looked at him with those beautiful stormy eyes. "Please, Aaslo, forgive me. I do love the home you're building for us, and it's not that far from town. I know we can be happy together."

Aaslo brushed a thumb across her cheek, wiping away a tear, and then took her face in his hands. He kissed her. He kissed her the way he had always dreamed of kissing her on the day she finally professed her love to him. Then he pulled her hands from his chest and said, "*I* could be happy with you, Reyla. You could never be happy with *me.*"

Aaslo felt as if his chest were being torn in two, but he didn't have time to mourn his loss. He moved to step around his lost love, and she reached for him.

"Aaslo—"

Mathias's words echoed in his mind. He said, "I cannot settle for being second, Reyla. It's over."

If she said anything more, it was lost to the wind. Aaslo increased his pace and jogged briskly until he reached the foot of the mountain. There were no roads or trails to the home he shared with his father, and they were careful to keep it that way. The first stars of the night could be seen beyond the treetops as they swayed to and fro, and Aaslo was frustrated that time rushed so quickly whenever he was in a hurry. Now that he knew the gods had a plan, he was sure they were sadists.

The lantern was lit when he arrived home. He could see it resting in the center of their table through the open doorway. The table had only two chairs, and one of them was occupied. He kicked and scraped his boots on a piece of rough pine by the threshold, then stepped inside the humble abode, probably for the last time.

"Pa."

Ielo looked up from his meal and gave Aaslo a lopsided grin. It had been some time since all of his father's face worked properly.

"Aaslo, a fine day for catching leaves, I see." The old man nodded toward him, and Aaslo brushed a hand through his hair, sending the brown and gold flecks fluttering to the floor.

"And boar, from what I hear."

Ielo stabbed his knife into the chunk of meat on his plate. "I took a bit off the flank for dinner and left some with Ms. Brelle. The rest is out in the meat shed."

Aaslo perused his father's form. "You're uninjured?"

"I'd've said so if I weren't," Ielo muttered.

"I'm not sure you would," Aaslo replied. "I'm leaving."

"It's dark now," Ielo said. "You don't need to be out in the forest at night. I shouldn't have to say that."

Aaslo crossed to his bed in the corner and pulled a small chest from beneath it. He put a few of the supplies from his pack into the chest and replaced them with items he thought might be needed for a journey.

"Where are you going?" Ielo said.

Aaslo glanced over his shoulder to see his father turned in his chair, staring at him with concern.

"I don't know," he said as he went back to packing.

"Then, you go with Mathias?"

"What do you know of it?" Aaslo said, looking back at him again.

"Only what you've told me, which is nothing," Ielo replied. "But, I doubt you'd leave this house at night for any other reason."

"A rider came into town. She'd been attacked and was nearly dead. It spooked Ms. Brelle, and now she and Mathias need to leave town." He paused, wondering how much he should say, then decided his father deserved the truth. "Mathias is some kind of prophesied hero, and she's taking him away to save the world. They're leaving at night"—he glanced up, looking at his father pointedly—"through the woods."

Ielo looked at him as if he suspected a head injury, then nodded.

"They'll need a guide, I suppose. I can do it. I'm more familiar with the forest on the route out of town."

"No," Aaslo said. "He's my brother. I may not be a part of his destiny, but our fates are intertwined. I will go with him."

"Then, you'll leave the forest?" Ielo said.

Aaslo smirked. "Someone has keep the *chosen one's* head on his shoulders."

Aaslo was abruptly reminded of the gods' sadism. He only ever got a half smile from his father, but he got a whole frown. Pausing, he said, "Before I go, tell me about Mother. Do you know where she went? Maybe I could find her."

Ielo turned his gaze toward the fire. "I don't see the point. You already know that after we married, she decided she didn't want to live in the forest. She was going to leave before discovering she was pregnant. I begged her to give it a chance. She agreed to stay long enough to wean you; then she was gone. I don't know where she went. She said she wanted to live in a big city. She wanted romance and fancy things."

Aaslo felt like he had been punched in the gut. First his mother, now Reyla. He shook his head. "What good are fancy things? Seems better to have practical ones."

Ielo grunted and nodded. He said, "How far do you intend to follow him?"

"As far as he needs to go."

CHAPTER 3

THE WARMTH HAD LEFT WITH THE SUN, AND MATHIAS WISHED HE HAD grabbed a warmer coat. Having never traveled beyond the town, he hadn't realized how cold it could get riding atop a horse in the wind. It had only been an hour since they left the house, and he was already wishing for a warm fire and cozy bed. His horse snorted, and Mathias cringed. He felt like every sound was a call to the bandits—or whoever they were. He rode the horse that had belonged to the mysterious rider, and it looked none the worse for wear. It was difficult for him to accept that his grandmother was a sorceress, but the proof was in the beast. Magdelay had healed and soothed the injured animal in a matter of minutes, and now Mathias was riding it away from his home.

"Grams," he said in a harsh whisper.

"What?" she said.

Although he couldn't see her, he could feel her tension. She was alert, her gaze constantly roving the dark forest that surrounded them. The road was narrow between Goldenwood and Mierwyl, barely wide enough for a wagon. During the growing season, the trees and plants had to be continually trimmed or the road would disappear in a matter of weeks.

"Is it safe to speak?"

"I sense no one in the area. Speak quietly if you must."

"You told us that magic is inherited. If you're the high sorceress, then that means I'm a magus, too, right?"

The silent minutes that followed seemed to stretch into infinity. Finally, she said, "I am not your grandmother, Mathias. You are not of my bloodline."

Mathias shivered, and it had nothing to do with the wind. Of all the things he had thought she might say, that had not been one of them.

Before he could rouse a response, Magdelay added, "You *are*, however, a member of one of the twelve bloodlines."

"But not *yours*."

"Correct. Your parents had been married little more than a year when you were born. Your mother was a young sorceress of the Sereshian bloodline. She possessed moderate power and had little experience. The Council of Magi agreed that it was in the best interest of the world for you to be taken into protective custody. Your parents protested, of course, but it was not their choice."

He yanked on the reins, causing the horse to snort loudly as it came to an abrupt halt. Mathias's face heated, and he shouted, forgetting the potential threat. "You *stole* me from my parents!"

Magdelay stopped and turned her horse so that she faced him. "It was for your own good. Your parents could not have protected you from those who sought your death. It was some time before they accepted that, but, eventually, they did."

"What happened to them?"

"Nothing happened to them," she said. "Your mother is the sorceress of Bellbry Court, a position she could never have earned on her own talent, except she married the earl."

"Wait, my father is the Earl of Bellbry?"

"Yes, although your mother is technically in the higher position, despite the fact that she received it by virtue of her marriage—and, I suppose, the council's guilt over taking their child."

"You don't speak very highly of my mother," Mathias said with accusation. His shoulders were tense, and he wanted to throttle something.

"Of course not. She is a Sereshian, and not just in name. She is fully committed to their cause."

"I don't understand."

"It's politics—politics with a long history." Magdelay guided her horse back down the road, and Mathias begrudgingly followed while she explained. "As you know, magic is only passed down the bloodlines. People without magic are called *seculars*. Although we live longer than seculars, it is difficult for us to procreate. We have more success if we mate with seculars. Doing so waters down the bloodline, though, so the practice is discouraged unless the bloodline is in peril. There used to be fifteen bloodlines. Now, there are only twelve. Not only that, but the oldest of us, elder magi like me, bear a fraction of the power carried by our ancestors. The younger generation—magi like your mother—dream of possessing even half that of an elder. In short, human-borne magic is dying."

"So, you hate her because she's weaker than you?"

"No, I pity her for that. I dislike her because of her cause. Each of the bloodlines approaches magic—and its impending expiry—in its own way. Some approaches are compatible. Others are not. I am of the Etrieli line. We pursue the advancement of applied magic through research and development. Your mother is a Sereshian. They use magic for profit and care nothing for its restoration. They believe their bloodline is best served by acquiring as much wealth as possible while they have the advantage. We have been at odds for as long as the bloodlines have existed."

"If you hate them so much, why did you raise me? Why not send me to someone else?"

"You are our savior. It was agreed that the strongest should protect you. Besides that, only I held the power to suppress your own for so long."

With every question she answered, with every explanation, Mathias's nerves burned hotter. "If I'm supposed to be this powerful savior, why would you suppress my power? Why not teach me to use it?"

"A little magic boy running around Goldenwood would draw attention. Each member of the bloodlines is known and registered. If some random child exhibits power, people will investigate. Only the council and your parents know of your existence, and we hoped to keep it that way until you were grown and fully trained. You have not yet realized this, but I *have* been teaching you magic. The dead languages, the artwork, the meditations, even some of the dances, are spells. You know them already. Once you learn to connect with your power, it will not take long for you to learn to apply them practically."

Mathias's anger finally overcame his curiosity. "You're saying that nothing in my life has been *real*?"

"Don't get snippy with me. I know you, Mathias."

Mathias started to protest, but the words died before reaching his lips. His grandmother—no, *Magdelay*—was right. He wanted this. He wanted it more than he wanted to have known his parents, and that made him angry.

"You're ri—"

"Shhh," Magdelay said with urgency as she drew her horse to a halt.

Mathias pulled the reins, then reached over to loosen his sword. The moon was but a sliver, and the stars were obscured by a thin haze. Darkness surrounded them such that he was unable to discern a single tree. He had no idea how Magdelay had managed to keep to the road, but as high sorceress, she had her ways, he was sure. Still, he heard nothing unusual over the rustling branches and hollow breeze.

It was the motion that caught his attention. A silhouette hurried toward them from behind. With blood pounding in his ears, Mathias barely caught the scuff of boots over the rough road. A flicker of light drew his attention away from the figure. Thin tendrils of purple lightning snapped around Magdelay's fist and twisted up her forearm as she turned to face their stalker. Her determined gaze reflected the violet light as she drew back her arm.

It was too late. Fire scorched his back as Mathias was thrown from his horse. The attack had come from the other direction. Before he knew it, shadows were converging on them from every side. Magdelay was screaming something, but he had no time to consider her words. He reached for his hilt and couldn't help crying out at the ripping of flesh across his back. The smell of roasted meat and burnt hair reached his nose, and he knew it to be his own. Somehow, it didn't hurt as badly as he would have thought. With the shadows getting closer, he knew he needed to get to his feet. He tucked his legs under him and drew his sword as he rose. The night was abruptly lit with the gold and purple of fire and lightning. Mathias's blade flashed in the light, then clashed with the weapon of the nearest assailant. It was then that he got his first look at the enemy.

Before he could wrap his mind around the truth, a searing pain tore through his calf, and he faltered. He caught a glimpse of the feathered shaft sticking from his leg as his assailant's axe fell toward his head. Struggling to raise his blade in time, he knew it was for naught. He jerked, falling to one knee, his lungs ceasing to take breath as something jabbed into his back. *Another arrow*, he thought. He watched in agony as the axe-wielding creature in front of him was suddenly split into two, showering him in milky white blood and gore. The tightness in Mathias's chest finally released, and he gasped to capture every bit of air he had missed in that eternal, excruciating moment.

His lust for survival overrode his pain, and Mathias struggled to his feet, then turned to meet his attackers. An arrow sliced across his arm as he lunged to stab one of the creatures through the throat. Grabbing the dying fiend, he used it as a shield to block two more arrows while simultaneously searching the forest for the archer. The only light now came from a few bushes set ablaze during the initial attack, and Mathias realized the flicker of purple lightning had gone.

"Magdelay," he called. "Magdelay, where are you? Grams?"

Mathias's head began to spin, and he blinked to clear his vision. If Magdelay wasn't there, then who was fighting the other creatures? Who had saved him from losing his head? He glanced around, seeking the source of the sounds of battle, but he could only see two dark silhouettes struggling in the trees just beyond the road. He wheezed, and then hot liquid shot up his throat. Black in the darkness, his blood spilled over the pale flesh of the creature behind whom he hid. Coughing and sputtering for breath, he could no longer hold his own weight, much less the weight of another. Mathias crashed to the ground, half buried under the fiendish corpse.

Movement from the trees caught his eye, and he grasped for his sword, which he didn't remember dropping. Pawing at the dirt, he searched in vain as another of the creatures scurried in his direction. A shout from his other side drew his gaze, and a dark figure ran toward him. He glanced back to his attacker just in time to witness the descent of the blade that would take his life. It happened so fast. The sword had impaled him, thrust deep into the ground beneath him, faster than he could have blinked. But he didn't blink. He saw every glint of firelight slither across the mottled blade. He sought the face of his killer, the foreign beast that had robbed him of life, of his destiny, but the creature was gone. Abandoned. The *chosen one*—alone in death, reduced to insignificance before his journey had even begun.

I'm real!

He blinked as the stars glittered above him through a break in the haze. How had he never noticed such brilliant beauty?

I'm real!

Was that a sound? It was so far away. Should he try to find it? The stars were winking out, one by one. Only one was now left, and he feared to look away lest it disappear, too. He didn't want to be alone in the darkness.

Something massive blocked his view of his last light.

"I'm real, Mathias! Don't die. Mathias, breathe! Mathias!"

He knew that face, and he knew that voice. He was not alone.

CHAPTER 4

"I'm real, Mathias! Wake up! No, Mathias, no!"

Aaslo shook Mathias, then grabbed his face. He looked into his friend's distant gaze and saw with brutal clarity that the light had left. Panic threatened to overcome him, but he knew he had to make it right. Somehow, he had to fix Mathias. He looked into the trees and saw a distant purple glow. It was far from the road—too far. He couldn't leave Mathias. If more of those creatures lurked nearby, they might take Mathias away. Then how would he save him? Mathias was the chosen one. It was his destiny to save the world. He couldn't die on the first day of their journey. The world needed Mathias to live. Aaslo needed him to live.

Aaslo pushed a creature's corpse off, then waited. Magdelay would return. She was the high sorceress. Of course she would return. As he surveyed the carnage, his gaze roved over the pools of blood, milky in the firelight and smelling of tannin, save for the one human corpse beneath him. Its blood was dark and held the sour scent of metal. He spied a familiar sword lying just inches beyond the reach of Mathias's outstretched hand, the fallen savior's fingers still gripping the dirt where they had searched for the weapon. Aaslo took Mathias's hand, warm as a living man's, and placed the hilt within it. Looking back to the trees, he could see the purple glow intermittently lighting the trees, so he knew Magdelay lived. He waited. He had to protect Mathias.

Eventually, his panic subsided, and a dull emptiness settled inside him. He leaned down to examine the creature he had pushed off Mathias, though the dwindling fire in the bushes did not provide much light. The fiend was unlike anything he had ever seen. With its saggy purplish skin and milky white eyes, it seemed otherworldly. It was monstrous, and its vague human likeness made the creature's appearance all the worse. This specimen wore leather armor, like most of them, and had wielded a sword. A few of the others were dressed like common folk, some bearing swords and hatchets or axes, and others wielding sticks and rocks.

When the sorceress finally returned, he had just finished searching the bodies nearest Mathias, finding nothing of use. When Magdelay saw him, the purple lightning erupted over her hands, but it was dim compared to the vivid blast he had seen earlier. Aaslo stepped in front of Mathias's body and paused.

Magdelay's voice hissed with vitriol as she said, "Why are you here, and how did you follow us without me knowing?"

"You know why I'm here. He's my brother. I came to join you, but I found their trail in the forest. They were following you, and I followed them. Their trail turned away from the road, and I realized they were taking a shortcut to ambush you at this bend. I tried to catch up to warn you, but I was on foot, and you were riding."

While she did not release her power, she did appear less likely to attack him. "Well, the horses are gone now," she said. "How's Mathias?" She nodded toward what she could see of Mathias's body. "He is injured. Is it serious?"

"I've been waiting for you—it seems like forever. You need to fix him. Use your magic," he said as he stepped to the side.

He knew she would be upset when she saw Mathias sprawled lifeless on the ground with a sword through his heart, but he didn't expect the shriek that erupted from the doggedly poised sorceress.

"No! What—No!"

Magdelay rushed to Mathias's side, glanced at the sword, and then slapped Mathias's face.

Aaslo said, "I left it in—the sword—you know, because they say to leave it in or it'll bleed more."

"It's through his *heart*, Aaslo! He's *dead*!"

"But you can fix him. You're the most powerful magus in the kingdom! You can fix him!"

"No, Aaslo, I cannot fix *death*!" She fell onto her rear in the bloody mud and buried her face in her hands. "I failed! All these years, the plans, the preparations, and I failed. We're doomed. There is nothing to be done. The savior is dead, and we have not even a fool's hope."

"What? *No*. You have to fix him! You fixed the horse. *Fix him!*"

She shook her head, her expression one of defeat. "I could heal his body, but I cannot return his soul. No one can. He's *dead*, Aaslo."

Aaslo had never felt anything like what he was feeling in that moment. Nothing made sense, and he had no desire to pick and choose his words. "You were supposed to protect him! It was *your* job. You left him here in the road, all alone with these, these, *things*!"

"He wasn't alone. I realized it was you right before they attacked. Mathias was trained for this. He could have prevailed but for the magus. The magus somehow masked their presence from me. I cast a wide net that should have sensed them from miles away. It should have sensed *you*. Yet, it did not."

"Not until I stepped from their path," he said. "You sensed me when I took to the road to warn you."

Magdelay sighed. "Yes, he must have masked their path somehow. He attacked Mathias first. I didn't see it coming. The magus was more powerful. I didn't think I could defeat him, so I led him away to keep him from attacking Mathias again and to give you two time to escape should I fall. It was only by luck that I prevailed."

"By what luck?" Aaslo said. "Does he live?"

"No, he lit a fireball while standing under a fiergolen tree."

"Why would he do something so stupid?"

She shook her head, but her heart seemed absent—defeated. "I don't believe they grow outside the Efestrian Forest. He likely didn't know it would explode. *This*—" She waved a hand over the slaughter. "We cannot stay here. I must inform the council. The king will also need to know. You should go home, Aaslo. There is nothing more you can do."

"Go home? What about the enemy? What about the impending doom?"

"We have already *lost*," Magdelay said. "It will probably be a while before they reach Goldenwood. Enjoy what time you have left."

Aaslo clenched his fist. "By the time they reach Goldenwood, there will be no one left to help us."

"No one can help anyone." She nodded toward Mathias, where he lay still as the dirt beneath him. "Only he could save us, and he is dead."

"That's absurd," said Aaslo. "If one man can do it, another can as well."

"No, I told you, *every* branch of the prophecy ends in defeat except his, but he has to be alive to make it happen. I don't know how or why, but it had to be *him*. He must have had some special skill or power or a connection with the enemy, or the blessing of the gods. . . . It doesn't matter anymore."

Aaslo growled, then said, "If you think I'm going to sit back and wait to die, then you don't know me at all. These things killed Mathias, and they're threatening to kill everything else. We need to stop them."

"You think to take up Mathias's banner? You are not the savior."

"No, I'm a forester. Foresters do what needs doing, even when no one else wants to. Beyond that, you don't know what I am. You said I wasn't in the prophecy."

"I said you weren't in *his* prophecy. I told you that I checked with the prophets. You have your own branch."

"Well, what does this prophecy say about *me*?"

"Death. Your branch is death. So say *all* the prophets."

"If my branch is *death*, then why did you let me befriend Mathias?"

"You did not cause his death, Aaslo. You are not responsible for this. If anything, you gave him a fighting chance." She waved at the corpses littering the ground and said, "You killed all of these, didn't you?"

Aaslo nodded, then tilted his head to stare at the night sky. He didn't want to look at the bodies. He said, "Mathias was severely injured. Otherwise, he could have done it himself."

"Yes, I know. That was my fault," she said, her voice quavering.

Aaslo finally looked at Mathias, his friend, lying there as if waiting only to be told to breathe. "I'm his brother in all things. That's what we always said. Brothers in all things that matter and those that don't. If this was important to him, then it's important to me. If he can't finish his destiny, then I'll finish it for him."

Rising to her feet, Magdelay said, "I appreciate the sentiment, Aaslo, but it is for naught. I must get to the council quickly. If you truly want to help, you can take the news to the king."

"The king," Aaslo echoed. "The king in Tyellí?"

"Yes, the King of Uyan, *our* king."

Aaslo took only a breath to contemplate the trip to meet the king, and he was greatly disturbed. "There are no forests near Tyellí."

"No," Magdelay said, with patronizing patience, "you will have to leave the forest, and you will need to take proof. The king does not know you, and this is something he will need to see for himself."

"You want me to take Mathias to Tyellí? *How?* That's weeks from here by horse, and we seem to be out of those."

"No, you are right," Magdelay said, looking down at the body. "You cannot take his body. Cut off his head."

Aaslo's stomach heaved. *"What?"*

"I will cast a preservation spell upon the head so that it won't decompose. The king will need to see the mark."

"I can't—I can't travel to Tyellí carrying my brother's head. What's wrong with you? You raised him. Don't you feel anything?"

Magdelay glared at him. "Of course I do. I grew to love that boy as my own. I regret that I didn't tell him that when I revealed truth of his birthright, but we must prioritize, and our feelings fall very, very far down the list. In fact, they're not even on this list."

She picked up the axe of a fallen creature and held it out for him. "You must do it."

Aaslo's stomach continued to flip and spin, and he thought he might become sick. He looked at the oddly shaped axe, crusted in old blood, and his lip curled in disgust. "No, I'll use my own."

"So be it," she said.

The sorceress created a glowing green orb over her head to light the ground in front of her. She walked to the side of the road and waved her hands in a strange pattern while muttering unintelligible words. The ground began to peel away in layers to form a deep trough with a mound at one end. Then the sorceress—Mathias's grandmother—turned away.

Aaslo said, "I'll be right back." He shuffled down the road a short way to where he had first stepped off the enemy's path. There, he found the pack he had discarded in his haste. All he could hear as he collected his belongings was *I should have run faster.*

His steps were noticeably slower upon his return to the scene. The scent of tannin soured the air around it, and he wanted nothing more than to turn and go back the way he had come. He tried not to think of what he was doing. *It's just like cutting a log,* he told himself. *It's Mathias,* his heart replied.

Releasing his pack, he grabbed the hilt of the sword in Mathias's chest and wrenched it from the ground before launching it into the forest with as much strength as he could muster. He then picked up his axe and stood over the body.

"I'm sorry. If it has to be anybody, then it should be me." After taking a deep breath—and then another—he raised the axe and brought it down with a *thwap*. Something broke inside him. It was as if he could hear the crash, like a glass shattering in his mind.

"Is it done?" Magdelay said.

Aaslo's gaze fell on the bloody stump of Mathias's neck. He looked up to see that the head had rolled a few feet away and was now staring at him. He didn't vomit. He was surprised. He had thought he would be sick, but his stomach felt like an empty pit. Aaslo picked up the head by its wavy golden locks and stared into the empty, lifeless eyes—not at all like Mathias's. They were the eyes of a man he didn't know.

"Yes," Aaslo said, "do you need to see it to cast the spell?"

"Unfortunately," Magdelay replied.

While Magdelay worked her magic, Aaslo pulled a burlap sack from his pack. He had intended to use it for gathering useful plants and herbs along the journey, but he supposed it would do for a head. Only once the head was placed inside did he realize how heavy it was. He grumbled, "A burlap sack is a poor burial shroud."

Magdelay's gaze was distant. "It is no longer of consequence. We are *all* dead and buried under the shroud of this prophecy." She pointed to the trench and said, "Do not bury him with his sword. It was a gift from the council."

"He needs a sword," Aaslo mumbled, barely able to force his voice past his lips.

"What's that?" she huffed.

Aaslo swallowed hard, his voice rising in anger. "He needs a sword. He needs his head, and he needs a sword." He gripped the bag against his chest and again muttered, "He needs a sword."

"Then bury him with yours," she said testily.

Aaslo had nearly forgotten about his sword. During the battle, he had used his axe, as it was his preference. Mathias had given him the sword because he had wanted a training partner. Aaslo supposed it was only appropriate to give it back. He removed Mathias's sword belt and wrapped it around his own waist before placing his sword in the pit with the rest of his best friend's body. Magdelay covered it over with dirt, and then they both stood in silence. After a few minutes, Aaslo began dragging the creatures' bodies into the woods where they wouldn't be easily found, while Magdelay continued to stare at the fresh grave.

Finally, she said, "We must go."

MYROPA WATCHED AS THE TWO SHADOWY FIGURES DISAPPEARED INTO the darkness. She would find them again; but, for now, she had another task. She studied the fresh dirt piled over the young man's headless body. It was a shame. He had been a handsome man with great potential. Still, he wasn't the first to die in this war, and he certainly wouldn't be the last. She turned her gaze back to the dark road. Was it coincidence that she had been sent there—at that very moment? Two of the travelers had been unknown to her, but the third she would have recognized anywhere. Never had she thought that one person could drive another to such madness, to lose herself, to utterly destroy her entire being until not even her soul was her own. Was it fate or destiny that had driven her back onto that path?

Turning away, she moved fifty paces into the forest with little more than a thought. On silent feet, she followed the iridescent path that twisted between the tangled branches rendered black by night. She felt neither dread nor thrill on the gloomy trek through the untamed wood. Long past were the days of threats by forest terrors. If only she had felt so dispassionate while she lived, she would not be in her present state.

The rich aroma of roasted meat tinged with the sour scent of charred hair and bone prickled her nose. While the taste of a savory meal or delectable dessert was denied to her, the scent of death was all the more pungent. It was a special torment for her kind, and a torture overshadowed only by the persistent, aching chill that suffused her body. She could feel the heat radiating from the wood still burning at its core, but never would her flesh be warmed.

She knelt on the sooty leaves, though they did not crackle beneath her—proof again that she was only a trespasser in this world. The wizard was dead. Well, he would be in a moment. A talented healer might have repaired enough of his scorched body for revival. It was too bad for him that none were present. She leaned down to whisper in his ear, and then he was standing in front of her, a luminescent man-shaped figure wrapped in a shroud of swirling light.

"Myropa," he said—a single word tainted with accusation.

She smiled with indulgence. "Disappointed? Trust me when I say that this is all my pleasure."

"Put me back, Myropa. You have gone too far."

She held her hand out to the charred mass of flesh on the ground. "You wish to go back to *that*?"

"What is this?" he shouted in alarm. "That woman! What has she done? It is impossible. She could not have bested me. I am far stronger than she."

Myropa *tsk*ed and said, "Obriday, you were always so arrogant. I told you it would be your downfall." She pointed to the ashy remains of the tree beside his corpse. "You killed *yourself*, actually, blew yourself up, to be precise. You should not have lit a flame near a fiergolen tree."

"What is a fiergolen tree? Bah, never mind that. Put me back and take me to Byella for healing."

"You know I cannot do that, Obriday. It is your time. You are marked." Myropa dragged one finger along the iridescent tether that bound her to him. "It will not break until you are delivered to the Sea—*if* it will have you."

"There has been a mistake. Pithor would not allow it. I am an incendia."

"Well, you certainly are *now*," she said wryly. "Remember, I do not work for Pithor."

Obriday curled his lip. "You should have more respect for the Deliverer of Grace and be grateful to His Mighty Light for assigning you to this team. It is likely your only chance for salvation, should you serve him well."

Myropa plucked the iridescent cord between them. "Yes, I have seen his light. Pithor may be a deadly force in this world, but he is nothing to me. He came begging on his knees for aid from Axus. He will pay a heavy price for my services."

"It is not a shame to subjugate oneself to the gods. Pithor is the Blessed Chosen. While others scoff with skepticism, he knelt at the feet of the temple's idol. With unmatched and undeniable faith and humility, he prayed for aid, and it was granted. Axus, the God of Death, demands you serve Pithor, and Pithor wants me alive."

Myropa brushed her long, dark curls over her shoulder. "I was not sent by Axus. I am here at Trostili's behest. Axus may be the God of Death, but he does not make the rules."

Lifting his chin, Obriday said, "The God of Death, the God of War— what difference does it make? They are both on our side, and theirs is the will of the gods."

"Are you so sure about that? Axus stands to gain much power from Pithor's war. I am not certain he has the other gods' approval."

"What do you know of the gods' desires? Most are just as eager as Pithor to see this world cleansed. The others don't care. Tell me, did any of them interfere in the realization of the prophecy? Did we succeed? Did we kill the Lightbane?"

From the dozens of thumb-sized marbles dangling on black cords at her waist, Myropa selected one that glowed with a pale blue light. She twirled it in the air before him and said, "Yes, he is dead." She indiscriminately grabbed a handful more and said, "So is your team." Dropping them back to her side with a clatter, she manifested a clear, empty orb in her open palm. With the vessel pinched between her finger and thumb, she placed it in the path of light between them and said, "So are you."

"Wait, you must inform the deliverer that the Lightbane is dead. He must know that he has already won."

Myropa hummed a slow tune, one tiny vestige of her past, and said, "You are not listening, Obriday. You are dead. The concerns of this world—Pithor and his plans—no longer matter *for you*. Have you nothing of *yourself* to remember?"

"I cannot be dead! I am an incendia. I am to lead our troops against the darkness that infests the hearts of man. I will help bring His light into the world."

With a deep inhale, Myropa activated the tiny sphere. "No, Obriday, your tasks are done. Now, you go into the Afterlife."

CHAPTER 5

AASLO AND MAGDELAY WALKED ALONG THE RUGGED ROAD FOR HOURS without a word. Aaslo was tired. He had spent the entire day tending the forest with Mathias, and now he was leaving the forest with Mathias's head in a burlap bag. That thought alone was enough to stay any complaints and keep him walking. It was a mindless task. He didn't think about his aching feet or windburned face. To keep from thinking about the burden he carried, he focused his entire attention on the sounds and motions of the forest.

"We'll stop now," Magdelay said, breaking the crisp barrier of reticence between them. "You need to rest as much as possible, for you have a long journey ahead. I'll keep watch until the dawn; then I must leave you."

"What do you mean, *leave*?"

"We are nearly to the crossroads. There we part ways."

Aaslo didn't like the idea of leaving the forest alone. He didn't like the idea of leaving the forest at all. What he liked no longer had bearing in his life, though. "First, tell me—what were those things, and where did they come from?"

"I don't know," Magdelay said. "I've never seen nor heard of them before tonight. The magus was human, though. He didn't speak, and I didn't recognize his spells. His clothes were strange, and he wore his hair longer than usual for a man. I think it's reasonable to conclude that these people are not from any of the known lands."

He was unsatisfied with the answer but accepted that it was the only one he would receive.

"Don't you need sleep?" he asked.

"Do not concern yourself with me. My magic can sustain me for a time."

Aaslo nodded, then dropped his pack. He stretched out on the ground, not even bothering with a tent or blanket. Worried that an animal might run away with his best friend's severed head, he wrapped himself around it and fell into a deep, dream-filled sleep. In that sleep, he was sure he had found madness.

✳

HE WOKE BEFORE DAWN AS USUAL. A SMALL FIRE WAS CRACKLING IN A pit, and half of a roasted rabbit was on a leaf in front of him. Aaslo sat up and collected the welcome food.

"You look different," he said as he wiped sleep from his eyes.

Magdelay had never looked her age. Although she was supposedly in her sixties, Aaslo had thought she looked to be no more than forty-five. Now, despite a sleepless night, she looked closer to thirty. The white streaks in her hair had disappeared, and where fine lines had marred her flesh, her skin was now smooth and vibrant.

"Magi are long-lived," she said. "We cast spells to rejuvenate our bodies. It would have appeared strange had I not aged while caring for Mathias, so I didn't cast the spells."

"How old *are* you?" Aaslo said. He knew it was rude to ask a woman's age, but she was the one who brought up the issue.

Magdelay replied with a smirk. "I'm one hundred and nine years old, so no matter how old you and Mathias get, you're both boys to me."

Her gaze fell on the burlap sack beside him, and she cringed. She tossed the map tube into his lap. He had no idea where it came from, since she hadn't had it the previous night after her horse escaped. He caught the small purse she threw next, then stared at her, his anxiety rising.

"Spend that wisely. I'm sorry, I don't have much on me. The rest ran away with the horse. I'm leaving now. Make your way to Tyellí as quickly as possible. There's a letter of introduction in the tube. If you have any trouble with the guards, show it to them. No matter what, Aaslo, don't lose the head. Make sure it gets to the king." She glanced toward the lightening sky and mumbled, "Not that it'll do any good." She gave him a withering smile, and he thought she might have wanted to hug him. Instead, she said, "May you ever walk in the shade," before she turned and strode away.

Aaslo couldn't find it in him to hurry through the simple meal, so he savored every bite. Then he kicked dirt over the fire and stomped on it to make sure it wouldn't spread to the forest. No matter his new responsibilities, he was first and foremost a forester.

What would have been a three-day ride to the next town became a five-day walk, and only because he took a few shortcuts. He ducked off the road once when a wagon passed, presumably on its way to retrieve lumber from Goldenwood. Since he didn't know if the enemy had spies, Aaslo wasn't taking any chances. He didn't even know who the enemy was, besides the fact that they dressed oddly and possessed strange creatures that bled white.

After days of trekking through unfamiliar woods, Aaslo abruptly stopped in the middle of the road. This was the moment he had been dreading. He stood between the last two trees of the forest halfway down the last foothill and gazed across the open land to the town in the distance. For as far as he could see, it was nothing but a flat plain with the slightest rises and dips, like a wrinkled swath of golden carpet. Here and there, tiny copses dotted the landscape, and nothing obscured the horizon, where gold met stormy grey. Aaslo had seen this scene once, from far atop a mountain. At that distance, though, the plains had looked like a tiny blotch on an incommensurable landscape. From here, it appeared that his despair would last for an eternity.

With his bow, axe, and pack strapped to his back, a sword at one hip, and a severed head at the other, Aaslo took his first step beyond the tree line. When his foot struck the ground, somewhere deep in his mind, in his heart, a bell tolled.

Shut up, he said to himself. *It's only a field.*

He nearly tripped twice as he walked the rest of the way down the hill. No longer was he surrounded by the haven of the trees that comforted him like a blanket. His gaze painted the sky in paranoia. There was too much of it—so much emptiness, so much unbroken blue and grey. He wanted dearly to crouch among the grasses that barely reached his knees. Out on the plain, he was exposed. Anyone—*anything*— could see him from miles away. It was a predator's dream. No longer did the branches crack and the leaves rustle. His mind was filled with the drone of grasses shifting in the wind. Worse yet, he was still a half hour's walk from Mierwyl when the sky broke open.

Aaslo shivered. He slogged through the mud. Alone. For five days he had been alone, and now he would drown under an open sky, cursed to walk beneath the clouds and sun. He was wet and cold, but at least he was somewhat obscured by the pouring rain.

"They can see you in the rain, too, you know."

He spun around, looking in every direction, but there was no one—no dark figures in the rain, no lumps crouching in the grass.

"Who said that? Who's there?"

No one answered. Thunder rumbled across the sky. Aaslo shook his head and continued sloshing through the puddles. It had to be in his mind.

"You're dreaming about me too? That's just sad, Aaslo."

The voice was followed by hollow laughter.

Aaslo paused and gripped the burlap sack tied to his belt. It hung heavier than all of his other gear combined. The hairs on the back of his neck and arms stood on end, and the scent of metal and mint filled the air just before a silver bolt from the sky struck less than twenty yards from him. Rattled by the concussion that reverberated in his chest, Aaslo picked up his pace. He couldn't remain exposed in the storm now that he was the tallest of anything between the forest and the town. He considered that it might be smarter to lie down and wait it out.

"We both know if you do that, you won't get back up."

"Shut up," he told the voice. "I'm not an infant. I won't drown in a field."

"You've never liked the water. I thought you were drowning every time Grams made you take a bath."

"I was *five*," he grumbled.

"Eight."

"I'm a grown man. I bathe regularly."

"Then you should invest in new soap. Yours must have soured."

The laughter that followed was too familiar, too painful to hear.

Aaslo stopped and jerked the sack from his belt. He shook as he held Mathias's head in his hands and pulled away the burlap. Clear blue eyes stared up at him, framed with the dark lashes that caused the girls to giggle, and perfect golden locks curled around his cheekbones. When they were younger, Aaslo had made fun of Mathias for being too pretty; and, in return, Mathias had laughed and told him that his mother must have been a bear.

"What did you say?" Aaslo yelled. "What did she do to you? Are you still in there, Mathias? Say something!"

But the head was silent. And the voice was silent. And Aaslo was alone, on a road, in the plains, during a lightning storm, yelling at a severed head.

The rest of the trek toward the town was quiet, save for the sloshing of his boots and the cadence of the rain. If he didn't think about it too hard, it almost sounded like leaves rustling in the wind. Of course, just before he reached the edge of town, the rain ceased. Mierwyl was a small town, according to Magdelay; but to Aaslo it was massive and overpopulated. A dozen streets crossed the main road, most of them cobbled, and those had streets crossing them as well. On every one of them were at least a few people. He wondered how so many people could exist in one place, and why they would want to. The buildings were all constructed of wood, wood he and his folk had helped to grow. He decided it was fitting that this forest's death should surround him in his time of despair.

"Don't be so morbid."

"Said the talking head," Aaslo snapped. He glanced around to see if anyone had noticed, but everyone was too preoccupied with their own business to concern themselves with a muddy traveler. He spied a man pinning back the shutters of an inn. Aaslo wanted badly to request a room, but he had little money and greater priorities. "Excuse me, sir, where might I purchase a horse?"

The man turned to greet him with a boisterous "Hello! Are you sure it's a horse you're wanting? It looks more like you could use a bath."

"Bwahaha! He's not wrong."

Mathias's laughter nearly made Aaslo jump, but the man didn't seem fazed as he continued his pitch.

"For two bits you can have one. It'll be ready in no time"—he waved with a flourish toward his establishment—"right in there."

Aaslo frowned and scratched at the scraggly beard that had erupted from his face during his five days without shaving. "And the soap?"

"Ah, well, that'll be another bit."

"Mm-hmm. And a towel?" he asked.

"That's a bit, too," the man said with a smile as if a bit meant *free,* except with pay.

"So, a bath is a copper," Aaslo said. "Why don't you just say a bath is a copper?"

Still smiling, the man said, "Because a bath isn't a copper. It's two bits. And, if you'd like a room, the bath is free!"

"How much is a room?"

"Five coppers," the man said, splaying his fingers.

"Five coppers is a silver. Why don't you just say a silver?"

The man gasped with dismay. "Well, you might not have a silver, but it's possible you have five coppers."

"It's the same amount of money," Aaslo grumbled. After five days of sleeping in the woods, a battle with white-blooded creatures, and slogging through the mud, he figured he probably smelled worse than the horse he intended to buy.

"Your acceptance of that fact diminishes its truth in no way."

"Shut up," said Aaslo.

"Excuse me, sir?" said the innkeeper warily.

"Ah, I said set it up. I'll not be taking the room, but I guess I'll have the bath. I'll need the soap and towel, too."

The innkeeper smiled with delight and waved him toward the bathing chamber. Aaslo paid an extra bit for more hot water to wash his clothes, which before long were hanging in front of the hearth on the other side of the small chamber. The rest of his belongings were gathered in the corner, except for the head. That, he had tucked between the tub and the near wall. The heat began to penetrate his muscles, and for the first time since Goldenwood, Aaslo thought he might relax.

He picked up his shaving kit from the shelf that lay across the tub and looked at himself in the small mirror. He scratched at his scruff and picked out a few leaves and chunks of dirt. At least, he hoped it was dirt. If he were honest with himself, he might have admitted that it had been seven days since he had last shaved—or bathed.

"I knew it!" Mathias said with a hoot.

Aaslo groaned. "Can't you just let me be in my bath? I don't need you in here with me."

"Oh, yes, sir. I meant no offense," said a small, squeaky voice from other side of the curtain blocking the doorway. "I was just seein' if you needed anythin' else. Sorry to bother you, sir." The curtain billowed as the door was pulled shut, and Aaslo groaned again.

AN HOUR LATER, HE WAS STANDING IN A RUN-DOWN STABLE YARD arguing with a gangly man who had a lazy eye. Aaslo rolled the numbers over again in his mind, and his stomach rolled with them as he considered his lightweight purse.

"What's so great about this one?"

"It's brown," said the man.

"You're charging ten extra silver for this one because it's brown?"

"Yes, sir. People like brown horses."

Aaslo surveyed the selection. Four horses. Of four horses, the man was trying to get him to buy this one—and pay extra—because it was brown.

"I need a dependable horse—one that can travel long-distance. I don't care if it's brown."

"I get that," said the man. "This one's as good as the others, plus it's brown."

"Sir, I'm a forester, and if you know anything about foresters, then you'd know I don't care one twig if it's brown."

"Jacobi, what are you tryin' to sell to that young man?"

Aaslo turned to find an older woman wobbling down the steps from the home into the attached stable.

"Ma, go back inside. Let me handle this," said Jacobi.

"Didn't ya hear the man? He's a forester. You'll not be tryin' to swindle no forester. Have some respect. I apologize, Sir Forester. I thought I raised him better than that. I've got a horse for you. He's a strong one—a bit stubborn and a little crusty, but he'll get ya where ya need to go. I'll give him to ya for five less than these others, too."

"Which one is he?" Aaslo asked.

"Oh, he's not in here. People are a bit uncomfortable around him on account of his looks. That's why no one wants him. I figure you don't care about that, though, do ya, Sir Forester? Just follow me."

"She's going to cook you and eat you for supper."

"I'm not good eating," Aaslo muttered.

"Oh, he's a good eater," the old woman called back to him. "A healthy weight—strong, like I said."

At best, the horse might have been considered strange, but most would say he was outright ugly. He could have been half boar, and Aaslo wouldn't have cared, so long as he took him where he needed to go. A line ran straight down the gelding's face from forelock to muzzle, one side black and the other white. More striking were the eyes, which were two different colors—bluish white on the black side of his face and brown on the other. It was as if someone had cut two horses down the center, then joined two of the halves. Beyond that, his coat was mottled with brown, black, and white splotches. Aaslo had never seen anything like it.

Mr. Poldry, the Goldenwood blacksmith, and Captain Cromley had taught Mathias what to look for in a horse. Aaslo had tagged along. From what he could tell, this mess of a beast seemed like a decent ride. If he was going to ride it, though, he'd need supplies.

"I'll take him," Aaslo said, "but I'll need to purchase some tack."

"That's all right. I'll have Jacobi clean him up for ya while you go up the street," said the old woman as they stepped out of the barn. She paused and squinted toward the stable. "Now, who's he talkin' to over there? My eyes ain't what they used to be, but that's a strange one if I've ever seen one."

A tall, thin man wearing odd clothing was deep in conversation with Jacobi. The man's black pants were tight around the legs, and his fitted white tunic hung to his knees. He wore a black sash around his abdomen, from which hung a curved blade, which was broader toward the tip and carried in an ornamented sheath. His straight brown hair fell to his waist, and his overall appearance was immaculate. The man nodded toward Jacobi and then walked away before Aaslo and the old woman had reached them.

"Who was that? What did he want?" the woman snapped, and Aaslo was glad she was there to ask.

"I'm not sure, Ma. He's looking for someone. A tall, blond fellow with a birthmark on his temple. Either of you seen him?"

"You know I'm not seeing much these days, Jacobi. What kinda question is that? Now let the forester get his things so he can be on his way."

From the street, Aaslo spied the stranger stepping into the linen shop. Quickening his pace, Aaslo scurried down the road to a general store. Just as he ducked through the doorway, he glanced back to see the man exit the linen shop and head toward the chandler's next door. Aaslo turned to survey the supply shop. It was dim, with dust motes floating in the afternoon sunlight that barely lit the front of the room. The shelves and crates stacked along the walls held an assortment of farm and ranch equipment, and the tack was piled in the rear, almost as an afterthought.

"Can I help you?" asked the shopkeeper as he stood from behind the counter.

Aaslo hadn't even realized the man was in the room. The shopkeeper's face was worn and leathery, as if he'd spent his life in the sun. He had a long mustache that hung past his chin and was missing one of his front teeth.

"I need some tack. Something good for a long journey," Aaslo said.

"Nothin' fancy, then? I've got a worn saddle, not *too* worn, mind you. Might be better than a new one if ya ain't used to ridin'. It'll be cheaper, too."

"That sounds fine," Aaslo said. "How much?"

The man narrowed his eyes, scrutinizing Aaslo's gear. "I'll give it to ya in trade. The tack for that axe."

Aaslo shook his head. "I need my axe. How much for the tack?"

"What do ya need more—the tack or that axe?" the shopkeeper said.

"He's got you there."

Aaslo clenched his jaw. "I need the tack more at the moment, but I'm a forester. I can't part with the axe."

"You're a forester, eh? I never seen a forester. Ya look normal to me."

Mathias hooted with laughter. *"That's because he doesn't know you."*

"Did you expect that I wouldn't?" said Aaslo.

"Well, ya ain't got no pointy ears or nothin', sir. I'm just sayin'."

Aaslo scowled. "Why would I have pointy ears?"

The man held up his hands. "Now, don't get a twist in your reins. I'm just saying some folks think you foresters've been dallyin' with the faeries. Others think maybe you *are* faeries—or some kinda fae folk, anyhow."

"I bet you're the prettiest faerie of them all, Aaslo. Show us your sparkle."

Aaslo huffed, "I'm not a faerie, and I don't know any fae folk. I couldn't say if they even exist. I'm just a man who needs a saddle *and* his axe."

"I suppose we can't be partin' a forester from his axe. It's a fine axe, though. If you're headin' south, you won't be gettin' much use outta it. No trees for a long while."

"How do you know I'm going south?" Aaslo said.

"Not much else ways to go, now, is there? I s'pose you could be goin' east, but ain't much reason to be going out that way. I figure you're answerin' the summons. The blight down there in Ruriton must be pretty bad if they're callin' for a forester from all the way up here. You'd think with all those magic folk, they'd be able to take care of it them-selves. Mayhap you'll be needing that axe when ya get there."

Aaslo knew nothing about a summons, or a blight, but at least he didn't have to come up with an excuse. The shopkeeper finally sold him the items he needed, and Aaslo hefted the whole pile, glad to be done with the mess.

"Good luck to you, Sir Forester."

He turned to leave and nearly ran into the man standing behind him. It was the stranger who had been looking for Mathias. The man looked at him with a piercing gaze that reminded Aaslo of a raptor siz-ing up its prey. Pale brown eyes rimmed in gold stared at him over sharp cheekbones bearing a waxy sheen. Pursing his thin lips, the man glanced over Aaslo, and it became obvious judgment had been passed.

"What . . . is a *forester?*" the man asked.

Aaslo wanted to ignore the question and leave, but the stranger was blocking the way.

Instead, he said, "Who are you? You don't sound like you're from around here."

The man grinned, baring teeth that looked a bit too pointed. He spoke slowly, as if he had all the time in the world. "I'm a visitor. They call me Verus. I'm looking for someone. Perhaps you've seen him? He's tall, young, with blond hair and a distinctive mark on his temple . . . right . . . here," he said, tapping his own temple with a finger bearing a long nail filed to a point and lacquered black.

"*I'm popular,*" cheered Mathias.

"You're dead," Aaslo muttered.

Verus's intense gaze searched Aaslo for everything that he was. He said, "I assure you that I am very much alive. It's interesting that you say that, though. Do you think of death often?"

"Only when planning my future," Aaslo retorted. "I can't say that I've seen anyone who fits that description, but I wasn't exactly paying attention. I mind my own business."

"Hmm, and what was that business, *Forester?*"

"None of *yours,*" Aaslo said.

The shopkeeper interrupted the exchange with an anxious cough. "Ah, kind sir, this here is a forester. They're highly respected, espe-cially in these parts. Ya see, they grow the trees, take care of 'em, make sure they're healthy—so as the loggers have somethin' to cut down. Without the foresters, none of us would be here. And, well, they don't leave the forests much, so they don't get talkin' to people much neither, if you understand what I mean."

Verus narrowed his eyes at Aaslo. "You are a gardener?" He turned to the shopkeeper. "This is a respectable position in your kingdom?"

"They say faeries love gardens, Aaslo. Maybe you are a faerie."

Although words rarely affected Aaslo, this Verus was likely the enemy, and he wanted to punch the man in his vicious little mouth. "I'm not a gardener."

The shopkeeper's grin faltered, and he glanced at Aaslo, presumably to see if he would say more. Aaslo attempted to step around the man, but Verus made no effort to move. He sized up the stranger as he considered shoving him out of the way. He didn't like Verus, and he decided any injury the man might incur would be acceptable.

"He might be a magus."

The thought gave him pause long enough for the shopkeeper to begin chattering again. Looking back to Verus, the shopkeeper said, "Yes, foresters are revered for their sacrifice. Even now, he's goin' to fight back the blight that's destroyin' the wilds in the south."

Verus leaned into Aaslo and sniffed. "What magic do these *foresters* possess to combat such a scourge?"

Aaslo didn't attempt to hide his contempt as he replied, "We don't have any magic besides hard work and experience."

With a malicious grin, Verus said, "Good luck with that." The infuriating man glanced at the shopkeeper and then dismissed them both as he left.

The shopkeeper rubbed his head and said, "He's a strange one, no doubt about that. Now that I think about it, seein' as how you're goin' to fight the blight and all, I kinda feel bad about chargin' ya for the tack. It's all used goods, after all. Here, let me return your money. If ya get a good reward, you remember me on the way back."

Although he had little money left, Aaslo had no desire to mislead or take advantage of the man. He was about to reject the offer when Mathias said, *"You're going to save the world, dimwit."*

"Right," Aaslo muttered. He took the coins from the shopkeeper and promised to return if he came back rich. Aaslo doubted he'd survive to come back at all.

"Well, you certainly won't with that attitude."

"You're right," he muttered as he left the shop. "I don't have to become the savior, anyway. I'll drop you off, and the king will find someone else—a knight or a magus or an entire army of knights and magi."

Aaslo didn't want to run into Verus again, so he quickly collected the remainder of his supplies and left the town astride his new steed. With his pack strapped to the saddle and Mathias's head secured at his belt, he took to the southern road toward the capital. It was not long before he realized the horse was an idiot. It first became evident when the gelding refused to turn left. No matter how hard Aaslo tried, he couldn't get the beast to go left, so he was forced to circle to the right every time he needed to change direction. Just as he reached the town limit, the moron spooked at a flowerpot beside the florist's stall; and, when Aaslo stopped to give him water, the damnable creature threw the water bucket into the air and then proceeded to stomp on it as if it were a rat.

The old woman had been true to her word, though. Dolt, as Aaslo had begun affectionately calling him, seemed to keep his pace indefinitely, even if it wasn't a fast one. The horse plodded along until well after dark. Normally, Aaslo would have stopped for camp at least an hour before sundown, but he was concerned about being followed. He doubted he had roused Verus's suspicions, though. The man seemed to have rejected him as inconsequential, but Aaslo felt it better to be safe. That night, he slept hidden in the grass far from the road.

MYROPA WATCHED VERUS STEP INTO THE NEXT SHOP. SHE HAD ONCE again found the Lightbane's former companion as he was haggling over the price of a horse, although the sorceress was no longer with him. She had not expected to find Verus in the village, not so far north. He had been assigned the central region, but the man was ambitious, perhaps more so than Obriday, who had at least gained his position through skill. What Verus lacked in strength and skill, though, he made up for in brutality.

Myropa might have considered updating Verus on the progress of the mission if he had been able to see or hear her, but the sorcerer had not been granted the blessing. She imagined the ignoble louse spending weeks looking for someone who was already dead and smiled to herself. With a thought, she was standing at the edge of town watching the young forester ride past. She had hoped the sorceress would join him once his business in town was concluded, but the woman did not reappear. Myropa realized the two must have parted ways, although she couldn't imagine why the woman would have left him alone. Even Myropa knew well that foresters were not equipped to handle tasks outside their beloved forests, and the significance of this one leaving his forest had not been lost on her. Glancing at the bag that dangled from the man's waist, she considered again the loss he—and his world—had suffered.

She knew the forester's destination, so she would be able to find him again. Releasing the breath of the living, Myropa passed through the veil into Celestria. The light was bright there, unlike the muted tones in the Realm of the Living, where she no longer saw the sun as the brilliant yellow star she remembered. Her heeled slippers tapped lightly over the jade tiles as she exited the receiving chamber of the fifth palace. The courtyard was empty, save for the twittering birds bathing in the fountain. Skirting the voluminous leaves and petals of the exaggerated foliage, she passed under the marble archway of the far portico, then padded through the corridor, colorfully lit with varying hues of flame atop man-sized torches. A breeze swept through the open archways, brushing her split skirt aside and exposing her legs to a chill. While she could not feel warmth, the cold never eluded her.

When she reached the swirling door of liquid light at the end, she pulled on a golden cord at its side. A moment later, the light stilled, and she was able to pass through without trouble.

"Really, Trostili, I don't know why you bother with them," said Arayallen. "They're so destructive."

"That's the point," said Trostili.

Arayallen pursed her perfect, pink lips, then smiled. "Yes, I suppose you would appreciate that." She waved a hand toward the doorway but did not grace Myropa with her gaze. "Your pet is here. See what she wants so we can get on with the preparations."

"You throw the same party every day, Araya. What more is there to be discussed?"

"It's not the *same* party. Yesterday, the theme was reptiles from the planet Teguei. The day before, it was the forest giants of Byganth. You know the easiest way for me to encourage growth and evolution in my wildernesses is by throwing a party. It requires less of my energy when the other gods are gathered."

The goddess admired herself in a full-length mirror, twisting back and forth as pale wings suddenly erupted from her back, the tips delicately brushing the floor. Myropa stared in awe at the misty fall of cascading feathers.

Trostili grabbed the goddess by the waist and kissed her slender neck as she giggled. He brushed a thumb across her clavicle and stared into Arayallen's golden gaze as he spoke.

"Human, do you find it strange that the God of War and the Goddess of the Wilderness should enjoy such devotion?"

It took Myropa a moment to realize he had been speaking to her. She ducked her head and said, "I wouldn't know."

He grinned sardonically. "No, *you* wouldn't know the value of love, would you?"

Myropa felt her heart clench. The words stung because they were true.

Arayallen playfully slapped his chest. "You antagonize her."

Trostili sighed and turned toward Myropa. "Yes, but she never bites. You would think she's intimidated by me." He chuckled and leaned down to look her in the eyes. She was not short for a woman—a human woman, anyway—but the top of her head barely reached the god's chest. His gaze nearly brought her to her knees as he said, "You're not intimidated by me, are you, Reaper?"

Myropa's mouth hung silent as she tried desperately for an answer. She wanted to please him, *needed* to please him.

"Turn it down, Trostili," said Arayallen. "I can feel your influence from here. The reaper can't even speak. Get on with this silly game so we can finish planning the party."

Suddenly, Myropa could breathe again, and she hadn't even realized she'd stopped. "I come with news," she sputtered.

Trostili turned and grabbed a couple of persimmons from a bowl before stretching out on a cream-colored divan positioned just barely within the shade of the open room. "Of course you do. Why else would you be here? Speak."

Myropa was overcome with the need to comply, and her lips began moving on their own. "The one Pithor refers to as the Lightbane has been collected." She held up the pale blue vessel that dangled from a cord at her waist. "Obriday and his team are also dead, killed by a sorceress and the Lightbane's companion. Verus still seeks the Lightbane in the north. He is unaware of the success of the mission."

Trostili nodded with a pleased grin as he gazed across the open expanse of lawn and gardens toward the lavender sea. "Excellent. I never cared for Obriday, anyhow."

Arayallen strolled over with a couple of goblets and handed one to Trostili. She took a moment to adjust her new wings as she sat and drew her legs up beneath her on the seat next to him. "Of course you didn't care for him, Trostili. He was human."

He looked at her in surprise. "What do you mean? I care for humans."

"Pff, you do not. You're always pitting them against one another."

"Ha! They do that on their own. Well, mostly. That's what makes them such wonderful creatures. I hardly have to work for my power."

Arayallen nodded thoughtfully. "Well, you do spend an *ungodly* amount of time on them."

Myropa's gaze bounced back and forth between the two gods. She was mesmerized by the power that radiated from them. She felt its calescent touch wash across her skin, which warmed the longer she stood in their presence.

Trostili leaned in to kiss Arayallen, then brushed the strap of her gown off her shoulder. The goddess placed her slender fingers over his wanting lips and said, "Your pet is still here, Trostili."

He sighed again and turned to Myropa. "Is that all?"

She stared at him for a moment, then shook herself free of his thrall. "Shall I inform Axus and Pithor of the success?"

Trostili twirled one of Arayallen's caramel curls around his finger as he absently replied, "No, let them figure it out on their own." Myropa didn't realize she was smiling until he said, "This pleases you?"

"Yes," she said, but stopped upon feeling the quaver in her voice. She gripped the silky skirt of her burgundy dress and bit her lower lip.

"What is it?" He flicked a finger at her. "You always do that when you are eager to speak."

Again, her mouth rambled of its own accord. "The Lightbane's friend has taken up his cause. He carries the Lightbane's head to the Uyanian king in hopes of finding another savior."

Trostili raised a brow. "Oh? Tell me of this friend."

"He is a forester from the village where the Lightbane was reared."

Arayallen sat up, her interest piqued. "A forester? One of *my* foresters?"

Trostili pulled her back into his embrace and said, "You suddenly care for the humans, dear?"

"Well, no, but the foresters are the least offensive. They, at least, respect me. I have little hope for, nor interest in, the rest."

Trostili waved his hand toward the portal. "You may go. Keep this between us."

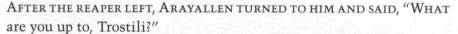

AFTER THE REAPER LEFT, ARAYALLEN TURNED TO HIM AND SAID, "WHAT are you up to, Trostili?"

He laid his head back and closed his eyes. "What I do best, dear— *war*."

"Why do you not tell Axus that his plan worked and be done with this already? If you keep it from him, he will delay the assault."

"The longer the war, the more power for me. Besides, I am not *keeping* it from him. I'm just not doing his work for him. Are you so eager to see the humans destroyed?"

Arayallen pursed her lips. "I have no interest in your little game. I had such hopes for the humans. They were my favorite, you know. Their design was nearly perfect—the closest to our own that I've made. I blame Iochtheus. He made them too self-aware. Not only are they aware of themselves, they are aware of *us*!"

Trostili rolled his eyes. "They are not aware of us."

"Well, they know we exist."

"They *think* we exist. There's a difference."

"Not by much," she said as she fisted her dainty hands. "Barbach. *He* filled them with ambition . . . and pettiness . . . and arrogance. They are nothing like us. What was he thinking?"

"He *is* the God of Desire. What would you have him do?"

"Keep it to himself," she said.

"It's good that they aren't perfect, Araya. We wouldn't want them getting it into their heads that *they* are gods, would we?" Trostili swirled the amber liquid in his goblet. "Axus won't be satisfied with the humans, you know. He intends to take the entire world."

She turned to him with hesitance. "All of it? All my creations? The plants as well?"

Trostili tilted his head, studying her reaction carefully. On which side of the war would she fall? If anyone felt an interest in challenging Axus for the welfare of Aldrea, it would be Arayallen. Discontent fluttered across her face; then she shrugged. She tugged a length of filmy material from a table and wrapped it around herself as she twisted in front of the mirror.

She said, "Aldrea is just one little world." She then turned to him with a burst of excitement. "Did I tell you? Olios has created a new sphere. It's a lovely blue with spots of green and swirls of white, and he's placed it around a golden star at just the right distance. Truly, the Worldmaker has outdone himself." Her eyes widened, and she slapped her hands together. "I could start again—with the humans, I mean. We could adjust the recipe, bring them better into balance with the wilderness."

Trostili smiled. "Think of the glorious battles."

"*You* will stay out of it," she said.

He laughed aloud and thought, *Not likely.*

CHAPTER 6

THE JOURNEY TO TYELLÍ WAS LONG, AND AASLO TIRED OF THE INCESSANT wind that rattled the prairie grasses. Beyond haggling with a few shop-keepers, he spoke with no one besides Mathias. He could not even escape the phantom in his sleep. His dreams were haunted by bloody battles, each of them different, but always ending the same—with a beheading. Sometimes it was Mathias's, sometimes his own. Day after day, Mathias droned on about the most trivial things. The phantom voice wondered about the origin of the stars, pondered why most animals had four legs, calculated random currency exchanges, and told the story of Parshia at least twice per day. Aaslo wondered why he chose that particular story. They had read it together years before, and it had only come up again on the last day they had truly spoken—the last day of Mathias's life.

"*You think I'm dead?*"

The voice roused Aaslo from his reflections. "Are you saying you're not?" he said as he stared down an empty road that was little more than a set of wagon ruts through a field.

"*I suppose that's a matter of opinion. What* is *death, anyway? I mean, you're alive and going about your business . . .*"

Aaslo did his best to tune out the monologue, as he had for more than three weeks. His horse tripped over a nonexistent rock—*again*—jarring him and everything else it carried. The heavy burlap sack smacked against Aaslo's thigh as it swung down from its perch. He kept it secured to his belt at all times, never certain the horse wouldn't run away. He pulled the bag into his lap.

"*You're not paying attention.*"

Aaslo sighed as the guilt churned in his stomach. "You're right. I apologize. Tell me again."

"*As I was saying, Bougliet never truly understood the Siderian cultural obsession with carrackac hats. I can't blame him, really. They look ridiculous. You should get one.*"

"You just said they look ridiculous."

"*Well, yeah, but it's not like you'll be worse off than you are now. Besides, you like functional things, and you like plants.*"

"I don't live in the desert. I can get water from the streams and rivers. We cross at least two every day."

"*But if you strap a carrackac plant to your head, you wouldn't have to wait to find one or clean the water before you drink it.*"

Aaslo said, "With this much water in the air, a carrackac plant would be the size of this horse within a couple of weeks."

"*I see your point, but it would still fit your head.*"

"We'd best not argue over who has a bigger head, seeing as how I'm bearing the weight of both."

Mathias did not respond, and Aaslo found relief in the silence that loomed over his guilt. At least, he did until his stupid horse mistook a porcupine for grass. The rest of his afternoon was spent plucking quills from the beast's muzzle. He couldn't imagine how the horse had survived for so long. By the time he was finished, the sun was nearing the horizon, so Aaslo decided to make camp. Thus far sustained by rabbits, squirrels, and even rats caught in traps he set each night, he decided to use the extra daylight to hunt for something more substantial. With his bow in hand, he left the road to seek prey near a small pond. He missed a pheasant on the way and realized the distance to his target was harder to estimate on the open prairie than it was in the forest.

"*And you always said you were better with the bow. That was pitiful.*"

Aaslo didn't protest, seeing as how it was true. He tied Dolt's reins around a thick stand of reeds on one end of the pond, hoping the horse didn't get himself stuck in the mud, then waited for something edible to appear from the other side. As the sun dipped below the horizon, six pygmy deer, small enough to hide in the thigh-high grasses, cautiously approached the pond in a tight group. Just as he released his arrow, the herd startled. He swiftly released a second, picking off the rearmost doe. He turned to see what had spooked the creatures just as the sound reached his ears. Not far in the distance, a group of riders was approaching from the north. They had likely spied him already—

or at least his horse, who had managed to get his bridle caught in the reeds so that he was pivoting in circles trying to free himself.

Aaslo figured that leaving the ideal campsite as the sun was setting would only raise the riders' suspicions. After collecting the doe and Dolt, Aaslo waded through the tall grass to make camp at least a hundred yards from the pond, hoping the riders would leave him alone. He had no such luck. By the time he had finished dressing the small deer and started a fire, two of the riders were headed his way. Nine men, seven of which appeared to be soldiers, remained at the pond watering their horses, unloading a wagon, or divesting themselves of their armor and clothes. Aaslo's sword was at his waist, and he gripped his axe as he awaited their arrival.

The two riders stopped several paces from him and dismounted. Each drew a sword, and the man in the lead, an officer, judging by the shiny medallions on his breast, said, "Throw down your weapons and identify yourself."

Aaslo glanced at the soldiers beyond these two. While they appeared relaxed and tired at that moment, he found it suspicious that they were bothering with him. He knew the small army would be upon him if he caused trouble. Still, he had a task, and he couldn't afford an inspection. If he killed a soldier, he'd be captured and hanged. "I have no problem with you, and I'm minding my own business. I'll move on down the road if it'll make you feel better."

"Drop the sword, too."

Aaslo straightened and lifted his chin as Cromley had taught him. He said, "You have no cause to divest me of my weapons. A man is entitled to arm himself on the road."

The officer stepped forward and motioned for the other to flank Aaslo. Reminded of his practices with Cromley and Mathias, Aaslo knew better than to let the soldier get behind him.

"Ha ha! They're going to take you down, just like I always did."

Aaslo backed away so both men stayed within his sight. The evasion did not sit well with the officer, who issued no further warnings. The man advanced on him, covering the distance between them in a few quick steps. Aaslo drew his sword in time to deflect the first overhead strike, then twisted and ducked beneath their joined blades to avoid a second attack from the other soldier. He quickly backed away, nearly tripping over a clump of grass, and collided with his horse, who had not been there when last he looked. Dolt chose that moment to nip at his hair. Aaslo pushed his muzzle away, then ducked beneath the beast to avoid the advancing soldiers. The horse stood swishing his tail and chomping on grass as if he weren't standing in the middle of a sword fight.

The officer skirted the horse's head, while the other soldier went to the rear. Without warning, Dolt kicked the soldier in the chest hard enough to send him sprawling and gasping for breath. Aaslo jumped back as the officer swiped at him from the side, then parried another high strike. The officer delivered a gut swipe and then a jab. Aaslo managed to avoid the brunt of both, taking only a small cut across his stomach. He parried another strike, then saw movement from the corner of his eye. He realized more men from the camp were headed his way. His best bet was probably to end the fight, jump on Dolt, and flee the scene. Unfortunately, on the open prairie, there was nowhere to hide, so he would have to ride until they gave up pursuit.

"Focus."

Aaslo ducked just in time to avoid decapitation.

"Come on, Aaslo. Stop playing around."

He swallowed the bile that had made its way up his throat and hardened his resolve. He gripped his sword and pounded forward. Taking the officer by surprise, Aaslo commenced a flurry of strikes he couldn't possibly maintain for long, but that wasn't necessary. If he didn't finish this quickly, he might as well drop his sword and let the man kill him.

"Remember that dead tree? The big one you took down in one swipe?"

With another glance at the approaching riders, Aaslo pummeled the officer with such ferocity that the man couldn't manage a counterattack. He gripped his sword and swung with all his might, smashing the man's sword from his grip and toppling him to the ground. Aaslo stood poised with his sword hanging over the man's head, ready to deliver a final thrust.

"Halt!"

Aaslo was too late. The riders were near enough that he wouldn't be able to run. Frozen with his sword in the air, he imagined how he looked in that moment, like the beast that had taken Mathias. Breathing heavily, he didn't take his eyes from the downed man as the others arrived.

"Drop your weapon!"

"This man accosted me with no cause," Aaslo said. "I was minding my own business."

When no response came, he glanced up at the newcomers. Mounted before him were five men. The man on the right carried a short sword and bore a smug expression over a haughty bearing, the impact of which was thoroughly ruined by his servant's livery. The one on the left was rough and wore heavy leather armor over chain mail. Two more had the appearance of personal guards. One of the guards circled around to Aaslo's rear. It became apparent that Dolt didn't appreciate the intrusion, since he proceeded to intermittently gnash at the other horse's tail.

The lead man in the center, a young man no older than Aaslo, calmly surveyed Aaslo's camp and then the scene of the battle. Sitting tall upon his impressive steed, he stroked his short, perfectly trimmed beard and adjusted the emerald-green felt hat that hung over his right ear. Then he tugged at the high collar of his cream-colored tunic, which was partially covered by a dark green, sleeveless overcoat. The man's attire appeared expensive but still practical for traveling. He said, "Is that a deer I spy? Shall I arrest you for poaching?"

"Obviously he's a noble. It's practically written on his forehead, not to mention the crest on his overcoat."

"Which one?" Aaslo said as he lowered his weapon and took a few steps away from the officer on the ground.

The noble surveyed the scene again. "Are you saying you killed more than one deer?"

"Come on, you remember. The wolf's head surrounded by a tangle of briar."

"I don't remember," Aaslo replied.

"You don't remember how many you've killed?" said the nobleman.

"You know the rhyme. Wolf-briar . . ."

"Dovermyer," said Aaslo.

The man straightened in his saddle. "If you know who I am, then you should know to sheathe your weapon in my presence. You will refer to me as the Most Honorable the Marquess of Dovermyer."

"That's quite a mouthful," Aaslo said, while maintaining the grip on his sword. "It was just one."

"One what?" said the marquess.

Aaslo pointed the tip of his blade toward the pile of deer parts. "It was one deer, and this is common land."

"Who are you to make such a claim?"

"*I'm* not claiming it. So says the map, and neither of us is granted the power to change that."

The armored man beside the marquess started to dismount, but the marquess held up a hand. He said, "You are impertinent."

"You're better at communicating with strangers than I thought. He already knows you so well."

Aaslo mumbled, "You were always better at talking to people."

The marquess replied, "Well, yes, of that I am certain. Are you not concerned that you are surrounded?"

Aaslo shrugged as he kept an eye on the officer, who was fuming after having regained his feet. "I have many concerns, most of which I can do nothing about. I *am* curious as to why the *Most Honorable the Marquess* of Dovermyer is traveling this way. Your land is to the south, is it not?"

The marquess looked to the sky and sighed with exasperation. "That *is* most vexing. I was sent by my father to recruit a forester—one of those elusive wood folk from the north. It is rumored they hold power over nature. They have ignored our summons for months, so I was entrusted with the task." He shook his head and clenched a fist. "I spent my father's last days searching for people who might as well be animals and still, they refused to leave their precious trees."

"The lot should be punished for their insolence," said the dark, armor-clad guard.

"The king's orders stand," replied the marquess. "The foresters are to be left to their own business, so long as their business is tending the forest."

"My lord," said the rugged guard with a disapproving grumble. "You have yet to learn anything about this man, yet you share our business freely. It is your prerogative to question him, not the reverse."

The marquess tugged at his collar again. "You are right, Greylan. I allowed my frustration to hinder my judgment." Turning back to Aaslo, he said, "Who are you?"

Aaslo looked the marquess in the eyes and said, "My name is Aaslo, Forester of Goldenwood."

"You—"

"My condolences about your father," Aaslo said before the marquess could complete his thought. "May he forever walk in the shade."

The marquess paused and then said, "Thank you. You are the first to offer as much to me, though I cannot say I understand about the shade."

A shrill squeal interrupted them, and the guard who had circled to Aaslo's rear shouted when he was bucked from his horse, which had apparently decided it had endured enough of Dolt's taunting. Dolt bared his teeth at the other horse and then abruptly lay down to roll in the grass.

"What is wrong with your horse?" the marquess said, obviously confounded by the display.

Aaslo said, "He's an idiot."

The marquess looked at him appraisingly. "How do I know you're a forester?"

Aaslo sidestepped a few paces to where he had dropped his axe, then stooped to pick it up. "Because I said so."

"Tell me something a forester would know, something that is not common knowledge."

Propping his axe against one shoulder and gripping his sword with the other hand, Aaslo said, "What could I tell you about forestry that is not common knowledge and that *you* would know to be true?"

After a lingering glare, the marquess smirked. "Touché. How do you intend to prove it, then?"

"I don't," Aaslo replied. "I don't care what you believe. Your business is none of mine, and mine is none of yours. You all can go back to your camp, and I'll be gone before you break in the morning."

The surly Greylan said, "My lord, you cannot allow this commoner to speak to you in this way."

Aaslo's gaze did not leave the marquess as he said, "I'd say that's not your call, *guardsman*."

Whatever the marquess had intended to say died on silent lips as he watched Aaslo thoughtfully.

Greylan didn't let up, though. "My lord, what would your father say? The marquess—dismissed by a vagabond! You should—"

The marquess abruptly turned to Greylan. "Must you always presume to tell me what *I* should do? You all go back to camp, and take him with you," he said, motioning to Dolt's first victim, who had lost consciousness. "I shall stay here to have a chat with Sir Forester."

"You believe this insolent fool?" huffed Greylan.

The marquess said, "Of the few foresters we have met in the past several months, how many were more respectful than this one? I'd say none. If nothing else, he has the bearing of a forester, and is he not that for which we have been searching? A forester who will leave the forest?"

"At this point, I am not sure I would trust a forester who leaves the forest," Greylan grumbled. "Still, I cannot leave you here alone with an armed man."

"He carries a wood axe, not a battle-axe," said the marquess.

"And a sword," Greylan replied.

The marquess stroked his beard as his gaze fell on Mathias's sword. "Yes, strange that. None of the others carried weapons of battle." He then met Aaslo's hard stare. "You defeated one of my officers."

Aaslo didn't reply to the observation and instead said, "Has the *Most Honorable the Marquess* nothing better to do than waylay innocent travelers?"

"What's in the bag?" barked Greylan, eyeing the burlap sack dangling from Aaslo's belt. One of the officer's strikes had slashed the sack open, but Aaslo didn't think they could see its contents through the small hole.

"A root," Aaslo said. "It was requested for a transplant."

"Liar."

"Hand it over," said Greylan, waving to the guard behind Aaslo, who stood panting after he had managed to settle his mount. "Bring me the bag and the sword, too."

Aaslo gripped his hilt and the haft of his axe and said, "I carry few possessions, but those that I do will not be taken. I'll die before that happens, and I don't die easily."

"A second lie in as many minutes."

Aaslo hissed. "It's not a lie. I carry death in my heart already. It'll not claim my soul so soon."

"As if you have a choice. I didn't."

"You are rather melodramatic for a forester," said the marquess, "but then again, your people are ever so protective of their plants. Go, Greylan. I wish to have a private discussion with the forester."

Greylan started to protest, but the marquess shot the guard a withering look. Greylan's nostrils flared, and his contemptuous glare toward Aaslo expressed more than a glint of enmity. Aaslo wondered if the sentiment had already been earned by his brethren long before his current predicament. None of the foresters he knew would react kindly to the demands of an obnoxious noble, particularly if those demands meant leaving the forest. In that moment, Aaslo felt the culmination of the bits of knowledge he'd been avoiding throughout the journey. He was in the wrong place.

Once the guards and servant had departed, the marquess dismounted and came to stand before Aaslo. As he removed his riding gloves, he said, "Well met, Sir Forester—or perhaps it is a rather coarse meeting. Considering the direction of the conversation thus far, I doubt you're inclined to tell me of your business this far south. Perhaps we can come to an arrangement? I can be very influential in most matters."

"I doubt it," Aaslo grumped. Deciding to make the best of the change in mood, Aaslo sheathed his sword. He said, "I'm tired. If you insist on staying, we can sit—or are you opposed to getting your fancy trousers dirty?"

"You can't talk to him like that. He's a marquess. You're going to get yourself hanged."

The marquess grinned and then settled on a clump of flattened grass near the small cooking fire. Aaslo sat as well, poking at the fire with a twig from the dead shrub that was his kindling. He fed the minuscule inferno with a few more twigs. He said, "Your men don't respect you."

The marquess crossed his legs, wrapped his arms around his knees, and leaned back. He said, "Why do you say that?"

Aaslo thought the man looked far too comfortable sitting in the grass for a man of his station. He said, "They seek to control you." Nodding toward Greylan, who had not returned to the camp but was instead hovering at the edge of the twilight's illumination, he said, "Especially that one. They think you're too young and inexperienced. They're probably working with someone else—perhaps one of your father's acquaintances."

The marquess glanced toward the silhouette. "That's very insightful for a man who not only rejects politics but the outside world in general and refuses to abide by its customs."

"I don't care about your politics, and I care even less for your customs. If you want to let them control you, that's your business. It's the same to me either way."

The marquess tilted his head and said, "How would you deal with such a problem? If you were me."

Aaslo reclined on his pack and crossed his arms. He was almost relieved to have someone to talk to besides a ghostly severed head—even if it was a pompous marquess. He considered the many options and how the marquess's people would react based on what he had learned from Magdelay. He suddenly wished Mathias would say something. Mathias was always better with these things. *He* actually *enjoyed* learning about people.

"Don't be daft. This isn't about people, Aaslo. It's about packs, and you know packs."

"Packs?"

"Excuse me?" said the marquess.

Aaslo looked up at the man. "They don't see you as the alpha."

The marquess stroked his beard and nodded. Then he said, "What is an alpha?"

Confused by the marquess's interest in anything he had to say, outside the subject of forestry, Aaslo considered his words carefully. "What do you know of wolves?"

The marquess scrunched his face with distaste. "Only how to kill them."

Aaslo shook his head, knowing it was common practice among flatlanders like the marquess. "Wolves run in packs. The alpha is the dominant wolf. He is basically free to do what he wants, and the others choose to follow his lead. If another wolf surpasses the alpha's dominance, three things can happen: the alpha may submit, he may leave the pack, or he may be killed. The alpha isn't necessarily the largest or the strongest, though. He or she displays the most confidence—charisma, if you like. If you want your pack to follow you, then you need to be the alpha."

"And you don't think I am?" said the marquess.

"What I think isn't important."

"Is this where you tell me I just need to believe in myself?"

Aaslo grunted. "This isn't a book of inspirational proverbs. There are plenty of people who think too highly of themselves, while everyone else sees idiots. It's what *they* think that matters."

"So, I have to make them *believe* I'm the alpha."

Aaslo nodded once. "You don't behave like an alpha. You act like a man trying to fill his father's shoes while looking to others to confirm that they fit."

"What do you suggest, then? How do I fix the problem?"

"Well, for one, you need to wear your own damned shoes. It doesn't matter if they look anything like your father's—only that they look good on *you*. Of course, they need to be functional, so you need to know what you're doing."

The marquess lifted his chin. "I know how to perform my duties."

"Good, then stop looking to others for approval. There's no one in the forest to tell you if you're doing it right, except for the trees when they live or die."

"That sounds like a sage piece of wisdom."

"Just a fact."

"You said that was *one*. You have other suggestions?"

"Tell him. He's going to love this."

Aaslo nodded slowly. "You need a beta."

"That is . . . ?"

"A right-hand man—or woman. Someone you trust that will speak highly of you, spread word of your deeds, and have your back in conflict. Just as importantly, you need someone to tell you when you're wrong—privately, of course. There's a risk with a beta, though, when it turns out that he or she isn't so trustworthy."

The marquess said, "How do I find this trustworthy beta?"

"How should I know? That's *your* problem."

Obviously displeased, the marquess said, "Do you have a beta?"

The fire popped, and Aaslo thought back to that terrible night. He said, "I had a pack—it was a pack of two. When we were performing his duties, he was the alpha. When we were doing mine, I was alpha. We both knew where the other stood in things of importance, and the rest was worthy of healthy competition. He's gone, now. It's just me."

"Not even in your dreams."

"I can't control my dreams," Aaslo mumbled.

"You dream of having that again someday?" said the marquess.

KEL KADE

Aaslo looked back to the man. "No, never. He was my brother in all things. That's not something easily found or replaced. Eventually, I'll follow him into death—probably sooner than later."

"Have you no hopes for the future? What of a wife? Children?"

Aaslo shrugged. "I had hopes for the future, but it seems the future didn't have high hopes for me. The woman I loved chose him, and she lost us both. I doubt there will be time for more. Why do you care about my life—or about anything I have to say, for that matter? Why are you even talking to me?"

"I find you intriguing, mostly because no one has ever spoken with me the way you do. You are straightforward—to the point—without concern for offense. While infuriating, it is also refreshing. None in my household would dare say such things, and I would not trust those outside of it. You, however, hold no stake in my success or failure. As to why I'm speaking with you, you already know. I need your assistance with the blight."

"I don't have time to deal with your blight. There are plenty of agriculturalists and magi in the south. Why don't they help you?"

"They've tried," said the marquess.

Aaslo shook his head. "A blight is a messy curse. Sometimes the only solution is to burn it out."

"That is not an option," said the marquess. "Our forests are not like yours, and neither are the flatlands like this. We can scarcely grow food. The trees are steeped in marshes and swamps bearing vapors that carry flame like the wind carries dust. They harbor rare plants used in potions and medicines that the magi say are found nowhere else in Uyan and even in all of Aldrea. These resources are invaluable, and they are what my people depend on for trade. It is uncommon for one in my position to beg assistance, especially from a commoner, but the other foresters had no interest in anything I had to offer. Do you need a better horse? You can take mine. Do you desire gold for your travels? Here's my purse. Do you require influence in a noble house? I will be your broker. What may I offer that will bring you to Ruriton?"

"Sounds like a good deal, Aaslo. Maybe you should forget this world-saving business and live it up."

"Is that what you would do?" Aaslo muttered, glancing at the burlap sack beside him.

"I'd do what I must for the world."

"I'll do what I must for my people," said the marquess.

Aaslo considered his response as he turned the roasting meat. The marquess didn't know it, but what he had to do *was* what was necessary for the marquess's people—and everyone else. He looked up at the illustrious man who had humbled himself to beg at the feet of a forester. "I think you're probably a good man. At least, you'll be a good marquess"—he nodded toward the other camp—"so long as you don't let them get to you. You'll not believe me when I say that my task takes precedence over your own—by your standards, not mine. I'd rather be dealing with a blight, and it pains me to turn away from such a scourge."

"Then, come help us. The task is urgent and fit for a forester."

"That may be, but I bear my brother's burden at the moment. I'll give you this. If I successfully complete my current task, then I will come to Ruriton and do what I can."

The marquess appeared conflicted, as if torn between anger and relief. Finally, he straightened and said, "Then I shall assist you in your task."

Aaslo felt the tiniest spark of hope ignite in his chest, and he realized how hopeless his quest had felt. He had just been granted a boon. He had found a spring in the desert.

"Yes, because that won't draw attention. You, riding at the side of a marquess."

The trickle of excitement evaporated. The spark fizzled. He couldn't accept the marquess's help. As circumstances were, he was a scruffy lone traveler with few belongings and an ugly horse—no one of consequence, not even worth robbing. Beyond that, accepting the marquess's generosity would be tantamount to theft, since his chances of ever addressing the blight were minuscule.

His words were heavy on his tongue as he said, "I cannot accept your gracious offer, My Lord Marquess. My present task is better served by me alone."

"It was a task for the chosen one, *brother. Your only job is to deliver the message to the king. He and the Council of Magi will find a new hero."*

Aaslo wiped a hand across his weary face and added, "I anticipate your services will be required in the future, if not by me, then by whomever takes up this mantle."

"It sounds like a heavy mantle to bear for a man alone." With a subdued chuckle, the marquess said, "I should have anticipated it. From what I can tell, nothing less than the fate of the world could drag a forester out of his forest."

Mathias hummed a knowing tune, but Aaslo said nothing. They sat in silence for a while, which was fine with Aaslo. He and his father had often gone days simply existing in each other's presence without uttering a word. Even Mathias had learned to occasionally hold his tongue when Aaslo was thinking.

Finally, the marquess said, "I look forward to the day you share with me your story. How is it that a forester is so skilled with the sword, and how did he acquire such an exquisite weapon? What drew him from his beloved forest, and what task is so important that he forgoes his calling?" He stood, brushing the straw from his pants. "Until then, I shall revel in the mystery." He pulled a small purse from the pocket of his overcoat and tossed it to Aaslo. "My thanks for your candid advice. Consider this an investment in the successful completion of your task. I have faith that we shall meet again, Sir Forester."

Still averse to taking the marquess's money for no reason, Aaslo offered the man a small pouch from his pack. The marquess looked at him uncertainly as he reached for it. "For your men," said Aaslo. "Have them mix it with a bit of water before application."

"What is it?" said the marquess.

"It'll help with the leeches."

The marquess's face blanched, and he gazed into the darkness toward the pond. He nodded toward Aaslo, then turned to leave. He paused. Turning back, he said, "You might have led with the fact that you are a forester, seeing as how foresters are exempt from poaching laws."

Aaslo smirked. "It was none of your business."

CHAPTER 7

MAGDELAY PEERED DOWN AT THE EVERGATE FROM HER HIDING PLACE in the rocks on the opposite slope. Besides a few larger boulders, there was little cover that high in the Cambor Mountains of northeastern Uyan. Spikemoss and lichen were most abundant, with a few scraggly junipers and sagebrush dotting the rugged hills. Clumps of grass and thorny brambles peeked from between boulders and talus in the lower crevasses and valleys.

It was early afternoon when she arrived, and the shadows were at a minimum, so she wrapped a spell of environmental mimicry around herself. At a distance, she was fairly safe from observation, but the closer she crept, the less effective the spell would become.

The evergate was surrounded by the same creatures that had attacked on the road outside Goldenwood. In the daylight, they were no less horrifying. Their wrinkly skin had the grey-blue hue of an aged corpse over the joints and bony parts but appeared pinkish around the muscles and softer flesh. It sagged as if it had been stretched too large for the creatures' thin frames. They were the size and shape of men but lacked hair and lashes, and their black-rimmed irises were nearly white. Behind bluish-black lips were tiny, pointed teeth, and every once in a while, sinuous black tongues slipped from between them to lick the air. Although they were dressed like mismatched soldiers or mercenaries and worked with purpose, she never heard them speak in a human tongue. Snarls, grunts, and hisses seemed to be their primary method of communication.

About fifty of the creatures were camped at the base of the evergate. Magdelay had been watching them for over an hour but had yet to see another magus. She needed this gate. The one nearest Goldenwood, which she used to attend the council meetings every month, had been destroyed beyond her ability to repair when she had arrived. She had been forced to travel weeks to the next evergate, only to find it under siege. Luckily, after the first attack her horse had not run too far, and her summoning spell had been successful in encouraging it to return with her supplies. She felt guilty about the state in which she had left Aaslo, but she could not have retrieved the other horse, which was unfamiliar with her magic. She wondered if the forester had changed his mind and gone back to his forest, then considered that he was far too stubborn for that.

A commotion captured her attention. The gate, constructed in the modified mouth of a cave, suddenly activated. A young-looking magus stepped through the prismatic crush of colors that glowed within the keyhole-shaped framework. The creatures skittered back, and the shaggy-haired magus, who looked to be no more than twenty, dropped a thick rope in their midst. After he retreated back through the portal, a number of creatures swarmed forward to snag the rope, then began pulling. As the rope slowly grew longer, more creatures came forward to assist. Finally, a train of two large wagons attached to the rope creaked through the gate. The young magus arrived again, this time in the company of two older magi.

The creatures tore the covers from the wagons, and Magdelay's stomach churned at the sight. Each was filled with human corpses. As she watched, the creatures dragged the cadavers from the wagons and laid them on the rough ground in three rows of five. The young magus pulled the lid from a barrel in the front wagon and began scooping a red powder into a sack. Meanwhile, one of the older magi carried an urn around the site, splashing the cadavers with a clear liquid that was so pungent, Magdelay could smell it from her perch, at least twenty yards away. The third magus muttered words he read from a thick tome, and the wind suddenly died on the crisp edge of a spell. The young magus tipped the sack over and carefully poured the powder in a thin line around the bodies. He then refilled the bag and rounded them in the opposite direction, drawing foreign symbols with the powder.

Magdelay had never seen the spell they were creating, but since it involved corpses, thought it safe to assume it was of a dark nature. She felt like she should disrupt it, but her chances of surviving against three unknown magi and a host of fiends were probably low. Aside from that, interrupting a spell in progress could have disastrous consequences for everyone. She couldn't risk damaging the evergate before she could use it. She needed to get to the council immediately, before Aaslo reported to the king.

When the young magus finished pouring the designs of the script, he joined the other two. Together, they chanted something unintelligible from the tome; then the younger one turned to face the magus who still held the urn. To her shock, the urn-bearer withdrew his belt knife and slit the younger magus's throat. The tome-bearer snapped the book shut and supported the young magus as he slumped, while the urn-bearer collected the young man's spurting blood in the vessel. After the flow slowed, the urn-bearer walked among the corpses, pouring blood into each of their mouths. Once he was finished, the tome-bearer raised his arms and cast a spell that released the wind. It quickly intensified into a tempest, furiously whipping over the bodies in a maelstrom of rocky debris and red powder. Static energy began to snap within the currents, eliciting crackling bolts within the dark air mass.

Magdelay's blood froze as the corpses' eyes popped open to reveal milky irises that stared wide-eyed into the storm. The hair was stripped from their flesh, which darkened as it began to sag. Then they began to move. Their joints bent awkwardly while their arms and legs awoke in jittery movements. As they bent and crawled, their motions became smoother. One by one, they stood upon wobbly feet while the storm raged around them. They turned her way as one and looked as if they were staring straight at her. The hairs on the back of her neck stood on end. The storm abruptly died, and where cadavers had lain sprawled on the ground stood fifteen more of the strange creatures.

The tome-bearer moved to stand in front of the group. He spoke to them in a language unknown to Magdelay. When he was finished, the monsters began acting the same as the others who were present when she arrived. The two remaining magi turned and strode back through the evergate, leaving the young magus behind. As soon as they disappeared, the creatures swarmed the magus's body, ripping it to pieces and fighting each other as they devoured every bit.

Magdelay knew she needed to get to the gate before the magi returned, and the distraction of the magus's body wouldn't last long. She scrabbled back up the slope, ducking behind boulders to hide her retreat. Once over the hill, she slid down the talus on the other side to where she had left her horse and gear. Balene was anxious, probably scenting the blood, but Magdelay whispered a soothing incantation in the mare's ear. She anticipated needing a number of spells if she was to make it through the fray, and she hoped to destroy the creatures in the process. While she was capable of more than most sorceresses, it was draining.

She emptied a small pouch of odds and ends into her larger pack, then led her horse into a gully at the bottom of the hill. She needed rocks that were smooth and symmetrical, but none would be found in the angular rubble on the hill. Upon first pass, she had noted an outcrop of poorly lithified conglomerate in the gully, a paleo-riverbed of smoothed river stones and friable clay.

She pried what she needed from the layer, then washed the stones with a splash from her waterskin. With an oil-charcoal mixture, she marked runes onto the stones, a technique she had learned from a runesmith who had once been a good friend. She then used the black paste to draw runes on her skin, clothing, and horse, imbuing them with spells native to witchcraft rather than sorcery. Traditionalists derided the use of magics nonnative to their disciplines, but she had not become high sorceress by being finicky.

Once finished, she mounted Balene and led her to the mouth of the crevasse. She could hear the fiends' savage cries echoing through the chasm. Balene stomped the gravel as her ears turned back and her nostrils flared. Magdelay patted the mare's neck but did not cast another calming spell. Balene would need all her energy if they were to survive. Magdelay exhaled a slow, steadying breath, then kicked the horse into motion with a shout. Balene thundered up the path as Magdelay activated her first spells. Purple tendrils of electricity crackled along her hands and forearms. As she held the spell, the tendrils grew, snapping up her torso to be released in sizzling zaps from the tips of her loose hair.

The creatures did not see her at first. In the absence of the magi, they had descended into a state of chaos. Worried that the magi might return to put them in order, Magdelay slapped the rune beside the horse's mane, spurring her forward with unnatural speed. The nearest creatures shrieked, and the horde turned.

Gripping the horse tightly with her legs, Magdelay raised her arms in both directions and released the purple lightning with a thunderous clap. Several of the creatures in the front line were knocked back, a few falling to the ground in convulsions as the lightning wrapped around them. She whispered a spell begotten of wizardry, which loosened the gravel on either side of her direct path to the gate. She then swiped another rune painted on the other side of Balene's neck. With every strike of the mare's hooves, the ground of the chasm shook. The vibration, caused by the consistent patter of footfalls, increased quickly, and the loose sediment began to behave as a liquid. Creatures howled as they sank into the liquefied ground. As they struggled, the shifting sediment built up friction. Magdelay stroked a rune painted on her own neck as she mumbled an incantation and raised her arm, drawing the static energy from the ground. She formed a spell in her mind but had no time to cast it before several of the creatures jumped at her.

Magdelay smacked the first creature away with unnatural strength, but the fiend managed to score her arm with its claws. She deflected an attack on her other side with an energy shield, then ripped a piece of rune-bearing fabric from her sleeve and dropped it in the midst of the gathering attackers. As soon as the fabric struck the ground, it exploded into dozens of linen tendrils that whipped around the legs of the nearest creatures. As they paused to tear themselves free, Magdelay rode past, tossing several of the enchanted stones into their midst. Some of the stones exploded, while others emitted dense fog or spewed an acrid liquid that melted flesh.

Creatures began crawling over their dead and those stuck in the talus quagmires. As Magdelay kicked and slashed at one with a whip of purple lightning, another leapt on her from the other side, nearly knocking her from the saddle. Magdelay screamed as the creature bit into her shoulder and dug its claws into her arm and thigh. She slapped a rune on her arm beside the monster's talons, but the script had been damaged and the spell wouldn't activate. She formed a ball of green mage fire in her palm and smashed it into the creature's face. It fell away from her, clawing at the enchanted fire that spread to cover its head, then dripped onto the creatures around it.

Magdelay mustered the energy she had been saving as she neared the evergate. When several creatures converged on her, she slapped the remaining runes on her arms and clothes. The combination of spells caused a burst of energy that threw the creatures back several paces. She then tossed the last of the enchanted stones behind her, clearing the creatures on Balene's heels with a variety of devastating effects.

Inside the gate, Magdelay was surrounded by a slush of colors that looked like broken mirrors. She quickly threw her cloak over the mare's head to keep her from panicking, then removed her packs and tack. When she was finished, she removed her cloak and looked into the mare's dark brown gaze. She whispered an apology as she threaded a mystical tether between them. She had little hope it would work. She then turned to the evergate, drawing tendrils of energy from the mass she had been saving and linking them to each of the runes that defined the portal to form a massive web of energy. The last tendril was linked to *her*. She activated the device and was transported across the kingdom. In the process, the link to the evergate was severed, releasing the accumulated raw energy and destroying the gate, which had stood for hundreds of years.

Magdelay shook her head as the colors of the receiving evergate fizzled. Her worries were confirmed. Balene had not made it through. The horse was lost to the realms, deposited somewhere on an unknown path, in a random world or in the vastness between them. Magdelay hoped the horse had found herself in a place where she could survive, but knew it unlikely.

She stepped out of the small, barren receiving chamber into the vast corridor. The soaring stone arches and the shadows they cast were a stark contrast to the rays of golden light that shone through the long windows between them. She had lived in the Citadel of Magi since she was a small child, and it had always felt peaceful, comforting to her. This was her home, but it was not the one she had shared with Mathias. Her heart ached with his memory. *Mathias* had been hers. In him, she had found a light that had made every trial worth it, and he was dead.

The soft shuffle of feet over the tiles alerted her to another's presence. She glanced down the adjacent corridor to spy one of the fledglings headed in her direction.

"You," she shouted.

The young magus, only a few years into his studies by his dress, lifted his head and blinked at her in surprise. He scurried forward, his face pale and his hands shaking. "Y-yes, High Sorceress. How may I assist you? You are injured. Shall I go for a healer?"

"No, there is no time for that. What are your duties at the moment?"

"I'm retrieving a sylph vessel for Wizard Motemer."

"This takes precedence." She pointed to the packs in the receiving chamber. "Gather those and follow me to the council hall."

"Yes, High Sorceress. The council is already gathered. I'm sure they'll be pleased that you could attend."

Magdelay rounded on him. "What are you talking about? Why are they meeting?"

Sweat beaded across the fledgling's brow. "I, um, don't know. I guess it has something to do with the visitors."

"What visitors?" she snapped.

"The foreigners from the new land."

"What do they look like?" she said.

"Um, I guess they're a bit strange. They all have long hair and black, pointed nails."

"They are here now?"

"Yes, High Sorceress. They're meeting with the council as we speak."

Magdelay was incensed. If these were the same *visitors* she had encountered on the road, then Mathias's killers had invaded her home. She stormed down the corridor, each bite, scratch, and bruise screaming with her every step. She was also drained, having used the last of her energy stores to destroy the evergate. She abruptly stopped and turned to the fledgling.

"Do you have any marmuck root?"

The young man shook his head vigorously. "No, of course not, High Sorceress. I would never—"

"Stop your prattling and give it to me."

The fledgling shifted, glancing at her anxiously. Finally, he dipped his hand inside his tunic and pulled out a pouch hanging from a cord around his neck. Magdelay snatched it from him and continued her trek toward the council chamber.

The fledgling hurried to keep pace. "Please, High Sorceress. I swear I don't normally use it. I was worried about the examinations, and Wizard Motemer has been working me tirelessly. I just needed a little boost to keep up, you know. Please don't expel me. I won't do it again."

Magdelay ignored the young man's rambling as she shoved a knob of marmuck root into her mouth, chewing with gusto so as to rid her mouth of the foul taste as quickly as possible. She felt a quickening, the zap of energy spreading through her limbs and filling the empty chambers that carried her power. She would regret it in the morning, but she had more immediate concerns.

A gaggle of youths were gathered at the chamber door when Magdelay approached. Every one of them was attempting to peer through the cracks or listen through the wood with shoddy spells. No one noticed until the fledgling carrying her bags coughed rather obviously. The others jumped and spun to face her, then began bowing and ducking when they realized who had caught them.

Magdelay scowled at the youngsters. "You all need to go to your rooms immediately. Lock and ward the doors. We have little time. If you hope to take breath in the morning, you will heed my words." She looked to the fledgling who had accompanied her. "Go with them." The young man dropped Magdelay's packs, and the fledglings all muttered apologies as they scurried away.

Magdelay took a deep breath. She nibbled another knob of marmuck root as she prepared a few nasty spells. Raising her hands toward the doors, she threw them open with a burst of power. The other council members, a number of staff members, and even a few senior students were gathered in their usual places, the visitors addressing them from the podium in the center of the circular theater. Everyone turned toward her.

With surprise, Sorcerer Goltry, who was leading the meeting, said, "Greetings, High Sorceress."

As soon as the visitors heard the pronouncement, one of them began summoning a spell to cast a fierce red javelin in her direction. Magdelay did not wait for its release. She thrust a bolt of sizzling power at the man. His javelin spell fizzled as he raised a shield in time to deflect the brunt of the attack, but he endured severe damage to his left side. Wooden debris blasted from the podium in every direction.

Shocked by the sudden violence, most of the attendees were slow to react. Magdelay released another attack as they recovered their wits. She summoned her familiar. Few had the power to bond with beings from the ether and even fewer with one possessing a hive mind. A swarm of black ice wasps dripped from the air upon her command, engulfing the five foreign magi in the center of the council hall. The injured magus and a second cast deflective wards, while the other three responded with attacks of their own. Multiple balls of fire whipped through the air, crashing into stone and causing the walls to shake as blocks were torn from their settings. Attendees near the aisle were thrown from their seats as their benches were ripped from beneath them. All the flying debris and power bursts were directed at Magdelay.

The black ice wasps burrowed through the deflective shields, while the councilors began casting protective wards and attacks of their own. Those nearest Magdelay doused enemy fireballs with conjured ice and water. Others weathered flying stones and wood to silt and dust in an instant. Multiple shields erupted around her as she directed her ice wasps through the invaders' wards. Meanwhile, the masters of the council engaged the visiting magi in a destructive battle that nearly brought down the hall. As soon as the first wasp made it through the enemy's protective ward, the others followed. They swarmed the visiting magi, blocking them further from their power with every sting. When the enemy magi could no longer maintain their wards, the council magi inundated them with ethereal webs and tethers. The magus Magdelay had injured in the initial attack shouted and slammed a vial onto the floor. Green smoke rose from the spot in puffs, surrounding the magi, then spreading outward. Crackles of lightning flickered within the fog as it expanded.

Magdelay shouted, "Shield them now!"

Every capable magus cast a shield ward toward the center of the room where the visitors were gathered, but their hasty efforts were insufficient to contain the explosion. People and debris were smashed against the walls, and Magdelay was propelled into the corridor just as the amber smoked glass of the domed ceiling crashed down onto the councilors.

Magdelay's head spun and her stomach churned as she shakily pushed herself to her feet. Holding her ribs, she failed to suppress a painful cough. She limped toward the doorway, which was mostly blocked by debris, then turned to lean against the wall as voices she recognized shouted orders to help the injured and clear the way.

It took Magdelay a moment to recognize the first person to come stumbling out of the room. The filthy, disheveled figure covered in sticky goo and dust was Enchantress Wenthria. The woman blinked as she wiped mess from her eyes and then brightened when she saw Magdelay. Wenthria hurried over to grasp her in a hug, which ignited a pained wheeze deep in Magdelay's chest.

"Oh, you're alive!" said Wenthria. "I was worried you'd been crushed. Thank you for not being dead."

Magdelay's voice was rough with grit as she said, "You're welcome. What of everyone else?"

Wenthria stepped back, her amber eyes still wide with shock. "I don't know. I was closest to the door. A massive beam fell from the ceiling behind me. They're still trying to move it."

An audible pop vibrated up Magdelay's neck and into her skull as she tilted her head. She exhaled in relief, not having realized the pain she had been enduring until it was released. She slumped farther against the wall and said, "Can you not enchant it to make it lighter?"

Wenthria blinked several times, then jumped as if stung by a bee. "Yes! Oh my, why did I not think of that?" The lithe woman, in what had once been a lovely peach day gown, turned back to the devastated room. "I'm just so rattled."

A moment later, a crash reverberated down the corridor, and Magdelay winced. The council hall had been a powerful room, a place of unification, a chamber dedicated to the celebration and proliferation of magic, regardless of bloodline or principle. It had been reduced to rubble in a matter of minutes. Magi began pouring into the outer corridor, and Magdelay was heartened that so many had survived.

Sorcerer Goltry, her greatest rival and most avid supporter, passed the wizardess he was assisting to another, then joined her. "How are you, Mags? You look terrible." His gaze fell on the bite and claw marks on her shoulder and arm. "You did not get those during this attack. What has happened?"

Magdelay glanced at the others, who had all turned to stare, their expressions a mixture of fear, curiosity, and anger. Wizardess Nomina stepped out of the crowd.

"Why did you attack our guests? They were invited to the hall under the assurance and assumption of hospitality. How many have we lost due to your recklessness?"

Magdelay gritted her teeth as she straightened. She hardened her gaze as she met the woman's accusations. "Do not forget, Nomina, that *I* am the high sorceress, and it is *my responsibility* to engage hostiles in our citadel . . . as it is *yours*."

The woman sputtered with indignation. "What hostiles? We were holding a *peaceful* introduction. They proposed an exchange of knowledge. All five of them were stronger than any of us. They obviously knew something we don't."

"Nomina, you are a senior master. I will not excuse your disrespect as a product of this devastation. If you cannot contain yourself during difficult times and hold to the traditions of this council, then you should not be permitted to lead."

Nomina pursed her lips, then begrudgingly said, "I apologize, High Sorceress. I am certain you had good reason for your attack on the visitors who had shown no signs of aggression."

Magdelay narrowed her eyes at the woman. "We will discuss your attitude later." She then turned her gaze toward the others. "I have traveled for weeks, hoping to arrive in time to deliver the news before you heard it from other sources." She met Nomina's gaze. "I was delayed because our *visitors* destroyed the seventh evergate and the sixth was under siege." Turning to Goltry, she said, "We must begin preparations at once." She took a deep breath, clutching her side and immediately regretting it. "The Mark of Aldrea is dead."

CHAPTER 8

IN THE MIDST OF THE OPEN EXPANSE OF UYAN WAS A HILL, THE remnants of an extinct volcano, according to the scholars. Atop the hill stood Tyellí, a robust bastion of culture and wealth, a testament to the gracious rule of a powerful line of kings and queens—or so Aaslo heard, *repeatedly*, as he was inundated with such declarations by criers at every crossroads within a few hours' ride of the city. He could again hear the calls from the road ahead as Dolt plodded over a short bridge that crossed a stream at the bottom of a gully. The horse huffed as he tackled the slope on the other side before resuming his steady pace at road level.

Shortly ahead, two men were on opposite sides of a convergence in the road. Aaslo might have been concerned for an ambush except that a large caravan of travelers was heading toward the capital city, joining his route from the other road. The man on the left side of the road stood on a wooden box holding a sign that professed the glory of Tyellí. Aaslo briefly wondered how much the crown paid for the service. The second man was sprawled on the ground to the right emitting giant guffaws as he taunted the first.

Aaslo fully intended to ignore the men and join the caravan, but as soon as he reached the two, Dolt stopped. Aaslo dug his heels into the willful gelding's sides and shook the reins while shouting, "Heeyah! Go! Get moving, you damnable beast."

"Are you looking to make new friends, Aaslo?"

"Maybe y-e-e-u-u sh-sh-should s-s-speak sweetly to 'im," said the raggedy man on the ground. "Ya know, flies an' honey and a-a-all dat." The man fell over in a fit of giggles that were interrupted by heavy coughs that ended in a gurgling wheeze. Alcohol tinged with body odor lingered heavily in the air.

"Silence, drunkard!" said the crier. Turning to Aaslo, the man bowed and said, "Fear not, fair traveler, for naught but an hour ahead, the mighty city of Tyellí towers in the light of Bayalin, god of our luminous sun." The man scowled at the old drunkard and said, "It is a stronghold in the fight against the shadows of intemperance, pestilence, and vagrancy."

"Ha! It's Tyellí that casts the sh-shadow," called the drunkard. "If your mighty city's s-so gr-r-reat, why am I layin' out 'ere in the dirt?"

"Because you're a lazy lout, you sot," said the crier.

"He has a point."

The man cackled and coughed. "That's t-true, but you'd th-think the *bastion of a mighty god* could f-fix a man like me, eh? Nay, your fancy magi an' nobles jus' want us to dishappear. *Kill 'em all! Let 'em die. Get rid of w-what we don't like, and all dat's left is beautif-skul.*"

"That's a valid claim, too. I don't know. Aaslo. I'm torn. Can they both be right?"

"I don't care," Aaslo mumbled. Frustrated with his horse, he dismounted and pulled on the reins. His struggles were in vain, and he was glad the two men were preoccupied with what seemed to be a well-worn argument between them.

"You wouldn't know something beautiful if it slapped you in the face," said the crier.

The drunkard donned a toothless grin. "I know a beautif-skul woman when I shees one. What say we asks the purdy lady, eh? I'd rather be talkin' to her anyhow."

Aaslo glanced down the road in each direction. The entire caravan had passed, and no one else was in sight. He and the crier shared their confusion with a glance and then looked back toward the drunkard. The man was gazing up at Dolt, his eyes filled with admiration. The crier chuckled and then began to laugh in earnest. Dolt bobbed his head, then started walking as if he had been all along.

Aaslo paused when the drunkard's eyes rolled back into his head. The man fell over with that silly grin frozen on his face. Aaslo tried to pull the horse to a stop, but Dolt yanked the reins from his fingers and continued clomping down the path. The crier stepped down from his box and hesitantly shuffled over to check on the man. Aaslo glanced behind him to see Dolt steadily plodding up the road. If he didn't catch up with the horse soon, he doubted he would ever find him.

The crier said, "He's dead!" The man blinked at Aaslo in shock. "We were just talking to him, and now he's dead."

"Yup, that's dead. Maybe you should take his head, too."

"That's not funny," said Aaslo.

The crier looked up at him with disgust. "I didn't say it was."

Aaslo searched again for Dolt. He said, "When I get to the city, I'll let the guard know to send someone to collect him."

Shaking his head, the crier said, "No one will come. The patrol will pass through here at dusk. They'll take care of it—probably just bury him off the road somewhere."

Feeling guilty for leaving, Aaslo bid the crier farewell, then hurried to catch up with Dolt, who was ambling along without concern.

"He wasn't your responsibility."

"I know that."

"Then why are you moping?"

"I'm not moping," Aaslo grumbled, "but I could have at least helped bury him."

"What if someone came looking for him? They wouldn't be able to find him because you buried him."

"You heard the crier. He was a lonely drunkard."

"Even drunkards have family."

"You're probably right, as usual. I just think I should have done more."

"You are *doing more."*

Mathias was blessedly silent for a while. Closer to the city, the roads were wide and paved and occupied by merchants and travelers from all over Uyan and beyond. Annual pilgrimages to the capital city were encouraged. The monarchy claimed it stimulated optimism and unity within a people who were strongly segmented by distance and topography.

Aaslo gazed up at the city that crowned a barren, rocky hill.

"Look, it's a thousand forests all stuffed onto the hilltop."

Few trees stood upon the hill, only those contained within carefully manicured gardens, so Aaslo knew that was not what Mathias had meant. He surveyed the houses and buildings constructed of wood and stone, some topped with wooden shingles, the more affluent with clay tiles. Fences, benches, sheds, stables, carts, stairs, and hitching posts were all composed of the trees that he and his brethren had nurtured.

"They're not forests—only memories. I don't begrudge them taking the wood, so long as they replace it."

"A life lost can never be replaced."

"Are you *trying* to make me miserable?"

"Only making a point."

Dark thoughts swirled in his mind as Aaslo rode through the streets toward the palace at the city's center, taking care to avoid the crowds near the market. He wondered what Mathias had meant but couldn't find the answer.

Aaslo was surprised by the number of tents and rugged shanties that had been erected near the road at the edge of town and in the alleys. Whispers and a few shouted castigations led him to believe most of the people were refugees of some sort from the south. He wondered if the prophecy was already coming to pass. If that was the case, he needed to hurry.

Once he was past the outermost perimeter, he realized that Tyellí was indeed beautiful—for a city. He was certain magi had helped build the soaring structures of white, pink, and grey stone. Each building reflected either one of the unique environments of Uyan or the building's particular function. A grey monstrosity had the appearance of a cave in the stark cliffs of the eastern mountains, while another structure resembled images he had seen in paintings of the sea to the west—a tide of blue marble with sea serpents, mermaids, and other sea life in bas-relief. He passed a white hall with tall pillars and striking geometric designs trimmed in gold. The massive placard proudly declared it to be the Ministry of Finance. The boulevard was lined with pergolas and fountains, but few people made use of them. He wondered at this, then realized that despite the efforts of the city planners, shade was at a minimum. The sun grew hot at midday this far south. *If only they hadn't cut down all the trees*, he thought. He was inclined to remove his jacket but needed it to cover Mathias's eye-catching sword and the patched burlap sack at his waist.

His gaze danced across the tips of two tall spires. He squinted, unable to make out the symbols that graced the flickering flags atop the pinnacles. He blinked several times to clear his vision, then dropped his focus to the building in front of him, only to be met with a surprise. A narrow tower was nestled in the crook of the larger structure to which the spires belonged. The smaller tower, carved to look like bark on a tree trunk, twisted in a spiral around an arched doorway. It widened into branches that looked like wood and leaves entwined around a central sphere resembling a giant seedpod. A sign over the door read FORESTER'S HAVEN.

After dismounting, Aaslo studied the building for a moment. Suddenly, it felt as if a great weight had been lifted from his shoulders—or, rather, his waist. His heart thudded in his chest, and he reached down for the sack. Only a tuft of burlap remained where the bag had been cut from the rope securing it. He glanced up just in time to see a ragged figure fleeing down an alley.

Aaslo dropped his reins and took off after the culprit. He knew that his horse and possessions would probably have disappeared by the time he returned, but nothing else mattered if he couldn't retrieve the chosen one's head. He ran down the empty alley and caught a glimpse of fabric slipping around the next corner. Skidding through a pile of muck, Aaslo rounded the building in time to see his prey scaling a rope toward a rooftop. Two others began hastily pulling the rope to the top as Aaslo closed the distance. The thief slipped over the ledge, and all three men ran toward the opposite end of the roof. Unable to follow them, Aaslo turned down the next street, colliding with a laundry cart and spilling the entire load onto the street. Ignoring the angry shouts, he quickened his pace, able to pick up speed on the downhill side of the street. He glanced down each alley and finally spied someone tumbling onto a lower rooftop on the other side.

Knowing he needed to get to the roof, Aaslo dashed into the next open doorway. He took the stairs of the apartment building three at a time, then ran through the first flat he found that had access to a balcony. He sped across the room, startling the elderly woman who was knitting beside a window. Upon entering, he could see another balcony beneath a low overhang on the other side of the alley. With that as his target, Aaslo jumped onto the banister and propelled himself with all his might. The fasteners on the iron railing broke under his weight, though, and he fell far short of his goal. He collided with an awning and then crashed into a pile of crates filled with fruit.

Gasping for breath, he struggled to his feet, his back and side aching from the fall. The stall owner shouted, then cracked him in the head with a board broken from a crate. His vision swam as his feet slipped across the paving stones. Aaslo stumbled down the street and barely avoided being trampled by a horse at the next intersection. The street tilted as he ran, and he was no longer certain he was going in the right direction.

"Mathias!" he called between labored breaths. "Mathias, where are you?"

Mathias was silent.

"You wouldn't shut up the entire trip here. Now, when I need you, you say nothing."

Half the spinning world turned pink, and Aaslo blinked. He paused to lean on the closest building and wiped sweat from his eyes. His hand came away crimson. Just then, a horrifying shriek broke through the hum in his ears. Without thought, Aaslo ran toward the sound of an angry horse and found the ugly beast blocking the escape of two men in an alley. It took him a moment to figure out that it was *his* angry horse, and one of the two men was the fugitive who had stolen his bag—the bag that now lay empty in the mud.

Aaslo took a tentative step forward, his right leg dragging along the ground. He looked down and shook it, but it didn't seem to respond the way it should have. He wondered if he had torn something important and hoped it was a temporary sprain. Looking back at the perpetrators, who were cowering against a wall, he wiped blood from his eye. Then he reached over to Dolt's saddle and drew the axe that had been strapped to its side. Aaslo stomped his right foot on the ground a few times and only felt a tinge of pain. He looked up and pointed the axe at the two men. The one on the left was young, only a boy. The boy sank to the ground, covering his head with his arms as he cried. Focusing on the one on the right—the one who had stolen Mathias—he said, "Where is it?"

The wide-eyed young man held up filthy hands wrapped in rags. "Look, man, I don't have it. I mean, that's messed up. Who carries around a head?"

Knowing he looked a terror at that moment—disheveled, dirty, and covered in blood—Aaslo allowed anger to fill his voice. "Where is it?"

"I—I threw it in the river."

"What river?" Aaslo snapped. He didn't recall passing a river; but, at that moment, most of the events leading up to his standing in that alley were a blur.

The thief tipped his chin. "Over there—on the other side of the building. I threw it from the roof."

Aaslo pulled his arm back, then thrust the axe through the air. It tumbled end over end. With a *thunk*, it sank deeply into the wall beside the young man's head. Aaslo followed in its wake, shoved the thief against the wall, and grabbed the man's throat. "You're going to find that head. If you run, I'll follow you until the end of your days, and it won't be just me. You have no idea how many enemies you've made, and *I* am the least of them. If you help me find the head, I'll let you live. Others will not be so accommodating."

It was a lie. Aaslo had never lied so much in his life as he had since leaving the forest. He knew no one would go after the thief, at least not directly; but if he didn't get the head back, he wouldn't have proof for the king. If the king didn't find a new hero, then this thief—and all the other thieves, and everyone else in the world—was doomed.

The thief tried to shake his head but settled for a pained wheeze of compliance. Upon release, he doubled over gasping, then looked up at Aaslo.

"The river's slow this time of year. Not much rain. It shouldn't have gone far."

"You'd best hope no one finds it before we do," said Aaslo.

The man nodded and coughed, then grabbed the boy by the back of his shirt. "Stand up, Mory. We gotta find the head."

Aaslo looked down at the patched burlap sack. Since it hadn't rained recently, he didn't want to think about what had created the mud caking it. His first thought was to find a new sack. Then he grabbed the one in the mud with a hard shake to remove the muck.

The thief grimaced. "Look, man, I'll find you a new one, okay?"

Aaslo held it to the man's face and said, "Does this look like something you'd steal?"

Covering his nose and turning away, the thief said, "It certainly doesn't *smell* like it."

"Precisely," said Aaslo. "Remember what I said about running."

"All right, as if I wasn't already convinced by your insane horse. How'd you train him to do that?"

As if unable to accept the praise, Dolt chose that moment to release his bladder, showering the alley—and their legs—with his pungent spray.

"Unbelievable," said Aaslo as he took up the reins and started down the side street toward the river.

The eldest thief caught up to him as the younger straggled behind, keeping his distance from Dolt. The thief said, "Hey, man, what's your name?"

"What does it matter?"

"Well, since we'll be working together, I'll need to know what to call you. I'm Peckett, but everyone just calls me Peck." As Peck spoke, he pulled the ragged wraps from his hands and shoved them into his pockets. Then he took off his raggedy jacket and turned it inside out before replacing it.

"What are you doing?" said Aaslo.

Peck brushed his hands down the soft black velvet and slipped two gold buttons through their loops. He ran his fingers through his dark hair and tied it back into a queue. "If I'm gonna be walking about the city in broad daylight, I gotta look respectable, you know? The city guard, the shopkeepers—they'll watch you like a hawk if you look like—well, *you*."

Aaslo reached up and wiped drying blood from his face, then looked down at his shoddy clothes. The thief had a point. He still had to retrieve the head from the river, though, so he'd worry about his appearance afterward.

"Don't listen to him," said Mory, his voice cracking with youth. "He just wants to look good for *her*."

Peck grinned and said, "I won't deny it." He waggled his eyebrows and said, "Lena works by the river. She sells seeds and herbs at an apothecary stall, and she smells as sweet as she looks."

Aaslo felt a stab in his gut as his thoughts turned to Reyla. She liked to make lotions and perfumes from the herbs and cuttings he had brought to her, so she had always smelled fresh like the forest.

"So, what's your name?" said Peck.

"Aaslo."

Peck glanced around, then leaned in and whispered, "What's the deal with the head, anyway? Are you a bounty hunter? It's proof of your kill, right?" Peck grinned and waved at a few people he seemed to know when they reached the river. Then he said, "So, um, what does something like that cost? I've got a few I wouldn't mind putting on your list."

Ignoring the questions, Aaslo said, "Where did you throw it?"

Peck looked up at the tops of the buildings and pointed to a two-story structure with a flat roof. "I threw it from up there. I was in a hurry, so I didn't throw it too far. The river's slower on this side." He pointed to a place a few hundred yards down the riverbank and said, "It probably hasn't made it to the fishing docks yet. It might've washed up on the shore."

Aaslo surveyed the bank beyond the paved street. Cobbles and boulders dotted the landward side of the long point bar. Scraggly bushes and grass had grown among them, and the mud nearest the river was thick with dark silt and clay covered in brush. Aaslo was relieved. There was a chance the head had gotten hung up on the plants, which might also prevent anyone from finding it. The river wasn't wide, though, and he worried that the head might have gotten swept into the faster current. Something about the river wasn't making sense, though.

"Where does the river come from?" he said.

"You're not from around here, eh? It comes from the east."

"We're on top of a hill. It slopes downhill to the east."

"So?"

"So, water flows downhill."

"Ah, you're not thinking big enough. There's mountains to the east. The water goes fast down the mountains, so it swoops up the hill," said Peck with a sweep of his hand.

"The mountains are hundreds of miles away. The river wouldn't come up the hill. It would go around."

Peck scratched at his temple, looked up at the sky, and then shrugged. "I guess it's the wizards, then."

"The wizards?"

The thief nodded. "Wizards, sorcerers, witches, whatever—they're always making weird things happen. A lot of stuff doesn't make sense around Tyellí. Try not to think about it too hard. It'll give you a headache."

"Do you know any magi?" asked Aaslo.

"Magi?"

"Magus, magi—they're the general terms for people with magic, in case you don't know which to call them."

"Huh, I didn't know that. We wouldn't know those types. We don't exactly run in the same circles, them being nobles and rich folk, and us being"—he tugged at his lapels and winked—"*entrepreneurs.*"

"We met a wizard once," said Mory. "Remember, Peck? He was in the city square. He made that man's purse disappear and come back filled with flowers."

"He wasn't a wizard, Mory. He was an illusionist. They use sleight of hand to make you think they're using magic. They're one step up from a pickpocket."

"But you said he was a wizard," said a crestfallen Mory.

"You were eight. I didn't want to ruin the excitement for you."

Aaslo shook his head, then secured the axe to his saddle before withdrawing a smaller hatchet. He pointed downstream. "The river always runs in that direction?"

Peck grinned and said, "Of course. Water runs downhill, doesn't it?"

Aaslo growled, "Come on. We're going into the water to search the bank from the river."

Mory practically shouted, "But I can't swim."

"Can't swim?" said Aaslo in disbelief. "You have a river in your city, and you can't swim? How old are you—twelve?"

Mory lifted his chin. "I'm fourteen."

"Hmm, you're small for your age." He glanced at Peck, then added, "No doubt from lack of proper food." He tossed the reins to Mory, who caught them on impulse and then held them at arm's length. Aaslo said, "You watch Dolt. If you try to take any of my things, he'll eat you."

Mory shook his head vigorously up and down, then seemed to think better of it and shook it side to side.

Peck removed his coat with a sigh and handed it to Mory. "Don't let anything happen to this or *I'll* eat you." Mory grinned, and Peck tousled the boy's shaggy brown hair before following Aaslo into the water.

Several moments passed in silence, and Aaslo's thoughts rolled freely through his mind. Finally, he returned to something that had caught his attention earlier. He looked over at Peck, who was within arm's reach. "Entrepreneurs, huh?"

Peck pushed a branch to one side as he inspected the bank and said, "Yeah, there's this other country where the people with the most money get the power. It doesn't matter how you grew up or who your parents were. They call it capitalism, and people who start their own businesses are called entrepreneurs."

"I know what an entrepreneur is," Aaslo muttered. "I'm just surprised you do."

"I heard it from a traveling merchant in a tavern. Truth be told, it sounded like a faerie tale, but I like it."

"Maybe not as great as it seems," said Aaslo. "Everyone doesn't come into this world on an even scale. People born to money usually end up with the money."

"Yeah," said Peck, "but it doesn't have to be that way. They might lose their money. More important is people like me and Mory—we'd not be limited. There'd be nothing stopping us, you know. It might be hard, it might take a long time, but it *could* happen. If we kept trying, eventually we'd find a way. Not like here. No matter how hard we try, we'll never be more than we are. It's the law."

"You'll always be commoners, but you don't have to be thieves."

"What else are we gonna be? We raise ourselves. We've never been trained to be anything else. No one's gonna pay for an apprenticeship. If we don't steal, we don't eat. Plus, there's dues to pay, you know. Being a thief ain't free."

"You'll pay with your life when you get caught. I doubt there are too many old thieves in Tyellí."

"That's true enough, but I don't intend to go hungry in the time I got. Besides, Mory's gotta eat, too, and I'm pretty good at what I do."

"Not so good you don't get caught," Aaslo said with a pointed stare.

"Ah, well, no hard feelings, right? I mean, it was too easy. A lonely bag just dangling there, no one paying it any attention. It was too good to pass up, and I'll probably be regretting it for the rest of my short life."

"You speak freely for a criminal."

"Don't see as I have much to lose. I figure I'll be lucky if you don't kill me when we find the head, and I know you'll kill me if we don't. How was I supposed to know you were a bloody blade for hire on a demon horse?"

Aaslo wanted to correct the man. He was a forester—an emissary of life, growth, and tranquility. He ultimately decided it was better for the thief to continue believing his own tale for the time being. Instead, he said, "Is Mory your brother?"

Peck reached into the water, pulled out a boot, and then tossed it aside. "Nah, I sort of found him. I guess you could say his mom gave him to me." At Aaslo's questioning glance, he continued. "When I was ten, I was nearly caught stealing a pan of muffins from the bakery. The pan was still hot. It burned my hands, and I dropped it. I ran for a while with the city guard on my tail, then ducked into a basement boiler room. It wasn't long before I realized I wasn't alone. A woman was there. She was pregnant, and she wasn't doing so well. She was trying to be quiet, so I knew she wasn't supposed to be there. There was a little boy with her. She told me his name was Mory, and he was four years old. She asked me to take care of him. Then she started scream-ing, and a whole lot of blood came pouring out of her. I grabbed Mory and got out before the city guard got there. I went back later and asked around, but everyone who knew anything said she had died. Turns out they didn't even try to get the baby out of her. They said it was better the baby die with her than end up as another street rat.

"It was the most horrible thing I've ever seen, and I'll never forget it. I keep up with my women, you know? At least for a few months, just to be sure. I'll never be responsible for a woman dying in pain, scared and alone in a basement. As far as I know, I've never gotten one pregnant. Well, there was one, but she said the baby wasn't mine. She married a city clerk's assistant, and I figure he's better off with them either way."

"The city guards, the officials, they just let the woman and baby die? They didn't call for a healer?"

"Why would they? There wasn't any money in it for them."

"How about basic decency—respect for life?"

"Says the hit man. Come on. Can you say that you've worked so hard to help others in need, especially when there wasn't anything in it for you?"

Aaslo considered his life before the past few weeks. If someone had asked, *anyone* besides Mathias, there would have been few, if any, rea-sons good enough for him to leave the forest. The very nature of his work was in helping people, though. He couldn't be expected to do everything. He knew he was lying to himself. He didn't do it for the people. He did it for the forest—for the trees and the wild land that needed to be preserved and protected. That had been his calling. Help-ing people was someone else's. Was he no better than the apathetic city guard or the common thief?

No, Mathias was dead, and he was trudging through a mystical river in Tyellí. He had left the forest and hadn't returned because the world needed a hero and didn't yet know it. When fate had called upon him, he had stepped up to the challenge. Mathias's calling had been to help people, and Aaslo was trying to see that through. He would get the head to the king so that a new champion could be found. Now, he just needed to find the head.

Aaslo spied a mass of hair floating beneath a briar bush. He used his hatchet to hack away the tangle of limbs and then grabbed the soft mess, plucking it from the water with ease. The putrid stench of decay hit him like a roaring bull, and he dropped the mass.

"Ugh! What *was* that?" said Peck.

Aaslo gagged and tried to expel the vapor from his nose and mouth. "Some kind of algae. I've never seen or smelled anything like that."

Peck said, "It smells like death. I think I'm going to be sick."

His eyes watering, Aaslo waved Peck downstream away from the algal source. When they passed the thicket, they found Mory standing beside the water with golden locks threaded through his fingers and a perfectly preserved face staring at them.

"I found it," said the boy through clenched teeth and a wry smile.

Aaslo spied Dolt standing placidly beside the road, his supplies still secured to the saddle. Slogging onto the bank, Aaslo pried the head from the boy's white-knuckled grip and stuffed it into the sodden burlap sack.

"It's about time."

Aaslo was both relieved and struck with stomach-churning anxiety at hearing his friend's voice again.

"What's wrong with it?" said Mory.

"What do you mean?"

Mory scrunched his face. "I've seen a head before."

Peck snapped, "When did you see a severed head?"

Mory looked only slightly apologetic, as he couldn't take his eyes off the burlap sack. "I went to the chopping block. I know I wasn't supposed to go, but I went anyway. After they cut off the heads, they put them on pikes for everyone to see. It doesn't take long for them to get pretty horrible. This one looks perfect. It might as well still be attached. I half expected it to start talking to me."

"Did it?" Aaslo said, a little too eagerly.

Mory released a nervous laugh. "What? Talk to me? Of course not. It's dead, and I'm not crazy."

"Is all my stuff still there?" Aaslo asked with a nod toward the horse.

Mory glanced at Peck. "Yeah, I didn't touch anything. Your horse is crazy. I tried to make it stop, but it insisted on following you along the river. And, it tried to eat my shoes."

"Your shoes?"

"Yeah, I don't know much about horses, but I don't think they usually eat leather."

"When did it try to eat your shoes?"

"Um, well, he suddenly stopped walking and started nipping at my shoes. He chased me around until I took refuge in the rocks. I guess it was a lucky break, because that's when I found the head."

Aaslo looked at the horse, which appeared to be either having a stroke or unsuccessfully attempting to lick its own ear. "Yes, lucky that," he said. He glanced between Mory and Peck. "You are free to go," he said, then started walking toward the confounding beast.

Peck bounded to his side. "That's it? You're not going to, you know, make us pay for your troubles or something?"

"I only wanted the head. Just tell me how to get back to the place where you found me, and I'll be on my way."

Peck appeared anxious as he said, "Right then, um, you just follow the river, and then you take the second bridge, turn left at the temple with the bell, then go two streets down and turn right at the stall with the flowers—er, sometimes it's potatoes. Maybe it's best if I just show you."

"Why would you do that?"

"Well, we wasted half your day, and you got hurt and filthy. I guess we kind of owe you."

"You're thieves. You owe everyone you've robbed."

Peck shrugged into his jacket and sucked air between his teeth. "Well, I can't say it's not in our best interest. Strength in numbers and all that. You know what I mean?"

"No, I don't. I need to get back to the place where we started, though. If you're willing to show me the way, then let's be on with it."

Peck grinned and hooked an arm around Mory's shoulders. He said, "The boy'll show us. I want to see how much he remembers."

Mory pushed Peck's arm over his head and said, "I know the way,

Peck. I'm good with the city." The boy bounded several paces ahead but frequently checked over his shoulder. Peck said nothing, and his mood seemed to sober the longer they walked.

"They're leading you into a trap."

"You think so?"

"Do I think what?" Peck said.

"Something's up with him."

"I noticed."

Peck glanced around anxiously and said, "Noticed what?"

"Don't say anything. He'll know you're on to him."

"I must. If I say something, maybe he'll call it off," Aaslo replied. To Peck, he said, "You're acting strange."

"Me?" said Peck. "Look, you can say whatever you want, but if he catches us, he's not going to call anything off."

"He's setting you up."

"No, he's scared," Aaslo said.

"You're not?" said Peck.

Aaslo gave him a sidelong glance, but Peck's attention was elsewhere. Mory had paused to chat with the young woman tending the stall, and Peck's mood brightened as they neared. He hand-combed his hair again and straightened his jacket, although nothing was to be done for his sodden pants and boots.

Peck bowed with a flourish and said, "Lovely Lena, how is your day?"

In his mind's eye, for the briefest moment, Aaslo saw Mathias in Peck's place. He had seen his friend do as much many times with the young women of Goldenwood.

"He's not me, Aaslo. You need to keep both our heads straight. He's up to something."

Lena's smile fell as she glanced at Aaslo. She said to Peck, "Who's your friend?"

"Ah, well, he's a visitor. We're showing him the city."

"That's nice, Peck." Lena appeared unconvinced, but she had kind eyes as she glided toward Aaslo. He ducked his head and averted his gaze as she brushed his hair aside. "You're hurt," she said.

Aaslo reached up to touch the cut at his temple, but she caught his hand. He said, "Am I still a mess? I thought I cleaned most of it off in the river."

Lena's eyes widened. "No, it's only a small cut, but if you washed it in the river, it'll get infected for certain. Here, let me give you something for it."

The young woman shuffled through several bottles and packets of herbs. She carefully poured them into a wooden mortar and ground them together with a pestle. She then added a bit of liquid to the mixture and transferred the glob onto a strip of waxed cheesecloth. After dabbing a bit of the ointment onto Aaslo's wound, she wrapped the remainder and handed it to him.

"Don't tell Master Gerredy. I'm not supposed to mix remedies on my own, but I've made this one with him enough times to know it well. You'll need to apply it at least three times per day until it's healed."

Aaslo retrieved the purse he had hidden inside his waistband and withdrew a few coins.

"No, that's not necessary. Any friend of Peck's . . ."

"I insist," Aaslo said.

As he tucked his purse behind his belt, he gave Peck a warning look. Peck did his best to appear innocent, but Aaslo was unmoved. He rested his hand on his sword hilt, the sword he had yet to draw. Peck's smile slipped, and he dipped his head.

"Thank you," Lena said with a genuine smile. "Master Gerredy will be glad of the sale, but I'll tell him you bought the raw herbs, if you don't mind."

"Of course," Aaslo said. He bowed courteously, then continued on his way. Peck had a few more words with Lena and then caught up with him as Mory bounded past.

Peck's disposition became more apprehensive with every step. He said, "You know, ah, it's nearing dusk. You never know what might come after dark. Maybe it would be better to keep your axe nearer."

Aaslo gave him a sidelong glance. His axe was strapped to the saddle beside his head. "It's right here. How much closer does it need to be?"

Peck laughed nervously. "No, no, it's fine. I'm sure it's fine." After a few more minutes, he said, "How good are you with the sword? You didn't even draw it before. Is the axe your weapon of choice, or are you good with both?"

"He's testing you. He's leading you into an ambush."

"An ambush."

"What? Where?" Peck said with alarm as he spun around in the road.

"Your ambush, Peck. The one you're leading me into," Aaslo said.

"Me? No, I wouldn't. I swear. But I can't guarantee—"

Peck's words were cut off as someone reached out from a shadow, grabbed him by the neck, and jerked him into the alley. Two more men converged on Mory, who immediately cowered on the ground and covered his head with his arms. A rough-looking man with a broken tooth and a scar across his cheek stepped into the waning light. The man flicked a knife end over end between his fingers and said to Aaslo, "We don't know you, and we don't care to. You stay out of this, and you're free to go on your way."

Aaslo took a few steps back so that he could peer into the alley. It was still dark, but he could see that Peck was being held against the wall by a hulking man with a wicked ten-inch blade to his throat.

The alley man said, "Hi Pecker, it's time to pay up."

"It's Peckett, and I don't have your money yet. You said by tonight. Just—just give me 'til the end of the night. I'll make good, I swear."

"Look, Pecker, I said by tonight or I'd start taking it out of your hide. You don't want to make me a liar, do you? I think I'll take a bit now to give you some incentive. You don't need your ears, do you? No, you can still hear without 'em."

"No, Jago, I'll get your money. It's fine. See, I've got someone with me now. We're working on it. It's all good."

"I hear you talking a lot, but I don't see any *proof* of your commitment. Maybe I should start taking payment from your little boyfriend over there. He doesn't seem to be pulling his weight." He jerked Peck farther into the light and forced him to look at Mory. He said, "Look at him, sniveling on the ground like a coward. Caris told me you'd been caught. I didn't believe him at first, but then he said it was 'cause your boy toy couldn't make the jump. *That* was believable."

"Caris would have known Mory couldn't make that jump when he chose the route. He set us up. He wanted us to get caught."

"The boy is your weakness, Pecker, and now he's gonna be your death."

Aaslo watched the exchange as Captain Cromley had taught them, surveying the thugs for strengths and weakness. There were four that he could see. They were all big men, brawlers, except the one who had warned him off. He was a wiry man with a big stick—one studded with metal shards. Aaslo couldn't hope to take them all. Mathias might have been able to, but probably not, surrounded as they were. Mory was a sitting duck, alone, on the other side of the road with the two thugs, and Peck was one twitch away from a slit throat. The weight of the bag at his hip reminded Aaslo that he had bigger problems. With an apologetic glance at Peck, he turned and led Dolt through the group.

When he reached the halfway point, Aaslo palmed the hatchet he had tucked into his belt, ducked around his horse, and threw it at the farthest thug who was hovering over Mory. As the hatchet sank into the man's chest, Aaslo drew his sword and gutted the second while he was still blinking in shock. He had no time to regret his choice of attack as the man's guts spilled over a squealing Mory. The wiry man rounded the horse's rear to inspect the commotion, and Dolt kicked the man in the head. As the horse turned to trample the downed assailant, Aaslo slipped his axe from the saddle. With a sparing glance, he lobbed the axe at the boss, severing the arm that held the knife to Peck's throat. Peck appeared frozen in shock as Jago collapsed to the ground screaming and gripping the spurting stump at his elbow.

Aaslo leaned over Jago, positioning the tip of his sword at the man's jugular. He said, "Do you know why I spared you? If I kill you, your men will keep coming after us, and I'll have to keep killing them until they're all dead. By sparing you, I give you the chance to recognize our bill of sale."

Jago blinked up at him, his face pale and covered in sweat. "B-b-bill of sale?"

Aaslo tilted his head toward Peck. He said, "This one and his friend are paid in full. I give you your life in exchange for theirs. Do we have a deal?" Aaslo pressed the sharp edge into the soft flesh of the man's throat, just below his double chin, eliciting a trickle of blood.

Jago shook his head. "Yes, yes, they're yours. They're small earners anyway. With all the refugees, I got plenty more. Just take them and go."

"He's going to stab you in your sleep."

Aaslo narrowed his eyes and searched the man's pasty face.

"What is it?" Jago blubbered. "I said they're yours!"

"Don't be an idiot, Aaslo. He's lying."

"Are you the kind of man to hold a grudge? Am I going to have to keep looking over my shoulder? It will annoy me if I have to hunt you down. Believe me when I say that I am a *very* good hunter."

"*Oh, that was a good one, and he doesn't even get the joke.*"

"No, no, we're all good. I don't ever want to see you again. Please, I need to get to a healer. I'm gonna bleed out."

Aaslo glanced behind him and said, "Your men are dead. You'll likely live—at least long enough to warn the rest of your men to stay away."

"*Oooo, scary. You're good at this, Aaslo.*"

Aaslo felt sick. He had never before killed a man. At least, he didn't think the white-blooded creatures were men. They weren't *human*, anyway. Now, he had killed three and maimed a fourth. He could no longer sit back in apathy, though. He knew Peck and Mory were thieves, but they weren't bad men. He had hope they could be redeemed if given a chance.

He stepped back from the injured boss, who immediately scrambled to his feet and stumbled down the alley with his bleeding stump gripped to his chest. Aaslo picked up his axe, kicked the arm into the shadow, then looked at Peck. The thief's gaze was steeped in fear and his face was nearly as white as Jago's in his shock. Aaslo wiped the blood from his sword and sheathed it before cleaning his axe and returning it to his saddle.

"Peck," came a haunted wail. "P-e-e-e-ck."

Peck shook himself from his stupor and rushed to Mory's side, giving Dolt a wide berth. Aaslo felt terrible upon seeing the boy drenched in the bloody gore of the thug's innards. Dolt's victim was smashed to a pulp, so Aaslo began dragging him by his ankles toward the river. Darkness had set, and no one was about by the river. If this was the typical welcoming party, then he could understand why. After dumping the first body, he returned to the scene to grab the second, from whom he retrieved his hatchet.

"*That was a good throw. You've improved.*"

"I could always throw the hatchet better than you."

"*I let you win. You needed the boost in confidence.*"

Aaslo sighed. "You probably did. You were better at everything."

"*Except the forest. You're best at forestry.*"

"Yes, but I'm not *in* the forest. There is no forest for at least a hundred miles."

"You grow things, Aaslo. You make sick and dying things well. Look at this city. It is like a forest, in a way, and it needs someone to make it well—to make it grow again."

"That's not my job. That's a job for you. That's a job for the king and the magi. I'll take you to see him, and then I'll go back to my old life."

"And them?"

Aaslo glanced at the two thieves as he returned for the final body. Peck had managed to rid Mory of most of the intestines, and the boy huddled within his arms shivering.

Aaslo said, "Help me with this mess and have the boy wash in the river. He'll feel better once he's clean."

Peck said nothing as he stooped to pile entrails onto the body. Then he took Mory by the arm and guided him toward the river as Aaslo dragged the eviscerated corpse. Mory and Peck both stood sheepishly at the water's edge as they watched Aaslo guide the body into the deeper water. Once he had sloshed back to the shore, he paused. They didn't move and instead stood staring at him.

"What?" he said.

Peck glanced to where the bodies had disappeared into the darkness.

Aaslo looked, too. He said, "Don't worry about them. They're gone. The river's carried them away."

Peck's voice wavered as he said, "And us? Is it going to carry us away, too?"

"What are you talking about?" Then it dawned on him. "You think I brought you over here to kill you?" Neither said anything as Mory began shaking harder. Aaslo sighed. He said, "I'm not a murderer. I'm not a hired blade." He waved a hand downriver and said, "I've never even killed a man before tonight, and the only reason I did was because they were going to kill you."

"What do you mean that you've never killed a man?" Peck said. "You carry a head in a bag!"

"Yes, but I didn't kill him. I needed proof that he was dead, and his body was too big to transport. I only cut off his head *after* he was dead."

"But you fight like a terror . . . and your horse!"

"My horse is an idiot," Aaslo said as he glanced sidelong at Dolt. The horse stared at him with one bright bluish white eye. "I guess he's good for something, but he's still an idiot." Dolt snorted as if he somehow understood. "It wouldn't have taken much training to defeat those thugs. Yes, I was trained to fight, but I'm no warrior. I guess you could say that I was a warrior's sparring partner. I wasn't meant for this."

"What's the difference between a trained warrior and a sparring partner?" said Peck. "Hired blade or no, you just killed three of Jago's men and cut off his *arm*. How did you do that, anyway? A few inches over, and it would've been my head!"

"I've spent a lot of time with my axe," Aaslo muttered. "Look, there's still bloody gore on the street. We probably don't want to be around when the city guard finds it. It's dark now, and I really need to get back to where I was before all this started. Since I just saved your lives, the least you can do is show me the way."

"Right, yes, of course," said Peck. "But, ah, just to be clear. You're not going to kill us once we get there, right?"

"Do you plan to attack me?"

"No, never that!"

Aaslo growled his frustration. "I told you, I'm not a murderer. That, up there, was self-defense—and defense of *you*. Now, get him cleaned up so we can go."

Once they were finally back on the road, Peck and Mory kept their distance, which was fine with Aaslo. Mathias had started talking again, and it didn't seem like the monologue would ever end. Every second of the fight was broken down into tiny pieces, which Mathias analyzed and criticized without reserve. By the time they reached the tree-shaped building, Aaslo's emotional attachment to the battle had been severed by his phantom friend's incessant drone.

"I won, okay. Can we just let it go?" Aaslo snapped.

"Yeah, sure, no problem," Peck said anxiously. "We're here."

Aaslo looked around. The tree building was dark now. In fact, the whole square was dark, every building closed to the night, and there didn't appear to be any inns in sight. Aaslo sighed. He should have asked them to take him to an inn. He turned, expecting the thieves to have disappeared, but they still awaited his approval. He hooked a thumb over his shoulder toward the Forester's Haven and said, "What's that building?"

Peck looked past Aaslo. "Ah, the left side is the Loggers' Union, and the right is the Carpenters' Guild."

Aaslo glanced back at the two tall spires, then shook his head. "No, I mean the one in the middle. It says 'Forester's Haven.'"

"Oh, that's for the foresters. They're tree folk, mostly from the north, from what I've heard. Some say they're magical gnomes that build their homes in the tree branches."

"I heard they swing from the branches by their long tails," said Mory. Aaslo was glad to hear the boy speak again, but he was still disturbed by Mory's haunted gaze.

Aaslo said, "What's it for?"

Peck said, "I guess it's for whatever the foresters need it to be for."

After wrapping Dolt's reins around a fence post and collecting his pack, Aaslo walked up the steps to the arched door. He knocked, but the tiny thud barely carried to his own ears. He smirked. The door was a forester's gong. Thick as a tree trunk and carved by a master, doors like these graced the hovels where the foresters met when group discussions became necessary. With the right amount of power, at just the right height, the door would resonate like a bell. He pulled back his arm and slammed the portal with a meaty fist. A deep peal reverberated up the entire structure as other gongs were activated.

Aaslo stepped back and waited. A tiny flicker lit near one window and then steadily grew. The light moved to the next window, and Aaslo watched it flash past each level of windows as it descended. A few minutes later, the massive door silently swung inward, and a tiny head wearing a bed cap peeked out from behind. The man was very small, barely rising to Aaslo's chest. He had narrow features, a pointed nose, and large, startled eyes. He pursed his lips and stared at Aaslo.

Aaslo said, "Greetings. I bring shade in my heart and water in my soul. May I enter?"

Somehow, the little man's eyes widened farther, and he sputtered, "Yes, yes, m-may the soil bear the fruit of your labors." He pulled the door open and stood back as his lantern shook in his upraised hand. The little man glanced back toward the others and then blinked up at Aaslo.

Aaslo said, "Is there a place to stable my horse?"

"Ah, yes, Sir Forester. It's not a stable, as such, but the woods are in the back."

"You have woods?" Aaslo said, a tiny blossom of hope in his chest.

"Well, not so much as a forest. But we have a small courtyard with several trees. It's the most trees gathered in one place in all of Tyellí, except for the palace grounds, of course. We have a fountain and a pergola that should do well enough for the horse. Will your men bring him around?" He pointed a finger toward a small gate to one side.

Aaslo looked back at Peck and Mory. Both appeared confused and anxious, but neither made to leave. He wondered why they hadn't yet disappeared.

Peck gathered Dolt's reins and said, "We'll take him to the back and brush him down."

"They might steal him."

Aaslo had no idea what the thieves intended, but he figured Dolt would do what he wanted, and there was little Aaslo or anyone else could do to stop him. He nodded toward the thieves and then followed his host into the hovel. It was more spacious than it had appeared from the outside. The ground floor contained several rooms, most of which had furniture for sitting or dining. In the back was a kitchen, and Aaslo could see the "woods" through the window. The loggers union and carpenters guild wrapped around three sides of the courtyard, with the Forester's Haven at the entrance. Although it was dark in the courtyard, he could see the silhouettes of the two thieves and the horse wandering through the trees.

He turned to inspect the kitchen and found his host staring at him again. The man shook himself, then bent to stoke the fire in the hearth. He threw on another log and then hooked a pot of water on the crane to boil. "I shall make you some tea, Sir Forester. Have you eaten? No? How about some stew? It won't be long." He pointed to the hearth with his wooden spoon and said, "The pot's enchanted. It takes less than half the time to cook than a normal pot."

Aaslo watched the tiny man move about his kitchen with ease. His host set to gathering vegetables and herbs from the cabinets, then started furtively chopping. The water began to bubble, and he ladled hot water into several cups before adding herbs from a ceramic jar. A subtle tap at the back door announced Peck and Mory's arrival. His host ushered them into the kitchen and bade them sit at the table with Aaslo. Aaslo wondered why the two were still hanging around, especially since they seemed hesitant to meet his gaze.

Their host paused and took a deep breath as if to center himself. He looked up at Aaslo and said, "I've never met a forester. None have

come here in all the years I've cared for this place. It's been, oh, fifty . . .
ah . . . fifty-seven years. Yes, that's right—fifty-seven. Oh, my Maralee would have been so excited to meet you. She passed away several
years ago, but she always told me you would come. When I began to
doubt my calling, she would say, 'No, Galobar, don't you doubt yourself. The foresters will come, and when they do, they'll need you.'"

"How do you know I'm a forester?" Aaslo said, and he saw Peck and
Mory blinking at him from the corner of his eye.

"Oh, well, I've had a few show up over the years claiming to be foresters," Galobar said as he sliced potatoes into the tiniest chunks and
tossed them into the pot. "They're usually looking for free food or a
place to stay, but no one has ever rung the gong. Truth be told, I wasn't
sure it really worked. My master claimed it would, but I don't think
he had ever heard it himself. Nor have any used the formal greeting.
My master taught the words to me long ago, but never have I heard
them uttered on the lips of a forester. No, not I. This is truly an exciting night."

He paused in the chopping of his vegetables and said, "Oh, I am so
sorry. I've forgotten myself. Silence is a virtue. Foresters like solitude
and quiet, and here I am talking my head off. What may I do for you,
Sir Forester?"

Aaslo said, "I need a place to stay." He pulled the purse from his
belt. "A bath and a meal would be much appreciated, too."

Galobar held up his hands and said, "No, no! You can't use that here.
This is the *Forester's Haven*. It's paid for by the crown. It's a monu-
ment for the people—to remind us of who the foresters are and why
we must respect and revere them."

"Did you feel revered every time I laid you out during practice?"

"No," Aaslo grumped. The keeper blinked at him. Aaslo said, "Why?
We're not mythical creatures. We're men and women who plant trees
and help them grow after the loggers cut them down."

Galobar looked at him in shock. "Oh, no, Sir Forester. You are so
much more than that. You may not realize how special you are because,
well, it's who you are, but do not doubt that you are worthy of our rev-
erence. You are all so secretive and aloof, it would be too easy for
people to forget."

Aaslo was unconvinced, but Peck and Mory seemed enthralled with
the keeper's claim.

"Why are the foresters so special?" Mory asked.

"Well, I must say, I feel a little strange talking about the foresters with one sitting right here in front of me." Galobar nodded to himself. "It's true that some fantastic tales have grown around the foresters. Some say they're a kind of fae creature or elves or the like. I even heard a tale claiming there was really only one forester, and he was actually a god that deigned to walk among men to make sure we didn't destroy the forests he had worked so hard to create."

"Did you hear that, Aaslo? You're a god."

Aaslo nearly joined Mathias in his laughter, but somehow laughing with a ghost seemed wrong. Then again, so did carrying around his best friend's head.

The keeper continued his discussion of foresters, while Aaslo retreated into the quiet space of his mind. He imagined he was lounging beneath the trees on his back porch, his father sitting silently beside him rocking in his chair and watching the stars twinkle between the swaying branches. He lost himself in the memory and even Mathias was silent. When he finally roused, he realized a significant amount of time had passed. Galobar was gone, and the steamy aroma of stew reached his nose from the bowl in front of him. He reached for his spoon, and Mory jumped.

"S-sorry. I thought you were sleeping with your eyes open," the boy mumbled.

"Not sleeping," Aaslo said. "Just caught up in another place and time."

"For real?" Mory said, his eyes widening.

Aaslo scowled. "Only a memory—like any other. Nothing magical about it." Turning to Peck, Aaslo said, "Why are you here?"

"Um, we're eating stew."

"No, I mean why are you *here*—with me? Why haven't you gone home?"

Peck glanced at Mory, then said, "You bought us, so now we're your men. We do what you want us to do."

"What are you talking about? I didn't buy you. You can't *buy* a person."

Peck nodded. "Yes, you made a deal with Jago. Paid in full, you said. Our lives for his."

Aaslo scoffed. "I only said that to get him off your backs. I don't *own* you. You're free to go your own way."

Mory grabbed Peck's arm, and Peck shifted anxiously. "Well, you see that's kind of a problem. You made the deal with Jago, but if he thinks you've let us go, he'll come after us. He doesn't recognize our freedom, only your protection. He's afraid of you."

"Then, why don't you leave Tyellí? Wouldn't it be worth your freedom?"

"Where would we go? What would we do?" said Peck. "If we go anywhere else, we'll just end up under someone else's thumb. I don't know how to do anything but thieving."

"You feed them once and they never leave."

"Well, what am I supposed to do with you?" said Aaslo.

"Your bath is ready, Sir Forester." Aaslo turned to see Galobar beckoning him toward the stairs.

He scarfed down the last few bites of his stew, collected his pack, and left the table. He could feel the thieves' gazes on his back. He turned and said, "Eat, bathe, rest. We'll discuss this further in the morning. If you rob me or this house, I'll find you."

Peck and Mory adamantly shook their heads, but he caught them grinning at each other as he ascended the stairs.

"How much of this house do you think they'll be able to clear out while you and Galobar sleep?"

"I hope the *crown* will cover the cost," Aaslo mumbled.

"Not good, Aaslo. The first forester to visit the Forester's Haven brings thieves with him."

"What was I supposed to do? I can't kick them out now. That crazy Jago is likely to kill them."

"Since when is that your problem?"

"It's what you would do."

The voice fell silent, and Aaslo knew his words to be true. Mathias would have helped anyone who needed him.

CHAPTER 9

A WHITE MARBLE FOUNTAIN STOOD IN THE CENTER OF THE SQUARE AT the front entrance of the palace. Despite the unreasonable heat that morning, the center square was bustling with patrons, merchants, and city officials. Shops lined three sides of the square, and a ten-foot wall topped with iron spikes occupied the fourth. A massive iron gate manned by four palace guards stood opposite the fountain.

Aaslo urged his horse forward. Upon reaching the feature of glistening blue water, Dolt refused to heed Aaslo's command to stop and instead hopped over the fountain's rim to stand beneath the frothy spray. He then proceeded to flick the water with his tail, flinging it several paces in every direction, seemingly delighted by the patrons' protests. Aaslo tumbled onto the fountain's ledge as he gracelessly dismounted while scolding the horse. Shouts from the crowd echoed his own, except that they were directed at him. By the time Aaslo had his feet firmly on the ground, two city guards had joined him.

"What do you think you're doing? Get that horse out of the fountain!" said the first, a brown-haired fellow with a thick mustache and a dimpled chin.

"Oh, you're in trouble now."

"Can't you see that I'm trying?" Aaslo muttered. "The infernal beast does what he wants."

"Well, he's your responsibility, and you'll be paying for any damages. If you don't get him out of there right now, we'll have to arrest you for disturbing the peace."

A crowd started to form, and Aaslo wanted to get away before attracting any more attention. He said, "All right, how about you help me get him out, and then we can both be on with our business."

The guard drew a baton from his belt and pointed it at Aaslo. "Do I look like a stable hand?"

"Actually, he kind of does."

"Stable hands are usually bigger," Aaslo muttered.

The guard stepped forward. "What did you say?"

Dolt snorted, turned his massive head, and nabbed the second guard's hat from his head. The young man shouted and hastily reached for the cap, but Dolt dodged the attempt with a pleased nicker. The crowd roared with laughter as the young guard toppled into the fountain.

Aaslo turned to the first guard with a heavy sigh, crossed his arms, and said, "Doesn't matter your position. You're a man, and a man can choose to make things more difficult, or he can choose to help. In the choosing, he decides what kind of man he wants to be."

"More sage forester wisdom?" called a familiar voice. Aaslo turned to find the marquess's party watching the display from atop their mounts. "It seems your horse is up to his usual antics."

Dolt turned as if he knew they were speaking of him. He abruptly vacated the fountain and plodded over to nip at the tail of his former acquaintance. The other horse was again disquieted by the attention and summarily sent its rider crashing to the ground. The patrons jeered while the marquess's guard collected himself and hollered epithets. The marquess watched the scene with apathy, but laughter danced in his eyes.

The marquess's servant tapped two hollow metal shafts together, causing them to ring louder than the boisterous crowd. He called over the din, "The Most Honorable the Marquess of Dovermyer."

The crowd hushed, and then everyone was bowing—everyone but Aaslo. He glanced around and suddenly felt awkward to be the only one standing erect in the presence of the marquess. He decided that a belated bow would be even more uncomfortable, so he stood his ground with a scowl.

"You rebel. Still seeking the noose, are you?"

"If it's not a noose, then it's a thief," Aaslo muttered.

"What are you going on about now?" said the marquess. "Has someone robbed you?"

"This city is full of thieves," Aaslo replied. "But I got back what was taken."

"And then some."

"I am pleased to see you standing here well enough, then. I hear tell that some of these thieves can be quite brutal." The marquess tilted his head to examine Aaslo. "It seems you did not escape unscathed."

Aaslo brushed his fingers across the sore spot on his split scalp. Although it no longer bled, the injury was bold enough to stand out from his hairline. He said, "I'll live."

"Quite so," said the marquess, "but did the thieves?"

"The noose grows tighter."

Aaslo said nothing, and the marquess hummed under his breath. Glancing toward his frustrated guardsman, the marquess said, "Perhaps I should hire you to train my guards."

With Dolt's reins in hand, Aaslo yanked the horse away from the poor man. "I'm not a soldier. You know that."

"I'm not sure that I do, Sir Forester. You seem qualified to me."

Aaslo's stomach churned with the marquess's use of the title. A wave of chatter rushed through the crowd of onlookers, who suddenly appeared hungry. People were jostled as others pushed forward to see the forester on display, and his personal space began to shrink. Aaslo wished Dolt would dash through the crowd and drag him away. The horse turned to look at him as if to ask if he was serious.

"May I address the Most Honorable the Marquess?" said the city guardsman.

The marquess looked to the man and said, "What is it?"

The guardsman straightened and said, "Shall we arrest this man?"

"I am almost inclined to allow it," said the marquess.

"What? Why?" said Aaslo.

"If you are arrested, perhaps I can convince the king to sentence you to service in Ruriton."

Aaslo crossed his arms and said, "More likely he'll scold you for allowing a forester to be mistreated."

The marquess sighed dramatically and said, "Yes, you are probably correct. You foresters are so very fragile."

Mathias burst into laughter, and Aaslo was almost glad of it. How he missed that sound.

Aaslo glanced at the marquess's guards, a couple of them still sporting bruises. He said, "Your guards can attest to our fragility."

The marquess's expression sobered. "Indeed. They have rigorous training in their futures."

"*They should've had Cromley.*"

"Cromley wouldn't put up with them."

"Marius Cromley?" said the marquess's guard captain, Greylan. He suddenly appeared much more interested in the conversation.

Aaslo didn't like that Greylan knew Cromley's name. Cromley had once served in the army, he knew, but hadn't been anyone of note—or so Aaslo had thought. If Magdelay was the high sorceress, though, and Mathias the chosen one, then it stood to reason that Cromley was more important than he knew. Electing once again to remain silent, Aaslo maintained his stubborn poise, but the marquess and Greylan shared a suspicious glance. The name Cromley was whispered among the other guards, and even the city guardsmen were looking at him strangely.

"What are you doing here, Marquess?" Aaslo said, knowing it would elicit a reaction. The redirection seemed to work, as the crowd gasped and chattered about the informal address and his questioning of the marquess. The soldiers seemed ruffled and tense.

The marquess smirked and said, "You do love to push the bounds, and so eloquently done, I might add. With every detail, things begin to make more sense *and* less. Perhaps this is not the appropriate venue for discussion, though. To answer your question, the news is all over the city—a forester came to call at the Forester's Haven. Naturally, I thought it to be you, so I paid the haven a visit. The keeper said you had inquired about the palace, and so here we are."

It was Aaslo's turn to smirk. "You do realize that the marquess just publicly admitted to personally following me about the city."

The marquess rolled his eyes. "Yes, but I knew if I sent a summons, you would not answer it. Therefore, I had to come to you. You foresters are a privileged lot."

Aaslo huffed. "You can keep your privilege. I'm here to deliver a message, and then I'm done."

The marquess grinned. "Excellent. I happen to remember you promising to assist me with a little problem once your task was completed. It seems my efforts have not gone to waste. To where must we deliver this message?"

Aaslo motioned over his shoulder. "There. My message is for the king and none other."

The marquess looked to the palace, then rested his gaze on Aaslo for longer than was considered polite. All mirth had departed, and the prospect of news that had not yet been delivered by the mysterious forester seemed to weigh heavily upon the man. The marquess glanced at the crowd and then whispered something to his servant. The servant clapped the metal tubes together again and hollered, "Clear the square! By order of the Most Honorable the Marquess of Dovermyer, clear the square!"

Guards directed the crowd away from the square, and the marquess dismounted. Removing his riding gloves, he approached Aaslo still deep in thought. Meeting Aaslo's gaze, the marquess said, "You told me your task was important, but is it truly important enough for the king? An audience is not so easily gained, even for a forester."

"We can't trust him. He's far too suspicious. He knows something."

"Trust is a luxury I cannot afford," Aaslo muttered, "but that does not negate my need. Perhaps the marquess can assist me, after all?"

The marquess shook his head. "If *I* am to request an audience with the king on your behalf, then I will need to know the nature of the request. I will not be made the fool in front of the king's court."

Aaslo nodded. He didn't trust the marquess, and he had come too far to be waylaid at the palace gates. He had come prepared, though. As he reached inside his shirt, Aaslo said, "You will not be requesting it." He handed the marquess the letter Magdelay had given him and said, "She is."

As the marquess read, Aaslo knew what caused his face to pale. He had read the letter enough times to have it memorized.

> *The bearer of this letter is to be delivered directly to the king immediately upon presentation and will not be barred by guard, gate, custom, or courtesy. Whether in the midst of court or private session, the king will see the bearer without delay. The bearer will be received in private audience insomuch as is possible and will be granted the freedom to speak plainly. These demands are hereby rendered and guaranteed by Magdelay Brelle, High Sorceress of the Council of Magi.*

The marquess looked back to Aaslo, seemingly at a loss for words. His gaze passed beyond the fountain to the palace guards, who had not left their post. "Open the gate!"

Greylan stepped to the marquess's side. "What is it, my lord? Why such urgency?"

"Not now, Greylan. We must get to the palace."

Aaslo eyed the marquess with suspicion. The marquess must have noticed, because he hastily folded the letter and offered it back to Aaslo. As he moved to take it, the marquess said, "I know not what news you bring, but this letter and the fact that *you* are its bearer fills me with dread."

Aaslo said, "Nothing I have to say will deliver you from it."

The marquess's servant brought his horse forward, and Aaslo took to his own. For once, Dolt was being accommodating, and Aaslo wondered if he hadn't worn himself out. As Aaslo rode through the front gate at the marquess's side, he wondered how he might escape if it turned out the king did not respond well to bad news.

The palace lawn was superbly green and kempt, and Aaslo wondered how it was done until he saw the trees that lined the boulevard. Each was perfectly symmetrical in its every branch and leaf. It was so unnatural to Aaslo's discerning eye that he thought he might be sick at the sight. These trees were empty shells generated by magic, devoid of spirit and out of balance with the chaos of nature that trees naturally endured. The struggle of adaptation and survival was an integral part of the tree, more so than its color or height or any of the features most people found appealing. In rejecting individuality, the magi had stripped these trees of something vital.

"You don't like them?" said the marquess.

Aaslo had not realized that he had been wearing his horror so openly. "They are an abomination," he said.

"I'm surprised to hear that. I thought foresters loved trees."

"We do. These are not trees. They are magically generated impostors—like a cadaver with no soul, propped up to decorate the lawn."

The marquess grimaced. "That is disturbing. I will have to trust you on that and be grateful that I cannot see it."

"Indeed," said Aaslo, a gloom settling over him.

His jaw tense, the marquess said, "You will not be coming to Ruriton, will you?"

Aaslo shrugged. "I'm not certain I'll leave the meeting with the king alive."

"He can be harsh, but he is not one to kill the messenger."

"*You see, nothing to worry about.*"

"No one has ever delivered *this* message," Aaslo said.

At the end of the boulevard was a circular drive, in the center of which stood a garden of topiaries and exotic plants that should not have been able to survive the central Uyanian climate. Nearly a dozen carriages were parked around the circle and down a side lane, and coachmen were gathered in clusters chatting and smoking pipes. The front of the palace glistened in the sunlight, the façade clear as glass, and Aaslo could see ladies and gentlemen dressed in silks and frills meandering about the front hall with liveried servants scurrying among them.

With the marquess in the lead, their party was admitted at the door without issue and ushered toward the opposite end of the hall. Aaslo paused to offer his condolences to the poor soul that occupied the center of the hall. A massive lellisa tree had outgrown itself at more than twice its naturally achievable height; and, although out of season, it was in full bloom, filling the hall with its pale, sweet aroma. As Aaslo watched, white leaves and pink petals perpetually showered the floor, and new leaves and blossoms replaced them.

"It is beautiful, yes? It blooms year-round," said the marquess. When Aaslo did not reply, he said, "You do not approve of this, either, I take it."

"It's sick," Aaslo said, "dying, actually."

"But the magi—"

"Have created an illusion of good health and prosperity. It will not last."

A thin man with a dour disposition stepped into Aaslo's view. He wore a smart black overcoat from which white ruffles blossomed up to his chin. He rapped a silver-topped cane on the floor and said, "In the king's court, it is best to never speak of things you do not understand. Rumors abound. A misspoken word will spread like fire, and those who incite unrest with false claims are dealt with most severely."

Aaslo crossed his arms and said, "I assure you, I did not misspeak, nor have I issued false claim. I know my business."

The man surveyed Aaslo's worn and earthy woven jacket, grey wool pants, and soft leather boots. His gaze stalled on the incongruous gold-and-silver-wrapped hilt at Aaslo's waist. A flicker of uncertainty passed over his face before he finally dismissed Aaslo altogether. Turning his attention to the marquess, he said, "My Lord Marquess, as the king's seneschal, it is my duty to inform you that a serf is not permitted to carry a weapon, nor may he speak without leave. Yours has not been granted the privilege, and his attempts to alarm the court with unwarranted and unfounded ill portents are cause for reprimand." The man flicked his fingers toward a couple of guards and said, "He will be taken into custody and dealt with accordingly. If you wish to claim him, you may do so when your business is concluded. As to your request for an audience with the king—"

"I did not request an audience with the king," said marquess. With a wave toward Aaslo, he said, "He did."

The seneschal looked back to Aaslo with open contempt.

"Are you going to let him speak to you like that? Weak, Aaslo."

Disinterested in receiving further insult, Aaslo proffered Magdelay's letter and said, "I'll save you the trouble of another rant."

After eyeing the folded letter with suspicion, the seneschal snatched it from Aaslo's fingers. As the sour-faced man read, the two guards stood prepared to take Aaslo into custody. The seneschal furrowed his brow but otherwise remained unmoved. As he refolded the letter, he said, "What is your name?"

"Aaslo, Forester of Goldenwood."

The seneschal grimaced, appearing slightly embarrassed, and said to the guards, "We shall escort Sir Forester to the throne room."

"You managed to shame the king's seneschal. That's an accomplishment worthy of our list."

"What list?" said Aaslo.

"What list? Our list of adventures and achievements."

The seneschal said, "Have no concern, Sir Forester. You have been moved to the top of the waiting list."

The marquess glanced at Aaslo. "I shall remain here in case you wish to find me when your task is complete."

The seneschal turned to the marquess. "On behalf of the king, I must insist that the marquess accompany us to the throne room. The forester arrived in your company, and the king may have questions for you."

The marquess tugged at his collar and said, "I barely know the man. I only provided escort from the square. I have not been apprised of his business, and I would prefer not to be held responsible for the news he bears."

"You seem to have a rapport, and you certainly know more than the rest of us," said the seneschal. "You will attend."

The seneschal led Aaslo, the marquess, and Greylan to the other side of the giant entry hall and then down a wide corridor toward a set of massive wooden doors that loomed at the other end. Guards standing at attention lined the hallway. Their uniforms of dark blue with gold brocade identified them as king's guards, and their sharp gazes betrayed their apparent dormancy.

"I wonder how we'd fare against them."

"You'd probably defeat any one of them, perhaps two at once."

The marquess chuckled. "I appreciate your confidence, but you are far more accomplished with the sword than am I."

"You are capable of wielding the weapon you carry?" said the seneschal. "I was not aware the foresters trained for combat."

"We don't," said Aaslo. "The sword I carry belonged to a fallen friend, a brother. It was he who wielded it with grace. I am a poor substitute."

The marquess said, "If you think your swordsmanship poor, then perhaps I should replace my entire guard."

"He got lucky," said Greylan.

"Perhaps, but his luck meant victory," said the marquess. "If he had meant harm, two of our guards would be dead, and he would have escaped."

"I was caught," said Aaslo.

"I am not blind," said the marquess, "and I may not be great with the sword, but I am an excellent strategist. You were caught because you were trying to spare their lives. Had they been *luckier*, they would not have afforded you the same courtesy."

The seneschal abruptly stopped in front of the doors and turned to Aaslo. He said, "I will enter first to deliver the high sorceress's missive to the king. The guards will tell you when to enter. You will remain at the entrance until your arrival is announced. Then, you will walk to the end of the blue carpet and stop. Do not go beyond the blue carpet. You will kneel and bow your head. Do not rise or speak until bidden to do so by the king. If you are given leave to speak, you will refer to the king as *Your Majesty*. Your business is with the king, so do not address the queen. Be warned—there are archers in the balconies. If you draw your sword in the throne room, you will be struck down without delay."

"Why would I have cause to draw my sword?" said Aaslo.

The seneschal feigned patience and said, "You would not."

"Then why the warning, and why do you look so agitated?"

With a glance toward the marquess, the seneschal said, "I seek only to prevent unnecessary bloodshed. Some visitors are less accepting of offense."

The marquess smirked. He leaned in, and in a hushed tone said, "A few years ago, the Baron of Yebury accused Sir Ciruth of sneaking into his daughter's bedchamber. Sir Ciruth forgot himself and drew his sword in challenge in the middle of the throne room. It was a terrible mess, but Yebury was satisfied with the outcome."

The seneschal said, "Sir Ciruth was a knight."

"Not a very good one," said Aaslo.

With a sigh, the seneschal said, "Regardless, he was trained in court etiquette. *You* are not. You should also take special care to mind your tongue."

"I told you your mouth would get you in trouble one day."

The man turned and walked several paces down the corridor before passing through a smaller door that Aaslo presumed led to a back entrance to the throne room.

Potent breath wafted across Aaslo's face as Greylan whispered in his ear, "I've got six gold pieces riding on you."

"For what? You don't even know my business."

"Doesn't matter your business. Hane says you're thrown in the dungeon. I bet you don't make it out of the throne room alive. Don't let me down."

"Hane. Is he the one I pummeled in the field?"

"Luck," replied Greylan, and then said nothing more.

Aaslo was grateful for the momentary silence. The marquess's restlessness and avoidance of eye contact caused Aaslo to wonder if he was intentionally avoiding conversation.

"He probably bet against you."

"That implies someone bet in my favor," said Aaslo.

"Not necessarily. They could all be betting on different methods of death."

He glanced over to see the marquess pointedly staring at the throne room doors. He was about to ask when a smaller door, which had not been visible, opened from within the larger one on the right.

"The Most Honorable the Marquess of Dovermyer may enter now," said the guardsman nearest the open door.

The marquess stepped through the doorway, and a list of titles echoed through the chamber beyond. Aaslo made to follow, but Greylan shoved him back with a grunt before following his liege. Aaslo was mildly surprised to hear that Greylan belonged to a noble house, although he held no titles. He knew it was common for nobles who would not inherit to enter into the service of someone in higher standing, although it was hard for him to imagine Greylan serving anyone by choice.

When Aaslo entered the grand chamber, most of the attention was focused on the marquess, and Aaslo was glad of it.

"Aaslo, Forester of Goldenwood," called the herald.

"So much for not drawing attention."

The courtiers ceased their chittering and turned to gawk at Aaslo. He could see the judgment in their gazes, each one deciding if he was worthy of the foresters' mystique. Most appeared to find him lacking, and for that he was grateful. He surveyed the archers in the balconies. They were difficult to see in the shadows cast by the light streaming through the tall windows lining the wall to his left in the chamber. Above the windows was a narrow walkway, over which towered a row of stained glass, which further obscured the lighting on the upper level. It appeared that there were six archers on each side of the hall, four of whom had their arrows trained on him.

His gaze roved over the dais as he reached the end of the blue carpet, and he knelt as instructed. He had noted that it was five steps to a second landing and then another five to the top, where the king and queen sat in intricately carved wooden thrones accented in gold and adorned with jewels. Aaslo thought it ironic that the Uyanian royal thrones were made of imported terandian-tree wood.

"Of course you notice the wood. Did you even see the king and queen?"

Aaslo winced as he stared at the floor. He thought he had gotten a decent look at the king, but he had barely noticed the queen. After what felt like forever, he began to wonder if he had missed the command to stand. His doubt had nearly overcome his sense when a smooth voice said, "You may rise."

Releasing his breath, Aaslo drew himself to his feet and met the king's gaze. King Rakith appeared younger than he had expected, even though he knew the king to be forty-three years of age. Every year, the king's birthday was celebrated across the kingdom as a holiday, so it was impossible to forget. From beneath a golden crown, silky brown hair swept in waves to curl just under his ear, and his kempt beard and mustache held a rusty hue. His dark gaze was sharp and demanding, but deep laugh lines defined his mouth and the corners of his eyes. A midnight-blue velvet robe, trimmed with the fur of a spotted hare, was draped over his shoulders and pooled at his feet.

The king had not yet given him leave to speak, and he held Aaslo's gaze with an intensity that alluded to a challenge. Aaslo decided to meet the challenge and dared not glance away, particularly toward the queen.

After an eternity, Rakith said, "What brings you to my court, Forester?"

"I bear a message, one that is meant for your ears alone."

"Yes, I read the missive. Your message comes from the sorceress, then?"

"More or less," Aaslo replied.

"What does that mean? Speak plainly, Forester. I have no interest in fae riddles."

"I am not fae," Aaslo grumbled. "I would be glad to explain, except that you have not yet dismissed the court."

The king leaned forward and pounded his fist on the arm of his throne. "Regardless of what the high sorceress believes, I decide what happens in my court."

"I believe you," Aaslo said.

"Careful, brother. You're cutting a path to the gallows."

Aaslo followed with, "I am confident that if you knew the nature of my message, an empty court would be your preference."

"You profess to know my mind—the mind of a *king*?"

"Not at all, Your Majesty. I profess to know my message."

A titter and a shuffle passed through the crowd, but Rakith's ardent gaze did not waver. He raised a finger, and the seneschal hurried to the king's side. Rakith's words did not carry beyond the dais, and the seneschal departed through a door to one side a moment later.

Rakith looked back to Aaslo. "To my knowledge, no forester has ever visited this court. How do we know you are who you say you are?"

"How do you know any man is who he says he is?"

"You aren't supposed to question the king!"

Aaslo internally cringed but felt it a valid question nonetheless.

Rakith drummed his fingers on the arm of his throne. He looked toward the marquess. "Lord Sefferiah. How do you know this man?"

"Your Majesty, I am only briefly acquainted with the forester. We met on the road south. I hope to acquire his services in dealing with the blight in Ruriton when his business here is concluded."

"Then, you did not witness his presence in the forest?" said Rakith.

"No, Your Majesty. I have had several dealings with the foresters in recent months. After speaking with Aaslo, I felt that his temperament, and, dare I say, *culture* were consistent with that of the foresters—with the fortunate exception of his willingness to leave the forest, that is."

The king turned his dark gaze back to Aaslo, and then proceeded to sit in silence for several minutes. The seneschal eventually returned with another man. The latter was of middle age with greying hair, but his form was fit and his forearms were thick. He wore a smock bearing multiple pockets over a sweat-stained shirt and had leather pads strapped to his knees. He held himself with the demeanor of a man used to subjugation but appeared anxious as he knelt at the foot of the dais.

Rakith looked at Aaslo and said, "This is Master Pettridge. He is the head groundskeeper for the palace." Turning his attention to the groundskeeper, he said, "Master Pettridge, you may rise. This man claims to be a forester. You will test the truth of his claim."

Pettridge blinked at Aaslo in surprise. "Your Majesty, I would be honored to discuss anything, anything at all, with Sir Forester."

"Perhaps you will have time for discussion later, but for now you need only to confirm or refute his claim."

"Oh, I wouldn't know what to ask, Your Majesty. A forester's knowledge is surely much greater than my own."

The king looked to the ceiling and sighed. "Then confirm that his knowledge is at least equal to your own."

Aaslo wanted to move on to business. Magdelay's letter had said *without delay*, but the king seemed less than eager to comply. Aaslo said, "Master Pettridge, allow me."

"Idiot."

Remembering too late that he was not supposed to speak without leave, Aaslo continued before he was called out for it. "Your lellisa tree is dying. Your magi have encouraged it to grow to at least twice its natural size, and its leaves are white. They are supposed to be red."

Master Pettridge's lips silently wagged before he sputtered, "It is a rare anomaly. That's why it's special."

"No, the leaves are white because the magic is forcing it into perpetual bloom. It should only bloom for two weeks per year in the spring. The rarity of the occurrence is what makes it special. The spells are sucking the nutrients, the life, out of the rest of the tree to keep up with the demand for flowers that your fancy nobles take for granted."

"Is this true?" said the queen, and Aaslo finally had an excuse to look her way.

She leaned forward so that the loose strands of her long auburn tresses hung to her knees. She was only a few years younger than the king, but her heart-shaped face glowed with a healthy youth. Her face lacked the lines of a life well-lived, but her hazel gaze held intelligence and knowledge. Aaslo was surprised that she appeared genuinely concerned.

Aaslo opened his mouth but paused. This time he remembered the seneschal's instructions. He was not supposed to address the queen. Glancing back at the king, he saw the hint of a smirk behind the man's beard. Aaslo thought it a challenge, and he accepted.

"Yes, Your Majesty," he said with a bow for the queen.

"Looks like I'll be seeing you sooner than you thought."

Aaslo ignored Mathias and delivered the rest of his answer for the queen. "It is hard to say, due to the magic involved, but I doubt the tree has more than a year or two to live."

The queen stared at the groundskeeper, who shifted uncomfortably. The man looked back at the king and said, "What he says makes sense. I defer to the forester's judgment in the matter, Your Majesty."

The king appeared contemplative for a moment; then his gaze flicked to the sword at Aaslo's hip. "Your sword looks costly for a man who lives a life sustained by the forest."

Aaslo glanced at the courtiers before answering. He had no desire to reveal information that should remain secret, but he couldn't lie to the king. He said, "I inherited it. My possession of the sword is further proof of the importance of the message I bear."

"I would see it."

Aaslo placed his hand on the hilt, then caught a motion on his periphery, and he was certain he was a breath away from becoming a pincushion. Instead of drawing the weapon as was his instinct, he untied the leather cord securing it to his belt. Then he held the sword in front of him across both hands in offering. No one moved to take it from him, and he was already at the end of the blue carpet. He glanced at each of the onlookers for some clue as to what he should do. His gaze passed over the queen, and he wasn't sure if he had seen it, but he thought her eyes had flicked to the floor. Slowly, he sank to his knees and reached as far as he could past the end of the carpet. He laid the sword, still in its sheath, on the stone floor and then resumed standing.

The king flicked his fingers, again, and one of the royal guardsmen beside the throne stepped forward to collect the sword. Rakith's visage darkened as he examined the weapon. He said, "I know this sword. That it is in *your* possession is concerning. Very well, Forester. I will dismiss my court. If you fail to provide just cause, though, you will become well acquainted with my dungeon master."

"Sounds fair."

"Whose side are you on?" Aaslo whispered as the courtiers shuffled out of the throne room. He could barely hear his own voice over the din.

"I am on *my* side. Always," said Rakith. "I have been lenient with you because of the high sorceress's *request*, but you test my tolerance. It is not appropriate to question your king, particularly with that kind of query."

"My apologies, Your Majesty. Would you believe me if I said I wasn't speaking to you?"

"Who were you speaking to then? The marquess? I assure you, he is also on my side."

"No, I mean, yes, Your Majesty—"

"Marquess Dovermyer!" called the king over Aaslo's head. "Do you think to escape?"

Aaslo turned to see the marquess following the crowd to the other end of the hall. The man turned at the king's call, appearing startled.

He hurried forward and bowed. "Your Majesty, I was heeding your command to clear the hall."

"Not you, Lord Sefferiah. You will stay."

"Your Majesty?"

Rakith pointed a finger at the marquess and said, "You are somehow connected to this."

The marquess held up both hands and said, "No, Your Majesty, I have no knowledge of the forester's message."

"You brought him here, did you not?"

"Well, yes, but only because I read the letter from the high sorceress."

"Then, you already know as much as I. My seneschal says you have built a rapport with the forester. You will remain."

The marquess looked at Aaslo with accusation.

"What?" Aaslo said. "I didn't invite you to my mission. You and your men forced your way in—at swordpoint, if I recall."

The large doors at the other end of the hall closed with a thud, and Aaslo turned his attention back to the king. The room was not completely clear, of course, but all that remained besides the king and queen were the seneschal, the guards, including the archers, the marquess, and Greylan. Aaslo was uncertain as to why the marquess's guard captain had been permitted to stay but figured it was some sort of court etiquette.

"Now speak, Forester. What message do you bear?"

Aaslo glanced at the queen, who looked on with interest. There was no easy way to break news of the world's impending doom. He untied the burlap sack from his belt as he said, "I come regarding the Aldrea Prophecy." Gripping Mathias's head by the hair, he held it up for all to see. "The chosen one is dead."

CHAPTER 10

MYROPA WATCHED IN WONDER AS THE FORESTER REVEALED THE evidence of their world's certain demise. He stood strong before his king, pushing, or outright defying, nearly every rule that he had been given upon arrival. He showed no fear nor willingness to acquiesce to the expectations of others, despite their standing or authority. Like all foresters, this one, Aaslo, was stubborn. She wondered if Aaslo's will was strong enough to withstand the gods. Myropa hated the way the gods made her feel small and incapable—like a child. She might have died a young woman, but she had been a reaper for over two decades. She had seen things she never could have imagined as a human. She hadn't been a strong woman, though. She had succumbed to despair, to the darkness that had promised refuge from her misery, but it was the darkness that had led her to this.

The king slowly stood. Myropa had been to this court several times, most recently to collect a young knight who had been stuck full of arrows. She knew the king never stood. Nobody cared now, though. They were all in shock—all but the forester. He held his ground, still gripping the head before him, as Rakith descended the steps and stopped in front of him. Rakith hesitantly brushed his finger across the mark on the dead man's temple. His nostrils flared, and he looked to the forester.

"You did this?"

Aaslo scowled. "Of course not. Well, I did collect the head, but he was already dead." Lowering the head back into the sack, he said, "Mathias was my friend, my brother. He and Magdelay . . . ah, the high sorceress . . . were attacked on the road their first night out of Golden-wood. I was hurrying to catch up with them when I found evidence they were being followed. I tried to warn them of the ambush, but I was too late. Mathias was injured in the first blast. While the high sorceress battled their magus, I fought off Mathias's attackers." The forester hung his head. "I failed to save him." After taking a deep breath, he raised his head and met the king's astonished gaze.

Rakith said, "*This* is the message the high sorceress sends?" His voice rose with frustration. "Why bother?"

Aaslo said, "Your Majesty?" Myropa was just as surprised as Aaslo.

"What was her point?" snapped the king.

"Um . . . because you are the king? You must find another savior—a knight or a soldier, one of the magi, or—*someone.*"

The king tried to turn, but the heavy cloak made it difficult. He furiously tugged at the pins holding it to his shoulders, and he wasn't satisfied until it lay in a puddle on the floor. He stomped up the steps to the top of the dais and sank into his throne. The queen reached over to place her hand on his. He looked at her with a sightless gaze more akin to the dead than the living. To Myropa, he looked utterly defeated, a feeling with which she was quite familiar.

"It is over," he said.

"No, husband," said Queen Kadia. "The death of one man does not mean defeat."

Rakith huffed and slammed his other fist on the arm of the throne. "Yes, it does! Such is the prophecy. Such is *every* prophecy! From *every* prophet! The best we can hope for now is to surrender and beg for mercy."

The queen's face fell, and she pulled back her hand.

"No," said Aaslo. "We can fight. I knew Mathias better than anyone. He would have wanted us to fight. He never would have surrendered. If anyone could have saved the world, it would have been he."

"And *he* is dead!" shouted Rakith.

"But we are not," replied the forester. "All of the enemy were killed, so the only people who know Mathias is dead are the high sorceress and the people in this room. Someone else—"

"No one can take his place," said Rakith. "No one else can succeed. Even those who might try would be better off spending their final days with their loved ones. Such will be my order."

"But, Your Majesty, we must fight. The battle has not even begun—"

"There will be no battle. We will wait and hope the enemy reserves a place for at least some of our people."

Aaslo did not hide his anger as he argued with the king. "The

prophecy says it will be the end of life—*all* life. There will be no reserve. What can it hurt to try?"

Rakith waved his hand. "If you want to try, Forester, then you may
do so of your own accord. I will not stop you, but I do not claim your
cause either."

Myropa was stunned by the turn of events, and it appeared that
Aaslo was, too. He stared at the king. He looked as if he would protest
again; then his jaw firmed and he raised his chin. "I *will* take up my
brother's cause. I may not be the chosen one, not even a mage or knight,
but I'll at least *try*, which is better than sitting around waiting to die.
I wish to reclaim my brother's sword so that it may meet the destiny
for which it was forged."

Rakith spat, "You ask a boon?"

"Give him the sword, Rakith," said the queen's soothing voice. "He
has carried it all this way. It is important to him, and you have no use
for it."

Myropa was unsure about whether she liked Queen Kadia. The
woman was sensible and compassionate, but she need not be so placating to her husband.

Rakith thrust the sheathed sword into his seneschal's hands. The
bumbling man nearly dropped it, and Myropa figured he had probably
never before held a sword. Aaslo was not shy about taking it from the
man, either. He tied it to his belt, along with the burlap sack.

Not even an ounce of respect could be found in his tone when he
said, "By your leave, Your Majesty?" Myropa couldn't blame him. King
Rakith had turned out to be a spineless coward. At least the forester
would go down fighting, and even that caused her sadness.

AASLO LEFT THE HALL WITH THE MARQUESS AND GREYLAN ON HIS
heels. He couldn't believe he had made it all the way to the royal
court in Tyellí and was walking away without aid. There would be no
savior, no hero knight, and no army. Some mysterious enemy would
swarm their borders, and the entire kingdom would lie down and
show its belly like a beaten dog.

"What will you do?"

He decided the biggest problem with the monarchy was that no one would stand up to the king when he was being an idiot.

"Sir Forester, what will you do?"

Aaslo could not understand what the man was thinking. It was his job, above anyone else's, to protect the kingdom.

"Sir Forester, wait!"

He wondered how anybody could be so—

"Someone's talking to you, Aaslo."

Aaslo shook his mind free of its brooding and noticed that the marquess was practically running to keep up with him. He slowed as he approached the exit, where he spied a young page delivering a message to the doorman.

Aaslo paused and turned toward the marquess. "What is it, Marquess Dovermyer? Pardon me, *Most Honorable the Marquess of Dovermyer.*"

The marquess blew out a breath and said, "I think we may dispense with that. Thank you for slowing. For a moment, I thought you'd not stop until you were back in your forest."

"Which is what you should do."

"Such is the dream," Aaslo muttered.

"Yes, well, what do you plan to do now?"

"I suppose I'll face an unknown enemy of unknown numbers with unknown power."

"How will you do that?"

"The high sorceress has gone to the Council of Magi. I will go there to see if anyone is willing to help."

"I see," said the marquess. "I have not been back to my estate since my father passed. I must return to set things in order. My brother is not the most dependable, and I am certain things have gone amuck." The marquess ceased his rambling when he realized Aaslo had stopped and was staring at him. "What?"

"Did you not hear what we were discussing in there?" He hooked a thumb toward the throne room. *"The end is nigh."*

The marquess cleared his throat. "Yes, well, I cannot exactly plan for that, can I. I figure it's better to keep things running smoothly until it is no longer possible. I must have faith that you—or someone—will do something to prevent that from happening. Otherwise, I think I'll go mad."

"Then you support my endeavor?"

"Wholeheartedly," said the marquess. "Unfortunately, I cannot go with you. I've always been more scholarly. It was no jest when I said your swordsmanship far exceeds my own. I can give you money, and you are welcome at my estate. When the time comes to recruit an army, my men will be at your disposal."

"That's assuming they haven't all abandoned their posts in fear."

"Desertion is not an option in the coming war," said Aaslo.

"No, I believe you are right in that. I will begin preparing them as soon as I return. They will understand what is at stake."

Aaslo patted the burlap sack tied at his waist. "You cannot tell them about this."

"Of course. No need to make things worse."

"I will find another way."

"I appreciate your determination. It makes it much easier for me to live in denial."

"I'm just being practical. It's not hard when the alternative is death."

The marquess leaned in and whispered, "You should probably keep those sentiments to yourself while you are here." Then, more casually, he said, "I shall bid you adieu, Sir Forester. I must return to my estate to begin preparations. If you accept my patronage in this endeavor, I will have my secretary arrange delivery of a few supplies to your guild house."

Aaslo scratched his chin and glanced around the receiving hall as he considered the possible outcomes of accepting the marquess's patronage. As a forester, he was relatively free to do as he pleased. Accepting patronage meant owing a debt. Magdelay and Cromley had taught Mathias and him not to trust people who offered much for seemingly little gain. The marquess seemed sincere, but nobles were practiced in manipulation and deception. Considering the circumstances, though, the prospect of continued life was a rather attractive boon—and there was still the matter of the blight. He noticed that Greylan seemed displeased with the proposed arrangement, and Aaslo's mind was made up.

"Very well, Marquess. I accept, on the condition that you recognize I am my own master. I will do what I believe necessary."

The marquess looked at Aaslo uncertainly—and expectantly.

"The blight, Aaslo. He wants you to fix his swamps."

Aaslo sighed and added, "And, I will do what I can to cure your blight as soon as it is manageable."

The marquess smiled. "Then we have a deal." He turned to Greylan, who seemed to be snarling at Aaslo with his eyes. "Come. We have much to do and little time, it seems."

Aaslo made to follow but was stopped by the doorman at the palace entrance.

"Sir Forester, I have received word that you are to remain in the palace."

"Uh-oh, Aaslo. The king changed his mind about throwing you in the dungeon."

"Am I being arrested?"

The doorman raised his brow and shook his head. "No, sir. You are a royal guest." Glancing up, the doorman waved toward a middle-aged, mousy woman in palace livery as she entered the hall from a servants' passage. A massive ring of keys jangled at her waist as she scurried toward them on slippered feet.

The doorman said to the woman, "This is Forester Aaslo. He is to be a guest at the feast tonight and will be quartered in the royal wing— the *Sapphire Room*."

The woman's eyes widened, and she surveyed Aaslo with a glance. "I will see to it immediately."

"I didn't like her reaction, Aaslo. Something's up."

"Probably just because I'm a forester."

The woman blinked at him. "Oh no, I don't believe that's true. Many illustrious visitors come to the palace. Not even princes and magi go to the Sapphire Room."

"Sounds nefarious."

"Why is that?" Aaslo said.

Glancing at the guard, the woman pursed her lips and said, "I couldn't say." She abruptly bowed, her manner suddenly formal, and said, "I am Helania, the keeper of the keys. It would be my pleasure to escort you to your quarters—if you would follow me?" Without waiting for an answer, she turned on her heel and began walking toward the corridor.

"Wait," Aaslo said as he caught up with the small woman in only two strides. "I must return to my guild house. What about my belongings?"

The woman glanced at his apparel out of the corner of her eye. "You will be provided with everything you require while you are a guest at the palace. Brontus will be your manservant. He and the master of the wardrobe will attend you shortly for a fitting."

"Fitting?"

"For your dinner clothes. With all due respect, Sir Forester, you cannot sit at the king's table in *those*."

Aaslo's head was spinning. He had no desire to remain at the palace any longer than necessary, and he certainly didn't want to dine with the king. He wondered—if he was suddenly being treated as a royal guest, perhaps the king had changed his mind about the prophecy.

"He probably decided he doesn't want you meddling in the kingdom's affairs. He must want something else. Look, you're heading for the tower dungeon."

Aaslo's momentary flutter of optimism was dashed as Helania turned toward a set of winding steps. He cleared his throat and said, "Are you sure *Sapphire Room* isn't another word for *dungeon*?"

Helania's foot slipped on the next step, and she fell back into his arms. As she straightened, she said, "Thank you, Sir Forester, and no. Why would you say such a thing?"

Aaslo grumbled, "I figure I'm more likely to be placed in shackles than offered a seat at the king's table."

She glanced back, looking as if she was suddenly concerned about being stuck in an empty stairwell with him. "Why? Have you done something to displease His Majesty?"

"I was only the messenger."

Her smile was one of relief. "Oh, I cannot imagine King Rakith holding that against you. He's a very reasonable man."

"And he will reasonably *lock you in a tower, so you don't go running around the kingdom spreading word of impending doom."*

"Who would believe me?"

"Apparently *someone* believes you," said the woman. "You are, after all, a royal guest."

"That's what concerns me." Passing another exit, he said, "This doesn't look like the route the king or queen would take to their quarters."

Helania laughed. "No, you wouldn't want to go that way. There are so many checkpoints with guards and even a few magi. Every one of them would want to confirm that you are who you say you are and that you're actually a royal guest. Not that they wouldn't believe *me*. They just like to feel important. It would take forever." She jangled the keys in front of his eyes and said, "That's why I have these. I can access any door in the palace, even the secret ones." She winked at him with a sly grin. "Don't go getting any ideas, though. I'm a witch of the First Order."

"I've never met a witch."

"No, I would be surprised if you had. We are almost as rare as sorceresses."

"What's the difference?"

"Do you never listen?"

"I must not have been there for that lesson," Aaslo mumbled.

"I suppose it isn't something that's generally taught," said Helania. "Few outside the bloodlines understand. A sorceress or sorcerer shapes raw power with the mind. Their spells are most powerful but usually lack finesse. A witch or warlock uses incantations or rituals. It takes more preparation to develop spells of equivalent power, but we are more efficient and accurate than all but the most powerful sorceresses. Unfortunately, it is also easier to bind our power, which is why we are permitted to serve in the palace."

"Then you are a member of one of the twelve bloodlines?"

"Of course. I am a Vivant."

Aaslo remembered the conversation he had overheard between Magdelay and Mathias as he had tracked the enemy outside Goldenwood. He said, "I heard that each bloodline believes magic should be used for a specific goal. If you don't mind me asking, what do the Vivants believe?"

The woman unlocked an unimpressive door on the fifth landing and led him into an elaborately decorated, albeit empty, corridor that curved. "You were told correctly," she said as she shuffled past the first set of intricately carved doors. "The Vivants believe magic should be used to honor and worship the gods."

"Do you worship a specific deity?"

She smiled as she stopped in front of a door painted blue and gilded around the edges. "I prefer to remain impartial. They are all worthy of our devotion."

"Even *Death*?"

Helania said, "Oh yes! Death is an inevitability. Of all the gods, he is the most important after we leave this world. It is within his kingdom that we will find paradise or terror. I think it is best to please him."

MYROPA WANTED TO LAUGH. SHE MIGHT HAVE IF HER FACE HAD NOT been numb from the cold. There was no pleasing Axus, and he cared nothing for the well-being of the humans before *or* after death. She knew firsthand the disdain he felt for humans. They were only a means to an end. Axus might be the God of Death, but he was not the Keeper of Paradise the witch believed him to be. Myropa had overheard the gods venting often enough to understand Axus's power. He gained it through the *process* of death, the passage of souls through the veil. If he had access to the shining souls themselves, Axus's power would quickly outshine that of the other gods. Only the tarnished souls destined for punishment ended in his care, but they did not provide him with much power.

Myropa, like the other reapers, was assigned to collect souls on Axus's behalf, then deliver them to the Sea of Transcendence. She wasn't sure what happened to them once in the Sea. She wondered if even the gods knew. The reapers were a safety measure emplaced by the other gods. Axus was not permitted access to the Sea lest he claim the souls and gain unfettered power. Only reapers could reach its shores.

Myropa kept following the forester, despite the pain of shame and guilt he inspired. In his presence, she felt a mixture of sorrow and joy. Given her present state of existence, the former could never be assuaged, nor could the latter be celebrated.

After following Aaslo through the doorway, she surveyed her surroundings. She had never before seen this room—had never needed to collect anyone from this place. Aaslo seemed to think he was in trouble, but nothing here spoke of punishment. If anything, the voluminous fabrics and pillows, in earthy tones, piled together and mixed with the sweet scent of musk and incense had a soporific effect. A pool of steaming sapphire water sprinkled with lavender and rose petals occupied the center of the chamber, and a spelled lute displayed on a golden stand in one corner played an enchanting melody.

Aaslo's expression turned to one of confusion; then he turned to look right through Myropa to the keeper of the keys.

"What is this?" he said.

The woman motioned toward the pool and said, "This is the Sapphire Room. Food will arrive from the kitchen shortly. You are expected to take advantage of the warm bath before dinner. Brontus will be here soon. He will assist you with anything else you might need."

Rising in fragrant curls, the steam was enticing. Myropa wished she could feel the hot bath melting the ice from her core. She felt a familiar sizzle in her chest and looked down just as a luminous tether snapped into existence. She wanted to remain with the forester, but she had a soul to collect, and it was not far. Turning from the room, she shuffled down the corridor past the queen's chambers and on to the king's. She took a second to admire the guards, both handsome men who were exceptionally appealing in their uniforms. With a thought, she stood on the other side of the door in the receiving chamber. She passed tables, sofas, tapestries, and flower-filled vases, all of which she was certain were delightfully colorful, but they appeared drab to her. Then she was in the king's bedchamber.

"Come, Your Majesty, I will cheer you up," said a young woman with strawberry curls, whom Myropa guessed to be his latest consort. The woman was half naked and kneeling on the bed behind Rakith where he sat still dressed in his court attire. He was at the foot of the bed, bent forward with his head in his hands.

"No, Alarie, there is no cheer to be found this day."

"It surely cannot be that bad," said the young woman. "We make our own joy, do we not?"

Alarie slid from the bed and turned to face the king. That was when Myropa saw it. A charcoal-grey creature no larger than a hunting dog had been hiding behind the woman. Veins bulged along the leathery skin that was stretched tight across its bony body, and its wispy hair flicked around its oblong head as if untouched by gravity. Bulging, mottled grey-and-black eyes without pupils blinked at Myropa. The vight hissed, bearing sharp little fangs within an overlarge mouth. It lunged with glistening talons toward Alarie's abdomen.

Myropa slapped her hands together and opened them to emit a burst of light. Her voice rang with power not her own as she intoned, "By the power of the Fates, vight, I cast you to the Alterworld."

The vight screeched and tore across the room, trying to reach the sliver that remained of its portal hidden behind a drapery.

"Stay out of this, Reaper," it hissed. "Axus will hear of your interference."

"Axus goes too far. This one has not been marked by the Fates, yet they warn me nonetheless." She plucked the tether, which had changed from the usual blue hue to pale orange in the vight's presence. "Neither you nor Axus have the right to meddle in the tapestry. The Fates decide which souls Axus may claim, not you."

"It will die anyway. They all will."

"Yes, but not by your hand."

She cupped her palms and felt the power build within them. When she opened them, a ball of light streaked toward the little demon. The light wrapped itself around it like a spider's web, and it was sucked through the veil along with the iridescent tether that had drawn her to the room. Myropa looked to the king and his consort, who were unaware of the ethereal battle that had threatened them.

Rakith rested his hand on Alarie's belly and said, "I am distraught that she will not have a chance at life."

Alarie's brow furrowed. Her smile appeared forced as she stroked his cheek. "How do you know it's a she?"

The king rubbed the baby bump adoringly and said, "I have five sons already. I think I am due a daughter."

Taking Rakith's hands, Alarie moved to sit on his lap. "You will give her the same life and joy you have given your sons. Why do you worry so?"

Rakith kissed her forehead and said, "Do not worry over it. Stress is not good for the baby."

She smiled and climbed back onto the bed. "Come. A nap will do us both good."

Myropa glanced toward the drapery to see that the vight's portal had completely sealed. She mentally groaned. This meant another report to Trostili.

CHAPTER 11

AASLO HAD JUST DISCARDED HIS CLOTHES WHEN THE CHAMBER DOOR opened to admit a willowy man with long, silvery black hair intricately braided down his back. The man's black suit was immaculate, perfectly fitted to his form and free of wrinkles and dust. He wore white gloves and carried a silver-tipped cane from which hung a small pouch overflowing with baubles. Aaslo grabbed a pillow from the bed, covering himself. The newcomer stepped aside to reveal another well-kempt middle-aged man. This one had grey hair and wore a haggard expression as he lugged a large basket to a side table. He was followed by two women and a boy carrying trays laden with food, wine, dishes, and table linens. The latter three went about setting a small table near the enchanted lute, while the two men approached him, unconcerned with his nudity.

The grey-haired man said, "I am Brontus, your manservant for the remainder of your stay at the palace. This is Master of the Wardrobe Akirini."

Akirini placed his hands on his cane in front of him and said in a droll voice, "There is no need for modesty. Your present state of undress is well suited for acquiring your measurements." Aaslo looked at the women and boy, and Akirini followed his gaze. The man said, "It is nothing we haven't seen before."

Aaslo scowled as he looked back at the man. "You haven't seen this one, and I'd just as soon keep it that way."

"The steward will be pleased to hear it," Akirini said, his expression unchanged. "Shall we continue?"

"Did he just make a joke?"

Aaslo glanced to where he had left the burlap sack on the floor a few feet from him. He doubted anyone who had not been in the throne room knew what was in the bag. He decided that, at that point, it was probably best not to call attention to it.

"You're not going to introduce me?"

"I'd rather not," he muttered.

Akirini said, "I am a professional, sir. I could estimate your size, but your dinner attire will fit better if I take your measurements."

The two women glanced back at him. One whispered to the other, who giggled behind her hand. Then both women and the boy collected their empty trays and left the chamber.

Aaslo looked back to the two men. "Fine. I don't want anything frilly, though. None of that ridiculous lace, and I'm not wearing hose."

"Of course not, Sir Forester," said Akirini. "You seem much too practical for that."

"His delivery could use some work, but he's quite funny."

While Akirini took Aaslo's measurements, Brontus arranged a number of bottles and hand towels on a tray beside the pool. When he bent to collect Aaslo's worn clothes from the floor, Aaslo snapped, "Don't touch the bag. It stays with me at all times." The manservant glanced at Aaslo, then wrinkled his nose as he withdrew his hand.

Akirini said, "That will not do. To carry such a filthy thing to dinner would be offensive—especially to anyone with a nose."

"I'm hurt, Akirini. I thought we shared a bond."

Aaslo said, "It stays with me."

The man's lips thinned in disapproval, but he said nothing more.

An hour later, Aaslo was fed, bathed, and dressed in a thick robe. He smelled like lavender and roses and—he sniffed his arm—sage? He sat on a padded stool mentally grumbling to himself as Brontus combed and trimmed his hair. His hackles rose when the manservant moved toward his throat with a straight razor, but he begrudgingly allowed the stranger to shave his face.

"There, that's better. Do you agree, sir?" said Brontus.

Aaslo stroked his smooth cheek. "Seems like a lot of trouble just to eat dinner."

Brontus chuckled. "A feast at the palace is much more than a meal, especially for one such as you. The feast is an opportunity to meet with your betters and to demonstrate to them whatever it is you have to offer. With luck, you may secure patronage."

"I already have a patron," Aaslo said.

"Well, then you are one of the lucky ones. Still, it doesn't hurt to gain support. The more the better, I say. Besides, as far as I know, no forester has ever visited Tyellí, much less the palace."

Aaslo crossed his arms as he presented Brontus with a dubious look. "I am being put on display like one of those exotic animals in the traveling fair, aren't I? I'm not so much a guest as the entertainment."

Brontus looked abashed, but he smiled and said, "It is not my place to question the motives of the monarchy."

He looked as confused as Aaslo when suddenly there was a heavy rap at the door. Brontus shuffled forward and opened it with practiced grace. One of the royal guardsmen stood on the other side. The guard glanced at Aaslo, then whispered something to the manservant. Brontus's eyes widened and he, too, glanced at Aaslo. Then he bobbed his head and closed the door as the guard turned away.

"Uh-oh, you're in trouble now."

Aaslo scowled down at the burlap sack, then looked back to Brontus. "What is it?"

Brontus spread his hands and said, "It seems you have been invited to observe the goings-on in the practice yard."

"What goings-on?"

"The practice, of course."

Aaslo huffed, "Whose practice of what?"

"Oh, pardon me, sir—the practice of the royal guard."

"Why would I do that?" said Aaslo.

Brontus's smile faded. Glancing at the sword Aaslo had tossed on the bed, he said, "Well, you are a swordsman, are you not? Would you not care to observe the kingdom's finest?"

"Not really."

"Oh," Brontus said with surprise, followed by an uncomfortable pause. He ventured, "If I may, sir, it would be considered rude to refuse the offer. It might not be a good idea to offend the royal guard."

"You should refuse. The consequences will be highly entertaining. Besides, I'd love to see the looks on their faces when he tells them you said no."

"You won't see anything," Aaslo replied.

"I am afraid I must," Brontus said with a shaky grin. "I am to attend to you at all times during your stay."

"You're keeping an eye on me—spying."

Brontus grinned again, as if he had just told a joke. Aaslo sighed. "I cannot go to the practice yard dressed in a robe. You took my clothes."

The manservant jumped into action, riffling through the large basket he had lugged into the room. "Of course not, Sir Forester. I have some things for you here—simple things. I thought you would be most comfortable in them until you are required to dress for dinner."

Aaslo looked at him sideways. "I appreciate that."

Brontus smiled up at him from where he knelt beside the basket. "I am not unaware of your circumstances, Sir Forester. I doubt you are accustomed to seeing many people out there in the forest, and now you are thrust into the Palace of Uyan itself. I cannot imagine your discomfort. Even our customs—those of your own kingdom—would seem foreign. That is why I was assigned to you. I usually serve visitors from afar, helping them and their retainers to understand our customs. Do not worry yourself too much, though. You will be granted much leniency for your ignorance."

"The fact that you're still breathing is evidence of that."

Aaslo donned a white linen shirt that laced up the front and a comfortable pair of brown wool trousers. He opened his mouth to refuse the embroidered, hunter-green velvet vest that Brontus held before him.

"He's here to help you stay out of trouble. Wear the vest."

By the stubborn set of the man's jaw, Aaslo knew Mathias was right. He sighed and slipped it over his arms. Brontus hooked the loops over the brass buttons and straightened Aaslo's shirt accordingly.

"I can dress myself," Aaslo said.

Brontus presented him with a pair of slightly worn boots. "Yes, I am sure you can, but then I would be out of a job."

"Let the man feed his family, Aaslo."

Aaslo grabbed the burlap sack and then turned toward the door. Brontus blocked his passage as he held up Mathias's sword.

"I am only going to watch," said Aaslo. "I don't need it."

"Best not to walk about the palace unarmed, sir."

Aaslo frowned at the man. "Am I in danger here?"

Brontus smiled, but it lacked sincerity. "It is custom."

With his sword and the severed head strapped to his belt, Aaslo followed Brontus through several corridors. The keeper of the keys had not been lying when she said there were too many checkpoints. Since they were *leaving* the royal wing, though, they got no more attention than curious glances and whispers.

The royal practice yard was located in the central bailey, and it was surrounded by platforms bearing benches for spectators. The benches were empty at that time, save for the guardsmen who occupied the first two rows, watching their comrades, making comments, and occasionally jeering. They turned as he entered, muttering to each other and drawing the attention of the others. Before he knew it, all practice had stopped, and everyone was staring at him.

"You've done it now, Aaslo. Perhaps they want to see you dance before they arrest you."

One of the men who had been sparring in the practice ring strode toward him. He wore pants, but his chest was bare and slick with sweat. He grabbed a drying cloth from one of the empty benches and wiped his clean-shaven face as he approached. He gazed at Aaslo with dark brown eyes, then held his hand out in greeting.

"I am Lopin, Captain of the Royal Guard."

Aaslo hesitantly shook the man's hand. "Aaslo, Forester of Golden-wood."

The man's smile exposed a full set of perfect, white teeth. "It's true then? You are really a forester?"

"A dancing monkey, more like."

"Yes, is that significant?"

"Everyone seems to think so," said Lopin. "I'm more interested in your skill with a sword, though."

"I'm not a soldier," said Aaslo.

"Perhaps not, but I hear you know Cromley, and the Marquess of Dovermyer seems to think you're quite the swordsman."

Aaslo glanced at the curious faces of the kingdom's best guardsmen. He said, "My friend trained with Cromley. I just helped with the practices. I prefer an axe and a spade."

"Can't see how a spade would be useful in a battle," said Lopin.

"Precisely," said Aaslo. "I help things grow. I don't go about fighting people. I don't even like people."

"Seems like a decent enough reason to fight them," said Lopin, to the enjoyment of his peers. "Perhaps you'd care to join us for a training session."

"I'd rather not," said Aaslo.

"Careful. These are the men who are going to be arresting you later. No need to make it worse."

Lopin's perpetual smile soured, and Aaslo glanced at Brontus, who shook his head in disapproval. Aaslo figured no swordsman in his right mind would refuse the honor. Then again, he was already in doubt over whether or not he *was* in his right mind. He surveyed the men, who were looking at him expectantly. "What is the point of this?"

"Who said there needed to be a point?" said Lopin. "A swordsman must hone his skills, keep them sharp."

"I never wanted to be a swordsman. I only learned to help my friend."

Lopin lifted his chin toward the sack tied to Aaslo's belt. "Is that the friend?" No one seemed surprised by the question, except Brontus, who eyed the sack warily. Lopin must have noticed Aaslo's concern. He said, "Yes, we all know. What I don't understand is why you continue to carry it."

Aaslo first thought to tell them that it was none of their business, but leaving the forest and losing Mathias had already cost too much. He would not turn his back on the ways of his people. So, he considered the question and the potential consequences of every conceivable answer before replying. "I will carry his burden so long as it is necessary."

Lopin nodded solemnly, then glanced at the others. He nodded once, and then the lot of them rushed him, knocking Brontus out of the way. Aaslo struggled against their grips as they hoisted him into the air with a multitude of hands securing his arms and legs. They dumped him in the dirt at the center of the practice yard. He kicked and shoved at them as they divested him of his vest and shirt. He was abruptly released when the men backed away, and he quickly scrambled to his feet.

Before he had even steadied himself, Lopin took a swipe at his head with a blade. Aaslo stumbled backward, falling to his rear, and rolling out of the way as Lopin's sword struck the ground where he had been lying. Aaslo glanced down as he reached for his hilt and realized the burlap sack was missing. He drew his sword just in time to deflect an overhead strike, then parried and dodged a few more aggressive swings. "Why are you doing this?" he asked as he backpedaled.

Lopin grinned, and it was decidedly less pleasant than when they had first met. He said, "You disrespected the king, and in front of the court, no less. You have already begun to develop a reputation as a swordsman, yet we have seen nothing to prove you are deserving of it. I would see if you are capable of more than slinging good names around."

"I don't want a reputation," Aaslo said as he continued backing away. "I don't want to fight you. I don't want to stay in the palace. I just want to be gone from here." He turned to run, but stopped short when he realized three more royal guards, swords bared, were blocking his way. He spun back around just in time to dodge another attempt to take his head.

"You did not strike me as a coward," said Lopin. "Fight back, or don't you want to see your *friend* again?" The guard standing behind Lopin jiggled the burlap sack in the air.

As Aaslo stared at the bag, the scent of pines and fresh fallen leaves inundated his senses. Mathias was silent, and the forest called to him. A million scenarios shuffled through his consciousness, more than one containing Reyla and a decent life—for a time. He blinked to clear the visions, then looked back to Lopin. "What are the terms?"

"First blood gets the bag."

Aaslo glanced to the sack again and then clenched his jaw with resolve. He nodded toward Lopin, who appeared genuinely pleased. They circled each other several times, and Lopin feinted, then feinted again. Just when the guard seemed to lose confidence that Aaslo would fight, Aaslo advanced. He slashed and jabbed as Lopin retreated. The tables abruptly turned when Lopin sidestepped as Aaslo thrust. He smashed Mathias's blade toward the ground, then backhanded Aaslo in the face as Aaslo withdrew his blade. Lopin grinned as Aaslo reached up to wipe blood from his lip. Aaslo nodded with a pointed stare, and Lopin inspected himself to find a small cut across his abdomen. The man looked at him in surprise, then set his stance again as he said, "A tie. Looks like it'll be second blood, then."

With a mental groan, Aaslo raised Mathias's sword. Lopin was good—very good, but then he'd have to be to have earned his position. Aaslo was already fighting to the best of his abilities. He knew Mathias could have taken the man down with a smile on his face, but he was not sure he could land another strike before Lopin. He needed the sack, though. He couldn't let them have Mathias.

Lopin did not hold back. He came at Aaslo in a flurry, and it was all Aaslo could do to defend himself. Cromley had taught them that in a situation like this, he should wait—wait until the other man wore himself out but Lopin did not seem to be slowing. If anything, he was getting faster. Aaslo ducked another swipe at his head and knew Lopin wouldn't have mourned his passing if it had landed. He began to wonder if the king had put the royal guards up to this. Was this their way of getting rid of him? It seemed a bit extravagant, but perhaps they needed the entertainment.

Aaslo swiped at the captain's legs, and Lopin jumped, bringing his sword down with a mighty force as he landed. Aaslo rolled out of the way, then slashed at the man's exposed side. Lopin twisted, avoiding the attack. He was as agile as Mathias, and Aaslo remembered that Mathias had still beat him two out of three matches. He had often wondered if Mathias had let him win those but had dismissed the notion due to his friend's competitive streak.

Lopin knocked Aaslo away when he stepped into the man's guard. As Aaslo fell, he caught a motion in the tower window. He had not expected the audience, and it was a momentary distraction that cost him. He pulled his head to the side just as Lopin's blade struck the dirt. He grabbed the man's arm and used his feet to hook Lopin's legs, dragging him to the ground as well. Aaslo rolled atop the captain of the royal guard and punched him squarely in the face. Rough hands grabbed Aaslo from behind, and then he was struck hard in the head.

He blinked up at the cloudless blue sky. His vision swam, and his stomach churned as it began to clear. Lopin crouched over him, his crooked nose dripping blood. He flicked Aaslo's ear, which burned like fire.

Lopin said, "I got you first," then spat a glob of bloody phlegm to the side. "It was a good fight, though. Most of my men could not have lasted as long. You'll have to settle for second best."

Aaslo shook his head and mumbled, "I'll never settle for second." He wasn't even sure why he had said it.

Lopin glanced up to the tower. He said, "Perhaps you wouldn't have, if not for the distraction. I can't say as I blame you." As the captain stood, he dropped the burlap sack onto Aaslo's abdomen, forcing the air from his lungs.

Aaslo pulled himself to a seated position. His head spun as he squinted at the retreating figures. There were twice as many as he remembered. Then two Brontuses filled his view. He blinked and stared at the men until the two manservants became one. Brontus helped him to his feet, and Aaslo leaned heavily on the man until he could focus. Then the manservant helped him dress.

"Did you know they were going to do that?" Aaslo said.

"He probably thought they'd do you in."

"No, sir, not as much. The royal guard doesn't tell their business to the likes of me. It was impressive, though. I think they approve."

"Approve? They tried to kill me."

"I'm no soldier, but I'd say they were testing you. You got your bag back, didn't you?"

Aaslo licked his split lip. "I guess so. How much of my ear did he get? I'm afraid to check."

"It's nothing, Sir Forester. Just a clip, barely noticeable behind your hair. I'm afraid you'll need another bath, though." Aaslo sighed. Two baths in one night. How had his life come to this? "You got distracted for a moment," said Brontus. "What was it?"

"I'm not sure," said Aaslo. "I saw someone in the tower watching."

"Many people were watching. I don't see how that made a difference."

"It was the queen."

MYROPA WAS PLEASED. SHE HAD BEEN CONCERNED WHEN THE GUARDS had tossed the forester onto the practice field. She could feel something pulling her there, so she knew someone was about to die. She had thought for certain it would be he, but then he walked away with a few minor cuts. The feeling was still strong, though, and it seemed to follow him, so she did as well.

Aaslo, and then Myropa, rounded the bailey wall, and she shrieked. The vight jumped in startlement. It hissed at her as it quickly thrust its talons toward a man just as Aaslo was passing him. It was the captain of the royal guard, and he was alone at the moment. Myropa slapped her hands together and whipped them apart, releasing a streak of light. Her attack had been sloppy in her haste, but it succeeded in knocking the creature back a few paces before his strike could land. She advanced on the vight, shouting as she prepared another attack. "By the power of the Fates, I cast you into the Alterworld!"

The vight dodged a ball of light and lunged, swiping at her. Its claws passed through her insubstantial form. It could not touch her here, for she was not truly in this world. She formed a glowing ball in her palms and then smashed it into his face. The tendrils of light wrapped around him; then he was sucked into another realm. Myropa would have been breathing heavily if she had needed breath. She hurried after the forester. She could guess at what would have happened if the vight had succeeded. Everyone would have thought Aaslo had killed the captain, and he would hang after an arduous torture. Had the forester garnered Axus's attention, or had it been coincidence? How many vights had Axus planted in this world? It was not an easy task, and it took a great amount of power to fully transport beings across the realms, especially those who did not belong.

She needed to report to Trostili. Glancing once more at the forester, she exhaled, releasing the breath of life that had been lent to her, and crossed over the veil. When she arrived in Celestria, she was not in the fifth palace. Her slippers brushed the manicured lawn as she followed the natural pull toward the god she served. She knew exactly where Trostili was, even though she had never been to this place. He was always there, wrapped around her soul until he finally released her.

Myropa took a well-worn path that meandered in the shade of the tallest trees she had ever seen. Their trunks were rough with rusty bark that peeled away in furry tufts, and their dark green boughs were so high, a skilled climber might take a half day to reach them. *Aaslo would love this forest,* she thought to herself. She missed a step, nearly tripping into a fern. As she recovered, she tried not to think about the forester or the reason for the errant thought. Her frozen nerves were a jitter as she realized that one part of her wanted to return to Aaslo immediately, while another wanted to never think of him again.

The path ended at a shore dotted with grey cobbles surrounding a pond that appeared black in the shade. On the other side of the pond were steps carved from white rock that led into the water. At the top of the steps was a small wooden temple that looked to be as old as the trees between which it was nestled. Myropa skirted the pond to where it narrowed before spilling into a creek. It was dammed behind a structure that looked to have been made by an animal rather than a person. Across the top were larger stepping-stones that barely peeked above the waterline.

As she stepped over the stones, set a bit too far apart for her comfort, she watched her feet carefully. When she was halfway across, she spied something out of the corner of her eye. She turned to look and nearly fell into the water. The face of a very large male was staring up at her from beneath the surface. He grinned, as if laughing at her, then slipped away in a giant watery streak. Myropa did not see the figure again as she approached the temple and ascended the stairs. Just as her foot touched the top step, a voice rumbled in her ear.

"What brings you to my temple?"

Myropa jumped and spun to face the god. Her heel struck the step, and she dropped onto her rear. Although he was standing several steps below her, she still had to crane her neck up to see his face. He stood there, towering over her. His taut muscles were slick with water, and a glorious grin graced a ruggedly handsome face as he reached for her. He pulled her from the ground and settled her on her feet as if she weighed no more than a feather. He said, "You're a pretty little reaper. Does your god give you the attention you deserve?"

His smile was inviting, and his tone suggestive. She was momentarily glad her body no longer held enough warmth to cause her cheeks to flush when she spied the evidence of his interest. She realized, though, that she felt none of his godly influence, and the glow of his power did not extend beyond the surface of his flesh. The fact that he was capable of keeping it so well in check meant that he was one *very* old god.

He tipped her head up with a finger, and she realized she hadn't answered—and she'd been *staring*. "Does my body offend you?"

"Um, n-no, it's just that h-humans usually wear clothing when meeting new people."

"An unfortunate tradition," he said with a smile. He stepped away and drew a small red drying cloth from atop a bench that was nestled beneath a cluster of colorful hanging plants. He wrapped the cloth about his waist and returned to her. The cloth didn't cover much more than the *important* bits, and part of her wished she hadn't said anything.

Myropa smiled at him and hooked a curl behind her ear. "I'm Myropa. I seek Trostili."

With a nod, he said, "I am Disevy, God of Virility." He took her hand and pressed the softest kiss to her knuckles. The spot continued to glow with a golden light after his lips departed.

She breathlessly whispered, "I didn't know there was a god for that."

"Of course. I am the god of strength and power. I endow men with their masculinity"—he brushed a lock of hair away from her face—"and compassion."

"Are those not conflicting sentiments?" she said.

"Of course not." He straightened proudly. "The strongest of men are capable of bearing the weight of others." He then leaned in and said more softly, "I also instill within them an instinct for the proper treatment of a deserving woman."

Myropa licked her lips anxiously, and his wanting gaze followed the path of her tongue. She said, "Who decides if they are deserving?"

A light flashed in his eyes. "They are *all* deserving."

She frowned. "I think you might be failing on that point, then." As soon as she said it, she wished she could take it back. She had never spoken to a god in such a disrespectful way. She blamed his unmatched control over his power. He did not smash her into the floor, though. Instead, he laughed. It was a hearty laugh that echoed throughout the temple.

"I try my best, but others interfere." He lifted his chin and nodded toward something behind her. "One of the guilty parties approaches now."

Myropa felt him before she saw him. His power suffused her being, and she struggled to remain standing as her soul begged her to wither and cower. She knew Trostili was capable of restraining his power almost as well as Disevy. He did this to torment her. She turned to watch his approach. He wore one of the many splendid sets of armor that he donned every time he left his quarters. This one had a silver breastplate and cingulum over a black tunic embroidered in gold. A golden scorpion graced the center of the breastplate, and a gold laurel wreath nestled in his dark hair. Myropa's knees began to shake, and by the time he reached her, she was a trembling ball on the floor.

"Pull it back, Trostili." Disevy's tone was far more commanding than any she had previously heard directed at the God of War. Myropa was surprised when the power began to ease. After a few minutes, she was able to stand again. Thoroughly embarrassed, Myropa avoided Disevy's gaze as she conducted a vigilant survey of the floor. Disevy brushed a finger over her cheek, and a tendril of his power suffused her flesh with a warmth that soothed her shaking nerves.

Trostili scoffed with disgust. He said, "Do not forget, Disevy, she is a reaper."

"Yes," Disevy drawled. "I have always felt that reapers are deserving of our care, our loving grace. I cannot help but feel that we failed them."

"You are in the minority, then. They spurn our gifts and for that they pay."

Disevy met Trostili's disgruntled gaze. He said, "What have you ever gifted them, Trostili? You fill them with the need to destroy each other. If anyone is to blame for their plight, you are certainly one of them."

"On the contrary," said Trostili. "With my influence, they fight to live. They fight so that others will live. These"—he waved at Myropa—"pitiful creatures chose to give up."

"You might be convincing if you only ever inspired them to protect themselves. You antagonize the aggressors as well, and they fight to destroy whatever their victims hold dear. Can you blame them for not having the strength to endure the loss?"

"Yes," said Trostili. "They have only one responsibility in that world, and it is to exist."

"It is our task to design the world and creatures that can thrive within it. If it is so terrible that they cannot do so, it is our fault, not theirs."

Trostili motioned to Myropa again, and she felt as if she were shrinking inside herself. "This one was perfectly capable of living in the world we provided. She was healthy, attractive, and had all that she needed and more. She was selfish, though. She thought she was *entitled* to more. In pursuit of it, she hurt those she should have cared for and destroyed her own life. *Her* choices. Not ours." He thrust a hand toward Disevy, holding in his palm a small, glowing orb. "Take it. Witness her self-destruction."

Myropa squeezed her eyes shut. She would have cried with mortification if she had been capable of it, but she had to settle for covering her face with her hands.

"No," said Disevy. "She wears the evidence of her shame openly. Still, if her sorrow and pain was so great, was it not selfish of us to require her continued existence?"

"That was between her and the Fates," said Trostili. "Now, I want to know why she's here."

Myropa pulled her hands from her face and quickly described the attacks by both vights, then described them again when both gods demanded more detail.

"Axus is determined," said Disevy, "I'll give him that. Why the willingness to expend his power on pulling vights from their realm in the Alterworld? Is someone protesting his claim of the world?"

"Only the humans," said Trostili.

Disevy seemed genuinely surprised. "Not even Arayallen?"

Myropa witnessed the hint of a smile on Trostili's lips at the mention of Arayallen. He said, "She has been preoccupied." Disevy shook his head at Trostili and then winked at Myropa, but she didn't understand the hidden message. "Vights," mused Trostili. "It is a strange choice. Such undependable creatures. They rarely hit the intended target. Perhaps he seeks only to seed a bit of chaos before the storm."

"I doubt he would spend power so frivolously," said Disevy. His gaze slid to her. "How is the Sea?"

She blinked at him. "The Sea?"

Trostili huffed with impatience. "The Sea of Transcendence, Myropa."

Myropa was momentarily thrown by the use of her name. He rarely used it. "Um, it is calm. It looks the same as usual."

Disevy nodded thoughtfully. He looked to Trostili. "If Axus spends power so freely, he may have found a way to pull it from the Sea." Turning toward Myropa, he said, "Please, let me know if it changes—in *any* way—if the tiniest pebble looks out of place."

Myropa's eyes widened, and she nodded anxiously. "Of course, I will—immediately."

"The Fates assigned her to *me*," said Trostili.

Disevy's approving gaze caressed her again. "Pity, that."

In her heart, Myropa agreed. He grinned at her, and she wondered if he possessed the power to read minds. She had yet to meet a god who claimed such powers, but she could not discount the possibility. He took her hand again and brushed his thumb over her glowing knuckles. He said, "Have faith, fair Myropa. The Fates have a plan for you."

She blinked up at him. "How do you know?"

"Because it is what they do." Then he looked at Trostili. It was clear that the God of Virility would brook no argument when Disevy said, "She will report to me if the Sea changes."

Trostili's nostrils flared, and he looked at Myropa with a penetrating gaze. "What are the king's plans for fighting back? Did he select a new champion?"

"No, he is ready to surrender."

"Already?" He glanced at Disevy. "Weak. I'm going to have a talk with Arohnu about his prophecies. It seems he and Axus are trying to cheat me of my power."

Disevy said, "I thought you supported Axus's little war."

"Precisely. His *war*. Where is the war in this? He attacks, they die. What's in it for me?" He turned to Myropa. "What is the forester doing?"

"He's trying to muster help. He's not ready to give up."

Looking to Disevy, he said, "At least one of them has a spine."

"Watch yourself, Trostili. I will not abide disrespect," replied Disevy.

"It was a compliment," Trostili ground out between his teeth.

Myropa wasn't convinced, and she didn't think Disevy was either. Trostili turned back to her. "Keep an eye on that forester." Then he spun and stalked back through the open corridor.

Myropa drew her gaze from his retreating form and realized Disevy was still holding her hand. He was perusing her with admiration. From any *man*, she might have felt disconcerted. From him, it felt empowering, as if his fathomless gaze was showing her how she should see herself when she looked in the mirror. She could feel that for *this* god to look at her with such adoration was a true blessing.

"What of women?" she said before realizing her lips were moving.

"What about women?" he said, tilting his head curiously.

"You spoke of men. What of women's power and strength?"

"Ah, *that* job belongs to my sister Azeria. We had differing opinions on how the blessing should be bestowed, so we decided to split it. She thinks my ways too brutish and prefers a more delicate touch. I believe she has truly perfected the art."

"But men are stronger."

He nodded. "In some ways. Women excel in others. We try to maintain a balance."

"I think your sister overlooked me when she was bestowing her blessings."

"This from the woman who fended off two vights?" he said with a smirk.

"It was the power of the Fates—"

"Yes, they grant it, but *you* choose to wield it." He tilted his head and looked at her curiously. "Do you know that not every reaper can?"

A whisper of self-approval fluttered deep within Myropa's frozen core. "No, I didn't. I've never met another reaper."

"Of course you haven't. Yours is meant to be a solitary existence. A dozen reapers could be standing here, and not one of them would be aware of another."

No one had ever explained these things to her. In fact, none of the gods had ever spoken with her for so long—or treated her as a person. Myropa glanced around her uncomfortably. "Are there others here?"

He stroked her chin. "You are the only one."

She pulled her face away. "Trostili was right. I am deserving of my punishment for my weakness."

A slight pulse of power caused her to meet his gaze. He said, "I am the god of strength and power, so you may believe me when I say that we all are weak. Our weakness is merely the vessel that holds our strength. If you choose not to look into the vessel, all that you will see is your weakness."

"You seem proud of the strength you have granted the humans. Do you not care what happens to them?"

He met her gaze as he pressed another kiss to her fingers. "What good is strength without adversity? Axus and Trostili have their parts to play in the humans' evolution. Life and death, peace and war—the first would not be appreciated without the second." He finally released her hand and said, "Do visit again." He then strode off in the same direction that Trostili had gone.

Myropa watched until Disevy disappeared. He was a sight to admire, and she was sure he knew it. She then closed her eyes and felt for the call of the Fates. It would be easier to cross the veil if she was pulled by a tether. One suddenly snapped into place, a glowing rope at her core. She abruptly inhaled, filling her lungs with a borrowed breath of life, and stepped across the threshold.

CHAPTER 12

Brontus pulled Aaslo to the side as he stopped before the open portal to the great hall where the feast was to be served. The two royal guards stationed there did not acknowledge either of them, but Aaslo felt their gazes when he wasn't looking.

"Sir Forester, please listen to me," Brontus said with a hint of concern. "I will be serving you during the meal. If anyone else tries to offer you food or drink, you should politely decline. It is not customary and should be considered suspect."

"Does that happen often?" said Aaslo.

"No, but it only takes one poison to kill you."

"You should listen to him. At least, if you die from poisoning, they'll know who to blame."

"Right," said Aaslo, glancing into the brightly lit room full of colorful characters.

"Also, do not address the royal family unless you are invited to the discussion."

"That should be no problem," replied Aaslo. "I have no desire to speak with anyone, much less *them*." He glanced into the room again. A dozen tables were already stacked with linens, glimmering place settings, and an array of trays, bowls, pitchers, and platters nearly overflowing with food and drink. No one was sitting at the tables, though. Everyone stood in migratory clumps, most brimming with chatter and laughter. One heated group, however, looked as if they were ready to discard their finery for a sparring match in the yard.

"That is Wizard Everly," Brontus said, following Aaslo's gaze. "He has an opinion about everything and thinks it's his solemn duty to put anyone who disagrees with him in his place."

"And the other one?" said Aaslo, nodding toward the younger man with whom Everly was arguing.

"Warlock Rastiv. He's new to Tyellí—arrived a few months ago from the Mouvilanian division of the Council of Magi. He's one of the few around here with the power to stand up to Everly, or so I've heard. I have no idea what brought him here."

"What is their point of contention?"

Brontus shrugged. "Everything. I'd suggest avoiding them both."

A crash of cymbals sounded, and everyone began moving toward the tables. Aaslo glanced at Brontus.

"Come," said the manservant. "You must be seated before the royal family arrives."

Brontus led Aaslo through the crowd. Most of the people were pre-occupied, but their gazes burned into his back as they settled. Passing table after table, Aaslo became increasingly discomfited. When Brontus mounted a set of steps that led to the table on a raised platform, Aaslo nearly groaned aloud.

"Ha ha! Your humiliation will be on display for all!"

Brontus indicated for him to take the seat on one side closest to the end of the table. Wizard Everly was already seated across from him. As Aaslo sat, Warlock Rastiv took the seat to his right. The rest of the chairs remained empty. Since he was facing the hall, Aaslo was graced with a view of all the people staring at him. Although he would have been more comfortable in his own clothes, he was somewhat grateful to Akirini for providing him with appropriate apparel. He wore a dark green surcoat over a honey-colored tunic and trousers. His sword was belted at his waist, and Mathias's head was in a dark green velvet sack tied to his belt by a golden rope. His knee-high boots had a slight lift to the heel, which he knew was popular with riders, but he was more concerned with stumbling over his own feet.

Aaslo surveyed the feast, his interest only partially feigned. He avoided looking at Wizard Everly, who didn't look like any wizard from the stories. He had short, greying hair, deep furrows across his brow, a hard stare, and a sour countenance. His dress was not unlike Aaslo's, except that his surcoat was longer and he wore many more embellishments. Multiple gold chains hung from his neck, each finger was weighted with bulky rings, and small gold studs and gemstones dotted the rim of each of his ears. Earrings and studs were apparently a popular look with the nobles, since almost everyone in the room wore them.

"Maybe you should get some, Aaslo. You can use sticks if gold is too shiny for you. You could even grow trees from your ears."

"That's absurd," he muttered.

"I agree," said Warlock Rastiv. Aaslo looked up and followed the warlock's gaze. A large cart was being wheeled up the aisle by four servants. Atop it was an entire roast boar dangling from a spit. Beneath it was a metal tub in which a small fire burned with blue flame. A thick rim of ice surrounded the tub, and piles of fresh fruit and vegetables framed the display.

Wizard Everly grinned at Warlock Rastiv, but it was not a friendly expression. "We like to make an impression."

"The only impression that man is making is an appreciation for gaudiness."

Warlock Rastiv grunted. "I've been here for months, and I've seen nothing of the sort. Who are you trying to impress?" He hooked a thumb at Aaslo. "This guy?" The warlock turned toward him. "Who are you, anyway?"

"That's the question we should ask ourselves every day."

Aaslo had learned from Magdelay that Mouvilanians were direct. It was an attribute he could appreciate. Before Aaslo could answer, Wizard Everly said, "It was the queen's idea. Apparently, it is a celebration of life or some such. It probably has something to do with the king's consort. She is expected to give birth soon. The king hopes for a daughter."

"They don't know it's a wake."

"A wake?" said Aaslo.

"To mourn the passing of life—all life—in advance, of course, since no one will be around afterward."

Wizard Everly's face reddened as he scowled at Aaslo. "It's a celebration. No one has died."

"Ha!" said Warlock Rastiv. He shook his head. "In Mouvilan, it might have been a wake, indeed, *and* a celebration. The queen would have the king's mistress put on the spit, not throw her a party."

"Our ways are different from yours. There are reasons for the way things are done. The king and queen had an arranged marriage. It is a business partnership. The queen was chosen because her character and skills balance those of King Rakith. They respect each other, rule together, and produce legitimate heirs. Beyond that, they are free to pursue their own interests. Such is the way with most of the nobility."

"It is disgusting," said Warlock Rastiv. "In Mouvilan, we believe in honor and fidelity."

Wizard Everly said, "They have already sacrificed for their positions. It would be cruel to ask for more. In Uyan, we honor sacrifice."

The warlock blatantly eyed Wizard Everly's garish attire and sniffed. "Yes, I can see that you are well acquainted with sacrifice."

"Perhaps Sir Forester has something to say with regard to sacrifice," said a familiar feminine voice from behind Aaslo.

He and the two magi, as well as everyone else in the hall, stood as the queen moved to take her seat at the end of the table beside Aaslo. The five princes, ranging in age from twelve to twenty, two of them being twins, filled the remaining chairs. The king presided over the other end of the table. All of the attendees were required to sit as one, since it was improper to be seated before the king or to be standing over him when he was seated. Each of the table guests had their own server who pushed their chairs in for them as they sat, with Brontus performing the task for Aaslo.

As soon as everyone in the hall was seated, the servers began setting platters in front of the guests. The queen sat poised with confidence, sipping her wine as her server spread the napkin over her lap. Once her server stepped back, the queen said, "Well, Sir Forester?"

Aaslo glanced at her, then at the other table guests. The king was ignoring everyone beyond his sons, who were engaged in some debate, and the two magi were both looking at Aaslo as if he were a strange insect to be studied. He glanced at the queen uncomfortably. He was supposed to avoid talking to her. He had been hoping to avoid talking altogether.

"She's the queen, Aaslo. You're keeping the queen *waiting."*

Aaslo cleared his throat and met the queen's amused gaze. "We have a saying. A tree that bends in the breeze does not bend for the sake of his neighbors."

Wizard Everly narrowed his eyes at him as if trying to determine if Aaslo had issued offense. "What is that supposed to mean?"

The queen wore a slight lift to her lips as she said, "I believe it means that someone who endures a loss due to coercion or expectation has not truly sacrificed. It is a question of motive, is it not, Sir Forester?"

His gaze shifted to the magi. "Yes, Your Majesty."

"And what of you?" Wizard Everly said to Aaslo. "Do you think yourself worthy of the honor you're given?"

Aaslo pondered his response.

"They're not foresters. They aren't that patient. Delay implies lack of confidence."

Stalling, he decided to ask a question instead. "Forgive me my ignorance, but what is the difference between a warlock and a wizard?"

"Warlocks are skilled," said Rastiv. "Wizards are brutes."

Everly scoffed. "That was uncalled for, Rastiv." He turned to Aaslo. "Warlocks use rituals and incantations to cast magic—"

"Like a witch," said Aaslo.

"The women are called *witches*," said Rastiv. "They don't like to be associated with us. It is an old grudge. The truth is, I don't think anyone remembers the reason."

Everly continued. "Wizards use an object—usually a staff, wand, or amulet—to focus their *own* power into spells—unlike a mage, who uses the power within the earth or other objects to cast spells. But, Sir Forester, you did not answer the question posed to *you*. Are you worthy of your honor?"

"They're on to you, Aaslo."

Aaslo was agitated by the necessity to answer before fully considering the question. He said, "If I am to be honored for my sacrifices, then being a forester should not be one of them."

"Then, you think the foresters should not be honored?" said the wizard.

"I do not speak for the others, only for myself. If foresters are to be honored, though, it should be for their work. It is an arduous task, a necessary one. It is one that few appreciate and even fewer choose to undertake. If it is *sacrifice* that must be honored"—he glanced at the queen—"I have endured others more trying."

The queen leaned toward him. "Have any of these sacrifices been in relation to you being a forester?"

Aaslo saw a pretty brunette with a stormy gaze in his mind's eye. He recalled how the wind had whipped loose locks across her tearstained face as she rejected him. He said, "Some, for certain."

The queen leaned back with satisfaction. "Then, the fact that you enjoy your work should not negate your sacrifice."

Aaslo blinked at her in surprise. He hadn't considered that, yet he didn't disagree. He tipped his head and said, "Her Majesty is wise."

She smiled in appreciation, then turned to a disgruntled Everly, changing the subject to something to do with enchanted bells. Aaslo blocked out the conversation, content to dwell in the memories of loss the conversation had evoked. He glanced to his right to see Warlock Rastiv pointedly staring at him.

He said, "Is something amiss, Magus?"

"I haven't decided. What's in the bag?" The warlock's gaze dropped to the velvet bag at Aaslo's side.

"That's none of your concern," said Aaslo.

Warlock Rastiv pursed his lips. He said, "I sense that it is something of great importance."

"Yet it is still none of your business," Aaslo replied.

"*You* are important," said the warlock, and Aaslo noticed that the man's gaze did not seem completely present.

"Are you a prophet?" said Aaslo.

"No," the man mused, "but I sense the importance of things and try to place them appropriately."

"Does that have something to do with your bloodline?" Aaslo said, fishing for information.

"Indeed," said the warlock. "I am a Saft."

Aaslo waited for the man to say more, but none was forthcoming. He glanced to Wizard Everly who grunted and said, "Safts think magic should be used for the advancement of the human species."

Warlock Rastiv's gaze cleared, and he scowled at Everly. "You say that like it is a bad thing."

"A waste of time," said the wizard as he shoved a chunk of roast boar into his mouth.

Warlock Rastiv said, "You think we should all be getting rich like you Sereshians?"

Aaslo glanced up at Wizard Everly with sudden interest. This man was somehow related to Mathias. Was he Mathias's grandfather? Maybe his uncle or a distant cousin? Aaslo didn't see the family resemblance.

Wizard Everly chuckled. "When magic ends, our progeny will be sitting comfortably in our estates while the rest of you toil in the fields and streets with the other common folk."

"*That's a bit harsh, don't you think?*"

"You are a selfish lot," said Warlock Rastiv.

"*Selfish?*" said the wizard, his face reddening. "We use what blessings we have to ensure that our children and grandchildren live in comfort, while you would sentence yours to poverty. It is *you* who is selfish."

"That's quite thoughtful of my grand-something."

Warlock Rastiv pointed his fork at the wizard. "We work to ensure that *everyone* can live in comfort, not just our own."

"Ah, he has a point. I'm torn."

Both men held their tongues as the queen said, "I am curious as to what Sir Forester has to say about this as well." Then all three looked at Aaslo.

"Think quickly."

"I'm not a magus. It's not my business how they use their powers, so long as they're not hurting anyone."

For the first time, the queen appeared disappointed.

"Too fast, Aaslo. Think better.*"*

"*But,*" Aaslo added hastily, "they should be unified for at least one singular goal."

"What goal is that?" said Warlock Rastiv.

"Life," said Aaslo, "human existence and the existence of every other species."

"Well, that's a bit dramatic," said Wizard Everly. "I suppose such naiveté should be expected of a man who spends his days in the woods. Listen, young man, magi do not go gallivanting off on grand adventures to save mankind. That kind of thing is for the stories alone."

Aaslo glanced at the queen and then said, "And the Aldrea Prophecy?"

The two magi and the queen all stopped to stare at him. Aaslo felt a heat rise on his neck and glanced over to see that the king was also looking at him, although the princes were still preoccupied with asserting who was the better huntsman.

Wizard Everly said, "What do *you* know of the Aldrea Prophecy?"

"More than I'd like," said Aaslo. "If it came to fruition, would you step up to help?"

Everly chuckled. "If you know anything about that prophecy, then you know it's up to the chosen one to fight and prevail."

"Yes," said Aaslo, "but as far as I know, it does not say he must fight *alone*. What if his effectiveness is in his ability to unify the people?"

Everly shrugged as he went back to cutting his meat. "Then I suppose we will be unified."

Aaslo said, "If the path of the prophecy foretelling the chosen one's victory should fail, what then?"

"Then we all die," said Warlock Rastiv.

"You would not fight?" said Aaslo.

"What would be the point?" said Wizard Everly. "It would be better to spend what little time you had left enjoying life's pleasures."

"On that point, we agree," said Warlock Rastiv. "Besides, all of the other paths lead to naught but terror and death. Why would we want to subject our descendants to that?"

Aaslo shook his head in dismay. He looked pointedly at Wizard Everly. "Is it not in your bloodline's doctrine to secure your family's wealth and privilege? Is *existence* not included in that?" Then he looked to Warlock Rastiv. "Every generation of your bloodline works to advance the species, yet you will just lie down and die when faced with extinction?" Glancing between them, he said, "The tenets of your bloodlines require you to fight with or without the chosen one."

Both men appeared disgruntled but also thoughtful. Wizard Everly eventually grumbled, "What you say has merit, but it is impractical."

Aaslo ground his teeth. "Is it not worth a moment's thought to consider what you might do if the chosen one fails?"

Warlock Rastiv chuckled. "The prophecy has been around for hundreds of years. Every generation thinks it will come to fruition during their lifetimes. Still, I suppose the subject is worth an academic consideration, or perhaps for a bit of whimsy."

Aaslo met the king's warning gaze as he said, "You had best think quickly."

"Sir Forester," said the queen. She held a goblet out to him. "Would you care for some wine?"

Aaslo froze.

"Ha ha! She's going to poison you, and there's nothing you can do about it."

What was he to do? He wasn't supposed to accept anything from anyone, but she was the queen. It would be terribly disrespectful to refuse. Perhaps he could accept it and not drink. Aaslo glanced at the king, who was still staring at him with fire in his gaze. He returned

his attention to the queen, and then slowly reached out to take the goblet. "Thank you, Your Majesty."

The queen nodded, then lifted her wine for a toast. She watched him
closely over the rim of her goblet as he drank. With her ardent gaze, it
was not something he could feign. King Rakith abruptly stood to an-
nounce the commencement of the dance. The magi ceased to pester
Aaslo, and the king claimed the queen's attention. Unfortunately, there
were plenty of ladies who wanted to brag about having danced with a
forester. One young blond woman by the name of Adne was particularly adamant. She was pretty, but she followed him everywhere,
sneered at the other women, and claimed at least half the dances for
herself. By the end of the evening, Aaslo was glad to have had the
chance to dance, since it meant he had survived the dinner, yet he
hoped to never do it again.

*"But you're so light on your feet. I'm starting to believe that you
really are a faerie."*

"I'm not a faerie," Aaslo grumbled as he arrived at his door.

Brontus slipped the key into the lock, then looked at him curiously.
"No, Sir Forester, I never considered that you were. Oh, I know the
people talk. Rumors abound, but I think you are only a man."

Aaslo turned to face the man directly. "You are probably the most
sensible person I have met in this city."

Brontus grinned and bowed before following Aaslo into the room.
"Thank you, Sir Forester. That means much coming from you."

Aaslo frowned. "Because I am a forester?"

"Ah, no sir. Because I think you are quite sensible, as well. Shall I
turn down your bed?"

"No, thank you. I can handle that."

"Of course you can handle it. He doesn't think you're incapable."

Brontus glanced about the chamber. "Is there nothing else with
which I may assist you?"

"He looks anxious."

Aaslo narrowed his eyes at the man. He did look anxious. "Is everything all right?" Aaslo said.

"What? Yes, sir. Everything seems to be in order." He looked as if
he might disagree with himself, and he did not attempt to hide his concern. "The room looks to be empty, and the doors are closed, so I'll be

on my way." The man bowed one last time, then slipped into the dim corridor, closing the door behind him.

Aaslo turned to survey the room. He felt like he was missing something. "What is it?" he said aloud, but Mathias did not answer. He moved to sit on the bench at the foot of the bed, where he shucked his fancy heeled boots. As a man who spent most of his time on his feet, he was surprised that they could hurt so much after a bit of dancing. He removed his belt, allowing it and the sword to fall to the floor; then his surcoat and tunic followed. He carried the velvet sack over to the table beside the bed. Although he felt it morbid to sleep with a severed head on his bed table, he wanted it within reach should he need to run. He glanced to the sword on the floor and decided he should keep it close as well. As he bent to retrieve it, he noticed the slightest breeze rustle the bed skirt.

Aaslo whipped the sword from its sheath as he stood, turning to face the door. The wooden structure was unchanged, still closed, and no intruders stood before it. He glanced around the dim chamber, lit only by an enchanted sconce near the bed. He wondered, again, what was wrong. There were no windows, and the door was closed.

"Doorsss."

Then he realized what Brontus had said. It had been a warning. Aaslo shifted around the foot of the bed and turned to survey the dark recesses behind the bed-curtains and tapestries, one of which swayed as his gaze passed over it. He gripped his sword and said, "Show yourself!"

A black-clad figure stepped far enough into the light that he could see it was a woman.

"Adne?" he said. "Whoever you are, you had best leave. I neither desire company nor will suffer an assassination."

The woman chuckled as she stepped closer and raised the black lace veil that covered her features. She said, "Adne is persistent, but she would never be so bold. *I*, on the other hand, can afford to be bold." She sidled closer, brushed her fingers along the knuckles that held his hilt, then placed her other palm on the bared skin of his chest. Her cheek brushed his as she spoke into his ear. "Do you know that it is an offense punishable by death to bare your blade at your queen?"

The sword produced a thud as it landed on the rug at his feet. The queen grinned and then slipped around him, heading toward the still water in the center of the room. As she neared, colored lights began to shift beneath the surface, splaying across the ceiling and walls in dancing drifts while the water began a lazy circuit of the placid loch. The bewitched lute awoke to play a haunting melody, and the crisp scent of evergreens suffused the air. The queen's black dress slid from her shoulders, dropping to the floor in a puddle of shadow beneath a captive rainbow. Colorful swirls of vibrant light played off her feminine curves as she slipped into the enchanted pool. She turned and beckoned to him with a flutter of her fingers, her russet locks made slick by her glistening flesh.

Aaslo was mesmerized, but mostly he was terrified. "I don't understand," he said, glancing around the room as if royal guards might swarm him at any moment.

The queen's laughter complemented the melody of the lute. "Come now, Sir Forester, you do not seem like the kind of man who does not understand *this*."

He stepped into the pool until the water reached his knees. She looked at him coyly and fluttered her fingers again, so he proceeded until he stood directly in front of her. "What of the king?" he said. "What if someone comes in and sees us?"

She ran her fingers over his shoulders, dribbling water down his chest and abdomen. "Rakith is with his consort in *his* quarters. No one is permitted in my chambers without my express permission."

Heat rose to Aaslo's face, and he didn't think it was from the water. "These are *your* quarters?"

"Of course. You are my guest." She ran her finger over his lips. "The Sapphire Room is where I enjoy my lovers. I have none at the moment, save for you."

"You don't even know me. What if I intended you harm?"

She shook her head. "I do not believe that of you, but I should probably warn you that Captain Lopin and several of his men are right outside the door. They seem to have mixed feelings about you."

"It was you, wasn't it? You put them up to the challenge."

She grinned wickedly. "They did that on their own. They are protective of me."

Aaslo groaned. "So, everybody knew why I was brought to this room but me." She giggled and splayed her fingers over his chest. He captured her wandering hands, touching her for the first time and wondering if it would be the last. He said, "Why me?"

She pulled her hands from his, then wrapped her arms around his neck and pulled him onto the submerged bench. After piling her lithe legs atop his lap, she looked him in the eyes. "I have always admired Rakith for his strength. Time and again he has stood against the tide, never one to back down. I think he would have led the charge himself for any other war without delay and without fear. The man you and I saw today was not the Rakith I know. To see him so forlorn, overcome with despair, defeated before the battle is begun, was terrifying. You, Aaslo, give me hope." She guided his hand to her face and pressed her lips to his palm. "This is a pleasure of the flesh. What you have given me is a pleasure of the soul."

"If it is false hope?"

She searched his eyes and then smiled. "I do not believe it is. I have faith that you will prevail. If I am wrong, then the rest of my days will still be filled with peace of mind."

CHAPTER 13

AASLO SLIPPED OUT OF THE CHAMBER BEFORE THE SUN ROSE. THE queen was still nestled within his sheets. By the soft upturn of her lips, she seemed to be safe within pleasant dreams. He wasn't sure he felt so pleasant about the experience. While the night was certainly enjoyable, the queen was a married woman; yet he could not have rejected her. Anyone with such power could not be denied. No, she was an intelligent and compassionate woman. He wondered if he was being unfair.

"You didn't try to deny her because you wanted her."

Aaslo knew it was true, and he didn't know how to feel about it. He drew up short when he turned to find Captain Lopin staring at him from where he leaned against the opposite wall. Two more royal guardsmen stood to either side of the door.

With a scowl, Aaslo said, "Why are *you* standing outside my room?"

The captain said, "You did not seem the kind of man who would sleep late."

"I was told I would be permitted to leave today."

Lopin nodded toward the closed door. "You would leave without so much as a farewell?"

Aaslo glanced back to the door, feeling a twinge of regret. "She doesn't need farewells. She needs to know someone is out there doing something to save all our hides."

Lopin stared at him unmoving. He said, "You think that should be you?"

"Absolutely not," said Aaslo. "I think I should be tending my saplings on the western slope right now." He looked at the man pointedly and said, "If someone else wants to step up, I'll be happy to pass the responsibility."

Lopin inhaled sharply as if frustrated, then averted his gaze toward the end of the corridor.

"I thought not," said Aaslo as he turned. "I wouldn't trust you to follow through anyway."

"*Brutal.*"

Aaslo was mildly surprised to hear Mathias's voice at that moment. He said, "I wasn't sure you were listening anymore. You were remarkably silent last night."

Lopin stepped into his path. "It's not my place to question the king. I am sure he will change his mind after his shock has dissipated."

"*His* shock?" Aaslo said. Ielo would tell him to hold his tongue, but his anger got the better of him. He didn't attempt to hide his disgust when he said, "The king wasn't the one who watched his best friend get stabbed through the heart. He wasn't the one who stood vigil over his body, only to be told by the *high sorceress* that nothing could be done. He wasn't the one who cut off his best friend's head and carried it across the kingdom!" Aaslo stepped toward Lopin. "Rakith is the *king,* and he is too shocked to act? Tell me, Captain, are you too shocked to act?"

Lopin clenched his jaw. "I am the captain of the royal guard. It is my duty to protect the king."

Aaslo shook his head. "Even if you could, what good is a king if all his subjects are dead?"

Aaslo made to pass Lopin, but the man reached out to grab his arm. Lopin said, "*If* that time comes, and should it become necessary, *I* will lead the charge. Do not get in my way."

Aaslo pulled his arm from the man's grip. "You forget that we will be on the *same* side. Keep in mind, if the king has his way and dismisses the army, you will have no one left to lead." He turned and continued down the corridor, this time without interruption. No one stopped him at the checkpoints or the door, so he strode straight to the palace gates before realizing he was forgetting something. He turned to one of the gate guards.

"Excuse me. How do I get my horse?"

The guard spied his worn traveling clothes, which he had found folded neatly in a basket inside his chamber door when he awoke. The man said, "If you came with a horse, he'll be in the guest stables." He glanced over to see a young boy running across the yard and hollered, "Hey, Fin, you need to get this man's horse."

The boy ran up to Aaslo. Still breathing heavily, he said, "Yes, sir, I can get your horse. Which one is it?"

"The ugly one," said Aaslo.

The boy laughed. "I know the one. The stable master was fumin' yesterday after Crazy Eyes ate his hat."

"His name is Dolt. Are you sure you can handle him?" said Aaslo.

"Yes, sir. He doesn't give me any trouble."

The boy ran away and returned a short time later with Dolt already saddled and ready to go. When they reached Aaslo, the boy tugged on the horse's lead to make him stop, but the horse kept going. Aaslo was forced to run after the beast, much to the guards' amusement. Dolt stopped to drink from the fountain, and Aaslo was finally able to get hold of him long enough to mount. The ride to the Forester's Haven was easy that early in the morning. The sky was beginning to lighten, and merchants were setting up their shops and stalls when he arrived. Dolt refused to stop, of course, and continued around to the back of the property without escort. Aaslo stomped up to the door, which opened just as his foot reached the landing. Galobar's bright expression greeted him.

"Sir Forester! I am so pleased that you have returned." He stepped aside to admit Aaslo. "I must say, I was quite concerned. A marquess came here looking for you. A marquess!" They entered the kitchen, but Galobar didn't stop for a breath. "I have never been in such illustrious company. I told his man that I had no idea where you'd gone, but they were not satisfied. Well, I recalled that you were asking questions about the palace—I do apologize. I didn't mean to divulge sensitive information. I hope it wasn't a secret."

Galobar shuffled through pots and gathered vegetables as he rambled. Since it appeared to Aaslo that he was going to make food, Aaslo was content to sit back and allow it to happen. He sat on a stool at the counter silently awaiting the rations.

"Your servants, though, they saw the guards and hid. Strange, that. Anyway, once Master Peck and Mory heard you might've gone to the palace, they left—in a hurry, I might add. I haven't seen them since. Perhaps once they hear of your arrival, they'll return as well."

Aaslo hoped not. He was ready to leave Tyellí, and he preferred to go alone.

"Without me?"

"Never."

Galobar blinked at him. "No? I cannot imagine anyone running out on a forester. It is a great honor to serve one such as yourself. I received a missive that you were to stay the night at the palace as a royal guest! Truly an honor." The man shook his head and continued mumbling.

Aaslo blocked out the rest of the chatter as he imagined he was ten again, sitting before the hearth with Pa, waiting impatiently for his potatoes and venison. *Never rush a meal, Aaslo. Some things in life are worth the wait. Some are worth a sacrifice.* His father had looked at him, then. It wasn't the first or last time he had seen sadness in his father's gaze, but it was the only time he'd seen regret. *Just be sure you know who will be making the sacrifice and who will be doing the waiting, for they are not always the same.*

He hadn't asked his father what he had meant. He figured Pa would have told him if he had wanted him to know. Pa had never told him, and now he wondered if he would ever have the chance to ask.

"There you go, Sir Forester. Perhaps not as nice as you'd get at the palace, but it's hot and hearty."

Aaslo was abruptly pulled from his memories to find a steaming plate of food in front of him. "Thank you, Galobar. This is a meal fit for a forester, and it's far less likely to be poisoned."

Galobar blinked at him in surprise. "Oh? Is that a common issue at the palace?"

"Apparently."

"Careful, Aaslo."

"I would go insane if I worried over every meal I ate," said Aaslo.

Galobar looked truly disturbed as he mulled it over. "I agree. Food should *nurture,* and poison can be so unpredictable. If one must kill, it should be done with certainty." The older man snapped up a knife from the butcher block, twirled over his fingers before jabbing the air in a move born of practice.

Aaslo paused with his food halfway to his mouth and stared at the man. Galobar set the knife down and continued cleaning the kitchen as if he hadn't just been discussing methods of taking a person's life. Setting down his fork, Aaslo said, "You seemed practiced with a knife."

Galobar nodded as he emptied the rest of the food from the pot onto Aaslo's plate. "Of course, Sir Forester. It is my duty to protect the haven and its occupants." He smiled and said, "The name would cease to hold meaning otherwise." He again picked up the knife and waved it around, pointing at nothing and everything. "The enchantments help as well. Most of them were placed or recharged by the high sorceress herself over the years."

Aaslo's ears perked. "Why would she do that?"

Galobar shrugged. "It seems she has a fondness for foresters. I imagine the enchantments are quite secure. She is a formidable woman."

"Not formidable enough."

"No one is perfect."

"Oh, I never said she was perfect, but anyone who cares for the foresters is deserving of respect."

Without responding to the zealous outlook, Aaslo scarfed down the rest of his food, then pushed away from the table. "I'll be leaving soon. Would it be possible to get some rations?"

Galobar turned to look at him with a pitiful expression. "You are leaving already? You only just arrived."

"I have duties to which I must attend."

"Of course, Sir Forester. I understand your folk are not the sort to dally. For how many days do you expect to be traveling?"

Aaslo paused, realizing he had no idea where he was going. He needed help, though, and since the army was out of the question, he supposed the magi were his best bet. "You don't happen to know where the Citadel of Magi is located, do you?"

Galobar pursed his lips in thought. "I believe it is east, but beyond that I have no idea."

"Perhaps," said Aaslo. "That's where the high sorceress said she was going."

Galobar's eyes widened. "You know the high sorceress personally? Oh my, you are fascinating. I had no idea the foresters were so well-connected."

Aaslo shook his head. "We are probably the least well-connected people in the kingdom."

"Except you."

"I'm just different, and it's all your fault."

"My fault?" said Galobar.

"No, not you," Aaslo grumbled. "Never mind. I'll ask around the city. Someone must know how to get there."

"*You should've asked at the palace.*"

"What if they tried to stop me?"

"Why would someone try to stop you?" said Galobar.

"Some people don't want me causing trouble," said Aaslo, "but sometimes causing trouble is the only solution."

"Another forester wisdom?" said Galobar.

"No, *that* was my friend. He lived to make trouble. He could get away with it, too. Everyone loved him."

"*Except the people who killed me.*"

His heart heavy with guilt, Aaslo said, "I'll ask around town today and leave tomorrow. It'll give us time to gather supplies, anyhow."

"Oh!" Galobar suddenly rushed to a side table and collected a stack of letters bundled with twine and sealed with a glob of wax. The wax was marked with a wolf's head surrounded by a tangle of briar. "I nearly forgot. This came for you last night. It bears the seal of the Marquess of Dovermyer."

"Thanks," said Aaslo, stuffing the stack into the velvet sack with Mathias's head. He then stalked out the front door, to find the streets filled with people going about their business. A cluster of curious busybodies was congregated at the fence. As soon as he stepped through the doorway, they erupted in a cacophony of cheers and chatter. Although he had always preferred to be alone, he had never disliked people. That was quickly changing. He walked down the path that crossed the lawn and then exited the gate. Keeping his head down, he avoided eye contact so he wouldn't have to talk to anyone.

"*What did you say before? A strong tree cracks in the wind?*"

"A strong trunk stands in the wind, but, when hardened beyond bending, breaks. Stop throwing forester wisdoms at me."

"*It's your wisdom, not mine. Don't forget who you are.*"

"I have no intention of forgetting, although I doubt anyone would let me. I need to find someone who can tell me where to find the citadel. Are you going to help or not?"

"Sure, but you'll have to tell me what citadel we're talking about." Aaslo turned to find Peck standing right behind him. Mory was waving off the crowd, telling them that if they didn't leave the forester alone, he might turn them all into trees.

"I bet a couple of experienced thieves could get the information quickly."

Aaslo sighed. Mathias was right. "I'm looking for someone who can tell me how to get to the Citadel of Magi."

Peck whistled between his teeth. "Why do you wanna know that?"

"Never mind. Do you know anyone who could tell us?"

"No, I don't know any wizards—er, magi, I mean." Peck brightened with a grin. "Best place to get information is taverns. People talk when they're drinking."

Aaslo narrowed his eyes. "Do you know of any taverns where magi drink?"

Peck's smile fell. "No, I think maybe they do their drinking in the Dragon District."

"Dragon District?"

"You know, because of their symbol—the dragon wrapped around a sphere? I guess it means something to them."

Aaslo recalled that both the wizard and the warlock at the palace feast had been wearing rings bearing a dragon wrapped around a spherical stone. He had never seen the symbol around Magdelay, but she had been in hiding.

"They all wear that symbol?" he said.

Peck shrugged. "Some do, some don't—at least, as far as I've seen." He paused and hesitantly said, "Did you really go to the palace? When that marquess showed up and I heard them saying you were going to the palace, I thought maybe you were being arrested for killing Jago's men."

"That didn't come up. I had business with the king."

"The king? Like, the *actual* king?" said Mory, having joined them after the crowd dispersed.

Peck eyed Aaslo suspiciously. "They'll not be putting up with the likes of us in the Dragon District, but if you know the king, then maybe they'll let you in." He glanced at Aaslo's clothes. "But not in what you're wearing."

"I told you that you should have taken the nice clothes from the palace. They were tailored for you."

"And have them accuse me of stealing?" he said.

Peck nodded. "Maybe. Those high society sorts'll say anything to get rid of people they don't like."

Aaslo shook his head. "It's too early to be drinking anyway. What about shops—places where they buy things for their spells?"

"Ah, those are also in the Dragon District."

He sighed again. Why did everything have to be so frustratingly difficult? "What about a library? Does the city have a library that's *not* in the Dragon District?"

"For sure," said Peck, "but it'll cost you a fortune to enter if you don't have a patron."

A thought occurred to him, and Aaslo tugged at the tie of the sack to retrieve the bundle of missives. Peck and Mory both backed away as he dug into the bag. He laid the sack between his feet and broke the seal over the twine. The first of the marquess's letters was a notice of patronage. The second provided directions for the bankers and information on an account from which he could draw funds. The third contained a map showing the marquess's estate in Ruriton and, of course, the location of the blight.

As he folded the letters and stuffed them back into the sack, he said, "I have a patron. Take me to the library."

The doorman—or woman, as it was—at the library took one look at Aaslo and tried to turn him away. Although she eventually accepted the marquess's letter of patronage, she made it clear that she did not approve of him. Aaslo spent the morning searching the maps and scrolls, but somehow the location of one of the world's most famous structures was nowhere to be found. Since neither Peck nor Mory could read, he sent them to ask around the city. If the information had been clearly and intentionally kept from the records, he doubted they would return with anything of use.

At midday, Aaslo left the library nearly as frustrated as he was hungry. The archivist who had been openly spying on him throughout his visit scowled every time the empty pit of his stomach growled. He headed toward the Dragon District but decided to stop for a meal before he got to a part of the city where they might reject him. He was starting to enter a tavern with a picture of a duck in a cauldron hanging over the door when a man suddenly came stumbling from the building into his path. The man clutched his chest as he collapsed to his knees. His panicked, pleading gaze turned toward Aaslo, then looked past him.

The man reached for the air and said, "Please, help me." Then he fell to the ground and released his last breath. The man's companions, who had exited the tavern behind him, cried out and grappled the man as if they could return him to life. Aaslo turned to look in the direction the man had delivered his last plea, but no one was there. He glanced back at the tavern and decided to find his meal elsewhere.

Backing away through the gathering crowd, he walked past a number of shops and then turned in to a tavern with an oversized wooden spoon over the doorway. The table nearest the kitchen was unoccupied and was also, pleasantly, the farthest from the other patrons. As Aaslo sat, he started considering that he might simply head east and ask for directions along the way.

"Because it's so often that people run into random magi that are willing to share the apparently secret location of their citadel."

"Do you have a better idea?"

"Go back and ask the queen? She seemed to favor you."

"Given the king's position, I feel I was lucky to escape the palace once. I'd not risk it a second time."

"I wouldn't want to go there either—bunch of slimy, back-stabbing snobs."

Aaslo lifted his head toward the speaker, a young woman with short, dark brown curls that bobbed around her almond-shaped face. Her eyes were nearly black beneath thick lashes, and her sun-kissed olive skin lent her an exotic appearance. Beneath her black server's smock, she wore a burgundy tunic that caressed her curves as it reached to her knees, which were covered by black hose. She leaned against the table and placed a hand on one cocked hip. "Who are ya talkin' to?"

Aaslo glanced at the sack he had set on the table in front of the seat next to him. He said, "No one."

The woman tilted her head curiously. "Yeah? I talk to myself sometimes, too." She grinned. "I'm the best company."

"She's cute."

"Shut up."

"What?" she said, appearing more surprised than angry. "Did you just tell me to shut up?"

"No, I wasn't talking to you."

She twirled a curl with one finger as she said, "Uh-huh. Well, maybe your personal argument can wait long enough for me to take your order."

"Great. You've known her for all of ten seconds, and she already thinks you're crazy."

"She's probably right," said Aaslo.

The young woman nodded. "I'm *always* right, but what am I right about *now*?"

Aaslo looked back at her. "Um, whatever I want to eat."

"So, it's up to me, then, is it? What about your friend?" she said with a nod toward the sack.

Aaslo glanced at the bag and back to her. "Can you hear him?"

She shook her head. "Nah, sweet lunatic. I'm pretty sure that's a blessing only for you, but since you keep talkin' to him, I figure he might be hungry, too."

Aaslo groaned. "He's not *real*."

"Hey, now!"

"I'm not sure if that makes it better or worse," she said, "especially considering you admit it. All right, I'll be back with some food in a few minutes. It won't be very good, and it costs too much, but you're gonna eat it because that's why you came here."

Aaslo was left in wonder as she walked away.

"She's strange."

As he waited, Aaslo tried to remember if Magdelay had ever mentioned anything that might give him a clue as to the citadel's location. It being east made sense, since it was supposed to be comprised of representatives of the twelve bloodlines from all over Aldrea. Somehow, he had always assumed it would be in Uyan; but, geographically, that made little sense. Then again, the citadel's location might not have been chosen for convenience. He wondered if it had been built in a place of great power. He couldn't remember her mentioning anything like that either—at least, not to him. He wasn't the chosen one, though. Mathias might have known more.

"Sorry, I took those secrets to the bag. Ha ha! Get it, Aaslo? You know, since I didn't have a proper burial or grave."

Aaslo's stomach churned. His guilt was threatening to bury *him*. He said, "I buried the rest of you. I even left you my sword."

"Cromley said to use your head before your sword, and you left me without one."

"I still have use for your head." Aaslo buried his own head in his hands. "I can't do this alone."

A *thunk* on the table startled him. "Sounds like you could use alone time. Seems to me you've got some unwanted company."

Aaslo glanced around to see who the server was talking about, then realized she was referring to Mathias's ghost. "It's not real," he said again.

"Seems like it's real to *you*," she said. She leaned forward and proffered her hand. "The name's Teza."

"Manners, Aaslo. Don't act like you grew up in the woods."

He cleared his throat. "It's a pleasure to meet you, Teza. I'm Aaslo."

She grinned and brushed a curl behind her ear, which he noticed had tiny little punctures lining the rim but no rings or studs. "So, what's the deal with your imaginary friend?"

At that moment, Aaslo was glad to have someone to talk to who was *alive*, and Teza's open personality made it easy. "He's not imaginary." Aaslo huffed and shook his head. "He's not real, either. He's gone, and I—I've taken up his standard."

She paused and tapped her lip thoughtfully. Narrowing her eyes at him, she said, "Let me get this straight. Your friend's dead, so you're taking on his responsibilities?"

"Yeah, I—"

"Hey, bar wench, where's our ale!" shouted a man from a table in the center of the room. Its occupants had gotten rowdier in the short time Aaslo had been waiting for his food.

Teza turned and hollered back at the man. "You'll get it when I feel like bringin' it, so shut your mouth and wait like a gentleman." Teza turned back to Aaslo and rolled her eyes. "They act like I'm some kind of servant."

"You're a server in a tavern."

She rolled her eyes again and rested her hand on her hip. "Well, yes, *right now* I am, but that doesn't make me a servant."

"Teza! Get in here, girl," shouted a husky voice from the kitchen.

She nodded toward Aaslo's food. "Best pay me now in case you decide to leave while I'm gone."

Aaslo settled his bill, then dug in as the woman walked off in a huff. She was right. The food wasn't good, and it was definitely overpriced, but it filled his grumbling stomach. Just as he pushed his plate away, the young woman tossed a bag on the table, plopped down in one of the other seats, and propped her booted feet on the chair next to him.

"So, where are we going?" she said.

Aaslo glanced around in confusion, then looked back to her. "Excuse me?"

She pulled a piece of crust from the hard bread he had left on his plate and popped it into her mouth. "Well, I figure if I'm coming with you, I'd best know where we're going."

"What are you talking about? Why would you come with me?"

"Since you got me fired, I figure you owe me."

He shook his head. *"I got you fired?"*

"That's what I said."

"I didn't get you fired."

She leaned forward and patted his hand. "Look, I know you like to argue with yourself, but I'm an actual person, so you'd best make up your mind."

"No, I mean, I didn't have anything to do with you getting fired."

"That's your opinion, and I respect that, but you still owe me."

"No, it's not an *opinion*. It's a *fact*. I had nothing to do with it, and I don't owe you anything."

She shrugged and sat back. "We'll just have to agree to disagree. I can tell you're a traveler, and I like your values, so where are we going?"

"What do *you* know about my values?" said Aaslo. "Look, unless you know how to get to the Citadel of Magi, I don't need your company."

Teza grabbed her bag as she abruptly stood. "All right, let's go." She took a few steps, then glanced back at him over her shoulder. "Well, are you coming?"

"Best get moving, Aaslo. She seems determined."

Aaslo grabbed the bag and tied it to his belt as he hurried to catch up with the woman. "Hey," he said as he drew up beside her. "Do you know where it is?"

She laughed. "Of course, but I don't know why you'd want to go there. They're worse than those snobs in the palace."

"She's lying. Why would she know?"

"No one else knows. It's not on any of the maps in the library—"

"You went to the library?"

"Yes. How do *you* know where it is?"

She raised a hand and waved toward her right. "It's in the center of the city. Everyone knows where the library is."

"No," Aaslo growled. "I mean the citadel."

"Oh, that's easy. I used to live there."

"What, like as a servant?"

She suddenly rounded on him, blocking his path, and that of every-one else who was flowing in their direction. She dropped her sack at her feet, stepped forward, and stuck a finger in his face. "I told you, I am *not* a servant!"

"Uh-oh, you've angered her."

Aaslo held up his hands. "I'm just trying to understand."

Teza leaned back and huffed as she crossed her arms. Then she grabbed her bag, flung it over her shoulder, and placed her hand back on her hip as she tapped her foot. "Fine, I'll let it go because you're cute, but don't make me tell you again." She abruptly spun and began walk-ing as she spoke. "I was a student there."

"You're a magus?"

She twisted her lips and said, "I *was* a *mage*, like most healers, but they kicked me out and bound my powers."

"So, you can't use your power anymore?" he said.

"I *can*, but only in an emergency. They'll know if I do, and they *do* investigate these things."

"Why did they expel you?"

"Careful, Aaslo. That's a sensitive subject, and she's batty."

"You know, most people are too afraid to ask. They said I cheated and stole someone else's project."

"Did you?"

"Of course I did! Stupid Gertridina did *two* projects, and I didn't have any. She didn't need both of them. The other would have gone to waste if I hadn't used it."

"Why didn't you do your own project?" he said.

"Look, it's not my fault that I'm not creative. I couldn't think of any-thing, so I put it off. Then, all of a sudden it was due, and I didn't have one. Gertridina should've been flattered that I used her work. It was kind of lame. I could've done much better."

"But you didn't."

"It doesn't matter. None of the teachers liked me, anyway. They all wanted me gone but couldn't figure out a way to get rid of me because I was too good. I would've been top of my class, if not for their stupid projects."

"But, the projects are the point of the classes, aren't they?"

She shook her head and waved a finger in the air. "No, see, you're as confused as the rest of them. The point was to learn to be a healer. It's not like a patient is going to walk up to me and say, *Hey, I need you to do a project.*"

"But, the patient *is* the project."

"Exactly, and I was good at healing patients. But the stupid masters said I had a terrible bedside manner. I hate most people, but you don't have to like someone to heal them or be healed by them. Just shut up and get it done, you know?"

"Now she sounds like you."

Aaslo nodded slowly. "Actually, that makes sense. So, how did you end up waiting tables in a run-down tavern in Tyellí?"

"How does any girl end up in a stupid place doing a stupid job? I followed a guy, of course. I met him after I got kicked out. He said we'd travel the world together. We took an evergate to Tyellí and then he stole my money and took off. Turns out he just needed my power to get through, since he was kind of weak."

"What's an evergate?" said Aaslo.

"They're these portals that are scattered all over Aldrea. They're like doorways that only magi can use. You step into one, cast a spell, and you come out in a different one. Distance is no matter."

Aaslo wished he had been able to use an evergate to get to Tyellí. He said, "Why didn't you use it to go home?"

Her expression was troubled as she glanced at him. "I was only allowed one evergate spell. I was supposed to use it to get home. So, I got stuck here, a complete stranger with no money and no way to get home. The truth is, I wasn't ready to go home. How am I supposed to face my parents after getting kicked out of the academy?"

Aaslo thought about how Ielo would have reacted if he hadn't wanted to be a forester. He said, "Your parents will love you whether you go to the academy or not."

"You don't know my parents," she muttered.

Aaslo pulled her to the side of the road, then looked around and realized he had no idea where he was. He looked back at her. "You can use your powers in an emergency, right? Well, I have an emergency. I need to get to the citadel. Can you use this evergate to get me there?"

She shook her head. "No, absolutely not."

"This really is an emergency. I promise, I'll get the high sorceress herself to excuse it."

Teza laughed. "The high sorceress would squish us both like bugs before we ever got near her. But, seriously, I can't take you through. You're not a magus."

"So, *I* can't use it, but can't *you* take me through?"

"Oh, I could take you in, but you'd not come out where you wanted."

"What do you mean?"

"The evergate connects to a magus's power to send him or her to the designated destination. *You* don't have any power, so it wouldn't be able to connect with you. You would be tossed out in some random place. It might not even be on Aldrea. You could end up in another realm, or in a volcano, or in a void with no air. You might even get lost in the pathways until you died of thirst or starvation. You simply cannot take anything living through the evergate unless it has magic of its own."

Aaslo rubbed the stubble on his chin. "You're right. That sounds terrible."

Teza grinned. "I like you. You tell me I'm right a lot." Then she bounced on her heel and started walking again.

"Where are you going?" he said.

"We're leaving. You said you need to go to the citadel."

"I don't have my things, and it's a little late to be starting out. I was planning to leave in the morning."

She paused and tilted her head. "Oh, I guess that makes sense." Then she glanced down the road. "Um, where are you staying?"

Aaslo glanced down the road, too. "I have no idea where it is from here, since I don't know where *here* is. I'm staying at the Forester's Haven."

She furrowed her brow. "That's a strange place to stay. I'm surprised the old man let you in."

"You know of it?"

She rolled her eyes. "*Everybody* knows of it. Well, come on. I'll take you to it—unless there was somewhere else you needed to go first?"

Aaslo shook his head slowly. "No, I guess I just needed to find you."

She smiled at him again. "Yes, I do like you."

It turned out that the Forester's Haven was not far, and Aaslo was sure the glances they received were not for him this time. Teza was quite attractive, and she held herself with confidence and openness. Unfortunately, that openness tended to explode on anyone who approached her.

"Did I ask for directions?" she shouted as she stared at the large man who had stopped her with just such an offer.

The man grinned. "No, but I wouldn't want a pretty thing like you to get lost in a big city like this."

"I think it's you who needs to get lost!"

"Who's gonna make me? *Him?*" The man glanced at Aaslo. "He doesn't look too keen about standing up for you, or maybe he just knows what's good for him." The man reached out to tug on one of Teza's short curls, and she abruptly walloped him with her pack. The man fell backward onto his rear. Before he could even sit up, a sword was at his throat.

Aaslo scowled at the sword wielder. He hadn't seen the man approach and neither did he have a desire to see him again. Captain Lopin leaned over the offender and said, "You'd best be on your way. The good forester here doesn't ruffle easily, but when he does, you'd not want to be at the end of *his* blade."

The man looked up at Lopin, noting the palace uniform, then looked back to see several more of the royal guard waiting across the square at the entrance to the Forester's Haven.

Teza looked at Aaslo. "You're really a forester?"

The big man on the ground crawled away from Lopin's blade, then got to his feet and took off down an alley. Lopin sheathed his sword and approached Aaslo, sparing a nod for Teza. He said, "For a man who rails against those who choose not to fight, you sure avoid it often enough. Would you have come to the woman's aid?"

Aaslo crossed his arms. "If she'd needed aid, she'd have said so."

Teza turned and harrumphed in agreement with a nod toward the captain.

Lopin looked at her again, nodded, then turned back to Aaslo. "I came to deliver your belongings you left at the palace."

Aaslo rubbed his stubble and mused, "The captain of the royal guard is running errands?"

Lopin tilted his head. "Not as such."

"I thought not. I left nothing at the palace that belongs to me."

Lopin's gaze flicked to Teza before he glanced back to Aaslo. "I think more at the palace belongs to you than you realize. Still, your clothes and a few other items have been delivered to your abode. The queen desires your company this evening. Shall I inform her that you will be joining her for *dinner*?"

"*Ask him, Aaslo.*"

"That depends. Do you know how to get to the Citadel of Magi?"

The captain raised a brow. "No, only the magi are privy to that information."

Teza suddenly stomped Aaslo's foot. "I told you I would take you! Do you think me a liar?"

Aaslo turned and chanced her furious gaze. "I think I just met you, and it's awfully convenient that you know how to get to a place to which no one else is able to direct me."

Teza raised a finger and opened her mouth to retort, then stopped. She dropped her hand and turned back to the guard with a shrug. "Touché."

Lopin glanced between them. "I see. You have found yourself a guide, but I think it will be for naught. No one will help you with this mission. You should go back to your forest—*after* you see the queen."

Aaslo stepped past the captain. "I'm not going back to the palace."

Lopin and Teza both followed at his sides. "It is not advisable to reject the queen."

"She told me what she really wants. I am doing it."

"What do you expect me to tell her?"

"Tell her the truth. Tell her I already left. Tell her I'll see her once she's safe again. Tell her I'm a scoundrel that ran off with another woman. Tell her whatever you want. I'm leaving in the morning, and I'll likely not survive to deal with the consequences. For your sake, you'd best tell her something pleasing."

"Wait," said Teza. "Are we talking about the *Queen of Uyan*? Why does she want to see *you*?"

Aaslo glanced at her and muttered, "She hopes I'll complete a task for her."

"Oh, *that's* why you want to go to the citadel. I'm sure she could have provided you with a guide."

"Perhaps, but not one that could be trusted to resist stabbing me in the back."

"I'm not sure this one won't."

Teza smiled. "I would never do that. If I stabbed someone, I'd want them to see it coming."

"You attract bloodthirsty people, Aaslo."

Lopin stopped when Aaslo and Teza arrived at the gate of the Forester's Haven. He said, "For what it's worth, I respect your decision to act, as misguided as it is. I think you'll do more harm than good, though. The king will do what's best for our people. I also think you're an idiot for rejecting the queen, but at least I know you're not using her for your own gain." The man shook his head with disappointment, then rejoined his men and left.

Teza turned to Aaslo as he opened the gate. "What exactly is your relationship with the queen?"

"It's not important," he said. "When can I expect you in the morning?"

"When you wake me up, I guess. I'll warn you, I'm not a morning person. Be prepared to get a fist to the face if you try to wake me before sunrise."

Aaslo paused. "You think you're staying here?"

"Where else am I supposed to stay?"

"I don't know—wherever you live? Don't you need to get your things?"

"I was staying in the attic above the tavern where you got me fired, and everything I own is in this bag. All my belongings from the academy were either sent directly to my parents' home or stolen by the cad who brought me here."

"Picking up another stray? You feed them once . . ."

Aaslo said, "First of all, I did not get you fired. Secondly, this is not an inn."

"Good," she said as she walked past him. "You know how I hate people."

CHAPTER 14

MYROPA FOLLOWED AASLO AND THE FAILED MAGE INTO THE FORESTER'S Haven. The girl was a mess, and Myropa once again cursed the Fates for their devious plots. She knew it was no coincidence that Aaslo and the girl had met. The tavern had not even been Aaslo's first choice. Myropa wondered if the man from the first would have needed to die if Aaslo hadn't initially chosen that tavern. The Fates were cutting strings and tying them together, and Myropa could not begin to understand their designs, but she was sure it had to do with the prophecy. Had they decided to use the forester to bring it to fruition? She admired him for his determination in the face of certain failure, but she wished he would just go back to his forest and spend his remaining days with his father. She was also disturbed by the fact that he continued to carry his friend's head. He seemed to think he needed it, but she worried it represented a touch of madness.

She wondered why Aaslo hadn't gone to the queen. She knew they had enjoyed each other's company the previous night, having accidentally popped in on him at an inopportune time. She had then spent the rest of the night trying to forget the image as she paced outside the chamber, keeping an eye out for vights. Myropa cared little for the queen, since she had set her sights on Aaslo, but she liked this wreck of a woman even less. Was he attracted to Teza? Had he stayed for her, or was he worried that she would run off and he'd lose his guide? Myropa figured the young woman was likely to hang around for a few days and then rob him blind.

"Sir Forester, I am glad to see you have returned in time for dinner," said Galobar upon opening the door, "and you brought another guest! This is wonderful. My Maralee would have been pleased to have so many visitors. Your young friends are in the back. I knew they wouldn't abandon you. They're seeing to your horse and replanting my herbs. I found him—the horse, I mean—munching on the plants this afternoon. I have plenty more than I need, though. I often sell the surplus at the market. Oh, listen to me rambling again. I do apologize, Sir Forester. I've become addled in my age and forgotten my training."

"It's fine, Galobar. You're a gracious host," said Aaslo.

Myropa smiled. Despite Aaslo's gruff nature, he had learned some manners.

"Host, Sir Forester? No, no. This is *your* home—well, yours and the other foresters'. I am only happy to serve."

Teza turned to Aaslo with her fists on her hips. Myropa bristled. The girl was going to berate him again. Teza said, "You don't seem the kind of man to have servants, and I wouldn't have pegged you as someone to be revered."

Aaslo frowned at the girl. Myropa wasn't sure if he was at a loss for words or just choosing them carefully. Finally, he said, "I'm not." Then he turned toward the stairs and took them two at a time.

Galobar turned back to Teza. "Mistress . . . ?"

Teza's glare shot daggers at Aaslo's retreating form, but she smiled pleasantly when she turned to the old man. "My name is Teza. It's a pleasure to meet you, Master Galobar."

"No, no," he said with a wag of his finger. "Galobar will be fine. Will you be staying with us, Mistress Teza?"

Teza dropped her bag on the floor, then plopped onto the seat at the table. "Yep, I'm traveling with Aaslo. We're leaving in the morning, I think."

Galobar's mouth twisted, and he looked out the window toward the courtyard just as Peck and Mory came tromping through the door. "Please, wipe your feet on the mat, if you don't mind!"

Both thieves looked surprised but slowly backed across the threshold to do as the man said. Myropa had witnessed Aaslo's meeting with these young men and found them to be quite entertaining. The older one, Peck, swaggered into the kitchen as if he were the master of the house. He straightened his velvety jacket and smoothed back his hair, then leaned one elbow on the table next to Teza. His smile was illuminating. Myropa liked the young man. "Greetings, lovely lady. To what do I owe the pleasure?"

Teza smiled sweetly, then shoved Peck's elbow off the table, causing him to stumble and strike his shoulder on its edge. She said, "What makes you think I'm *lovely*? You don't know anything about me, and I'll be perfectly happy for it to stay that way."

Peck straightened and rubbed his bruised shoulder. He looked at Teza with surprise and an overly dramatic sense of hurt. "My lady, whatever did I do to earn your ire? Please tell me so that I may make amends."

Teza's smirk turned to a pout—or was it a frown? Myropa wasn't sure. She begrudgingly admitted to herself that the girl was pretty no matter her expression. Teza said, "I know your type, and I'd like to keep my purse, thank you very much."

Peck glanced at Mory, who was still standing in the doorway with his shoulders hunched and his hands in his pockets. Mory shrugged and gave Teza a half-hearted smile. Peck swallowed and said, "All right, fair enough, but that's not who we are anymore—not unless Aaslo wants us to be. We're his men now."

Teza turned to face them both, crossed her arms, and said, "So you didn't steal *anything* today? Not *one* thing?"

Peck and Mory shared a glance, and Peck rubbed the back of his head. "Well, we got hungry at midday. . . ."

From out of nowhere, Galobar smacked Peck. "I'll have none of that, now. You serve the forester, and you'll do so honestly. He's a reputable man. There is plenty of food here in the kitchen. And if you think to steal anything from the Forester's Haven, you'll be dealing with worse than a knock to the noggin. There's enchantments in this place that'll put a curse on you."

Mory whimpered. "I don't wanna be cursed, Peck!"

Peck frowned at the young man. Then his expression softened, and he patted Mory's shoulder. "Don't worry about that. We haven't taken anything that wasn't offered, and we don't plan to, all right?"

Mory nodded, then looked at Teza as if seeking approval. Teza rolled her eyes and huffed as she returned to her seat. She turned to Galobar and said, "So where am I staying?"

Myropa turned as Aaslo tromped down the stairs gripping a piece of paper, a pen, and an inkwell. He had a map tube hanging from a strap over his shoulder. She shivered when he walked through her while crossing to the table, not because she felt anything but because she still found the experience creepy.

"All right," he said. "Where is the citadel?"

Teza laughed. "If I tell you how to get there, you'll leave without me."

Aaslo sighed. "Well, at least give me the general direction and how long it'll take. We require supplies, and I need to know what kind."

She pursed her lips and crossed her arms as she sat back in her seat. "It's east."

"I know that," said Aaslo, "but how *far* east?"

Teza shrugged. "I don't know. I came here by evergate."

Aaslo slapped a hand on the table. "You said you could tell me how to get there."

With a smile and a nod, Teza said, "I can—once we get to Copedrian. That's in Pashtigon."

"So, it's near Copedrian?"

"No, but I know how to get there from Copedrian. How long will it take to get there?"

After a questioning glance at the others, Aaslo pulled the map from the tube, then rolled it out on the table. Myropa peered over his shoulder at the map. It looked like it was probably very nice, but aside from her fateful move to the city, she hadn't been much of a traveler in life, and she hadn't needed maps in death.

"It looks like it'll probably be a few weeks' ride," said Aaslo.

Teza said, "Since neither of us knows the land, it might be worth joining a caravan. It'd be safer."

Myropa would have agreed if she didn't know what was coming.

"No," said Aaslo. "We'll ride alone. Considering my task, I think it would be safer."

Teza tilted her head and looked at him curiously. "Is it dangerous, this task of yours?"

Aaslo met Teza's gaze. "Perhaps not at the moment, but it may become dangerous." Although she respected him for it, Myropa thought it a mistake for him to warn the girl. Teza nodded, seemingly unaffected by the news. Aaslo abruptly mumbled, "Will you please be quiet? I'm trying to think."

"Sir Forester! I must protest," said Galobar. "That is no way to speak to a young woman."

Teza laughed. "It's okay. He's not talking to me."

Galobar and the thieves shared a look of confusion, since no one else had been speaking. Myropa realized what Teza had already known. Aaslo was speaking to Mathias again. A chill swirled in her stomach. She had a sinking feeling that Aaslo was losing his mind.

After a few minutes of silence, Peck ventured, "So, we're going somewhere?"

Aaslo looked up at the young man. "No, she and I are going. You two are staying in Tyellí—or don't. It's up to you, so long as you don't go with us."

Peck appeared genuinely hurt, and Mory looked scared. "But we're your men," said Peck.

"Look, I don't want to attract attention. A single man and a woman traveling together are no one important, and they probably don't have anything worth stealing. Two more and it looks like we have guards."

Peck nodded. "I guess I get that. We could follow you, though. It wouldn't look like we're together."

"Look at yourselves. If you saw the two of you riding alone cross-country, would you think yourselves targets? We've already established that you're not good at protecting yourselves. It's too dangerous."

Mory's voice shook as he said, "But, if you leave, Jago will come after us."

Teza lurched to her feet and shoved her hands onto her hips. "You two work for *Jago*?" Then she turned on Aaslo. "You should make them leave. Jago's bad news."

"I already took care of Jago," said Aaslo. He glanced toward Galobar. "How would you feel about taking on a couple of apprentices?"

Galobar raised his brow and then looked at the two thieves. "Yes, I suppose that would do. I should have taken one on long ago but never got around to it." To the thieves, he said, "There's much to learn about foresters. I'll take you in if you're willing to learn and work. You must vow to carry on the calling once I've passed."

"So, we'll be serving Aaslo?" said Peck.

Galobar said, "Not just Aaslo but all the foresters."

Aaslo grunted. "You'll likely never meet another, so it should be an easy job."

Myropa felt a tug at her core. She sighed just as the luminescent tether snapped into place. Somewhere not far from the Forester's Haven, someone needed to be collected.

A ASLO RUBBED THE SOFT FABRIC BETWEEN HIS FINGERS. HE HAD NO USE for such fine clothes, especially while traveling. The master of the wardrobe could have easily adjusted them to fit another man, and they could have been delivered by any servant or runner. Aaslo knew that these were not just clothes, though. They were a gift from the queen. He knew she carried no love for him. Any attraction or desire she felt was born of desperation. At least he would have something decent to wear to the Council of Magi. He ran his finger over the embroidered edge, then shoved the pile into his travel pack.

After surveying the room one last time, he turned toward the stairs and then vacated the building. Galobar had prepared a hearty breakfast and said his farewells long before dawn, and Peck and Mory were still abed. Teza made her distaste for rising at the early hour quite clear when she smacked him in the head with her pillow for waking her.

Aaslo reached the end of the walkway leading from the haven to the road and could tell by Teza's stormy visage that she was fuming again. He stopped in front of her, and she did not leave him waiting.

"A donkey?" she growled. "You want me to ride a *donkey*?"

"Mages ride donkeys," Aaslo said.

"*No*, we don't. Whatever gave you that idea?"

Aaslo shrugged as he strapped his belongings to the pack mule that was already laden with other supplies. "I don't know. I must've read it in a story."

"Well, I don't want to ride a donkey."

He turned to her. "Look, there weren't any horses for sale at a decent price. We're in Tyellí. Workers use mules and donkeys. The horses in this city are bred for show. Besides, we'll probably be riding over rough terrain. The donkey will be better."

Teza pursed her lips into a pout and eyed the donkey. "I guess she's not *that much* smaller than your horse. And, she's kind of attractive for a donkey. Fine, but I get to name her."

Aaslo tipped his chin and said, "Thank you for being reasonable."

Teza's short curls bobbed as she shook her head. "I'm always reasonable." She turned and mounted the donkey with ease as she said, "I think I'll name her Aaslina."

"She named her donkey after you."

Aaslo said, "I don't know if I should be offended or flattered."

Teza smirked, then leaned over the donkey's mane to stage-whisper into her large ear. "Don't take it personally, Aaslina. He's just surly because his horse is so ugly."

Aaslo mounted Dolt and said, "I don't care if he's ugly. It's his idiocy that grates on me." Dolt must have been listening, because he seemed to think it was the perfect time to lie on the ground.

Teza laughed and said, "You can't blame him. He's just a horse."

"He does it on purpose," Aaslo grumbled as he tugged on Dolt's bridle until the horse relented and stood.

"You're finally developing an imagination."

"I'm not imagining it. There's something off about him."

Teza nudged Aaslina closer and said, "I believe you, but I'm pretty sure the source is his rider."

Aaslo ignored Mathias's hoot of laughter as he mounted again and tried to turn Dolt down the road. Dolt refused to turn left again and instead spun to the right, becoming entangled in the mule's lead line. Teza laughed heartily as Aaslo dismounted and worked to free the beasts. She and Mathias echoed each other's taunts, but Aaslo chose not to heed anything they said. Instead, he listened to the noises of the city, mentally transforming them into forest sounds. The creaking of carts morphed into the crashing of boughs, shouting workers were the warning and mating calls of wild animals, and the city's underlying drone became the rustle of wind and water. It was a task, but he eventually settled into a peaceful place, albeit a smelly one. He briefly wondered why the mages didn't purify the air better, then realized most of them were probably used to the putridity.

The air was more pleasant outside the city, although the bold sweetness of evergreens and cool earthiness of rich, moist soil to which Aaslo was accustomed had been replaced by the spice of dried grass and delicate nectar of wildflowers. Aaslo and Teza rode in silence through the morning. They broke for lunch under the shade of a lone tree.

"So, why'd you leave the forest?" said Teza as she lounged against the tree's trunk.

"A friend of mine had business in Tyellí. He couldn't go, so I went in his stead."

"The friend you lost? He must have been some friend. I didn't think foresters *ever* left the forest." A heavy stone dropped in the pit of Aaslo's stomach. She said, "Actually, I never thought about foresters having friends—besides other foresters, I suppose. It sounded to me like you're a bunch of recluses." Aaslo took a swig from his waterskin but said nothing. "If there's trouble, can you protect us?"

He shrugged. "I guess that depends on how much trouble. Why?"

"You seem to be expecting it, and you're running with thieves. Are you up to something illegal? Are you a smuggler? A grifter?"

"I'm just a forester. I'm going to the Council of Magi to request assistance. There are some who would prefer I didn't."

"Why would anyone deny assistance to a forester? No one wants the forests to die."

He glanced at her, then turned his gaze to the never-ending prairie. "Some do."

Teza narrowed her eyes at him. "Are we under attack by another kingdom? Are they trying to destroy our resources? That's why the queen wanted to see you, isn't it? You're carrying a secret message because they don't want to cause a panic."

Aaslo scratched his scruffy jaw. "Something like that."

"Why you?"

"She's got you there."

Aaslo stood and stuffed the remainder of his meal into his saddlebag. "I was the only one willing to take on the task."

Teza did the same and mounted her donkey as she said, "That's strange. Aren't the soldiers and knights supposed to do that kind of thing?"

"She doesn't think you're up to the task."

"Maybe I'm not, but it has to get done." Once he was mounted, Aaslo turned in his saddle to look back at Teza. "Why are you so eager to go with me?"

"I'm not," she said. "At first, I just needed to get out of Tyellí, especially since you got me fired. It turns out you're headed toward my home, though."

As Dolt began plodding down the road, Aaslo said, "You're ready to face your family?" When she didn't answer, he glanced back to find her lost in her own thoughts, and by her expression, they weren't good.

On the fourth day, it started to rain. Aaslo had hoped that Teza's presence would allow for a more enjoyable ride, since he'd have someone to talk with besides a severed head. She was unusual, which he found interesting. He had hoped Mathias would be quieter with her around, particularly if the voice was truly a manifestation of his own insanity. He had wondered if he only heard the voice out of guilt and the fact that he was alone outside the forest. Mathias was relentless, though. While Aaslo wanted only to forget the incessant drizzle that soaked him to the core, Mathias sang songs about it, most of them designed to implore the gods for more. He also told stories, all of them about tragedy and heartbreak, and most of them took place in the rainy or winter seasons.

Teza's disdain for the weather was evident in her every word, and she had developed a sniffle. By the time they reached Yarding near the eastern border of Uyan, Aaslo decided they needed a respite.

Yarding was one of the largest cities in Uyan. It was a major hub for trade, and its proximity to the Tisiguey River provided indirect access to the Endric Ocean. Merchant houses, countinghouses, banks, and legal offices lined the main road through the city. Aaslo glanced down the side roads as they progressed toward the city center. Craftsmen, smiths, carpenters, and the like occupied one road, while shops and merchant stalls of the *affordable* variety were available on the next. Beyond that were two streets of taverns, pubs, and inns. Aaslo stopped in front of the second inn after they turned onto a side street.

"We shouldn't stay here," said Teza.

Aaslo looked over at her. She was shivering, her lips held a slight blue tinge, and her nose was almost as red as her watery eyes. He said, "Why not?"

"This is the kind of place that charges too much for subpar rooms. It's close to the main thoroughfare, and they use too much bright paint."

"You have something against bright colors?"

She pointed to the patio cover that was leaking almost as much as the sky. "They use it to cover the rot."

Aaslo looked at the building again with a more critical eye. It was difficult to be discerning when all he wanted was to get dry in front of a warm fire. The shutters hung awkwardly, nails stuck up from the floorboards on the steps and patio, and the front door didn't completely close. "I see your point."

As they rode, the buildings became progressively worse. Aaslo turned to Teza. "I think we should try to find a better part of town." Teza nodded but said nothing. Aaslo thought she seemed sicker than she had the last time he had looked, only minutes before. Just as he tugged Dolt to turn around, a woman came running out of a doorway and up the steps from a sublevel.

"Please!" she screamed as she tugged at his pant leg. "Please help me! There's a fire," she said, pointing at the smoke that had just begun spewing from an open window.

"A damsel in distress! This is your chance to impress her."

"Who?" said Aaslo.

The woman shook her head. "No, it's not a person. It's my home!"

Aaslo sniffed the air. He looked down at the woman and said, "You'd best go back inside and rid yourself of that brew before your whole house fills with smoke." The woman's pleading expression soured, and Aaslo led the pack mule back the way they had come. Teza was still staring at the woman as he passed.

"Now she thinks you're a monster."

"What does it matter?" he mumbled.

Teza sneezed. It wasn't a dainty chirrup but a full-bodied call to the god of strength and power. She wiped her nose and said, "I'm surprised you caught that." Pedestrians lurched out of the way to accommodate her donkey beside his horse in the narrow lane.

"Why?" he said.

"I didn't think that you, being a recluse and all, would recognize a con like that."

He said, "Who do you think invented the concoction she was using?"

"What do you mean?"

"We call it smoke oil. It doesn't usually burn hot enough to catch fire to green wood, but as you saw, it creates a good amount of smoke. We use it to rid the trees of pests."

"You're boring her, Aaslo. Women don't want to hear about bugs and smoke."

"She's smart, and she does," Aaslo muttered. Then, to Teza, he said, "A woman might burn it in her house if it has an infestation, but that was obviously not the case."

"You keep talking like that, and I might actually start to believe you're a forester."

Aaslo smirked. "I'm still not convinced you're a mage."

Teza sneezed again. "I'm not either right now."

"*She doesn't look so good. If she dies, are you going to take her head too? It'd be nice to have company.*"

"She's not going to die," Aaslo muttered.

"I might," said Teza. Then she fell off her donkey.

Aaslo jumped from the saddle and lifted Teza's head out of the mud. As he wiped her face, he realized she was burning with fever. People called for him to move the animals when the roadway became more congested. He tied the donkey's reins to the pack mule and then hefted Teza into the saddle. After securing her to the creature's back, he stopped to ask a city guard where he could find decent lodging. He then led the beasts by foot toward the nicer side of the city. The rain started falling harder as he reached the porch of an inn with a blue door. He doubted there was more than one inn with a blue door, unless it was the fashion in Yarding. He figured the guard would have described it differently if that had been the case.

Two young women emerged from a gate beneath an overhang to one side of the inn. The two looked to be of the same age, and they were strikingly similar in appearance. Although they were feminine, both were dressed in men's clothing and had their hair stuffed beneath brimmed caps.

The first said, "Greetings, sir. I'm Dia—"

"—and I'm Mia," said the second.

"Welcome to the Silver Sky Inn," said Dia.

"Would you like a room?" said Mia.

"They're pleasantly accommodated—"

"—and clean."

"We have space in the stable—"

"—and hot baths are readily available."

Aaslo's gaze bounced between the two as they finished each other's sentences. Finally, he said, "How much?"

"You'll have to take that up—"

"—with the mistress, sir."

Dia nodded toward the silhouette of a woman standing in the doorway where the blue door stood open. Aaslo handed the reins to one of the young women, knowing he would never be able to tell the two apart, and untied the unconscious Teza. At their concerned expressions, he said, "She's sick." Then he turned and carried Teza up the steps to the porch, stomping his feet to remove as much of the mud as possible and eliciting a nod of approval from the mistress.

"Greetings, Mistress," he said. "I bring shade in my heart."

"Just talk normal, Aaslo. No one speaks forester."

The portly woman pushed her spectacles to the bridge of her nose as her head turned upward to look at him. Her curious grey eyes stood out over rosy cheeks, and her silver-streaked auburn hair glimmered in the warm light from the inn. She said, "Good afternoon, sir. I'm Mistress Nova. I've never heard such a greeting. I'm afraid I do not know the proper response."

Aaslo glanced past her to the warm, dry common room. He said, "If you are offering hospitality, you might say, 'I have cool water to lift your spirits.'"

The woman tilted her head toward the street. "Seems a bit redundant on a day such as this."

"She has you there."

Aaslo granted the woman a rare smile. "A keen observation. Perhaps an invitation to your hearth, then?"

The woman smirked, then said, "We have hospitality aplenty, but it'll cost you. This is a business, after all." She paused to survey the unconscious woman in Aaslo's arms. "She is unwell?"

He briefly wondered if Mistress Nova would put them out if she learned Teza was sick, then decided they'd be best served by the truth. "We've been riding in the rain for some time. She's taken ill."

The woman brazenly stepped forward and placed a palm on Aaslo's forehead. "You seem well enough."

He said, "I'm used to working in all kinds of weather. She is not."

"Very well. Bring her inside where it's dry, and we'll discuss the price." As they walked through the entryway toward the front desk, the woman said, "Normally we wouldn't have any rooms on such short notice, but travelers are often delayed by the rain. Now we're just hoping to fill the empty rooms before curfew. How long will you be staying?"

"Curfew? Why do they have curfew?"

"I don't know," he muttered toward the floor. He looked back at Mistress Nova. "We had originally planned for one night. Now it seems we'll have to wait until she's well enough to travel."

"I should say so. Shall I send for the apothecary?"

Aaslo looked down at Teza's flushed face and damp brow. By the amount of heat radiating off of her, he knew not all of the moisture on her skin was due to the rain. He said, "Yes, that would be ideal."

Mistress Nova held out a key on a chain that dangled from a wooden figure of a purple horse. "Take her on up, then." She motioned toward the stairs on the far side of the common room. "The door to your room is painted with the image of a purple horse."

Aaslo shifted Teza so that he could take the key. "The cost?"

Nova made a shooing motion with her hands. "You get her dry and settled in a warm bed, and we'll discuss that later. I need to send for the apothecary before he closes shop. The girls'll be up shortly with your things."

As he turned toward the stairwell, a man and a woman walked through the door.

"Look, it's some of our new friends."

Aaslo's shoulders tensed, and he clenched his jaw upon noticing that the man wore the same strange white and black attire that the foreigner named Verus had worn. The woman's was similar in style but all black. Both wore their hair long and straight. Where the man wore a sword at one hip, the woman carried a baton with a brilliant red gemstone the size of a walnut atop it. Most remarkable, though, was the fact that both were completely dry.

They gazed into the common room like foxes in a henhouse. The woman drummed her pointed, black-lacquered nails on her baton, then turned to the man with a sour look. They muttered to each other in a foreign tongue, and by the heated tone, it seemed they were arguing.

Aaslo met Mistress Nova's gaze with a warning and shook his head. Then he turned toward the stairs. As he crossed the nearly empty common room, he heard her politely inform the newcomers that all of their rooms were occupied. The foreign woman had the nerve to suggest the mistress ask the other patrons if they would be willing to part with their accommodations in exchange for a fee. When Mistress Nova rejected the proposal and sent them on their way, Aaslo was relieved. Still, he was disturbed that the foreigners already had a presence in the farthest reaches of Uyan.

He carried Teza up the stairs to the room, which he found to be quaint but clean, and he was glad that it had two beds, even if they were fairly small. He laid Teza on the floor so as not to wet the bed, then stood back and stared at her. He muttered, "What am I to do now?"

"She's sick. Help her."

"She needs dry clothes."

"Just take the wet ones off and put her in the bed."

"I should remove her clothes?"

Aaslo jumped at a knock at the door. Glad to put off making a decision, he pulled it open. Mistress Nova stood there with her fists on her hips. She narrowed her eyes at him and said, "Now why am I turning away paying customers?" Then she noticed Teza on the floor and swept past him with indignation. "Why would you leave the young woman on the floor sopping wet?"

"I didn't want to get the bed wet, and I was still considering how to change her without causing offense."

Mistress Nova pursed her lips. "You two are not *together*? Well, no, it wouldn't be appropriate, and I appreciate that you're not the kind of man to take advantage. I've already sent for the apothecary." She waved toward the changing screen in the corner. "You get changed and then go on down to the common room to get some food. I'll take care of her."

Before Aaslo could respond, the twins tromped into the room lugging his and Teza's belongings. He thanked them and then riffled through his pack to retrieve a change of clothes. Nothing was particularly *fresh*, but he kept the pack well-oiled, so its contents were mostly dry. When he stepped from behind the screen, Mistress Nova wrinkled her nose and said, "I see we need to have your clothes laundered as well."

"Seriously. You smell worse than a corpse."

"How would you know?" he grumbled.

"My nose is one of the few body parts I still possess."

"I'm not blind," said Mistress Nova.

Aaslo glanced down at himself and nodded. "Yes, I see your point."

"All right," she said. "Just pile everything by the door, and one of the girls'll fetch it while you're gone. I'll see to this one's things. It'd be best if I know her name in case she wakes."

"Teza," he said. "And she's a bit temperamental, so if she does wake, you might want to stand back."

"Thanks for the warning," the woman said as she began unbuttoning Teza's overcoat.

Aaslo tromped down the stairs to the common room. He had most of the tables to choose from, so he claimed the one nearest the hearth. A couple of ladies and their gentlemen escorts were chatting animatedly at a table in the corner nearest him. Another table was occupied by an older gentleman with an oiled mustache wearing an ornate coat and a golden scarf tied into a giant bow that flopped over his chest. The man glanced his way, and Aaslo quickly averted his gaze lest the man mistake his observations for an invitation to converse. One of the twins passed by his table, dropping a plate and mug in front of him without pausing for questions or requests.

"She probably doesn't want to smell you for longer than she must."

"Food smells good," Aaslo mumbled.

It looked good, too, so he ate it without complaint. He knew he should employ the dining etiquette taught to him by Magdelay, but he was hungry and tired, so he inhaled it. After finishing, he sat wondering how long he should wait until he returned to his room. Although he didn't make a habit of eavesdropping, the conversation of the group sitting near him became louder and heated.

A brunette woman in a dark grey dinner gown had the kind of voice that grated on a person's ears and carried to fill the room. "I am quite dissatisfied with Antilius, our new wizard. I know he is young, but he cannot seem to do the simplest tasks. Why, the other day, I requested he retrieve a case of mountainberry wine from the north, and he failed to even operate the evergate!"

The bearded gentleman seated next to the second woman said, "That is strange. Just yesterday, our sorcerer could not get the third evergate in the southwest to respond. Perhaps they are temporarily out of service for repairs?"

The brunette huffed. "Well, if that is the case, I suppose I should not have been so hard on Antilius. I do hope the matter will be resolved swiftly."

"I am sure it is of the utmost priority," said the second woman, whose auburn hair matched her dress. In a moderating tone, she said, "The magi understand the importance of the evergates. If not for them, we would wait weeks or months for news and goods."

"They should build more," said the brunette. "Even with a reservation, the queue in Tyellí is sometimes hours long."

"I think they do it on purpose," said the blond gentleman next to her. "They keep the demand high, so they can charge more and keep us dependent on their services."

"I am sure that is not the case," said the auburn-haired woman. "I doubt they are so simple to construct. Besides, we would still be dependent on their services since none of us could hope to operate one."

"Which is also part of their plan," said the blond man. "They could find a way for seculars to operate the evergates, but the magi keep the gates to themselves to retain power over us."

"They would have power over us regardless," said the bearded man. "The Council of Magi prevents them from exercising it in a meaningful way."

"*Meaningful*, ha!" said the blond. "You mean enslaving us."

The brunette woman turned to her escort. "Now, now. I hold little love for the magi, but that seems a bit extreme. I may not like *them*, but I enjoy the amenities they provide."

"Which is precisely what they want. Mark my words," said the blond with raised finger, "a war is coming, and those magi will destroy us all."

"Is that so?" said an older man with a deep, gruff voice.

Aaslo glanced up from where he had been resting his eyes on the table. A thin man stood at the entrance to the common room, near where the group was seated. He wore a long black coat with gold buttons and a golden amulet in the shape of an inverted raindrop. The ensemble identified him as a magus healer. The man's pale grey gaze was sharp beneath bushy grey eyebrows. He removed his wide-brimmed hat and bowed to the ladies. He turned to the blond man and said, "Since you feel so strongly about our intentions, I expect you will not be requiring the services of me or my brethren at any time."

The brunette lurched to her feet, forcing the men to follow by custom. She said, "Please, Magus, you must excuse my husband. I am afraid he has consumed too much wine and has spoken out of turn."

The healer said, "I believe the problem is not that he has spoken out of turn but that he has spoken from his heart, and his heart is filled with contempt for my people. I hope you consider that the world would be much harder without us, just as we recognize that it would be harder without seculars."

"Yes, of course," said the brunette, glancing at her husband, whose jaw was set in stubborn defiance. The woman said, "I find no fault in your logic," and with a clenched smile and a nudge for her husband, added, "I am sure my husband agrees."

When the man said nothing, the healer shook his head, then turned toward the stairs. Aaslo followed after him, ignoring the mutterings of the people who retook their seats in the corner. He knew that some people resented the magi, but to think that those with magic would wage war on seculars was ridiculous. The Council of Magi was the oldest governing body in the world. If they had not organized a hostile takeover already, he doubted they ever would. The man was right, though. A war was coming—just not against the magi.

Aaslo arrived at the room just as Mistress Nova was greeting the healer. Both turned to him. He said, "Greetings, Magus. I am Aaslo. May your path be blessed with thick boughs and deep roots."

The old healer and the mistress both stared at him in confusion. Then the healer said, "Yes, ah, greetings to you as well. I'm Mage Soter. I've lived a long time and never heard such a greeting."

"He's a bit of a strange one," said Mistress Nova, narrowing her eyes at Aaslo, "and he still owes me some answers, but the girl is the priority at the moment."

Aaslo and Mage Soter followed Mistress Nova into the room to find Teza snuggled under a pile of blankets in the bed farthest from the window. Her face was flushed, with sweat beading on her brow. She coughed a few times but appeared to be unconscious. Without warning, the pile of dirty laundry by the door slid across the floor. Then a small pillow from the other bed flew at Aaslo's head, only to collide with the ceiling when he ducked.

The frown Mistress Nova offered Aaslo was filled with rebuke. "You didn't tell me she's a magus. It nearly gave me a heart attack when things started flying around the room on their own."

Aaslo held his hands up and kept a roving eye on the loose objects in the room as he replied, "I'm truly sorry, Mistress Nova. I didn't realize that would happen. I've never seen her perform magic." He glanced at the healer and said, "She's been banned from using it."

The healer's brow stretched toward the ceiling. "Why is that?"

"She said she was expelled from the academy for cheating."

Soter stroked his dry lips as he looked more closely at Teza. "I see. I remember the story from not so long ago."

"You heard of it?"

With a nod, Soter said, "Expulsion is rare and even more so for a future healer. That is the kind of news that gets around. A shame, really. The whole event was blown out of proportion, but the girl was too stubborn to make amends."

Aaslo looked at him in surprise. "You mean she could have returned?"

"Of course. The magus academy wouldn't destroy the life of a hopeful young healer for such a minor infraction. Suspension, extra duties, repetition of the school year—those are the usual punishments in such cases. I think this one, though, would not relent."

Aaslo glanced at the unconscious Teza and nodded slowly. Suddenly, he was struck in the back of the head by one of his extra boots. He rubbed the sore spot and said, "Yes, I can see that. Even when she's unconscious she's difficult."

The healer chuckled, then pulled a chair over beside Teza's bed.

Aaslo turned to Mistress Nova. "I thought you were sending for an apothecary."

Soter said, "He was out on a call, so I came in his stead. It's a good thing, too. A secular could not have dealt with this problem. It looks like she's stricken with a case of selkesh fever."

"Selkesh fever? I've not heard of it," said Aaslo.

"Is it contagious?" said Mistress Nova.

"Nothing to worry over for the two of you. It only affects magi. I'll need to inoculate myself as well, now that I have been exposed. Still, it is unlikely the apothecary would have recognized it, and he could not have treated her even if he had."

"What are the symptoms?" said Aaslo. "How do you recognize it?"

"Well, it looks as you see, much like a cold or flu." He pointed to some faint, barely visible purple lines that stretched like branches up Teza's neck and around her hairline. "We call these marks *dowdry branches*. Their presence is indicative of selkesh fever."

"I didn't see them before," said Aaslo.

"You wouldn't have," said Soter. "The lines only appear when the subject is using magic. They would have been evident long before the illness progressed this far but for her ban."

As the healer ministered to Teza, Mistress Nova turned to Aaslo. "I had a bad feeling about those two foreigners that came in earlier. You seemed to know something about them."

Aaslo considered how much he should tell the woman. If the purpose of his quest was to save people, it would best be served by warning them of the dangers.

"That's not a good idea. They'll panic. The kingdoms will fall into chaos."

"I won't tell them that part," Aaslo mumbled.

Mistress Nova crossed her arms. "Tell us what?"

Aaslo sighed. "Those people are dangerous. I believe they're slowly invading the kingdom. I came from the north. The first night away from home, my companions and I were attacked by people like them. They killed my best friend."

Mistress Nova looked sincere as she said, "I'm very sorry to hear about your friend. I know the pain of loss. But what makes you think they're *all* enemies? Maybe you just happened to run across a few bad ones."

Aaslo glanced toward Mage Soter, who had turned to listen. "I was with the high sorceress at the time. Although I cannot discuss the details, she confirmed the threat."

"The *high sorceress*?" said Mistress Nova.

Soter stood and walked closer. "Describe her," he said.

"Why?" Aaslo said with a groan.

"Because I'm not convinced you know her."

Aaslo said, "I appreciate your help with Teza, and I'll pay you for your services, but I don't care if you believe me."

Mage Soter said, "The Citadel of Magi was recently attacked by a group of foreigners. Word of it came through the fifth evergate days ago. The news was . . . disturbing. It wasn't something I wanted to believe."

"I hadn't heard that, but it's not surprising," said Aaslo. He nodded toward Teza. "She's my guide to the citadel."

"I see," said the old man as he returned to his chair. He appeared dejected and deflated. He said, "I've known Mistress Nova for a while, and you already seem to know more than you're saying. I will tell you something I probably shouldn't." He nodded toward Teza. "For her sake. The magi have been recalled."

"What do you mean?" said Mistress Nova.

Soter looked at her with aged grey eyes. "We have received orders to report to the citadel—*all* of us. I thought my place was here, helping the people. If what you say is true, young man, a war is brewing, and it seems this is where we'd be needed—amongst the people. I don't understand why they'd send us elsewhere—unless it's already worse there."

Aaslo tried to consider all the reasons Magdelay might recall the magi. "Perhaps she wants to put up a unified defense. The threat is dire. Spread out as you are, you are weaker."

Soter nodded. "Perhaps, but it leaves the people defenseless."

Aaslo couldn't imagine that the situation had already reached the point where they would sacrifice the masses for the defense of a central stronghold. He had heard of no attacks besides the one they had endured on the road outside Goldenwood.

"Where is the army?" said Mistress Nova. Her eyes were wide as she busily wrung her apron in her hands. "If the magi are abandoning us, the army should be stepping in, but I have four young men staying in another room claiming they've been granted leave." She looked to Aaslo. "They wouldn't grant leave if we're under attack, would they?" Her expression firmed, and she shook her head as she dropped her apron. "No. No, they wouldn't. There's been a mistake. We're misinterpreting the events. I'm sure there is a reasonable explanation, and all will be put back to normal soon."

She straightened primly and turned to Aaslo. "Breakfast will be served at dawn. I'll take your laundry now, and we'll see how your young lady is feeling in the morning." She gathered the laundry in her arms and left the room, her head held high, content in her denial.

Mage Soter stood and crossed to the door. "I've done what I can for now. I'll return tomorrow to check on her. There's a bottle on the nightstand. Have her drink it when she wakes in the morning. In a few days, once the contagion has passed, I'll take her through the evergate to the citadel."

"But she's my guide!" said Aaslo. "If you take her, I won't be able to find it."

Mage Soter shook his head. "The long way will take a few weeks. By then it will probably be too late."

"Too late for what?" said Aaslo.

The man shook his head sadly, his gaze filled with regret, then left without another word.

Aaslo sat in the chair and stared at Teza. She was sleeping peacefully, and the feverish appearance had dissipated. He was also relieved that the objects in the room were staying in their places.

"You should take her."

"What are you talking about?" he mumbled.

"Leave before the old man steals her away."

"I think that's her decision, don't you?"

"It's a war, Aaslo. The world needs you, and you need her right now. You're going to the citadel anyway."

"Yes, but the mage said it'll be too late by the time we get there. We don't know what he was talking about. What if she misses something important?"

"What could be more important than saving the world?"

Aaslo hung his head and ran his hands through his hair. In the forest, he would never have considered doing something so deceitful. Mathias was the golden boy, though. He was the savior. His choices would have led to victory. Aaslo said, "Would *you* take her?" When Mathias didn't answer, he asked again. "Mathias, what should I do? What would *you* do?" Mathias was again silent, and Aaslo growled in frustration. Mathias had suggested taking her, but Mathias was dead. Was it his own insanity talking? Would Mathias really have absconded with an innocent woman to save the world?

"She's the one who refused to tell you how to get there."

"I should give her a choice."

"You'll place the fate of all life on the decision of an ignorant, stubborn young woman?"

"I could find someone else."

"Who? They've all been recalled."

Aaslo snuffed the candle and stretched out on the other bed.

"How can you sleep?"

"There's nothing to be done for it tonight. Difficult decisions should be made by a rested mind."

CHAPTER 15

MYROPA COULD SEE THE WAR RAGING BEHIND AASLO'S DISTURBED gaze, but she could do nothing to assist. Even if she could, she wasn't sure she should. The gods had plans, and Aaslo was likely to get in the way. She abruptly felt a churning sensation swirl through her mind. With it came heat, blessed heat. The momentary warmth was worth the dizziness, and it seeded her with an uncontrollable desire for more. She released the breath of life and stepped across the veil into a hall so vast she couldn't see the farthest wall. The black ceiling that soared far, far above was dotted with stars swimming in a milky soup, and the floor beneath her feet felt soft, like walking across layer upon layer of blankets. As she walked with her arms out for balance, her feet sank, as if into sand.

She startled when she looked up from her feet. Windows lined the hall, but beyond them was not the luscious greenery of a garden or frothy waves of an ocean. Instead, creatures stood in display cases, as if preserved through taxidermy. Animals she had never before seen, strange things, things that made no sense, looked at her from behind crystalline glass. Some of them appeared more like people than animals. Their empty gazes looked as if they had once held intelligence. Her frozen heart leapt into her throat when she came across one that looked like her—not in coloration, body shape, or height, but as in *human*. Myropa's feet were rooted to the soft ground as she stared at the lifeless form that could have easily been her sister or mother or friend. It was soulless, empty, and alone.

A presence of strength and resilience pressed at her from behind. The power radiated through her, melting her frosty blood as it shifted to stand beside her. *"W-why?"* she said, and she thought she might have produced a tear if they had not been frozen.

"This is my gallery," said Arayallen. "Isn't it exquisite?"

"But they're all dead," Myropa said. "Why would you want to look at such things?"

Arayallen's laugh was lovely, like bells on a warm, sunny day. "Oh, they're not dead." She laughed again upon seeing Myropa's horrified expression. "They're not alive, either. They never were. They're just shells—prototypes, you could say. They were never blessed with a soul."

Myropa shivered, and it wasn't from the cold. "They're disturbing."

Arayallen tilted her head as if trying to see them from another perspective. "I suppose they could be if you think of them as equals. They're not, though. They're just raw material, formed by yours truly into something beautiful." She grinned impishly. "Or grotesque. Whatever suits my mood."

Myropa stared at the young woman who was never really a woman. "Did you really design me?"

"Of course," said Arayallen. "Well, not you, specifically. I do occasionally dabble with an individual, but for the most part, I let my creations proliferate how they may." She reached out and stroked Myropa's hair with a look of admiration and self-satisfaction. "You came out lovely." Her pleasant smile fell away. "It's a shame you didn't appreciate my hard work."

Myropa shook her head. "No, it wasn't like that. I looked okay." Upon seeing Arayallen's disgruntled look, she said, "No, better than okay. I mean, I was happy with my appearance. It was everything else I couldn't abide."

Arayallen raised an eyebrow. "*Everything*?" Myropa swallowed but didn't get a chance to respond as Arayallen began walking. "Come along. I don't have all day. Well, I do, but not to spend on *you*."

Myropa held up her skirt as she struggled to keep up with the towering goddess while sinking into the floor. They passed through an archway and were once again on solid ground. It was jarring. After walking so far on a squishy cloud, it felt as if the hard stones were striking back at her feet. In the center of a round courtyard was the biggest statue Myropa had ever seen, and it was a depiction of Trostili—naked—and *proud*. Myropa averted her gaze from his superb form and nearly bumped into Arayallen, who had stopped to admire it.

"I know." The goddess sighed. "It gets me every time. He doesn't know it, but I designed him. He is everything I wanted him to be."

Myropa couldn't help but glance up at the statue again. "You are older than Trostili?"

Arayallen sighed again, this time with feigned patience. "Life had to exist before it could start fighting with itself. I was rather upset when I found out he was the God of War. It was so unfair that the one I chose for myself would be brother to Axus."

"He's Axus's *brother*?"

"Yes, but at least Disevy's strength keeps them in line. I can't imagine how destructive they would have been in anyone else's pantheon."

"So Disevy is Trostili and Axus's superior? But he's so kind."

Arayallen glanced toward her in surprise. "You've met him?" She nodded without waiting for a response. "Yes, he can be—if he likes you. You must have made an impression on him."

Myropa shifted uncomfortably. "I think it was you who made the impression. He seems to appreciate your work."

Arayallen smiled. "Was that it? Yes, that makes sense. He likes to visit my gallery. I keep waiting for him to ask for a design, but he never does."

"A design?" said Myropa.

"For a partner," replied the goddess as she began walking again. "He's very old, older than I am, and he has never chosen a partner—at least, not for any length of time." Arayallen walked through another doorway into a small chamber that looked like an empty tomb. The walls were white marble, the floor was white marble, and the ceiling was white marble. Arayallen turned to look at Myropa, and the door suddenly shut behind her. It, too, was white marble. Nothing else was in the room.

Myropa tensed under Arayallen's powerful gaze. She felt like a mouse caught in a cage, and she began to shake from the intensity of the goddess's power. Just when it became unbearable, it relented. Arayallen said, "I don't particularly like you. I don't dislike you, either, although I think you have poor judgment." She paused and waited. Finally, she said, "Have you nothing to say?"

Taking a deep breath that she didn't actually need, Myropa said, "You've never spoken to me before. I don't know what you want to hear."

Arayallen hummed under her breath. "I see what Trostili was talking about. You're a timid little mouse, aren't you?"

Myropa once again wondered if the gods could hear her thoughts. She thought if they could, they surely would have destroyed her already. "I, um—"

"Never mind that. The only reason I'm speaking with you is because you are assigned to Trostili."

"He has a task for me?" said Myropa, relieved to finally have direction.

"No, I do."

"But I am not assigned to you."

"I realize that, but I think you'd prefer to do my bidding. You care about your little world, don't you?"

"My world?"

Arayallen sighed and spoke as if to an ignorant child. "*Aldrea.* You were once a part of it. I realize you left *of your own accord*, but surely there is *something* there that calls to you?"

Myropa shifted her feet. "I suppose—"

"Good. Then you will want to help me. I want you to report everything to *me.* Anything you tell Trostili or Axus—anything you *don't*—I want to know it."

"But I thought you didn't care—"

"Of course I care," the goddess snapped. "Axus wants to claim all the life I created. It's an affront to nature and a direct attack on *me.*"

Myropa said hesitantly, "I don't think he sees it that way—"

"Whether he does or not is of no consequence. Those are my beautiful creations, not his. If he wants them, he should wait for them to die by the Fates' design. *You* serve the Fates. *You* are from Aldrea. That is why *you* are ideally suited for this task. It doesn't hurt that you're also deeply entrenched within the enemy's ranks."

"Enemy?"

Arayallen shrugged. "It is what it is."

"But Trostili—"

"Shouldn't know," said Arayallen with a burst of power that socked Myropa in the gut. "This doesn't affect him. He gets his war either way. I intend for the outcome to be in my favor."

"But the prophecy—"

"Yes, yes, the prophecy. They can be so troublesome. You don't still have the Lightbane's soul, by any chance?"

"Lightbane?"

Arayallen huffed as if becoming frustrated with having to explain everything. "That is what you called him—what the followers of Axus call the *chosen one.*"

"No," said Myropa. "I already delivered it to the Sea."

Arayallen sighed. "Very well. I'll have to figure a way around that. Arohnu will feel my wrath if this isn't resolved. I cannot imagine how Axus convinced him to design a prophecy so terribly one-sided. I've always appreciated the prophecies in the past. I thought it intriguing and challenging that once emplaced, they must come to fruition. Our existence is long, and Arohnu makes things interesting, but this one is ridiculous." She paused and frowned at Myropa. "Well, what is it?"

Myropa abruptly stopped fussing with her skirt. She had too many questions and probably would only get the chance to ask one. Unfortunately, her mind had gone blank under the goddess's arresting gaze. "Um, why this room?" Myropa chided herself as soon as the words left her mouth. It was a stupid question, and there were so many others more pressing.

Arayallen glanced around the chamber that might as well have been a mausoleum. She frowned at Myropa and said, "I like this room." Myropa blinked at her, waiting for more. Arayallen rolled her eyes and said, "No other god has stepped foot in here—*ever*. Do you know how rare it is to find a space like this?" She spread her arms wide. "Everywhere else is saturated with the power of others. I know you've felt it. It seeps into you, contaminates you. *This* is mine alone. *This* is where I create, free from the influence of anyone else."

Myropa was shocked. She spun slowly, gazing at every marble block in awe. When she turned back to Arayallen, she said, "*This* is where all life was created?"

Arayallen pursed her lips. "Not created in that sense. I suppose *designed* is more accurate. I don't make *life*."

"Still, this is the greatest honor—"

"Enough of that," said the goddess, waving Myropa away. "Go back to your duties. Don't tell anyone about this."

"Of course," said Myropa as she slipped through the doorway that had opened behind her. As she whispered to the Fates and inhaled, she was suddenly very glad she had asked the stupid question.

"YES, I CLOSED IT," SAID PECK. IT WAS THE THIRD TIME THE OLD MAN had asked him to close the window, but Peck tried not to get frustrated. Over the past several days, he and Mory had barely left the guild house. During that time, it had become obvious the forgetfulness was genuine. Peck didn't think the keeper addled. Galobar was sharp as a needle. No, the old man seemed preoccupied to the point that he might forget his own name. Peck watched as Galobar sat on a stool by the open back door churning butter. He could tell that the keeper's thoughts were far away, though, because his motions would gradually slow until they stopped altogether. After a moment, Galobar would catch himself and go back to churning.

"Would you like me to do that?" said Peck. He hoped Galobar said no. He really didn't want to churn butter, but he felt bad for watching the old man do it.

Galobar blinked up at him. "What?"

Peck pointed to the butter churn. "Shall I?"

"Oh. No, the work's easy enough. I'm afraid I'm a bit lost in my thoughts today."

Taking that as an invitation, Peck decided to further the investigation. He pulled up a chair and straddled it as he rested his arm across the back. "What's bothering you?"

"Bothering me? No, I suppose you could say I'm nostalgic. I used to sit here with Maralee on evenings like this. I'd be churning butter or sharpening the cooking knives, and she'd sit there reading to me or knitting as she sang. She had a lovely voice—at least while she was younger. It became weaker with age, and she stopped singing. To hear her songs again . . ."

The old man's gaze was full of mourning when he looked over at Peck. "I can no longer remember them. It's like they're there—just beyond my grasp. Almost . . . almost, but no."

Peck didn't know what to say. He had never been close enough to anyone to feel the pain of their loss. He knew he would be devastated if something happened to Mory, but he refused to think about that. He said, "Do you think about her a lot?"

Galobar smiled fondly. "All the time. I've missed her every moment since she passed, but now it's different."

"How so?"

The old man began churning the butter again. After a moment, he said, "Maralee and I were content. We had our share of squabbles, as married folk do, but I never had a want to stray and neither did she. You know what kept us going? It was the mission. We had a shared purpose, one that we believed in more than anything else. We were to serve the foresters in their need. Maralee never got to meet a forester. After she passed, I began to wonder if I would share her fate. Well, now I *have* met one. He came here, and I served him as best I could, and then he left. You see? Two lifetimes of preparation between Maralee and me, all to serve a forester for two days. And now? I don't believe I'll be seeing one again."

"You don't think Aaslo's coming back?" said Peck, trying to hide the panic that heated his blood.

"Why would he?" said Galobar. "He's gone east to see the magi. After that, I figure he'll return to the forest."

"But he could come on the return trip."

Galobar shook his head. "There's more direct routes, and he didn't seem too fond of the city. Although, I suppose he may desire to visit the queen again."

Peck tipped his chair toward the old man. "Did you say the *queen*?"

Galobar grinned, then waggled his brow. "According to the rumors, she favored him one night."

"*Aaslo* and the *queen*? I don't believe it. You're trying to pull one over on me, aren't you?"

With a shrug, the keeper said, "That's the rumor. Take it as you want, but a marquess shows up at my door one day and the royal guard the next. I'd not dismiss the possibility so quickly."

A sudden crash upstairs was followed by a wail from Mory. The boy stumbled into view at the top of the stairs and then fell backward, tumbling end over end. When he reached the bottom, Peck heard a metallic clatter before Mory began moaning and crying hysterically. Peck rushed to Mory's side and found that the boy was not only injured from the fall, but bleeding profusely from his right shoulder. Peck pressed his palms to the wound to stop the bleeding and called to Galobar for help. His gaze caught on the shiny edge of a knife that had landed not far from Mory. The blade was coated in blood.

The whole building suddenly shook with a massive blast from one of the upper stories. The forester's gong began to toll of its own accord, never fading. A man dressed in a servant's smock came running down the stairs. Before he could reach them, though, large splinters of wood shot from the wall, impaling him in multiple places. He slid the rest of the way on his back, his sightless gaze fixed on the ceiling.

"The enchantments!" said Galobar. "We are under attack. Quickly, now! We must evacuate."

Peck tried to help Mory stand, but the boy screamed out when he put pressure on his left leg. "No, Peck! I think it's broken."

Peck turned at a shout from behind him. Another man, dressed like the first, rushed through the open doorway from the dark yard. Galobar stepped in front of the man, holding his arm up. "Please, sir. I am only an old man."

The attacker grinned with a feverish glint in his eyes. He raised his arm, prepared to strike Galobar down with a wicked serrated knife. Peck shouted, but he was too late. Galobar stepped forward and shoved a kitchen knife into the man's chest. He pulled the knife out with a gurgling pop, then paused. More footsteps could be heard stomping around the upper levels and pounding down the stairs.

Galobar said, "You take the boy. I'll hold them off. The enchantments will help keep them busy."

Peck threw Mory's arm over his shoulders and took the majority of his weight as he practically dragged the boy from the Forester's Haven into the night. Galobar suddenly shoved them both to the ground, and it was only after Peck rolled over and gave his eyes a second to adjust to the dark that he saw the attacker. In that terrifying instant, Galobar was struck down with a sword through his chest.

Running on instinct, Peck scrambled to untangle himself from Mory. He collected the knife from where Galobar had dropped it on the lawn and lunged at the intruder. The knife slipped into the man's back, but not with sickening ease as he had imagined. The sensation was rough as it collided with bone that crunched under the pressure. Peck stumbled back, startled by the blood that coated his hands. He had experienced violence—he had seen death and witnessed the taking of lives—but he had never committed it himself. It was terrifying—*liberating*. Although his heart pounded with the danger of the attack and the threat of more, he felt relief that in that moment he was free, safe.

"Peck!"

Peck rushed to Mory's side. He removed his jacket and shirt and twirled the lighter linen between his outstretched hands until it resembled a bandage. As he wrapped it around Mory's shoulder, hoping to stanch the bleeding, a rumble began within the house. He could hear the shouts of men and women in pain and terror. The windows began to flicker with golden light that grew brighter, then darkened with smoke. Glass panes shattered, and smoke and flame billowed from the structure, consuming the most majestic-looking tree Peck had ever seen—even if it hadn't been real.

Peck laid Mory back on the ground and then hurried to check on Galobar. The keeper's eyes stared toward the stars, which were quickly becoming obscured by the black haze of smoke. Peck jumped when the old man blinked. He turned Galobar's face toward him.

"Galobar, just hold on. It'll be okay. Maybe the sword didn't hit anything important. Stay with me, Galobar. Please—"

Galobar reached up and gripped his hand. The man's lips quivered as he spoke. "Find Aaslo."

Peck nodded vigorously and wiped the moisture dripping from his face, not realizing until that moment that he was crying. "You can come with us. We'll get you patched up, and you'll be good as new."

Galobar's gaze became distant. He whispered, "I remember now. I hear her song. She's beautiful, my Maralee." The old man's grip loosened as the light left his eyes, and Peck realized that something else was in his hand. It was a Galobar's purse. Although it wasn't large, it was more than Peck could have hoped for and more than he thought he deserved.

The Forester's Haven began to groan as the wood broke and shattered. Dust and debris exploded through the doorway when one of the upper levels collapsed, and Peck knew it wouldn't be long before the rest of the building tumbled to the ground. He peered into the dark, unable to make anything out clearly due to the spots of light in his eyes. A few people had emerged from adjacent buildings and were shouting for buckets and assistance, but Peck couldn't tell if any were enemies. He grabbed his jacket and threw it over Mory as the boy shivered. He then gathered the boy, who was nearly unconscious and delirious with pain, and dragged him the rest of the way down the path and across the square. Everyone was too preoccupied with the fire to pay them any attention.

Peck could only think of one person he might ask for assistance, and he was loath to involve her in his mess. He knew it was *his* mess. If he hadn't clipped a sack from a traveler's belt, none of this would have happened, and Mory would be safe and well—at least until Jago got ahold of them. Jago was another problem. They had to get out of the city before Jago found out about their misfortune. As Peck stumbled with Mory through the dark alleys, he suddenly heard a whisper in his ear.

"Follow the pretty lady," said Mory.

Peck paused and surveyed the passage in both directions. "There's no one here," he said.

Mory pointed down a pathway to their right. "Follow her, Peck. She knows where we're going."

Peck peered down the alley and saw no one, not even a rat.

"Please, Peck. I'm tired."

Peck took a deep breath, then dragged Mory in the direction of his imaginary woman, figuring at that point one direction was just as good as another. They needed to find a place to hide, somewhere where he might tend to Mory's wounds. He had never seen anything so bad as what Mory was suffering, though.

"We need to find a healer," he muttered between heaving breaths. Mory said nothing, so Peck continued. "You're hurt bad, Mory, but we'll get you better. Maybe it's not as bad as it looks. You're young and strong. You'll pull through." As he struggled down the alley, Peck was tiring. Mory seemed heavier than in the beginning, heavier than he had ever been. Mory didn't talk, and Peck was fine to let him rest. Peck stumbled as his fatigued legs gave out beneath him. He struggled to stand again, but Mory hung limp. Finally, Peck said, "Okay, Mory. Let's rest."

MYROPA SAT IN THE DARK ON A CRATE BESIDE THE YOUNG MEN. THE tether was strong. It bound her to the boy, but she didn't want to heed its call. She had already claimed the kind old keeper of the Forester's Haven. She didn't want to take Mory, too. She waited, hoping the tether would fizzle. It happened occasionally, usually due to the ministrations of a healer or apothecary. Peck had neither of them. If what Mage Soter had said was true, there might not be any healers left in Tyellí—or anywhere outside the Citadel of Magi.

For the rest of the night, Myropa sat beside the young men, refusing to claim the soul that called to her. Mory didn't see her at first as he sat on another crate across the alley staring at Peck holding his body in his arms. He seemed unwilling to look away from his companion's pain, as many were when their time came. Myropa didn't push him, but eventually, he turned his tearful gaze on her.

"Who are you?" he said.

"My name is not important," she said. "I am a reaper. I am here to take your soul to the Sea of Transcendence."

"I don't want to go," he said.

She nodded. "That's common." She followed his gaze to Peck, then said, "I'd rather not take you if I don't have to."

He looked back at her. "You mean I'm not dead?"

With a shake of her head, she said, "Not yet."

"Then, I could get better? I could go back to him? He needs me. If I die, who will take care of him?"

"I understand," she said. "Shall we wait awhile?"

He nodded solemnly. "Yes, as long as you can."

They sat for hours in silence, both of them visitors in the other's realm, neither fully intact. In this place between realms, all was not dark as it was in the living realm. Wisps of light danced in the air, people and animals shimmered with the power of their souls, and the stars shone like beacons, guiding lost travelers and lending them the comfort of knowing they were not alone.

The sleeping world came alive with the orange and pink glow of dawn. Myropa and Mory watched a woman shuffle down the alley to stop beside Peck, who had succumbed to sleep. She bent and brushed a hand across Mory's face, then shook Peck.

Peck startled and blinked but seemed lost in his fatigue.

"It looks like your friend needs help," said the woman. "Bring him inside. He has little time, if any at all."

Peck groaned as he worked his way to his feet, supporting Mory beneath the arms. He glanced at the sign over the stoop where he had fallen in the dark. It held the image of a mortar and pestle, the symbol of an apothecary. He grinned and gripped Mory tighter before dragging him backward into the establishment.

Mory looked over at Myropa as they followed Peck into the building. "You led us here?"

"You followed," she said with a sad smile.

"You mean, I don't have to die?"

"If your body can be saved, sometimes the Fates will spare you. It is up to the talents of the apothecary and the Fates now."

CHAPTER 16

"So, I'm good to go?" said Teza.

Aaslo averted his gaze, busying himself with tying his boots. "Yeah, the healer said you should drink the contents of that bottle and then you'll be okay. It's best if we get moving."

Teza looked out the window. The sky was implementing a full-on assault, seemingly holding nothing back. "Are you sure we shouldn't stay another day? Maybe we can wait it out."

His stomach churning, Aaslo said, "It's really important that we get there as soon as possible."

She turned back to him. Although she looked much better, her face was still pale, and dark circles made her eyes appear tired. "One more day?"

Aaslo stood and turned to her. He was suddenly captive to her dark gaze. She reminded him of a haunting woodland creature, the curious kind that desired a connection but was too fearful to allow it. He said, "I'll leave it to you. If you don't feel well enough, we'll stay."

She nodded and sat on the bed, silent in thought, as if assessing her own health. His stomach churned again, and he lost his resolve.

"Don't do it."

Aaslo ignored Mathias and said, "If you had a choice between going with me and returning through the evergate, which would it be?"

She looked at him and frowned. "I told you I can't go through the evergate."

"But if you could . . ."

"Why would she want to go the long way when she could be there in a second?"

She appeared thoughtful; then her expression hardened. "I'd go with you." She nodded toward the window. "But not in this weather."

Aaslo released a breath and nodded. "Very well. We'll stay another day."

"You could've lost your guide. That was stupid."

"She wants to go with me," he mumbled.

"What happens when she finds out you lied to her?"

"Good point," he said. He looked at Teza, who was staring at him with a knowing grin. She probably thought he was talking to himself. Maybe he was. He said, "The healer wanted to take you through the evergate. I was hoping you'd go with me before he returned."

An amalgam of expressions crossed her face as she finally replied. "Good call."

His breath rushed out of him before he realized he had been holding it. "What?"

Her dark curls bobbed as she spoke matter-of-factly. "If I'd gone with him, you wouldn't have had anyone to take you to the citadel."

Aaslo dropped his gaze to the floor again.

"You couldn't do it, though, could you?" she said. "The guilt is written all over your face. It's kind of cute." He glanced up to find her grinning at him again. She winked and said, "From now on, leave the lying to me."

"See? It's better this way," he said to Mathias.

"I agree," she said, then paused. "Oh, were you not talking to me?"

"Of course I was," he said, blatantly surveying the room. "Who else would I be talking to?"

She shrugged. "You haven't told me yet." She waited and then said, "It's your friend, isn't it? The one you talk about—Mathias?"

He looked out the window to avoid seeing the judgment that was surely in her gaze. "Yes, I've heard him since I left the forest."

"That was hard for you, wasn't it?" she said.

He turned back to look at her. He wanted to know what she was thinking. Would she run screaming from the madman? She didn't seem the type. Would she try to heal him? He didn't even know if problems of the mind could be healed. He said, "I thought never to leave the forest—never, for *any* reason."

"So, you endured two great losses at once."

"And more," he said. The sadness, the pain, the overwhelming sense of dread welled up inside him, threatening to drown him worse than any storm. He took a deep breath to steady himself, then cleared his throat. He grabbed his cloak and stomped toward the door. "Let's go to the common room before they stop serving breakfast."

The common room was empty when they arrived, so they had their pick of tables. Teza chose one nearest the stairs, but Aaslo shook his head before crossing the room to take a seat near the hearth.

"Are you cold?" she said.

"It has three seats," he muttered before settling the sack in front of the chair beside him.

"Are we expecting someone?" she asked.

He looked at the bag and realized that she probably already thought he was crazy. "No," he said. "Maybe. You never know."

"Okaaay," she drawled, and he was glad she didn't press him for more.

One of the twins brought their meals, a combination of the previous night's dinner and fresh eggs and bread. As they were finishing, Mistress Nova entered the common room with Mage Soter on her heels.

"The guide thief is back."

Mistress Nova took Mage Soter's wet cloak and dripping hat, then disappeared into another room. Mage Soter stepped up to their table and smiled as he held his hands in front of the hearth next to them.

"Greetings, Fledgling Teza. You look much better today."

Teza shifted uncomfortably. "Who are you?"

"Oh, I apologize. I forgot you were unconscious when I treated you last night. I am Mage Soter, Healer."

"Greetings, Mage Soter. You should know, though, that I'm not a fledgling anymore."

Mage Soter's expression fell. "Yes, I know of your problems at the academy. For what it's worth, I think they were too harsh."

"Outright *wrong*," she said.

He looked surprised and then shook his head. "Maybe I was mistaken. It seems you still have not learned your lesson."

"Are you going to let him talk to her like that?"

"It's not my business," Aaslo muttered.

"No, it's not," said Mage Soter. "But that's no longer important, considering the news. It's kind of funny how perspectives change on individual failures when the community as a whole is threatened."

"What are you talking about?" she said.

Mage Soter turned to Aaslo. "You haven't told her?"

Aaslo met the man's accusatory gaze and grumbled, "It's not my business."

Teza abruptly stood and placed her fists on her hips. "He told me you want to take me back through the evergate. What makes you think I would abandon my friend to go running back to those sanctimonious, hypocritical slanderers?"

Mage Soter's brows rose toward the ceiling. "Slanderers? I heard you admitted to cheating."

Crossing her arms with a huff, Teza said, "Yes, I cheated. I admit it, but it's not like anyone got hurt—except *me*."

Mage Soter furrowed his brow and looked at Aaslo questioningly. Aaslo shrugged. He didn't understand the woman either. Her reasoning made no sense, but she was passionate about it. All he cared about was getting to the citadel. To the healer, he said, "Would you be willing to tell me how to get to the citadel?"

Teza reached over and flicked his ear. "I *told* you I would take you!"

Aaslo rubbed his ear and looked back to the healer, who shook his head. "I'm afraid I can't do that."

"See? He's hiding things. Plotting."

"Is it some big secret?" said Aaslo. "No one seems to know, and I can't find it on any maps."

Mage Soter looked embarrassed. "No, I don't think it's a secret, as such. It's just that I've never gone the long way. In truth, I don't actually know its location."

"He's lying."

Aaslo stood, frustrated by the man's lack of assistance, considering he appeared to know more about what was happening than what Aaslo had told him. "Forgive the observation, Mage Soter, but you don't look to be a young man. Assuming your appearance is indicative of your true age, you must have spent quite some time at the academy and citadel. During all those years, you never once asked *where* you were?"

Mage Soter lifted his chin. "I've never been a curious man nor an adventurous one. I was perfectly satisfied with my life as a healer in Yarding. All of that is being upset now, and I'm only trying to do what's right."

Aaslo dipped his head and said, "Please forgive my harsh tone, Mage

Soter. It seems you and I are more alike than either of us thought. I, too, have a task I'd rather not be doing; but it must be done, and I need her to do it."

Mage Soter's mouth was set stubbornly as he looked at Aaslo. "I'll not force the young lady to do anything she doesn't want. It's up to her." He turned to Teza and held out another bottle. "This is the second treatment for the selkesh fever. You may still be contagious for another day, so it's not safe to take you to the citadel yet. I'll leave tomorrow at midday. If you want to go with me, be at the evergate."

Teza took the bottle and thanked the healer before he left. She turned to Aaslo. "What was he talking about? Why was his life upset, and why does he want to take me back through the evergate?"

"Death, Aaslo."

Aaslo shook his head. "I don't know. He didn't tell me the details, but the Council of Magi was attacked, and all of the magi have been recalled."

Teza dropped into her chair and stared at him. *"All* of them? Even *me?"*

He scraped at the grain in the table with his thumbnail. "So it would seem."

She stared out the window for a long while, watching the rain and humming to herself. Finally, she said, "Well, we're going to the citadel anyway."

Aaslo nodded. "He seemed to think there was some time constraint, but he wouldn't say why."

Teza turned to him. She met his gaze with eyes so dark he thought he might get lost in them if he looked too long. She said, "Why should I stick with you? What's in it for me?"

He was jarred by the question, which he knew should not be answered lightly. Leaning back, he mulled it over in his mind. With every second that passed, the corners of her lips dipped lower. Finally, he said, "You know I need to get to the citadel and that it's a matter of great importance." She nodded. "As for what's in it for you, I guess not much."

"Not helpful, Aaslo."

"I don't know you well," he said, "but what I do know of you is interesting." She continued to stare at him, as if waiting for more. "You're a different sort of person than any I've known. You're strange and sometimes frustrating, but I think I'd like to know more of you."

After a moment of silence in which she continued to stare at him, Teza jumped to her feet. She crossed the room and skipped up the stairs, calling back, "We'll leave in the morning, rain or shine."

"*I suppose that was well done.*"

"You're not Mathias," muttered Aaslo. "He wouldn't have been cruel. He wouldn't have lied."

"*Are you sure? Being the chosen one, having the fate of all life on one's shoulders, is a heavy burden to bear. It changes a man.*"

Aaslo looked down at the sack next to him and wondered how the small table could hold its weight. It took all his strength to lift the bag and tie it to his waist. His seemed to sink into the floor as he crossed the room, and his legs threatened to buckle under the intensity. Once he left the porch, liquid splashed over his face, blurring his vision. He sucked in a breath as his heart leapt through his chest. Everywhere he looked, the streets were filled with the white-blooded creatures that had killed Mathias. He took a step back and stumbled, collapsing onto the porch. When he looked up again the monsters were gone. The streets were nearly empty as the rain pummeled them into a murky mess, and not a single leaf of green was visible among the dreary grey. He buried his head in his arms and held his breath to stave off the tears that threatened to drown him.

"*Are you okay?*"

He nodded. "I'm fine. I guess—I guess it was an attack of conscience."

"*More like panic.*"

"Can you blame me?"

"*I never have.*"

"I should have been faster."

"*Are you okay?*"

"I said I'm fine," he snapped as he looked up.

Teza held up her hands. "Okay, I was just checking. Where are we going?"

"You need better travel gear," he said as he pushed to his feet. "Maybe you should stay here. It wouldn't do for you to get sick again."

Teza crossed her arms and lifted her chin stubbornly. "And let *you* shop for me? I don't want to imagine how that would turn out."

Together, they sloshed through the mud and rancid muck that Aaslo had come to realize was common in city streets. On the next street over was a market. The stalls were closed, but a few of the larger shops welcomed customers. He entered a shop that looked to specialize in clothing.

"Hello, I'm Jennis. May I help you?" said a young woman wearing an apron with multiple pockets filled to nearly overflowing with pins, spools, scissors, measuring instruments, and other baubles. She had long, mousy brown hair, a sharp nose and chin, and a smile to light the room.

"Yes," said Aaslo, gently pushing Teza in front of him. "She needs a waxed cloak."

Jennis looked down at the muddy puddle around his feet and said, "It looks like *yours* is doing the job fine."

"Oh," he said, removing his cloak and hanging it on a hook by the door. "My apologies. Do you have a mop and bucket? I'll clean it up."

Jennis laughed and shook her head. "Don't bother. It'll give me something to do later. No one's been in all day. A cloak?"

"Yes," said Teza, stepping between them. "Something warm, please."

"Sure thing. If you'll follow me?" Jennis led them past racks and tables stacked with items. "We don't have much that looks nice, mostly functional things."

"That's fine. We're traveling," said Teza.

Jennis looked back at her and grinned. "I know what I'd want if I were traveling."

"What's that?" said Teza.

Jennis grabbed a cloak from a hook on the back wall and thrust it out so that it fanned over another stack of clothing. "Pockets!" More than a dozen pockets were hidden in the inner lining of brushed black wool. The outer fabric was heavily waxed and the color of honey.

Teza pursed her lips and said, "Do you have anything more colorful?"

Jennis shook her head. "Not much, I'm afraid. You'd have to go to the dressmaker for that, but she's closed today."

Aaslo leaned against a wall watching in amusement as the two women settled into a practiced dance of bargaining. Teza made a show of browsing through the small assortment of waxed cloaks, grumbling over things she didn't like about each one, while Jennis pointed out the tiny differences that were sure to make each one better than the last. Finally, Teza held up the first one and sighed as if disappointed for having to settle.

Jennis peeked around the cloak and said, "Look, we can save the bartering. I know you like this one. It's the best we have. I'll give you a good deal on one condition."

"What's that?" said Aaslo, earning a scowl from Teza.

"Keep me company for a bit? I'm so bored I've actually started talking to the clothes. No joke." She pointed to a rack of hats. "That one is Orn." She turned to a display of scarves next to Aaslo. "That's Lady Lona. Orn wants to ask Lady Lona to join him for dinner, but he's afraid she'll laugh at him."

"Will she?" said Aaslo.

Nodding solemnly, Jennis said, "Probably. She's way above his station."

Teza huffed. "I don't get it. They're just hats and scarves."

Jennis waggled her eyebrows. "Don't let them hear you say that. They might take offense." She lifted her chin toward a hanger bearing petticoats. "Maid Arisha has been in love with Orn since she first laid eyes on him. I'm sure he'll realize her love is true and greater than anything Lady Lona has to offer."

Aaslo studied the scarves with interest, running the soft material between his fingers appreciatively. "I don't know. Lady Lona looks quite warm and soft. I might want her for myself."

"Aaslo!" said Teza with indignation.

Jennis laughed and winked. "She can be yours for the right price."

"I didn't realize she was that kind of lady," he said.

"Those are the only kind of ladies we have in here," she said. Then her eyes widened, and she sputtered, "The clothes, I mean. I didn't—not *me*, of course." She glanced at Teza, who doubled over in laughter. Jennis quickly hid her face behind a coat hanging on the rack next to her.

A sensation Aaslo hadn't felt in a while burbled up from his core, and he burst into laughter. It wasn't his usual subdued chuckle, but a full-bellied laugh. With it came the release of so much tension that he felt drained afterward. Teza stared at him in concern throughout the entire episode.

Aaslo enjoyed chatting with Jennis. She was easy to talk to, and to his relief, she did most of it. He was reminded of the times he and Reyla would stroll around the lake gossiping about the nonsensical mischief the other young people got into, mischief often headed by Mathias. Aaslo had always felt free with Reyla. It was the only time he felt that it was okay to stop working and relax. His father had told him that courting a woman was like tending the forest. When you were in the midst of it, it required your full attention. Unfortunately, relationships hadn't worked out for him *or* his father.

Teza paced anxiously around the store as he chatted with Jennis. She finally grabbed the cloak and left, claiming she needed to look for something in another shop. A short time later, Aaslo paid for the cloak with the marquess's money and went to look for her. He searched the shops along the path back to the inn, but she was nowhere to be found. By the time he returned to their room, he was ready for dinner. When he arrived, he found a tub filled with water sitting in the middle of it.

"You came back," said Teza. "I was beginning to wonder if you would."

Aaslo glanced at the pile by his bed. "All my belongings are here, and you're my guide."

She waved a finger at him. "I know, but I thought maybe you had decided to abandon your quest and stay with *Jennis*."

"She's jealous."

"Jealous?" muttered Aaslo.

Teza laughed. "Oh, no. She seems a sweet girl, if you're into *ordinary*. A man who settles for ordinary isn't a man for me." She placed a hand on her hip and smirked. "You should be glad *I* didn't take off. Really, you need to keep a closer eye on your prisoners."

"Prisoners?" Aaslo said, thoroughly stumped.

She crossed her arms and rocked back on her heels. "You *were* considering kidnapping me, weren't you?"

"*What?* No, I wouldn't—"

"Kidnapping by omission?"

"I, uh . . . That's not a thing," he said. "Besides, you chose to stay."

She shrugged. "I figure you still owe me for getting me fired."

Aaslo shook his head. "Also not true."

She abruptly handed him a small package.

"What's this?" he said.

"It's nothing—just something I picked up. It's no big deal. Here," she said, holding out several coins, "for the cloak."

"Don't worry about it," he said as he unwrapped the package.

"You think I can't pay for my own cloak? I'm not a beggar, you know."

"I never thought you were," he said as he pulled the item from its burlap wrap. It was a cloak pin. The small wooden disk was inlaid with tiny bits of quartz, feldspar, onyx, and jasper, which were surrounded by shiny black resin. "It's an ocelot," he said.

"Is that what it's called? I didn't know. It reminded me of you."

"It's a creature of the wild," he said. "They're solitary and mysterious."

"Solitary, yes. Mysterious, no—stubborn, ornery, work obsessed—"

"Yep, sounds like you," she said. She held up the cloak and narrowed her eyes at him. "I know what this is. You feel guilty."

"For what?" he said, surprised again by her reaction.

"For lying to me and trying to kidnap me by omission."

Aaslo sighed and shook his head. "That *didn't* happen." Then he said, "If I bought you the cloak out of guilt, why did you buy me a cloak pin?"

"It's poisoned. Don't let it poke you."

She winked at him, then pointed to the tub. "I already bathed. I'll ask the twins to bring up more hot water."

"Thank you," he said as he peered into the tub.

"Don't thank me. I *insist*."

"Ha ha. She thinks you smell."

Aaslo sighed. "I know what she's saying." When he turned back, Teza was already gone.

"I'm sorry, Mory," said Myropa.

Mory hung his head and covered his ears as Peck cried.

"I'm sorry," said the apothecary, leaning back against the long workbench covered in bottles, pouches, and bowls. "I stitched his shoulder and set his leg, but his internal wounds were extensive, and he lost a lot of blood. He was too far gone. If a healer had been here, maybe, but I couldn't help him."

Peck looked up, his eyes filled with grief and torment. "I'll get a healer! Where do I go?"

The apothecary shook her head. "They're all gone."

"What do you mean *gone*?"

"I mean they left. All of them, and not just the healers. *All* of the magi are gone."

"No! There has to be one left. I only need *one*!"

She laid a hand on his heaving shoulder and gazed at him with sympathy. "It wouldn't do any good. He's already dead."

"No, I'm not," shouted Mory, jumping to his feet. "I'm right here!"

"Where's the serum?" Peck shouted. "You said you had a serum that could cure nearly anything."

"It doesn't cure death," said the woman.

Peck pushed to his feet and raised a finger to her. "You don't decide if he's dead. *I'll* decide if he's dead. He's not dead. Give him the serum."

"I've never used it. I don't even know if it works. It's rare. I didn't make it. I couldn't. It requires the power of a magus, and I've met none in Uyan who even knew what it was. It shouldn't be wasted on a corpse."

"He's not a corpse! He's still warm." Peck pulled a purse from his pocket and threw it at the wall. Coins spilled over the floor, mostly copper and silver with a few gold. "Give him the serum!"

The woman jumped, and it was obvious she was becoming frightened by Peck's outbursts. "Okay, okay, but if this doesn't work, will you leave in peace?"

Peck grabbed his hair and said, "Yes! Just give it to him, *please*."

The woman used a tiny gold key to unlock a cupboard. She selected a red bottle and removed the stopper as she returned to Mory's side. "Hold him in a sitting position, and tilt his head back," she said. "Yes, like that." She tipped the contents of the bottle into Mory's mouth, and they waited.

Myropa stepped up beside Mory. She wanted to hold his hand or put her arm around him, but it was impossible. Mory turned to her with a pleading gaze. Myropa had seen the same look on countless faces. In the short time she had been following Aaslo and gotten to know Mory and Peck, she had grown fond of them. She had spent more time with these people than any since her death. Although they couldn't know her, she felt as if she knew *them*, and this one hurt more than most. She hated to separate the pair and felt even worse for taking another of the forester's companions. It was inevitable, though, that he would lose more. *Everyone* was going to die.

She held up a small, clear orb, and Mory shook his head as if he understood what was happening. She wondered if perhaps he did. She couldn't remember her own, but she thought maybe people could recognize their deaths when they saw them. Just as she moved the orb into the stream, the light fizzled out. She glanced up to find that Mory had vanished, and the orb was clear. The ice in her veins shifted when Mory's body began to convulse. It coughed and sputtered and shook in massive spasms. Then he inhaled deeply, and she recognized it for what it was. He had been granted the breath of life once again. She smiled to herself, knowing that Mory would no longer be able to see her. His gaze looked through her just as she released her breath and stepped into the Afterlife.

It always amazed her that with a single breath, she could be transported to another realm and be standing on a rocky butte or digging her toes into shimmering pink sand beside an endless sea—a sea of souls. *Breath* was perhaps the most magical of all the gods' powers, she thought. She held up the dangling orbs she had collected that night. There had been many. Most of them, she knew, would be rejected by the Sea and sent into Axus's service until they were deemed worthy. There was one among them, though, that she was both sad and glad to deliver.

She held the orb in her palm over the Sea as it lapped at her toes. Each time it touched her, she felt the most pleasant warmth mingled with cheer, excitement, desire, and love. The light within the pale blue orb began to pulse and swirl. Far in the distance, another light glowed, brighter than the rest. It shimmered, shifting between every color imaginable as it floated closer. Myropa enjoyed this part of the job more than any other. When the Sea light finally reached her, she bent and dipped the hand holding the orb into the water that wasn't water. The orb dissipated, and the blue light joined with the other in a frenzy of joy that seeped into her through her feet. Myropa collapsed into a fit of giggles as the water danced around her legs.

Once it receded, Myropa stood frozen in an icy shell, no longer capable of feeling the joy of the Sea. She turned to leave and paused. Glancing back, she studied the churning waters. It wasn't uncommon for them to stir, but something wasn't right. She stood for a long time trying to discern the problem. She finally focused her mind on the subject of her destination and took a step into Celestria.

The steps leading to Disevy's temple hadn't changed, but the temple itself looked different. The stone was black and shone like a mirror, and the soft greenery of the forest was replaced with deep red roses. A marble statue of a beautiful woman stood in the foyer, and white petals were scattered across the floor.

Myropa felt his presence behind her. She spun to find the God of Virility towering over her. He was clothed in a cream-colored silk robe over loose black silk pants. His feet were bare, and the robe hung open, but she was thankful he was clothed at all. He smiled at her and said, "My lovely Myropa. I am pleased you have come to see me again. Shall we dance?"

"Dance?" she said. "There's no music."

She closed her eyes as he leaned down to whisper in her ear. "There is always music if you care to listen."

Myropa realized that she could indeed hear music playing ever so softly on the breeze. Disevy took her hands, and when she opened her eyes, she found that he had shrunk to a human size. He danced her gracefully around the foyer, and Myropa thought she might lose herself to the breeze. When the dance ended, he stepped back and bowed.

"Thank you, my dear lady, for a most invigorating dance."

"No, thank *you*," she said.

He tilted his head. "You did not come to dance on the breeze with me. No, you are one consumed with duty, which means it must be the Sea."

"Yes," she replied. "Something feels wrong. It's not obvious. In fact, I couldn't see it at all, but I can *feel* it."

"Hmm, it is possible. The reapers are most attuned to its dispositions. What do you sense?"

"It's the souls. There are so many, the numbers greater than I could ever comprehend, but I am sure of it. Some are missing."

As Disevy's expression darkened, the roses that filled the foyer turned black as the stone.

Myropa was suddenly afraid. This god was more powerful than Trostili, more powerful than Axus. "I-I could be wrong—"

"No," he said softly. His touch was as delicate as ever when he brushed a kiss across her knuckles, but she could see the fury simmering in his gaze. "It is a shame this meeting is so brief, but I must go. I hope to see you again soon, lovely Myropa."

The god's form grew to fill the corridor as he walked away, his power lingering behind him, giving Myropa the sensation that he was still with her. She didn't want to imagine what it would feel like to experience the wrath of Disevy.

CHAPTER 17

AASLO GRIPPED HIS THROBBING ARM. HE GRITTED HIS TEETH AGAINST the pain and breathed heavily through his nose. Bile swept up his throat, but he swallowed it down before he lost his breakfast.

Teza looked down at him with a disgruntled yet amused expression. "Are you sure you don't want to get a different horse? Maybe one that doesn't kick and bite?"

He picked himself up off the floor of the stable and met Dolt's challenging gaze. "What is your problem?"

Teza crossed her arms and looked at the horse thoughtfully. "Maybe he's mad at you for not spending time with him yesterday."

"He didn't lack for care," Aaslo said. "The stable boy looked after him."

"Well, *I* know that, but it doesn't seem to matter to *him*."

Aaslo's hand came away from his forearm covered in blood. The skin was savaged around bite marks that extended deep into the muscle.

Teza's face scrunched. "Ew, that looks bad. You need to see a healer."

"*You're* a healer. Why don't you fix it?"

She shook her head. "Can't. Banned, remember?"

Gripping his arm again, he said, "The magi have been recalled. They're not going to come investigating. Besides, you used your power enough while you were unconscious to bring an army of investigators down on you."

Teza pursed her lips. "I didn't know that. Healer Soter can testify that I wasn't in control of my powers at the time. *This*, however, is not exactly an emergency."

"It will be if I get an infection," said Aaslo.

She shrugged. "Then we'd best go find a healer or apothecary."

"That won't be necessary," said a familiar voice.

"Grams!" Aaslo shouted as he spun to face the sorceress. "I mean Magdelay . . . ah, Ms. Brelle—er, High Sorceress?"

"Grams or Magdelay is fine, Aaslo. Greetings, Fledgling Catriateza."

Teza rounded on him. "The *high sorceress* is your grandmother?"

"Not by blood," he said.

Magdelay's fierce gaze was familiar enough, even if her appearance wasn't. Her formfitting clothes were the same, but her hair was jet black and pulled into a tight ponytail. She wore a familiar smirk on her glossy red lips. Aaslo was shocked. She looked no older than he at that moment.

Magdelay stepped forward and placed her hands to either side of his wound. They heated, and the pain, blessedly, dissipated as the flesh began to knit back together before his eyes. He cleared his throat and said, "I've been trying to get to the citadel to speak with you."

"I know," she said as she stepped back. She nodded toward Teza. "Mage Soter came through the evergate last night. I overheard him talking to her mother, and he mentioned you."

"My mother?" Teza said with a whimper.

Magdelay raised an eyebrow at Teza, then looked back to Aaslo. "Why were you looking for me?"

"I was coming to ask you for help. Not just you. The council. King Rakith will do nothing. He's ready to lie down and die and take the rest of the kingdom with him."

"The council won't help you," she said. "Although we hated to consider it, we prepared for this eventuality. We're implementing the backup plan. The magi are recalled. We're leaving this realm."

Aaslo's heart threatened to burst through his chest. "What do you mean, you're leaving the realm?"

"We are settling in another world, Aaslo. I'm sorry."

"You're *abandoning* us?"

"Believe me, this isn't what I want. If we could, we would take the seculars with us. You can't go through the evergate, though. You'd be lost in the pathways."

"No! You can't just *leave*. If Mathias were here, you wouldn't be leaving. You would fight beside him. I know you would. And what about *me*? You helped to raise *me* as much as him. Do you no longer care?"

"Of course I care," she snapped. "I am left with little choice."

"What if this is exactly the reason the prophecy leads to the death of everything? What if it's only because you all turn coward and leave?"

"We don't know that," she said. "The prophecy is clear. All life in this world *will* die. We must save those we can. Unfortunately, only the bloodlines will survive."

Anger overcame Aaslo's sense, but he didn't care at that moment. The fate of all life was at stake. "Isn't that what you wanted all along? A society without seculars? You abandon us so that your precious bloodlines will no longer be watered down?"

"You know that isn't true. I care about you, Aaslo. Believe it or not, I came to think of you as my own, just as I did Mathias. I would take you with me if I could, but I can't. The truth is, the bloodlines may not survive either. We find it increasingly difficult to produce offspring between us. We need seculars as much as you need us."

"Except that you have a *chance* at survival without us, but we don't without *you.*"

Magdelay looked away. He could tell she was trying to put on a strong face, but he saw the glisten of tears in her eyes. She glanced at the sack hanging from his waist. "You still have it."

"Of course. I would never leave him behind—especially not with the king. That man is a coward."

Magdelay shook her head. "Not a coward, just realistic. Give it to me, and I'll take it to his parents."

"Don't let her take me, Aaslo."

"No. They don't even know him. *I'm* his brother. Besides, I still need it if I'm going to find help from someone with a spine."

"What are you two talking about?" Teza said nearly in a panic. "You act like the world is ending."

Magdelay turned her attention to Teza. "The path of survival in the Aldrea Prophecy has failed. The chosen one is dead. You must come with us if you want to live."

Teza's golden skin became pale, and her wide-eyed gaze stared at Aaslo as if he were a monster she had never before seen. She glanced at the sorceress and then back to Aaslo. "What's in the bag?"

Aaslo swallowed his anger toward the magi and pulled Mathias's head from the bag, holding it up for Teza to get a good look. She quickly averted her gaze with a groan. Slowly, she turned back to peek at it out of the corner of her eye, as if somehow that would make the image less gruesome.

"That's him, isn't it?"

Aaslo nodded. "Yes, he's the chosen one."

"No, I mean, he's the one you're always talking to."

Aaslo said nothing as he placed the head back into the sack.

Teza turned back to Magdelay. "I can't go. If the prophecy has truly failed, then people will need me here."

"They're all going to be dead," said Magdelay, eyeing Aaslo with concern.

"Yes, I suppose," said Teza. "We all die someday." She lifted her chin stubbornly. "I'm a healer, though. It is our duty to bring relief and comfort to the dying, even if they can't be saved."

"We're not talking about a patient, girl. We're talking about the world—about *life*."

"The prophecy never said how *long* it would take everyone to die." Teza's color returned with her anger. "Besides, why would I want to survive with all of *you*? You turned me out, sent me away, *banned* me from ever using my power, even *after* I served my punishment."

Magdelay rolled her eyes. "All you had to do was apologize."

Aaslo turned to Teza. "You only had to apologize, and you could go back to the academy?"

Teza balled her fists. "I had nothing to apologize for!" She pointed at Magdelay. "*They* were in the wrong, just as they are now."

Magdelay sighed and called out, "Come, Gertridina. It seems I'll need your assistance after all."

A young woman Teza's age stepped into the stable. With her chestnut hair and rosy cheeks, she had a prim, bookish look. Her voice was soft and reserved as she said, "Hello, Teza."

"You!" said Teza in outrage. "How can you even face me? I told you I never wanted to see you again!"

Gertridina blinked at Magdelay for encouragement, then looked back to Teza. "I'm sorry, Teza. Nothing happened the way it should have. It was all a big mistake."

"You're right it was a mistake. It was a mistake to ever think you were my friend." Teza pointed at Gertridina as she turned to Aaslo. "*She* was *my* best friend, my *only* friend, and she betrayed me."

"I thought you stole her project," said Aaslo.

"I did, but it was only because she wouldn't help me."

"That's not fair," said Gertridina.

"It's true," said Teza, turning back to her. "I *asked* you for help. You knew I was struggling to come up with an idea. You said you were too busy to help me!"

"I *was*."

"You knew I couldn't do it on my own. Instead of helping me to think of something, you did *two* projects, and left me with none."

"I didn't think the first would get me a superior rating, so I tried for a better one. You know how strict my parents are about my ratings."

Teza appeared furious, and tears began to fill her eyes. "I know it was wrong to steal your work, and I knew you'd be upset with me, but I thought you'd understand. I thought we could work it out between us, but you *reported* me. You got me *expelled*!"

"I didn't mean to," said Gertridina. "Really, Teza. I saw the project sitting there, and I was surprised. I blurted out that it was mine. Wizard Tofrey just happened to be standing next to me at the time."

Aaslo said, "If you knew what you did was wrong, why didn't you just apologize?"

She pointed at Magdelay. "Because they care more about their rules and ratings than about the students. Nobody liked me. The instructors wouldn't help. They were just waiting for me to fail. They didn't care if I could become a good healer." She looked at Gertridina. "They're paltry and superficial." She looked back at him. "Even now, they have powers that could shape the world, possibly even save it, but they're running off to hide in another realm, leaving their fellow human beings to die. I won't do it! I'm not like them."

She turned back to Magdelay and gripped Aaslo's hand as she spoke. "Aaslo intends to fight this. I know he will because he's a *good* man, and he knows what it means to be a friend. Now he's *my* friend, and I'm staying to help him because that's what friends do."

Gertridina stepped forward. "Please, Teza. You'll die."

Teza lifted her chin again. "Then I'll die doing something worth dying for."

Tears spilled from Gertridina's eyes as she looked to Magdelay for help. Magdelay was staring at Aaslo, though. She said, "How do you do it? You inspire such strength of bond. Truthfully, I think Mathias expected that you would follow him. I don't think he would have left otherwise."

"Mathias would have done what was necessary," said Aaslo, "a trait that none of you apparently share."

"You have never spoken such harsh words," she said. "It's not like you."

"You have never left the world to die," he replied.

Magdelay shook her head. "I knew this would be difficult and disappointing, but I had hoped we could part on better terms."

"Then don't."

"I must. If all that we can save is ourselves, a small population of the human race, then it is my duty as high sorceress to see that it is done."

"Well, it's not *my* duty to save the human race. It was Mathias's, but he's dead because *you* failed to protect him." He hefted the sack and said, "I carry his burden because no one else will, but it is *you* who will be crushed under its weight."

Magdelay nodded sadly. "I think you are right, Aaslo. I wish I had some token to give you to aid you in your quest, but I'm afraid nothing will suffice."

He said, "You don't know what will suffice until it's been tried."

She looked troubled, and he could tell she was struggling with a decision. Finally, she said, "I would never suggest this to anyone under normal circumstances. In fact, it is forbidden." She took a deep breath and exhaled slowly. "The magi are not the only beings with power in this world. There are those called the fae."

"I've heard of the fae. People think *foresters* are fae," he said with disgust.

"The fae are real," she said. "They were here long before humans. Their power is mysterious. It's wonderful and terrible and far beyond our comprehension. The fae will know of the prophecy. Perhaps you can convince them to help. Be warned, though. Seeking them out, making deals with them, is forbidden because there are *always* consequences. Usually, the prize is not worth the price, but we're talking about the death of everything. I cannot see how it could get worse."

"High Sorceress?" Teza said hesitantly.

"Yes?" said Magdelay, turning to her.

"Would you tell my parents I'm sorry? Tell them I'm sorry for disappointing them."

Magdelay shook her head. "I know your mother, Catriateza. She'll be devastated."

"Ha! Not likely. If she was so worried, she would be here beside you."

Magdelay looked at her sadly and said, "I hope, with time, she'll be proud of the woman you've become. You're more like her than you know. If not for your siblings, I believe she'd stay too." She glanced at Aaslo, then returned her gaze to Teza. "You could not have chosen a better friend."

The high sorceress stepped forward, placed her hands on either side of Aaslo's face, and kissed his forehead, as she had so many times when he was a child. She said, "I know you're angry with me, but know that I love you as I loved Mathias. You are the sons I never had. I wish I had told him that. My family is bigger than *us*, though, and I must see to their safety. Give your father my regards if you see him again."

Aaslo gripped her hand as he pulled it away and swallowed a lump in his throat. He couldn't seem to clear the blockage, so he nodded. He knew the pain he felt wasn't just for the loss of the world or from the loss of the only mother figure he had known, but also for the fact that she was probably right. It was selfish and cowardly of the magi to leave, but it might be the only chance for the survival of their species. He was angry and envious that they had the option to leave and a place of refuge awaiting them.

He said, "For what it's worth, Magdelay, I wish you well in the other realm. Does it have trees?"

She smiled and reached into her pocket before placing a smooth, black lump in his hand. "More than you can imagine," she said. "And some of them talk." He glanced up from the seed to judge if she was kidding, but she looked sincere. She said, "Perhaps someday we'll learn to speak their language." She and Gertridina then stepped into the first sunlight Aaslo had seen in days and left the stable. The latter was heaving with great sobs.

Teza abruptly led her donkey from the stable and mounted. Aaslo followed with Dolt and the pack mule. He looked up to see tears streaming down Teza's cheeks. "Teza?"

She wiped her face with her sleeve and said, "I don't want to talk about it. Let's go."

"All right," he said as he mounted, then paused. He had no idea where to go.

"Well, where to?" said Teza.

"I guess we go to Ruriton."

"Why Ruriton?"

"Because it's the only place I know that we might find help."

CHAPTER 18

MYROPA'S FROZEN HEART ACHED WITH THE COLD. SHE CURSED THE
Fates for forcing her into this role. She hated watching the forester's
heart get broken again, and she knew it would happen over and over as
the world died around him until he, too, succumbed to the dark
prophecy. Although she didn't care much for the young woman, she
admired her strength and appreciated that she chose to stand with
Aaslo. Were the Fates being merciful in lending him a companion, or
was it a sadistic plot to exact a toll for his refusal to submit? What
pain could they impress if he had nothing to lose?

She followed them out of the stable and watched as they took the
road leading southwest, toward Ruriton. Since she knew where they
were heading, she took the opportunity to report to Trostili. She found
him in his home in the fifth palace. The furniture had been moved to
the sides in one of his rooms, and he was swinging a strange weapon
comprised of a curved metal shaft, half of which was lined with rows
of blades that looked like fish fins. He performed several maneuvers
with the frightening weapon before stopping to admire it.

"Hmm, I must decide who will be inspired to invent this. It needs
a vicious name. What do you think, Arayallen? Which world is best
suited for this weapon—Myrellis or Poupilon?"

Arayallen frowned. "If you put that thing on Myrellis, everyone will
be dead after the first battle."

"Good point. Poupilon it is." His expression brightened. "It will give
the Nodics a fighting chance against those wretched creatures you put
there—the big, grey, hairy things."

"They're called do'undigas," said Arayallen, looking up from the
book she was reading, "and I'm not sure even *that* thing will bring one
down."

Trostili grinned fiendishly. "It will be so much fun watching them try."

Myropa stood waiting patiently as the two bantered back and forth about whether Arayallen's creatures or Trostili's weapons would prevail. He seemed to revel in the competition, but she supposed such was his prerogative as God of War.

Arayallen glanced toward Myropa, and without the slightest acknowledgment said, "Your pet is here, Trostili. Do send her away quickly, please. I've invited Barbach over to discuss his role in the design of the new world—or the lack of it, hopefully."

Trostili tossed the magnificent weapon aside as if it were a rotting stick and strode over to sit beside Arayallen. He said, "Without Barbach's influence your creatures will never do anything. Without desire, ambition, drive, your creations will be the most boring in all the worlds."

"I'm not planning to ban him *completely*," she said. "I just want him to use a bit of restraint."

"Restraint is antithetical to his nature. He's the God of *Desire*, or does that concept escape you?"

"Don't patronize me, Trostili. I understand his power better than *you*. The only *desire* you understand is the want for destruction."

Trostili abruptly wrapped his arms around Arayallen and dragged her into his lap. "Not true, my dear." With a stroke of his finger across her collarbone, he said, "I'll be glad to show you the many kinds of desire I understand."

Arayallen giggled as she slapped at his chest. Her gaze slid sideways toward Myropa, and she grinned. "Perhaps you could demonstrate on your pet."

Trostili finally looked at Myropa and frowned. "The reaper? Why would I want that?"

Arayallen shrugged and stroked his strong jaw. "Oh, you don't like her? Disevy is enchanted, it seems. He has placed a statue of her likeness in his entryway."

Myropa's icy blood rushed through her veins. She had thought the statue looked familiar, but it had been a very long time since she had seen her own reflection.

Trostili furrowed his brow and studied Myropa again. She shifted uncomfortably under the scrutiny. He looked back to Arayallen. "Really? Disevy?"

She ran a finger over his lips. "Mm-hmm. *He* appreciates my work. Why do you insist on destroying it?"

It looked as though Trostili was about to argue the point when a chime rang through the air. Trostili picked Arayallen up with one strong arm and settled her back on her seat as he stood. He said, "That would be Axus. We have a standing engagement to discuss the war on Aldrea."

"*What?*" Arayallen shouted. "What of Barbach? You know they can't be in the same realm together, much less the same *room*."

"Then it seems we have an embarrassing conflict of schedule." He flicked his fingers through the air and said, "Enter!"

Myropa shivered as the God of Death stepped through the portal. He was a monstrous being of impeccable beauty. His dark skin covered taut muscle over a slender frame. The light reflecting off his flesh glistened like gold, as did his hazel eyes. His slick black hair was replete with amber highlights that would make the vainest lady envious. He wore a wrap made from the pelts of several spotted cats. It was wrapped around his waist and then over one shoulder so that one of the beasts' heads rested over his chest.

He met Myropa's wanting gaze for the briefest moment, and she once again knew the delicious desire that had driven her to seek her mortality prematurely. In his gaze was a promise—the end of pain, the sweet release from guilt, the escape from the agony of failure, the acceptance of loss and hope for another chance—

"Stop it, Axus," snapped Arayallen.

Myropa was abruptly dumped from the pit of despair she had found in Axus's knowing gaze. She inhaled several unnecessary, deep breaths to steady her nerves, which felt as if they were crackling with frost.

"You know I hate it when you use your power on one of my creatures in my presence," said the goddess. "And are those my ocelots you're wearing?"

Axus's attention snapped toward Arayallen. "That is the problem with the rest of you. You always act as though my power is less deserving just because it interferes with your petty plans for your toys."

Arayallen sidled up to him. "If we didn't make our *toys*, you wouldn't have anything to break!"

"And such a joy it is," Axus said, but his expression held no joy. In fact, the only time Myropa had seen any expression but apathy on Axus's face was when he was convincing her that *his* power was the only cure for her destitution. He said, "If you don't want them to be so susceptible to my power, perhaps you should make them stronger. Oh, that's right. You don't know *how*."

Arayallen said, "It's not a matter of not knowing *how*, Axus, but rather the fact that we recognize a need for your power if our creatures are ever to progress."

"Yet you are all thieves, limiting my power with endless restrictions, and the noose continues to get tighter."

Arayallen shrugged. "It's your own fault. You don't know how to restrain yourself, so we must do it for you."

"You had no right to withdraw my access to the Sea," he snapped. He pointed to Myropa and said, "You ripped away a piece of my power and divvied it up to these weak atrocities."

"You should never have claimed so much power in the first place," Arayallen said. "Dozens of us pour our power into making these creatures and the worlds in which they live, yet only *you* gain power through their deaths."

Axus waved a hand toward Trostili, who had so far seemed pleased to sit back and watch the conflict. He said, "That was why you all created *him*, isn't it? You let him steal away some of my power before I can even claim it."

"It's not *your* power, Axus," said Arayallen. "Just because you decided you wanted it doesn't make it *yours*."

"No one else came up with a solution. The rest of you created and created, throwing away power, and none of that power was returned. It was *I* who discovered the power released during a soul's crossing of the veil. It was *I* who learned to capture it and thus gain power through *death*."

"You were not the first god to think of *destruction*."

"No, but what about your precious creatures—the ones that were living forever—like *gods*. How did you expect to get that power back? You didn't have a plan. *I* came up with a solution. You should be thanking me."

Arayallen leaned into Axus's face, and Myropa envied her that she was not affected by his power. "The problem is not that you found a way to reclaim the power but that you refused to give it back! *That* is why we took away your access to the Sea, and don't forget that we *all* made the sacrifice. We couldn't take away *your* access without also giving up our own. Thus, we *need* the reapers. Without them, the souls wouldn't make it back, and we would grow weak. The Sea empowers us *all*."

As Arayallen turned from Axus, she met Myropa's gaze so briefly that she wasn't sure it had been intentional. Somehow, she felt like Arayallen wanted her to understand something, and she did—much more than before. Myropa began to wonder if hers was not just a position of servitude but perhaps one of power. The thought had only just formed when she caught Trostili looking at her intently. It felt as if her heart stopped when she once again wondered if the gods could hear her thoughts.

Without regard for Axus and Arayallen, Trostili said, "Reaper, why did you come here?"

Axus and Arayallen abruptly ceased their quibbling and looked at her.

Myropa felt herself shivering and swallowed to clear her throat. She looked at Trostili and said, "I came to report on recent events."

He narrowed his gaze at her, then threw his arms over the back of the settee on which he lounged. "Very well, report."

Myropa glanced at Axus and Arayallen, then back to Trostili. She wasn't sure how much she was supposed to say to each of them. She decided to speak truth and let them sort it out. "The magi have escaped the realm."

Trostili glanced at his viewing pool and leaned forward. "Interesting. Where did they go?"

Axus turned to Trostili with a frown. "You expect me to believe you haven't been watching?"

Trostili spread his hands, then motioned to the discarded weapon on the floor. "I've been busy with other things."

They all turned back to Myropa expectantly. "Well?" said Trostili.

She shook her head. "I don't know." Upon seeing their disgruntled gazes, she turned to Arayallen and said, "It has lots of trees . . . and some of them talk?"

Arayallen appeared thoughtful as she tapped her lip. Then she waved noncommittally. "There are hundreds, *thousands*, that fit that description, and the magi could be in any *time*."

Axus clenched his jaw. "I *will* find them, Arayallen."

"Not likely, but you're more than welcome to look. It will keep you too busy to claim the rest."

Axus slammed his fist into a wall that didn't exist, and the air in front of him shattered. "I cannot believe Enani gave those ridiculous human magi access to the pathways." He turned and raised a finger. "She did this on purpose."

Arayallen rolled her eyes. "She didn't give access to *all* of them, and how was she to know you would get the itch to destroy everyone's hard work?"

"She's the Goddess of *Realms*. She can access any realm during any *time*. She would know."

"It doesn't work that way," said Trostili. "She's not Arohnu. She doesn't dispense prophecies. If she saw that you destroyed the world in the future, then what she saw would be what happens in truth—without the possibility of alternative outcomes. Therefore, anything she did in response wouldn't affect the outcome."

"That's what she *says*," said Axus. "I am still not convinced her power works that way."

"Only *she* knows," said Trostili. "Now let the reaper finish her report."

They all turned to Myropa again. "There was an attack on the forester." Glancing accusingly at Axus, she added, "The old servant died, and the youngest of the companions almost succumbed to his injuries, but he'll live. They've decided to seek out and join the forester."

"Who is this forester?" said Axus. "And why should I care about him?"

Myropa had been sure the attack on the Forester's Haven had come from Axus but conceded that he might not have had direct knowledge of it. She doubted his agents sought permission for every attack.

Trostili clapped his hands together. "Excellent. That's a *nearly* ideal outcome." He appeared thoughtful. "It may have been better had the youngest died. Revenge is a superb motivator." He glanced toward Myropa. "Then again, *too* much loss could have broken their spirits, and we can't have that so early in the game."

"*You* sent the attack?" Myropa said, so mortified that she forgot her station. Trostili seemed too consumed with reveling in his accomplishment to reprimand her.

"Of course," he said. "The forester can't put up a fight if he has no one to fight for him. He keeps leaving them behind. It may seem petty now, but a few pawns can seed an army."

Axus said, "What are you up to, Trostili? Are you pitting this forester against me?"

Trostili turned to him in amused dismay. "He's not the *chosen one,* Axus—not your Lightbane. He's just a human *forester.* He's not even a warrior or a magus. He plants trees! How much damage can he do?"

"*I* like the foresters," said Arayallen.

"So you have said," replied Trostili. "You should enjoy watching this one flounder around for a while."

Axus turned his full attention on Trostili. "What if he finds the Lightbane before we do? If you screw this up for me—"

"How could I?" said Trostili, raising his hands with innocence. "The prophecy is very specific, and the Lightbane is dead."

Axus looked genuinely surprised. "He is?"

Motioning toward Myropa, Trostili said, "The reaper took his soul to the Sea."

Axus grinned at her, and Myropa immediately felt drawn into him. The sensation abruptly stopped as he turned back to Trostili. "Then I can send my forces to cleanse the world immediately."

"Just give it a minute," Trostili replied. He sat back again, resting his head in his hands. "*Someone* needs to put up a fight or there's nothing in this for *me.* It won't do Aldrea any good in the end." His sharp gaze narrowed on Axus. "If I don't get anything out of this deal, I won't be so accommodating on the next one."

Axus balled his fists. "Fine, but I'll not hold off forever."

"I don't need forever," said Trostili as he sat forward and rubbed his hands together. "I just need a few terrible battles and one good war."

AASLO STRUGGLED TO DRAW BREATH. NO MATTER HOW HARD HE TRIED, his lungs wouldn't respond. After a few agonizing seconds, they finally expanded, and the blessed breath of life filled his chest cavity. He blinked the tears from his eyes and rolled just in time to avoid a massive tail strike. He tumbled over the rubble, ignoring the sharp edges and thorns digging into his flesh. Finally, he caught sight of his sword where it had fallen over the embankment. He glanced back in time to dodge a swipe of the creature's talons. This time, he rolled right over the embankment, his descent barely slowed by multiple briar bushes. Upon reaching the bottom, he quickly untangled himself, ripping the briars from his skin and clothes, then skittered over the debris to reclaim his sword.

The giant lizard paced along the edge of the embankment as if trying to decide if Aaslo was worth the effort. The beast was the size of a horse, with thick, green-black scales, long talons on its front and back paws, and giant spikes protruding from its head and spine. As it looked at him, Aaslo considered again that he might have made a mistake in damaging the beast's wings. If he hadn't, the monster might have flown away by now. The creature seemed dead set on making him the midday meal, though. He hoped Teza didn't come looking for him. While he knew she had magic, he had no idea if it would be useful in a fight, and he didn't want her getting eaten, too.

The monster finally lurched, jumping from the top of the embankment straight for him. Aaslo raised the sword, tightly gripping the hilt with both fists, and thrust upward just as the creature fell atop him. He felt the scales give, and the blade sank deep into the creature's chest. The beast reared, its colossal shriek crashing off the canyon walls. Blue blood spurted from its chest as it inhaled deeply, then inhaled some more. Just when Aaslo thought the creature might burst, it exhaled. The air striking his face heated in an instant. Aaslo dragged himself from beneath the beast, scrambling backward as he stared into the creature's maw. There, deep in its throat, was an orange-yellow light. The light grew rapidly, turning deeper red, then purple and blue before it came swirling out of the beast's mouth, a flame caught in a wind current. Aaslo raised his left arm to shield his face as he rolled to his side, but he wasn't fast enough. The most intense pain he had ever felt shattered his consciousness, and he instantly dropped into peaceful darkness.

Myropa screamed as the fire consumed Aaslo. She had arrived just as the fire beast released its deadly torrent. After the initial shock, her first thought was that Axus had reneged on his word. Aaslo was dead, and the war would be over before it started. Trostili would be furious. He might even exact payment from *her*, but nothing he did could compare to the pain she felt deep in her chest in that moment. It was a sensation she had thought impossible for her to experience. After decades of emptiness, she was suddenly filled with the worst longing and terror she had felt in both life and death. Not only was Aaslo hope for the world of Aldrea, he was *her* hope.

The monster succumbed to Aaslo's fatal blow after releasing its final breath—the breath that had taken the forester from her. Although no tears fell, she wept, her chest heaving with the pain of her loss. She lowered herself to the ground beside his charred body and waited for the tether that would draw them together. She was the closest. It had to be her. The Fates could not be so cruel as to attach him to someone else. The longer she waited, the worse her dread became. Had they truly forsaken her? Had he already crossed the veil with a stranger?

A motion at the edge of the chasm drew her attention. A woman's scream filled the air, but it didn't come close to echoing her own. The forester's companion, Teza, came sliding down the embankment. She hurried to his side, calling his name. Teza rolled Aaslo over, and Myropa wanted so much to stroke his peaceful face. Aaslo's left side was badly burned, his arm charred to a crisp, but his handsome face had suffered only what looked like a sunburn.

Teza laid her hands on the burned flesh of his neck and shoulder, muttering to herself. "No, no, no, no, no. Not a burn. Aaslo, I can't heal a burn. I'm sorry. I don't know how. Please, let this be a bad dream. Please, this can't be happening."

Myropa shook her head as the young woman tried to deny what was right in front of her. Teza turned her attention to the monster that had taken Aaslo from them. A desperate look came over her, and she lurched to her feet. She stomped on the monster as she pulled the sword from its chest. Then she began hacking at the beast. Myropa understood the need to lash out at something. With the chosen one dead, she had thought Aaslo her only hope—her world's only hope. She knew the prophecy, but she wanted to believe as much as Aaslo that it could be changed. Now, he was gone.

In that moment, Myropa wanted only to destroy Axus. She began to heave a tearless cry all over again as she simultaneously laughed. What would Aaslo say about a simple little reaper challenging the God of Death? Would he say it was useless fantasy? No, Aaslo would applaud her courage in fighting for what was right.

Myropa's entire attention had been consumed by her thoughts of

Aaslo and the gods, so when Teza suddenly stepped into her, she was shocked. She scurried away from the disturbing situation, then watched in horror as the girl stood over Aaslo and raised his sword over her head. Myropa and Teza screamed in unison as the blade descended, and Myropa knew the young woman had gone mad.

CHAPTER 19

PECK'S BOOTS SCUFFED THE DIRT ROAD AS HE GLANCED BACK AT MORY again. The boy was different since he awoke from death. He had the same genuine humor, the same eagerness to please; but, somehow, he seemed less . . . *innocent*. There was knowledge in his youthful gaze, knowledge that had not been there before. Whenever Peck stared too long, he was overcome with a sense of depth, of otherworldliness. Mory never spoke of it, though, and Peck consoled himself with the prospect that it was he who was cracked. When he had thought Mory dead, he had broken inside. He had felt pain that he had never thought anyone could bear, and if Mory hadn't returned, he didn't think he could have. It was in the moment of Mory's demise that Peck had learned how much he truly needed Mory.

"How are we going to find him?" said Mory for the hundredth time since they had left Tyellí.

"I told you. We'll go to that marquess. He's paying Aaslo's way, right? Aaslo's gotta end up there eventually."

"Right, but where's the marquess?"

"In Ruriton."

"Where's that?" said Mory.

"Pretty much due south," said Peck, pointing down the road. "Should I draw you a map?"

Mory shrugged. "I wouldn't know how to read it."

Peck grinned and ruffled Mory's shaggy mane. "That's okay. I wouldn't know how to draw it."

"I've never seen a map," said Mory.

Peck rubbed his chin, trying to think of the map he'd seen. "There was part of one hanging in the Rusty Nail. You remember? It was in the rear by the back door. I think someone mighta used the missing part in the outhouse."

"Oh right. That was a map? It just looked like squiggles and dots to me."

"The squiggles are supposed to show the kingdom borders, I think. The dots are places, like cities."

"How do they know where to put them?" said Mory.

Peck shrugged. "I don't know. Maybe they count their steps."

Mory looked at him aghast. "You mean they count their steps all the way to Ruriton? There's gotta be hundreds."

"More like millions," said Peck.

Mory shook his head. "How much is a million?"

Peck rubbed his chin again. "I don't know. Can't say that I've ever counted a million of anything, but I know it's more than thousands. That's what people mean when they say it."

"That makes sense," said Mory with a nod. "I counted a thousand once. I wanted to know how much it was, so I made a pile of pebbles by the river. It took a long time."

"When did you do that?" said Peck. "I think I would've remembered."

Mory shrugged. "I was supposed to stay home since I was too little to help you in the streets. I got bored and went down to the river."

"Mory! Something could've happened to you. You shouldn't've left the den by yourself."

"It was years ago, Peck. Nothing happened. I'm fine."

Peck glanced into Mory's deep gaze and swallowed what he was about to say. "Yeah, I know you're fine. It's okay now." He scuffed his boot on a rock as he looked down the road and then glanced behind them. Fields of grass swayed peacefully as far as he could see in every direction, and the road was empty. It felt like he and Mory were the only people in the world. For a moment, he felt safe.

The sky was burnt orange fading to dark purple. A few stars shimmered directly before his eyes, and Aaslo wondered if they were calling to him with their pulsating lights. He blinked several times, then coughed. Suddenly, his view was blocked by a dark-haired beauty. Her intense gaze was darker than the night and devoid of the stars' sinister enchantment. His vision began to clear; and, no, he wasn't looking at a goddess. It was—

"You're awake! Oh, Aaslo, I'm so glad you're awake. No"—Teza pushed him as he tried to sit up—"don't move. Just rest for a minute. You were hurt badly. I didn't think I could save you, but I did, Aaslo—I *saved* you. You're going to be okay."

He was relieved. It didn't feel like anything was wrong with him, but he was glad to have her assurances that all was well. He tried to lift his arm to wipe his face, but it didn't respond as it should have. It felt heavy and moved awkwardly. He felt a pressure on his arm and realized Teza was gripping it.

"Don't—don't move this one right now," she said. "It's, um, not finished. It'll get better, I'm sure. It just needs time to adjust."

"What are you talking about?" he said as he tried again to lift it. He then attempted to turn his head, but it, too, didn't seem to move right. "What's going on?" he said. "I thought you said I'm okay."

"Well, you are," she said, but by the way she worried at her lip, he was not convinced. "I had to make a few adjustments. Don't panic, okay, and I'll show you."

"All right," he said, "What is it?"

Teza helped him to lift his arm into his field of view, and his heart nearly jumped out of his chest. "*What did you do?*" he shouted as he whipped the appendage out of her hands. It slammed into the dirt beside him with a *whomp*, and dust was thrown into the air, causing him to cough. Teza scrambled backward as he struggled to sit upright.

"Now, now," she said in a placating voice. "You said you wouldn't panic."

"Panic? *Panic?*" he said. He looked down at the green-black scales that covered the bulging muscles of an appendage that ended in two-inch-long black talons. "This is the arm of a *monster*!"

"Well, it's *your* arm now," she said with a grin that failed to appease.

"*Why?*" was all he could muster among his chaotic thoughts.

"You were horribly burned—worse than anything I've ever seen. I don't know how to heal a burn that bad. I never got that far in my lessons, but I know how to reattach an appendage."

"You can reattach an *arm* but not heal a burn?" he said.

"Healing a burn is very complicated. I'm not even sure a master could have healed your arm. The only way to save your life was to remove it. I didn't want to leave you without an arm, though, so I cut the arm from the beast and attached it to you." She wrung her hands. "Um, we're not supposed to attach parts of different animals together. It's forbidden, actually. Most of the time the animals don't survive; and, well, the ones that do usually have serious side effects."

"Like *what*?" he said, his heart racing. He searched for his sword. He wanted nothing more than to hack the foreign appendage from his body.

"Well, you see, the healing magic encourages the body to regrow the links between the part and the whole. Your *part*, though, isn't human, so your body is trying to . . . um"—she pointed to his torso—"*consolidate* . . . the two."

Aaslo hesitantly traced the scales up the arm, but they didn't stop at the shoulder. Smaller scales covered the left side of his neck, under his jaw, to just below his ear. Then he looked down as his hand explored additional scales over his left pectoral muscle, across his ribs, and around to his back.

"Am I turning into one of those monsters?" he said with alarm.

Her dark curls bobbed as she adamantly shook her head. "No, not at all. Your body is changing the arm more than it's changing you. You see? It has scales, and it's stronger, but it's shaped more like a man's than a beast's."

Aaslo tried again to move the appendage. The motion felt foreign, but it did move similarly to his other arm. He opened and closed the long, muscular fingers, accidentally stabbing himself in the palm with his talons in the process. The sharp nails barely scored the thick scales that covered his flesh. At a loss for words, he looked up at Teza. "Will it stop?"

"Oh, yes. It's slowed considerably already. I don't expect it to spread much more. As your body adjusts, the motion will become more natural. I expect you'll be able to use it just as well as your old arm." She smiled and, with forced enthusiasm, said, "This one even has some improvements, don't you think?"

"I look like a monster, Teza. People will run screaming."

"That's true."

Aaslo nearly jumped when he heard the unexpected voice. Had Mathias been giving him the chance to come to terms with his new reality, or had his mind finally calmed enough to produce the phantom voice again?

"Well, you might need to wear a shirt with long sleeves . . . and a glove. But, you're a forester. You don't see many people, right?"

Aaslo groaned. This was only going to perpetuate the foresters' mystique. People already thought the foresters were mysterious creatures that swung from trees by their tails. A chill rushed through him, and Mathias began laughing uncontrollably.

He looked Teza directly in the eyes and said, "Am I going to grow a tail?"

Teza tilted her head and winked at him. "Do you *want* to grow a tail?"

"What? Of course not!"

Aaslo had to work hard to stand up. His body felt off-balance and kept tipping toward the left. He took a deep, steadying breath. Trying to ignore the piece of monster attached to his side, he looked around. They were still in the chasm, but the rest of the creature was farther uphill. He could see the heavy drag marks where Teza had pulled him downslope, and he understood why. A number of scavengers were picking at the carcass of the beast. Aaslo wondered if his arm was over there somewhere. He looked back at Teza. He could see the worry in her gaze. She was still waiting for his approval . . . or was it forgiveness? He knew she wouldn't have cut off his arm if she didn't think it was necessary. He couldn't imagine what insanity had driven her to attach the beast's arm to his body, but he knew she had tried her best to save him in the only way she could.

He solemnly said, "Thank you, Mage Catriateza."

Tears welled in her eyes, and she shook her head. "I'm not a full mage yet. I'll never be."

"You may be the only one left in Aldrea. That makes you the greatest magus in the world, and you've saved my life." He lifted the disturbing arm and squeezed the hand again. "You gave me a new arm. You didn't have to do that."

She said, "I imagine it would be pretty hard to be a forester with only one arm."

Aaslo nodded but continued to avoid looking at the part of him that had been replaced. He wasn't ready to process that trauma. He said, "Where's Dolt?"

Teza shrugged. "He grabbed my hair and practically dragged me from the cave. Then he ran off. That's when I saw the monster in the

distance. I worried that it had gotten you while you were out hunting."
Tears welled in her eyes again. "I thought you were dead when I found
you. You can't imagine how bad it was." Then she burst into heaving
sobs and threw herself into his arms. He wrapped his good arm around
her as she cried. "I'm so sorry, Aaslo. I didn't know what to do. I don't
even know what made me think to do it. I just reacted."

He patted her back. "It's okay, Teza. I'll learn to cope. You did your
best, and I appreciate that. You didn't have to do anything at all, and
probably no one else in the world would have hatched such a crazy plan."

Teza wiped her eyes and looked upslope to where the scavengers
were savaging the carcass. "I didn't know dragons really existed. I
thought they were myth."

"So did I," he said. "Do you really think it was a dragon?"

"Are you blind?"

"It has scales and wings and breathed fire," she said. "What else
could it be?"

"I thought dragons were bigger. They're always much bigger in the
stories."

"Maybe the stories exaggerate." She suddenly turned to him with
worry. "Or maybe it was a baby dragon."

Aaslo looked toward the sky with mounting anxiety. "We should
get as far from here as possible."

"Agreed."

"Agreed," said Teza.

"Agreed," whispered Myropa.

She couldn't believe what she had witnessed. That mess of a mage
had cut Aaslo's ruined arm from his body and replaced it with that of
a monster—a *dragon*. She didn't know if she should be pleased or horrified, but she was ecstatic that he had lived. She wanted to stay with
him to make sure he was truly well. If he took a turn for the worse,
she wanted to be the one at his side when he crossed. That was why
she became particularly flustered when she felt the nagging call of a
certain goddess.

Arayallen wasn't in her white marble room or her disturbing gallery. She was in a garden filled with the most vibrant flowers Myropa
had ever seen. The color seeped into the muted hues that had consumed
Myropa's vision since her death, and she was immensely grateful for
the brief opportunity to see something so intensely beautiful.

The goddess waved her hand over a cut blossom. The petals elongated and turned a darker shade of crimson-orange. She tilted her head thoughtfully, and long yellow stamens shot from its core. Leaning over, she placed the blossom back onto the plant, which eagerly accepted it. The entire shrub erupted with the same crimson-orange blossoms a moment later.

Myropa stood mesmerized. She was certain she had just witnessed the creation of new life. She couldn't imagine why the goddess would bless her with such an honor. Arayallen meandered through the garden without acknowledging her, and Myropa realized the goddess probably didn't care that she might be interested or impressed.

"Well?" said Arayallen. "How did it go?"

Myropa drew her thoughts back together and said, "How did what go?"

Arayallen stopped to look at her as if she were dense. "The encounter with the dragon, of course."

"That was *you*? *You* sent a dragon after Aaslo? I thought you *wanted* him to win."

Arayallen rolled her eyes. "It was only a *little* dragon. He did survive, didn't he?"

Myropa was furious. She wanted to scream at the goddess, but not only would it be foolhardy, it would be futile. "I thought he had died at first. He was very badly injured."

Arayallen frowned. "Is he that weak?"

"He's *human*," said Myropa. "And he's not a magus. Plus, he's never *seen* a dragon and wasn't expecting it."

"Well, if he's going to fight Axus's forces, he's going to have to start expecting the unexpected. And he's going to need to be stronger. What happened?"

"The fledgling healer he travels with replaced his charred arm with that of the dragon."

Arayallen tapped her lip as she nodded thoughtfully. "Interesting. I can work with that. I need you to do something."

"Yes?" Myropa said hesitantly.

"I need you to visit Disevy to ask him for a boon."

"What do you ask of him?" Myropa said.

Arayallen shook her head. "Not what *I* want. The request must come from you. He won't even see me right now. I think he's in one of his moods."

"What makes you think he'll see me or that he'll do anything *for* me?" cried Myropa. "I'm just a reaper."

Arayallen sighed. "I don't know. I think it's ridiculous, too, but you seem to have plucked his heartstrings. Or he's playing some game with Trostili. I can't tell, but I think he'll see you, and you might have a chance at getting something out of him."

"What is it you want me to get?" said Myropa.

"Strength," replied Arayallen. "Not for *you*, of course. For the forester."

"That's it? Just *strength*?"

"Disevy decides how to distribute his blessings," said Arayallen. "I just want him to decide to gift one."

"But Axus and Trostili are members of his pantheon. Why would he work against them?"

"We're not asking him to work against them." She grinned at Myropa knowingly and said, "We're only asking him to bless your Aaslo."

Myropa dipped her head. "He's not *my* Aaslo. He doesn't even know me."

"He could—*someday*," said Arayallen.

"When he's dead," said Myropa, "for a minute. Then he and everyone else in my world will go to the Sea, and I will still be cursed."

"Perhaps," said the goddess. She waved a dismissive hand. "Go now. Go to Disevy."

Before Myropa knew what was happening, she was standing in a forest surrounded by the most massive trees she had ever seen. A scuffle behind her caused her to turn, and she saw Disevy ambling up a path. He wore clothes not unlike those of a forester, but he seemed to have no interest in the trees. He appeared troubled as he stared at the ground lost in thought.

Myropa jumped out of the way as he nearly walked right through her. He abruptly stopped and turned as if just noticing something was near. His eyes widened, and his expression softened. Reaching for her hand, he bent low to press a kiss to her fingers.

"Lovely Myropa, it pleases me to see you again."

Myropa thought she would have blushed furiously if she had been capable of it. She said, "Greetings, Disevy. You look troubled."

He suddenly bent down and swept her off her feet. She wrapped her arms around his neck as best she could, considering his massive size, and he carried her through the forest as he spoke. "My dear, you have no idea. Difficult decisions weigh heavily on me."

"I understand," she said. "I, too, have many, although I rarely possess the power to make them of my own accord."

"Is that so?" he said. "Which decisions would you care to make?"

She grinned up at him. "All of them."

His booming laughter reverberated through her. "Would you not care to share *some* of them?" he said.

She tilted her head. "Perhaps, but that would also be my choice."

He stroked her cheek and said, "I believe you had that freedom once, and you did not care for it."

Myropa looked away in shame and whispered, "I cannot change the past."

"Would you if you could?"

She said, "I have seen how hard others fight for lives worse than mine. I think I might have made a rash decision. I thought I was trapped. I thought I could never make up for my failures. I thought I didn't deserve a better life, yet I couldn't live with what I had. I can't honestly say that I feel differently about that now, but I do think I could at least help others more deserving to succeed."

When Disevy didn't respond, she finally looked up at him. He wore the same concerned expression as when she had greeted him, and she thought he must have lost interest in her rambling. Then he met her gaze, and his own was filled with such grief, she thought she might fall into the pit of despair all over again.

He said, "It saddens me that you feel that way, Myropa, for when I see you, it is as if the sun has begun to shine on a vast, frozen wasteland. I feel like, if you just stayed long enough, it would completely melt, and life would bloom in places only ever touched by emptiness."

Myropa stared at him, unable to form a response. From any other man or god, she would have thought the words trite, but Disevy delivered them with such sincerity, she could not help but believe them.

He said, "I feel it is a failure of mine that I cannot show you your value."

Again, she was stunned into silence. He eventually settled her on the ground under a cascade of purple flowers that flowed from a massive wisteria. She lay back on a carpet of soft petals, and he settled beside her. As the branches directly above them separated, the sky darkened to a night unlike any Myropa had ever seen. It was a swath of purple and pink and blue and white, and it was bursting with stars that sparkled among brilliant swirls painted with artistic flare.

Disevy said, "Do you know what that is, my dear?"

"It's wondrous," said Myropa. "I've never imagined anything like it."

"The people who first saw it called it *nebula*. It's where Olios the Worldmaker creates new worlds and stars to light them. It's a rather messy process, I gather, but the end result is worth it, I think." Myropa stared in awe at the mix of colors and shimmering light. Never had she thought to see the place where worlds were born. Disevy finally turned to her and said, "Why did you come here, Myropa?"

She hesitated. She kept her gaze on the nebula as she said, "I must ask a favor."

"I see," he said with resignation.

"I'm sorry if I upset you."

From the corner of her eye, she saw him shake his head. "I know you did not come because you wished to see me."

"No, it's not that—"

He nodded. "Yes, it is. You do not think well enough of yourself to think I might wish to see you." He looked at her and waited until she met his pointed stare. "Nor would you expect a favor from me."

Myropa clamped her mouth shut. It was true. She would never have entertained the idea that Disevy, God of Virility, might want to see *her* or give her anything.

"The truth is, Arayallen sent me. She wishes a boon but thinks you more likely to grant it to me for some reason."

Disevy propped himself up on one arm to look at her. "She wanted you to pretend it was your idea?"

"Yes, but I don't want to lie to you."

"I appreciate that," he said as he plucked petals from a blossom. "What does Arayallen desire of me?"

"A blessing for a human on Aldrea."

Disevy nodded. "Tell me. Do *you* desire this blessing as well?"

Myropa tilted her head and smiled, thinking of Aaslo. "I do."

He hummed under his breath. "Arayallen knows you would never ask on your own."

"I would never think of it," Myropa said with a shake of her head.

He gazed deeply into her soul. "*Why?*"

Myropa was surprised by the question, sure he already knew the answer. "What have I done to deserve a blessing of a god?"

"But you do not ask for yourself," he said. "You ask for someone else. Someone living."

"Yes," she replied. "I ask for someone I care about—someone who could save my world if given a chance."

"You believe that?" he said.

"I do."

"You speak of this forester that vexes Axus. I know who he is, and I know what he means to you." He placed his finger under her chin and tilted her head up, ensuring that she was paying attention. He said, "I will grant him this blessing, Myropa, but I grant it for *you*."

Her frozen heart fluttered, and she smiled cautiously. "What will you grant him?"

He stroked a thumb across her cheek. "That is for me to decide. Now, I need you to do something for me." He held out his hand, opening it to reveal six shining stars. Myropa jumped in shock. She had never seen souls free of their vessels *and* uncontained.

"How did you get those?" she said in alarm.

"Do not concern yourself with that. I need you to carry them for me. It is imperative that Axus not get hold of these. Do you understand?"

"You want me to keep souls from Axus? How can I? He has only to look at me, and I am destroyed all over again."

He stroked her hair lovingly with his free hand and said, "I know, fair Myropa. You will learn. Axus is strong, but he is not all-powerful. Regardless, he will have no idea that you have them, so you need not worry about him asking."

"Demanding," she muttered, and then glanced at him, abashed. She had no idea what he meant about learning to deal with Axus, and it didn't seem as if he was willing to expound. She said, "Am I to take these to the Sea?"

"No, absolutely not," he said with a cut of his hand through the air.

"You must keep them with you. Don't tell anyone you have them. This is between you and me."

Myropa looked down at the souls in his hand and nodded. She opened her palm and manifested a clear orb. She pinched the orb between her thumb and forefinger and very carefully laid it over one of the loose souls. The orb pulsed, then turned pale blue once the first soul was contained. She repeated the process five more times, then attached them all to the string of souls that dangled from her belt.

When she looked at Disevy, he appeared fascinated. He met her gaze and said, "I've never seen this power in use. We don't usually have loose souls in Celestria."

"I didn't think you had *any*," she said.

He tilted his head and grinned with chagrin. "We don't."

"You—the gods, I mean—don't create the souls, do you?"

"No, we do not—just as we did not create the realms or time."

"Then who did?"

With a shrug, he said, "I suppose whoever created *us*."

"You mean there are *other* gods? Gods greater than *you*?"

"Perhaps. There are beings unlike us with great power—beings like the Fates. Who is to say there are not greater gods?"

"But, Arayallen said she designed Trostili."

"Yes, she designed his body but not his soul."

"You have souls as well?" Myropa said, thoroughly floored. "They must be very strong souls to hold so much power."

He reached out and stroked her cheek again. "Souls are infinite, Myropa."

Beginning to put the pieces together, she said, "Which means human souls hold power as well." He nodded. "But humans cannot access it," she said.

"To varying degrees," he replied with a shrug. "Some, like your magi, have been gifted the ability to tap into a small amount."

"But reapers have access to the Sea that's filled with innumerable souls," she said.

"So they do."

"Axus does not," she said, thoughtfully, "but he wants it badly."

Disevy's soft expression became serious. "He must never get it," he said.

Without thinking, Myropa grabbed Disevy's hand as she became filled with anxiety. "If Axus gains power through the process of death, then he stands to gain much power from destroying all life on Aldrea. What if this is his attempt to regain access to the Sea?"

He said, "My dear, *that* is why you must protect those six souls."

CHAPTER 20

"How much longer?" said Mory.

"I don't know," replied Peck.

"But I'm tired of walking. We've been doing it *forever*. I think my feet are about to wear through my soles."

Peck sighed. "I've told you five times already that we'll be there soon. The man with the potato wagon assured us that we're in Ruriton. He said it's only a couple days' walk to Dovermyer. That's where the marquess has his estate."

Mory stuffed his hands in his pockets. "Walking is boring. We might as well be walking in circles. The land looks the same here as it did this morning and yesterday and the day before. It's *all* the same. I thought things would be more exciting outside the city."

"Maybe it'll be more exciting at the marquess's estate."

"Do you think he'll let us stay?"

"I doubt either of us will see the marquess. He has men to deal with the likes of us."

"But they won't hurt us, right? I mean, we haven't done anything to them."

Peck shrugged. "The marquess seems interested in Aaslo, and we're Aaslo's men."

"What if Aaslo owes him money?" said Mory. "You know what Jago did to people that owed him money."

Peck frowned. "I don't think Aaslo owed the marquess money. According to the rumors, the marquess wanted to hire him to do something."

Mory danced in front of him to walk backward with his finger held high. "*You* said not to trust the rumors."

"Well yeah, but sometimes rumors is all you got. Just don't believe them until you know for sure."

Mory tilted his head to look over Peck's shoulder. "Hey, there's people coming. *A lot* of people, it looks like."

Peck glanced back to see a caravan of riders and wagons kicking up dust in the distance. He grabbed Mory by the collar and dragged him off the road. "Come on," he said as he gently pushed aside the tall grass. "We don't know who that is, and I don't like getting caught out in the open like this."

"Maybe they'll think we're refugees from the blight we keep hearing about."

"The refugees are all walking the other way. We are the only people I've seen for two days going this direction—besides *them*."

"Maybe they'll give us a ride," said Mory as they ducked down in the grass to watch the procession pass.

"Maybe they'll capture us or leave us for dead by the road," replied Peck.

"Why would they do that?" Mory whispered, although it was unlikely their voices would have been heard over the clamor of wagons and horses.

"I don't know. People do strange things. Someone tried to kill us, remember."

"How could I forget?"

Mory's haunted gaze felt like a punch to the gut. Peck couldn't imagine what Mory had gone through. "Do you, um—"

"What?" said Mory.

Peck shook his head and stood again as they trudged back to the road. "Never mind."

Mory fell back in line beside him. "No, what?"

Peck looked sideways at him. "Do you remember being dead?"

"I was *dead*?"

Peck immediately felt bad for bringing it up. "I'm not sure. The apothecary said you were. I didn't believe it, though. It's just that, ever since you got better, you look different—like you know more. I thought maybe you remembered what it was like—being where you were."

Mory scratched his head. "I don't *feel* any different." His eyes lost focus as he gazed into the not-so-distant memory. "I might remember a woman. She was kind. She sat with me, I think. We didn't talk much." He shrugged. "Maybe I'm just remembering the apothecary."

Peck shook his head. "You and the apothecary didn't talk at all. You were too far gone by then."

Mory shrugged again. "Maybe it was a dream. I'm glad I didn't die, though. Who else would take care of you?"

Peck nodded. "You're right. I'd be getting into all kinds of trouble."

"I keep you honest," said Mory with a cheeky grin.

Peck laughed. "There's nothing honest about either of us."

With a troubled expression, Mory said, "Are we bad people, Peck?"

He didn't answer for a long while. Finally, he exhaled and said, "Maybe a little. Mostly, I think we're just desperate people. I like to think we'd do good if we could."

"Would you really give up thieving?" said Mory.

Peck grinned. "I don't know. I'm pretty good at it. Seems a waste to give up being so good at something."

Mory nodded. "That makes sense." After a long pause, he said, "So, how much longer till we get there," which elicited *another* groan from Peck.

Peck had to console Mory when they didn't get *there* that night. In fact, they were forced to stop long before dark. The caravan that had passed them earlier in the day stopped on the side of the road, beside a creek. Since Mory didn't know how to swim, they had to make camp as well. They stayed far from the caravan, but Mory was eager for excitement after weeks of walking and begging rides on rickety wagons.

"Please, Peck. We'll stay in the shadows. They won't even know we're there."

"What's the point, Mory?"

"I'm *bored*. It'll be exciting."

"What's so exciting about spying on a bunch of strangers? If we get caught, they'll think we aim to rob them."

"Well, maybe we do," said Mory. "I know I could use better shoes, and you've been grumbling about getting some real food since we left the last village."

"We have nowhere to run or hide. If they see us, we're as good as caught."

"All right, so we won't rob them. Can't we just *look*? Even if they catch us, they won't be able to say we did anything wrong."

"And if they're the kind of people that don't care for facts?"

Mory sighed heavily. He stood and paced in a circle, then crouched back down. After he repeated the cycle four more times, Peck finally gave in. "Fine. We'll stay far out of the firelight and downwind. Don't even think about taking anything."

Mory bounced up with glee. "That's great, Peck. Maybe they'll invite us for dinner."

"No!" said Peck, raising a finger. "We're *not* talking to them."

"All right, all right. I was just joking."

They grabbed their packs in case they had to make a quick escape and circled wide to the east. They hid their packs behind a few scraggly bushes and got on their hands and knees to inch closer to the camp. The grass and shrubs along the creek covered their stealthy approach, and they were able to get a decent view of the camp from just within hearing distance.

Peck immediately knew something was wrong. He placed a hand over Mory's mouth when he started to speak. Then he pointed toward the center of the camp, where several people were gathered. None of them looked like the kind of people Peck was used to seeing. The men wore strange clothes and had hair down to their waists. He couldn't understand what they were saying, but it was obvious they were having an argument.

One of the men waved to the side, and several grotesque monsters with grey, saggy skin stalked forward, dragging a line of bound people behind them. The terrified people had gags in their mouths and ropes tied around their necks and wrists. A taller man, wearing a long white tunic and fitted black pants, withdrew a small stick about the length of his forearm from a bag. He pointed it at the first person in line. Nothing happened, so he went to the next. After several more, he became angry and shouted something. Then the first man drew a long knife and slit the first prisoner's throat.

Mory squirmed behind Peck's hand, but he held the boy tight. Peck was afraid to move. The first man went down the line, killing each of the prisoners. When they were all dead, the monsters brought out another line of captives. The taller man pointed the stick at each of them. On the fifth person, an older woman, the tip of the stick began to glow. The man looked pleased. He tested each of the others before having them all killed except the older woman.

The taller man placed the stick into a bag, from which he withdrew a book. He read a passage from the book aloud, then dragged his hand through the air in a squiggly pattern. The first man stepped forward and used his knife to carve a symbol on the woman's forehead. She cried in pain, but when he was finished, she no longer possessed the look of terror. Instead, her eyes were vacant and her jaw was slack, as if she had lost all awareness of her surroundings. The taller man placed the book into the bag and handed it to a younger man, who ducked into a tent. Then the taller man began to ask questions that Peck could understand.

"What manner of magus are you?" said the man.

The woman's voice was hollow as she answered. "I'm a runesmith."

The man growled in frustration and turned back to the first. "This is a waste of time. She is only a runesmith."

The first said, "Some runesmiths are quite powerful."

"Not in this land," muttered the taller man. To the woman, he said, "Where are the other magi?"

She said, "I don't know."

"You lie!" he shouted.

"She cannot," said the first.

The taller man inhaled deeply, then said, "Why are they missing?"

"They were recalled," said the woman.

"Why?"

She said, "Because the prophecy has failed."

He laughed. "The prophecy has not failed. Everything is happening exactly the way it was foretold. You just don't like the outcome."

"Get on with it," said the first man.

The taller man said, "Why are you not with the others?"

"The evergate nearest me was destroyed. I couldn't join them in time to leave."

"So they left?" said the first.

"Gone to another realm," said the woman.

Both men appeared pleased. They grinned as the woman slumped forward, and the taller of the two dragged the blade across her throat.

Peck motioned to Mory, and they crawled back the way they had come. Once they were far enough away, they began running along the creek as fast as their feet would take them. After several minutes, they stopped to catch their breath.

"Who—who were they," Mory said between gasps.

"I don't know," said Peck, who was bent forward with his hands on his knees. "But I bet it has something to do with Aaslo."

"Why would you say that?" said Mory.

"He's a forester. *For-e-ster.* They live in the *forest.* Why was he in Tyellí? There are no forests anywhere near Tyellí. Why did he go to the palace? Why was he carrying a head? Why did the marquess want to see him? *He's* weird." Peck hooked a thumb over his shoulder. "*They're* weird. It's probably related."

Mory's eyes glinted with fright in the moonlight. He said, "You think they had something to do with the people who tried to kill us?"

Peck shook his head. "I don't know." He shook with fear and anticipation. "What I do know is that we need that bag."

"What bag?"

"The one with the book and stick."

"Why do we need it?" said Mory. "I don't want anything to do with that stuff."

"I know. Neither do I, but Aaslo might need it."

"Why would Aaslo need it?" said Mory. "He's not slitting people's throats—at least, not as far as I know."

"They're full of magic," said Peck. "That means they're power, and the enemy has it. If we can steal it, then we can give it to Aaslo."

"But Aaslo's not a magus. What would he do with it?"

"I don't know. Maybe nothing. But at least we can prove to him that we're useful. He might decide to keep us around."

Mory's voice quavered with fright as he said, "Is that something you worry about, Peck? Would he turn us away?"

Peck regretted his words. He said, "Don't worry about that. I'll take care of things if that happens." He didn't want to admit to Mory that he worried about it often, especially since they had finally gotten up the courage to leave Tyellí. The apothecary had let them keep most of Galobar's money, but it wouldn't last forever. Also, Peck wasn't much of a fighter, and he knew Mory felt safer with Aaslo.

After working out the plan, Peck and Mory summoned their courage and slunk back toward the camp. The two men who had performed the horrid ritual were seated at the fire with their heads bent over a map rolled out on a folding table. The monsters patrolled the perimeter seemingly at random. Two of them nearly collided with each other, then stood for several seconds studying one another, as if confused about whether or not they had found an intruder. The creatures weren't completely oblivious, though. They scanned the darkness using all their senses, tilting their heads toward sounds, sniffing the air, even licking it every so often. At one point, a raccoon dared sneak too close to one of the wagons. A grey monster was on it within seconds, ripping its flesh apart and eating all it could stuff into its mouth before another of the monsters stole the carcass.

Peck shivered with disgust and anxiety, already regretting his decision. He was determined to go through with it, though. He waited until there was a gap in their patrol, then darted toward the target tent, the one with the magic stick and book. He got the same thrill every time he approached a mark. It had the sweetness of excitement and the sourness of anxiety all wrapped into a tasty package. He controlled his breathing with practiced ease and listened for movement from within the canvas structure. As one of the monsters passed, he held himself against the side of the tent in the darkest shadow. The monster wasn't looking *into* the camp, though. Once it had passed, Peck untied two of the laces that held the material to a corner post and peered inside. It was dark, with only the smallest amount of light from the campfire glowing through the canvas and streaming in through a gap in the front flap.

He released a few more ties and slipped through the opening. As soon as he was inside, he knew he'd made a mistake. He hadn't looked for the younger foreigner before entering the camp. The man was lying on a bedroll with his back turned, but Peck doubted he was asleep. No one could fall asleep that quickly with so much grunting and growling just outside the tent. Peck didn't think he'd be able to sleep knowing those monsters were within fifty miles.

As Peck inched closer, he realized the man had stuffed wads of material into his ears. Peck wondered how anyone could feel secure enough to intentionally dispense with their ability to hear while sleeping alone. He searched the tent, moving as little as possible, and came up with nothing. The only place he hadn't yet looked was with the man. He knew nothing about these people except that one or more of them was a magus and they liked to kill people. Suddenly, a shadow was just outside the flap. It yelled something in a foreign language, but the young man didn't move. Just as the flap was pulled aside, Peck fell back into the corner, curled into a ball, and pulled a half-empty sack over himself.

He recognized the voice of the man who had wielded the knife against the innocent victims. Peck peeked between the folds of the sack. The man rattled off a few words, then growled as he stepped into the tent. He grabbed the younger man by the foot and yanked him off his bedroll. The younger man shouted, then pulled the fabric from his ears as he scrambled to his feet. They had a brief exchange; then the younger followed the other one out. Peck nearly jumped out of his skin when something jabbed him in the back. He lurched and turned to find Mory blinking at him through the opening.

He was furious that Mory had come into the camp, but he couldn't voice his feelings at that moment. They needed to find the bag and get out. The younger man hadn't taken it with him, so Peck scrambled over to the man's bed. There, beneath the roll, was the bag. He grabbed it and almost ran into Mory as he turned back to the opening he'd made. He pushed Mory toward the opening but forced him to a halt before the boy ran right out in front of one of the monster sentries. Once the thing had moved on, Mory stepped out of the tent. He suddenly drew up short with Peck on his heels. Mory had come face-to-face with one of the monsters.

The monster looked at Mory curiously, and Mory stared back. Peck knew Mory was probably frozen with fright, just as he was in that moment. The monster abruptly turned and walked the other way. Peck was so shocked, he forgot to move. Mory had already made it into the grass before Peck started to breathe again.

After making it out of the camp, they didn't stop to chat. They ran the rest of the night. When they were so worn they couldn't possibly take another step, they took turns napping, then got up and ran some more. They bypassed every town they saw, avoided every traveler, and stole food from barns, silos, and chicken coops along the way. The farther they got into Ruriton, though, the rockier the highlands and boggier the lowlands became. Goats and swine were more prevalent, but farms were fewer and mostly consisted of rice or potatoes.

Besides their grumbling bellies and overworked muscles, Peck's greatest worry was that magi could somehow track their stolen possessions. He had never before stolen from a magus. That was one line he never would have crossed in Tyellí, and he had made sure Mory knew it, too. He hadn't made many mistakes as a thief. Thieves who made mistakes didn't live long. His greatest folly had been stealing a nasty old sack from a worn traveler with a crazy horse outside a building that looked like a tree.

CHAPTER 21

"WHAT'S THAT IDIOT DOING?" SAID AASLO.

"I think he's scared of your arm," replied Teza.

"I would be, too."

Aaslo tried to ignore the offensive appendage as much as possible. He clenched the fist and then released it. He didn't know which was worse, the fact that it felt foreign or that it was becoming more familiar. "I can't blame him there," said Aaslo, "but he's being ridiculous."

Teza nodded. "Yeah, it's kind of weird behavior for a horse."

They were both on foot as they led the donkey and pack mule down the road. Meanwhile, Dolt kept pace with them from at least twenty yards away. When they stopped, he stopped, and when they continued, he did as well. The donkey and pack mule had been wary when Aaslo first made it back to their campsite, but both had quickly adjusted to the foreign smell. Dolt, however, was being stubborn as usual and wouldn't allow Aaslo or Teza near him. Unfortunately for Aaslo, his pack was tied to the horse's saddle, so he hadn't been able to change his clothes in two days. He was glad that at least the rain had stopped, but he worried every time he saw dust in the distance that they were about to encounter other travelers. With his new physique, he figured they were most likely to kill first and avoid asking questions.

Dolt abruptly turned down a rough path that led away from the road. Aaslo shouted, but of course his calls were ignored. Aaslo was about to give up on ever seeing his belongings again when Teza said, "Hey, look at this." She had bent down to retrieve something from the path. After brushing off the dirt, she held up a rotted sign. "It says 'Ruriton,' and it has an arrow."

Aaslo searched the brush beside the road and eventually found a broken post that had been consumed by plants. He lined up Teza's piece of the sign and groaned. "Of course that infernal horse knows the way. There's something off about him."

"*Yeah, he's yours.*"

Teza said, "Maybe he used to belong to a magus. I've seen them use spells to teach their horses to do unusual things."

"Well, he certainly *looks* weird enough to be bespelled."

"*Says the dragon man.*"

"I'm not a dragon man," Aaslo grumbled.

"*I wonder if you can breathe fire.*"

"That's absurd."

"Yes, it is," said Teza. "*Dragon man* sounds like some bard is trying too hard. How about *man dragon*—or *mandragon.*"

Aaslo groaned, "That's even worse. You two please stop."

Teza glanced around, then leaned in and whispered, "Is he speaking to you *now*?"

Aaslo rubbed his temples with his fingers and yelped when he nearly put out his own eye with a talon. Mathias laughed, and Aaslo said, "He never stops."

Teza said, "Do you think you really hear him, or is it a manifestation of your guilt over not being able to save him?"

He glanced toward her uncertainly. "I don't know. Mostly, I think I'm crazy."

"Well, then you're not. If you know you're crazy, then you're not really crazy."

"I'm not sure that's true," he said. "Magdelay cast the preservation enchantment. I sometimes wonder if she trapped his soul inside his head."

"I don't think it works that way," she said.

Aaslo shook his head. "I doubt it's true anyway. He doesn't sound like himself. I mean, his voice is the same, but he doesn't *act* like Mathias."

"How so?"

"Mathias would tease in good fun, but he was always positive and encouraging. Even though he was far better than I was at almost everything, he always told me I could be just as good if I worked at it. *This* Mathias—the one in my head—he's harsh."

Teza shrugged. "Death could change a person."

"He said something similar," said Aaslo.

"Then he has a point."

They both paused when they noticed that Dolt was standing across the middle of the road unmoving. He seemed completely unconcerned as they approached and even let Aaslo take his reins. Aaslo was so relieved that he told Teza to close her eyes and shucked his filthy clothes right there in the road before putting on a fresh set.

"Um, Aaslo?" said Teza from behind him.

"Yeah?"

"I think you need to see this. Hurry."

He slipped the clean shirt over his head and stepped around Dolt to join her. Not far ahead was a man sitting beside the road on a folding chair. His head was bent, and a book was open in his lap. A horse grazed next to him, and both appeared unfazed by the creatures encroaching on them from either side of the road.

"Does he not see them?" said Teza. The man licked his finger, glanced up, then looked back down and turned the page. "Maybe he's with them," she said.

"No," said Aaslo. "They're preparing to attack."

"Are those the things you told me about? The things that killed your friend?"

"Yes," he said, his stomach churning.

"You told me the others were controlled by a magus. Maybe he's their magus, and they want you to *think* they're going to attack him."

"I don't think they've seen us yet," said Aaslo.

"I'm surprised they haven't smelled you yet."

"How could they not?" said Teza. "We're standing out in the open, right in the middle of the road."

"Can you tell if he's a magus?"

"Can *you* tell if someone's a fisherman by looking at him from a distance?"

Aaslo scowled at her. "No, I just thought maybe you could use your power to detect if he has any. You know, cast a spell or something to sense when a magus is near."

She shook her head. "That would have been wonderful at the academy. I would've avoided being the butt of so many practical jokes."

Aaslo watched as ten of the disgusting, saggy-skinned grey things drew closer to the man on the chair. Most were wearing clothing like any commoner, although some were dressed as soldiers complete with leather and plate armor. Aaslo didn't recognize the uniforms or the crest, a white ring containing a white starburst on a black field. In the light of day, the creatures looked more grotesque than sinister.

"They were certainly sinister when they killed me."

Aaslo's guilt rolled over in his stomach.

"Well?" said Teza.

"Well what?" he replied.

"Are you going to help him or not?"

He frowned at her. "Of course I'll help him. I'm not going to just stand here and watch a man get slaughtered. I'm thinking of a plan."

"Taking your time again, I see. Will you be too late to save him as well?"

"A plan?" said Teza. She huffed with frustration, then raised her hand toward the monsters. A tight ball of white light manifested in front of her open palm. It suddenly streaked toward the monster closest to the waiting man. When it was about ten feet from him, the white ball struck and shattered a magical barrier before colliding with the creature. The monster was knocked off his feet but recovered quickly. All the creatures turned in alarm, as if just seeing them. The man in the chair continued to read, seemingly without concern.

Aaslo spun and grabbed his axe from Dolt's saddle with his monstrous arm. He was surprised that, in its strong grip, the axe felt as if it weighed almost nothing. He drew his sword and held it out for Teza. "Here, take this!" he shouted as the monsters closed the distance.

"What am I supposed to do with this?" she said as she took it. The tip immediately dropped into the dirt. "I don't know how to use a sword, and I can't even lift the thing."

Aaslo growled and took the sword from her, offering his belt knife in exchange. "You won't have any reach with this. It's only for an emergency. Stay back or use your powers to attack them."

"I tried that," she said. "It didn't work."

"Don't you have any other spells?"

"Um . . . probably. I just can't think of them at the moment. I wasn't training to be a warrior. I was training to be a healer."

Aaslo ground his teeth. "Then why did you attack them?"

She pointed to the man in the chair. "I was afraid they'd eat him!"

Without responding, Aaslo leapt in front of Teza to meet the first creature. He slashed the unarmored monster across the chest and then kicked it backward into one of its comrades. He ducked as one swiped at his head with a rusty sword and smashed his axe through the creature's leg. It screeched as it fell to the ground but continued to attack despite the egregious wound. Aaslo hacked at another of the creatures that was attacking him from the side. A third was abruptly knocked back by a brilliant ball of light, which gave him the chance to smash his axe through the head of the monster crawling toward him. From the corner of his eye, he caught sight of an armored monster sneaking up on Teza. He threw his axe as he turned, lodging it in the back of the creature's skull just before it reached her. As it fell, Teza blinked at Aaslo in shock, then screamed and pointed behind him. Aaslo got his sword up in time to stab his immediate attacker, but the blade became lodged in the monster's chest cavity. He placed his boot on the creature's chest and yanked, but the blade wouldn't budge.

A female creature flanked Aaslo, bringing a saber down toward his head. He raised his arm as the blade flashed in the sunlight. The sword struck the green-black scales and was deflected, casting sparks as it slid to the side. Something inside him stirred—something foreign. He instinctually lashed out, raking the razor-sharp talons across his attacker's sagging face, then sank the claws into her neck and ripped out her throat. When he realized what he'd done, bile swept up his throat. He tossed the white, bloody mess aside, then reached again for his sword. The blade finally came free, and he swung with the strength of both arms to lop the head off the next foe. He was showered in white blood as he engaged the final attackers amid a stream of white sparks that dazed and delayed them.

When nothing remained but mutilated corpses, Aaslo slunk back to join Teza. She looked up at him with wide, frightened eyes, then smirked as she pulled a piece of gore from his hair, discarding it with a flick.

He said, "I'm so frustrated."

She glanced at the mess behind him. "Why? You were amazing—much better than I expected."

He shook his head. "It's not that. I need to change again." As he turned to grab fresh clothes from his pack, Teza started to laugh, then doubled over as she became hysterical.

She wiped her eyes and said, "I'm sorry. I don't know what came over me. I was just so scared."

Aaslo didn't change right away. Instead, he grabbed a rag and wiped the worst of the milky blood and gore from his face and hands. He cringed as he cleaned the black scales, remembering how he had ripped out a woman's throat with nothing more than the claws of a foreign beast—*his* claws. As he scrubbed his neck, he strode over to the man in the chair, who was still reading. When Aaslo stopped, the man finally snapped his book shut and stood. He raised his face and met Aaslo's gaze.

"Greetings, Sir Forester. It is a great honor to finally meet you."

"I feel like I shouldn't have to say this, but never trust a man who reads through a battle."

Aaslo studied the man's fresh face. He appeared to be near Aaslo's age, but he looked to have never spent a single day in the sun or laboring. His hair and skin were immaculate. His pale grey eyes stood out in contrast to his thick black lashes and dark mahogany hair and brows. His face was clean-shaven, his teeth white and straight, and his smile seemingly genuine. He wore a black and brown tunic over black trousers, and his polished, knee-high black boots looked too new to be comfortable.

Aaslo said, "You seem to know who I am. Who are you?"

The man tilted his head. "My apologies. Sometimes I forget that we do not yet know each other. My name is Ijen. And yours?"

Eyeing him skeptically, Aaslo said, "I thought you knew who I am."

"So did I, but now you're something else, aren't you?"

The man tapped the book he held against his chest, seemingly out of habit. He said, "I know much about you, but I've never caught your name."

"Lie."

"I'm not going to lie," Aaslo muttered. "I'm Aaslo. She's Teza," he said, pointing with his axe.

The man eyed the black scales on Aaslo's hand. He appeared thoughtful as he tapped the book. He said, "Hmm, interesting." He opened the book, lifted the pen that was pinched between the pages, and made a notation. He muttered, "I didn't realize that part came first. I was certain it happened afterward."

Teza cautiously traversed the battlefield and came to stand beside

Aaslo. She crossed her arms and said, "Who are you? Tell us now or Aaslo will rip out your throat."

Aaslo looked at her aghast. The man glanced toward her, nodded, mumbled another "Interesting," and made another note in the book. He blew across the page, then snapped it shut before gripping it against his chest again.

"I have not done a good job of introducing myself," he said. "I apologize again. I'm not used to interacting with people."

"What do you mean?" said Teza.

The man bowed in formal greeting and said, "I am Ijen Mascede. I—"

Teza pushed in front of Aaslo and placed an accusatory finger in Ijen's face. "Don't listen to him, Aaslo. Don't talk to him." To Ijen, she said, "He's mine! I won't let you experiment on him."

Ijen raised his brow. "It looks to me like you already have."

With a stomp of her foot, Teza said, "It wasn't like that. I did what was necessary to save his life."

Ijen said, "Truly, I mean neither of you any harm."

"*Likely story.*"

Aaslo pulled Teza back to his side. He said, "What's going on?"

"He's a Mascede," she said angrily. "Their bloodline believes in observation and experimentation, both physical and social. They think seculars are their playthings. They toy with them to see how they'll react."

Aaslo looked at Ijen with disgust. The man held up his free hand and said, "That is true. Most of the Mascedes do feel that way, but I am not like that. I cannot be, due to the nature of my power."

"And what's that?" Teza snapped.

He bowed again. "I am a prophet."

Teza took one step back, and then another. She held up a hand as if to ward off impending evil and said, "Don't you dare tell me how I die. I don't want to know."

"*I already know how I die.*"

Ijen tilted his head at her and said, "You need not concern yourself with that. I do not know how you die at this time."

Aaslo interrupted the exchange with a more pressing question. "Why are you sitting in the middle of nowhere on the side of the road?"

"I've been waiting for you."

"Why?" said Aaslo.

"Because this is where and when we meet," replied the prophet.

Teza said, "Don't talk to him, Aaslo. Don't ask questions. Nothing good comes of speaking of prophecy."

Aaslo looked back at her. "My entire life has become prophecy, Teza, and yours now as well. It cannot be avoided." He turned back to Ijen. "Why didn't you run or fight against the creatures?"

Ijen tapped his book and said, "Because that's not how it happened."

"In the prophecy," said Aaslo.

Ijen smiled. "Yes, you understand."

"No, I don't," said Aaslo. "You would just sit there and trust your life to this prophecy?"

"Oh, not at all," said Ijen. "There were lines in which I did not survive. Sometimes you do not arrive in time, sometimes not at all. Once I saw your horse, I knew you would defeat them."

"But you didn't think to help?" said Aaslo.

"Coward."

"No, no. That would have been bad. In all of the lines that I fought or ran, I died. It was best to sit quietly while you worked it out."

"Wait a minute," blurted Teza as she pushed in front of Aaslo again. "Prophets aren't supposed to see their *own* lines."

Ijen nodded. "Yes, that is true. That is my curse." He looked toward Aaslo. "If a prophet sees his own line, it creates paradoxes and self-fulfilling prophecies. I came here to await you because I saw it in the prophecy. If I had not seen it ahead of time, I would not have been here. The results of the prophecy could not, or would not, have occurred without the prophecy itself. Hence the reason I am not good at interacting with people. I have spent the majority of my life studying the events of the future, the events from this point forward, rather than actually living."

"Why would you do that?" said Aaslo.

"Because I am a Prophet of Aldrea."

Teza gasped. "*You* study the Aldrea Prophecy? You can't be." She looked at Aaslo. "The Prophets of Aldrea are revered and kept under close guard. They aren't permitted to communicate with anyone except, under supervision, with those who have been approved by the council." She turned her attention back to Ijen. "They would never have left you behind."

Ijen tapped his book and averted his gaze. "I didn't tell them."

Teza shouted with dismay, "You didn't tell the council that you were receiving the Aldrea Prophecy?"

"I didn't tell *anyone*—until now," replied Ijen. "They would have locked me up, and I wouldn't be here to meet with you, although I'd rather be with them right now."

Aaslo growled, "If you've seen the future, and you know what will become of this world, why would you abandon it to that fate?"

Ijen blinked at him. "I haven't seen the whole future, but what I have seen is dark. Why would I want to live in a world of death?"

Aaslo slapped the filthy rag into the dirt and said, "Here I was thinking you were going to tell me how to save it."

Ijen shook his head. "I'm afraid that's not possible." Then, with a glance toward the sack hanging from Aaslo's waist, he said, "Death is an inevitability at this point." He tapped the book again. "It's good you didn't change your clothes yet."

"Why?" said Aaslo.

"Because this line means we still have a chance of survival. Now, if you would please unsheathe your sword?"

"Why?"

Ijen met his gaze and said, "Because you forgot to kill the magus."

The prophet abruptly ducked and scrambled to hide behind his folding chair as a sleek red javelin shot through the air where his head had been. It collided with the rock outcrop on the opposite side of the road and exploded. Aaslo spun and began running toward the attacker with Teza on his heels. Just as he shouted for her to go back, another javelin struck an invisible wall in front of him, ricocheting backward to obliterate a swath of boulders.

The air became a haze of ashy sediment, but Aaslo made out a darker figure shifting toward another pile of rocks. He leapt forward just as flame filled the air in front of him. His heart skittered as he remembered the last time he had experienced such a sight. He twisted to lead with his left when the fire struck. The scent of burnt fabric reached his nose, but he felt no discomfort from the heat where the scales provided protection.

Aaslo reached out and grabbed the shadowy figure by the heel as he tried to scramble up the slope. He dragged the man down to his level, raised his sword over his head, then thrust it through the foreigner's face. The magus bled red like any other. As the dust finally settled, Aaslo considered the brutality of the attack. He had never wanted to be a killer. He wanted to be a harbinger of life and growth, but something was squirming inside him, something that relished the hunt.

Backing down the slope, he nearly slid into Teza. "I saved you again," she said. "You owe me your life twice over."

"What are you talking about?"

She looked at him like he was daft. "The *shield*? You would have been itty-bitty little bits if I hadn't thrown that up."

"Yes," he said, "I didn't know you could do that."

"It's one of the first spells we learn—for protection," she replied.

"That might have been helpful earlier when I was fighting."

She shrugged as she led the way back to where Ijen was sitting again in his chair. "I forgot about it."

"How could you forget that?" Aaslo groused.

"Don't snap at me. *You* try thinking under pressure."

"*I do*," he said. He looked at Ijen as the man stood and said, "Well, Prophet, what do we do now?"

Ijen shook his head. "I cannot tell you which paths to take. It's forbidden. There are very specific rules for prophets."

Aaslo huffed. "Is it safe to change my clothes now?"

Ijen smiled. "I think so."

Aaslo grunted and then looked at Ijen's horse, who hadn't moved during the entire encounter. "Your horse is remarkably well-behaved," he said.

"As is yours," replied Ijen, eyeing Dolt where he stood in the middle of the road. "Mine is bespelled."

"Mine's an idiot," said Aaslo as he realized Dolt was actually asleep.

He used the fresh clothes that were now rags sodden with monster gore to wipe the rest of it from his body and then donned new ones. He rounded Dolt and said, "All right, we'll continue with the plan, then." He turned to Teza. "Are you ready?"

She stared at him thoughtfully. She tilted her head, and placed her hand on her hip, then stared at him some more.

"What?" he said, concerned that he might have missed some of the ick.

She said, "A little fancy for traveling, don't you think?"

Aaslo looked down at the clothes gifted to him by the queen.

"They're the only clothes I have that aren't torn, burnt, or covered in blood."

Ijen walked over, leading his horse by the reins, and waited expectantly.

"What do you want?" said Aaslo.

"I'm going with you."

"Why?"

Ijen tapped the book he had tucked into his belt. "That's how it happens in the story."

"It's not a *story*," said Aaslo. "It's our lives."

"Right. Sometimes I forget," said Ijen. "Where are we going, then?"

Aaslo gritted his teeth. "You should be telling *me*."

Ijen wagged a finger in the air. "No, no. *You* must decide."

He sighed. "Fine. We're going to find one of these fae creatures Magdelay told us about. You don't happen to know where to find one, do you?"

Ijen lifted his chin. "I might, but I wouldn't do that if I were you."

"Why not?" said Aaslo.

"It's not a good line of the prophecy," said Ijen.

Aaslo threw his hands in the air. "You just said that *I* have to pick. Do you have a better line?"

Ijen tapped his lip. "No, they all lead to death, but that one is particularly disturbing."

Aaslo raised his dragon arm and clenched a taloned fist in front of Ijen's face. "I can deal with *disturbing*. What I can't deal with is sitting around doing nothing. Mathias was the chosen one. He was supposedly a powerful magus. Therefore, it stands to reason that anyone with a chance of success needs to also be a powerful magus. We seem to be all out of magi, save for the two of you, and I have no power. These fae sound like our best bet at acquiring some allies with real power. So, where do we find one?"

Ijen sighed. He flipped through the book, read a few lines, then flipped to another page. After doing the same thing three more times, he finally snapped the book shut and said, "Ruriton."

Aaslo groaned as he hung his head. Then he began to chuckle. He couldn't help it. Mathias's laughter was contagious.

Teza crossed her arms. "What's so funny? It's convenient, right? That's where we were going anyway."

Aaslo shook his head. "Ever since I left the forest, people have been trying to get me to go to Ruriton. I've traveled for weeks and weeks looking for help, and all along I needed to go to *Ruriton*."

Teza tapped his nose. "Yes, but if you hadn't gone all over the place, you wouldn't have met *us*."

He shook his head. "Let's go."

As they mounted, Ijen muttered, "I *really* don't like this line of the prophecy."

CHAPTER 22

MYROPA SAT WATCHING THE ROAD STRETCH INTO THE DISTANCE behind them from the back of the prophet's horse. Of course, she wasn't really on the horse, but imagining it to be so meant less work on her part to keep pace with them. She wondered if the presence of the prophet had significance. Arayallen was livid with Arohnu for creating the imbalanced Aldrea Prophecy, yet he had also been delivering his messages to *this* prophet, who was apparently destined to become one of Aaslo's companions. What was the man's role? Was he to be a guide through the darkness, or was he meant to steer Aaslo from a path that might upset Axus's plans? Aaslo had insisted on pursuing the fae despite the prophet's warnings, and Myropa was most proud of him in that moment of forester stubbornness. She wondered how he had become so fearless.

The marquess's estate was set upon an escarpment that overlooked the ocean. Most of the surrounding land, in fact most of Ruriton, was either too rocky or boggy marshland. She understood why the marquess had been so adamant about acquiring any assistance he could. Myropa felt a familiar chill as they entered the town at the base of the escarpment. At the same time, the horses stopped. She glanced over her shoulder to see what had caused the abrupt halt. The city was completely devoid of life. No people manned the stalls, no children ran through the streets, no dogs begged for scraps, and no birds swooped down to steal what was left. Even the topiaries had shriveled into black masses. The grass and scrub that surrounded the town was brown and dried to halfway up the slope that led to the marquess's estate.

"What happened here?" said Teza. "Are they all dead?"

Aaslo said, "I don't think so. Besides a few overturned carts, everything looks in order. Look, the shutters are locked, the doors closed, and the laundry pulled from the lines. I think the people left."

"What about everything else?" Teza said.

Aaslo gazed at the sky and surveyed the ground. "I'd say everything else is either dead or it ran away." He dismounted and crouched by the side of the road to examine the dead foliage more closely.

"Don't touch it," blurted Teza.

Aaslo looked at her and shook his head as if he needn't be told. He turned back to the brush and considered it for a while. Finally, he remounted and directed Dolt down the path to the marquess's estate. He said, "Stick to the road. Don't touch the plants and keep the animals from them as well."

Teza said, "Is this the blight?"

"It would seem so," said Aaslo.

"Oh no," said Ijen. He pulled out his book and flipped through several pages, muttering, "Not good. Not good at all."

The slope around the marquess's estate was covered in tents, lean-tos, and hastily constructed huts. Displaced people and animals were everywhere, yet the makeshift town seemed quite orderly in its design. Many of the hardworking peasants stopped in their tasks to watch them pass, and some even smiled or waved.

"They seem to be in high spirits," said Ijen. He flipped a few pages in his book, lifted his head again to narrow his eyes as he observed the scene, then went back to reading. "No, this is strange. Someone has been meddling."

"What are you rambling about?" snapped Teza. Then she held up a hand. "No, don't tell me. I probably don't want to know."

Ijen blinked at her and then seemed to remember himself. "It's nothing terrible. Quite the opposite, really." He waved to the surrounding area. "This was supposed to be chaotic, the people in abject misery. That's the way it happens in the story."

Aaslo grumped, "*Life*, Ijen."

"Right, yes, I meant *prophecy*."

"Does this mean the prophecy is changing?" said Aaslo. "Is there a chance of creating a new line in which everything doesn't die?"

Ijen tapped the page with his pen. "No, nothing like that. Small differences happen all the time in prophecy. It's like the telling of a story from one generation to the next. We all know how it begins and how it ends. We know some of the major details in the middle, but the small things change with each telling. The outcome is the same, though."

"You could have let us *believe* it was changing," said Teza.

Ijen shook his head as he closed his book. "I do not believe the forester cares to live in fantasy."

Teza snickered. "I've seen him fantasize before."

Aaslo said, "What are you talking about?"

"Something about a love triangle between items of clothing," she said with a roll of her eyes.

Aaslo chuckled. "You're talking about the shop in Yarding. I suppose I did. Jennis had an excellent imagination. Mathias had such an imagination. When we were boys, he would make up these great stories about pirates and knights and dragon slayers and such. He always wanted to act them out."

"Who won?" said Ijen.

Shaking his head sadly, Aaslo said, "It wasn't like that. Mathias insisted we fight other kids or imaginary foes together, always on the same side. We were *brothers in all things,* he would say." He exhaled heavily. "I complained every time. I told him such fantasies were pointless wastes of time, that our efforts would be better spent on meaningful tasks."

Teza smiled at him. "But you still did it," she said. "You wasted your time with him because it's what he wanted to do."

Aaslo nodded. "Yes, he taught me how to imagine." His gaze roved over the encampment. "If not for that, I wouldn't be able to imagine the possibility of succeeding against all odds."

"Interesting," muttered Ijen as he made a note in his book.

Myropa was intrigued. She wanted to know more about Aaslo's life before that fateful night on the road. She wanted to hear about his childhood and his friends. She felt terrible for her part in claiming Mathias's life. She hadn't had a choice, though. The Fates would not be denied.

Teza said, "I thought you were having so much fun because you thought the shopkeeper was cute."

Aaslo grinned at her. "She was." Teza's expression turned bland, and Aaslo said, "But she reminded me of someone I'd rather not think about."

"Who's that?" said Teza.

"Ah yes, the brunette," mumbled Ijen, flipping back several pages.

"Must you do that?" said Aaslo. "I don't appreciate you digging into my life like that."

"Oh, I apologize, again." He held up his book. "It's just that this is the only life I've ever known."

Aaslo said, "It's not *your* life, Ijen. It's other people's lives—mostly *mine*, it seems."

As they neared the front gate of the estate, a half-dozen guards in plate armor stepped across the road, while another half dozen waited on the side. The lead guardsman held up a fist and said, "There's a blight on the march of Ruriton."

Aaslo frowned as he looked down at the man. "We are aware of that. How could one miss it?"

"Everyone must pass inspection. Did you venture off the path?" said the guard.

"No," said Aaslo as he reached into the sack tied to his waist. He pulled out a packet of papers, shuffled through them, and handed one to the guard.

The guard's eyebrows rose, and his face brightened. "Sir Forester!" he said. He waved the paper in the air and looked back at the other guardsmen. "It's the forester! He's come." He looked back to Aaslo and saluted before handing him the paper. "It's an honor to have you here. The marquess said you would come. There are those who doubted him, but I know him to be a man of his word, and here you are."

"Yes, I am here," muttered Aaslo.

Word spread quickly through the camp, and Myropa watched from the back of Ijen's horse as people gathered behind them. Myropa's icy core stirred with a thrill as people smiled in excitement, hollering to their friends that the forester had come to the march.

THE PARLOR WAS OPEN, AS WAS MOST OF THE ESTATE. THE WALLS WERE folded and stored in the corners so as to allow for the most efficient airflow, a necessity in the humid south. Aaslo sat uncomfortably on a fine divan as he and his companions awaited the marquess. Although his clothes were nicer than any he would normally have worn, he could no longer call them clean following several days of riding. He had hoped to procure a few new sets in the town, but that obviously wasn't going to happen.

"Look at you, finally concerned about your appearance."

"I'm not as concerned about my appearance as I am about damaging the marquess's fine possessions."

"I know what you mean," said Teza. "I need a bath."

"In due time," said the marquess as he entered the room. Greylan followed but stood watching them from the doorway. "Greetings, Sir Forester and companions. Welcome to Dovermyer. You have no idea how pleased I am to see you."

Aaslo couldn't help staring at the gaudy gold and purple atrocity on the marquess's head. After a prolonged pause, he realized the marquess was waiting for him. "Ah, sorry. I was distracted."

The marquess reached up and removed the coronet. "I was holding court. The people have many concerns these days. I forgot to remove this in my haste. Your presence has elevated my spirits greatly, and I did not wish to put you through the trouble of a formal greeting."

"You were afraid I'd embarrass you in front of the court," said Aaslo.

The marquess grinned. "Direct as ever, Sir Forester."

Teza whispered, "That's terribly rude, Aaslo."

The marquess said, "The forester and I have an unusual rapport. He says whatever crosses his mind, and I refrain from having him flogged."

"For how long? Shall we place a wager?"

"You were never a betting man," muttered Aaslo.

"No, not usually," said the marquess, "but I've found that betting on you is most profitable. Greylan, however, never seems to learn." Greylan sighed and looked away in disgust. The marquess said, "In the matter of the blight, I have placed all I have to wager on your success. Greylan believes you will fail." The marquess strode over to the window and gazed toward the desiccated town. "This is the farthest edge of the blight. It has spread across the entire march to the south and west. When first we met, it was still miles west of here."

"I've never seen anything like this," said Aaslo, "and if it's as vast as you say, I don't see how a single man can help."

"Perhaps not, but one becomes many. Speaking of which, we found a couple slinking around the estate. They claim to belong to you."

"They?" said Aaslo.

"Bring them in, Greylan."

Aaslo could hear the commotion long before the subjects reached the room. "I'm telling you, we're not here to cause trouble. We're just looking for a forester. He's probably—" Peck stumbled into the room as Greylan released his collar. "Aaslo! Are we glad to see you!"

"They'd be happier to see me. Everyone would be."

"I've never had so many people glad to see me in my life," Aaslo mumbled. He studied Peck and Mory. Peck certainly seemed excited, but Mory stared aimlessly into the air beside Aaslo with an odd expression. Aaslo said, "Why are you here?"

"Right," said Peck as he straightened his coat. "I guess we can save the greetings for later. The Forester's Haven was attacked. It's burnt to the ground."

Teza stepped up and grabbed Peck by the lapels. "Galobar?" she said accusingly.

Peck gently pulled her hands away. "He's dead."

"What did you do?" she shouted. She waved a finger in his face. "I know this was your fault, you scoundrel. You brought trouble to that sweet old man."

Peck shook his head. "No! I swear, it had nothing to do with us." He nodded toward Aaslo. "I think they were looking for *him*."

Ijen shuffled through his pages, looked up, narrowed his eyes at Peck, studied Mory more closely, then went back to his book.

The marquess glanced between Aaslo's companions. He said, "We have not been introduced."

"Right," Aaslo grumbled. He pointed to a couple of chairs beside a tea table just inside the opening of one wall. To Peck and Mory, he said, "You two go sit over there. Don't touch anything." Then, to the marquess, he said, "This is Mage Teza—"

"Fledgling," she said with a practiced curtsy, "healer, to be specific."

"—and this is Magus Ijen."

Ijen's nose was in his book again. He glanced up as if just realizing others were in the room. "Prophet, My Lord Marquess. It's a pleasure to finally meet you. Your role in the story is most unique."

The marquess looked back at Aaslo with delight. "You've brought a healer *and* a prophet. You, most unusual forester, have surpassed my expectations. These must be two of the last magi in Aldrea. It seems the rest have abandoned us—at least, those who made it to a *working* evergate in time."

"It's true," said Aaslo. "The magi crossed to another realm and left us for dead. I heard some of the evergates weren't working."

"I'm afraid not," said the marquess. "The latest is that the third evergate, in the southwest, was destroyed. Two others in the north and east are not responding."

"They've also been destroyed," said Ijen. He seemed surprised when everyone looked at him for further explanation. He said, "One was destroyed by the enemy, the other by the high sorceress." He flipped through his pages, read a passage, then muttered, "No, we don't know who they are yet." He looked back at the marquess. "Once the enemy gains access to an evergate, they can create a *key*, a map of its paths. They will be able to access any paths still intact."

"Wait," said Aaslo. "Do *you* know who the enemy is?"

"Ah, no," said Ijen. "We haven't figured that out yet, so I can't know."

Aaslo crossed his arms and turned toward the prophet. "But you've seen the prophecy."

"Yes," said Ijen, tapping the book.

"Then you know who the enemy is," said Aaslo.

"Ah, I've read the story."

Aaslo growled. "Well, who is it?"

Ijen shook his head. "I can't say. I won't know that until"—he flipped through the pages, then pressed his finger to one of them—"here"—he flipped again—"or here. Actually, in most of the lines, you find out before I do."

Everyone stared at him; then Teza shouted, "See? I told you nothing good can come of talking to a prophet."

Aaslo shook his head and said, "So, if they have control of one of the evergates, they can use it to access the others?"

"Yes," replied Ijen as he tapped his book. "It is one of their methods of invasion."

"*One* of them?" said Teza.

Ijen shrugged. "It depends on the line of prophecy."

The marquess pursed his lips. "With the magi gone, the evergates are useless. We should destroy the rest. How long will it take for the enemy to create these keys?"

"I couldn't say," said Ijen. "It happens differently in every story. They must key each gate independently. Destroying the gates may cause delay, but it won't prevent them from creating new ones once they know the paths."

"Is it safe to assume that takes a while?" said the marquess.

"It depends on the strength of the magi. Working together, the strongest of the present-day magi might require a decade of intense effort to create one. The *first* magi, though, were said to travel the pathways in an instant, without need of evergates. As the power dwindled with each generation, the magi lost the ability to independently travel the pathways, so they created the evergates. Now, there are barely enough magi with the strength to keep them in good repair."

"You mean there are none," said Aaslo.

"Ah, yes," Ijen said, "I suppose we have arrived at that part."

Aaslo said, "The high sorceress told me the foreign magus she fought the first night was much stronger than she. We should assume they possess the ability to create evergates in less time." He looked to the marquess. "Can you disseminate this information and see that the gates are destroyed?"

"I'll send out riders immediately, but without use of the evergates, the missives won't arrive at some of them for many months. There is also the small problem of compliance. I am only a marquess of Uyan, and most of the evergates are kept by people in far more powerful positions. Additionally, I hold no power in the other kingdoms. I doubt the authorities in Mouvilan will consider anything I have to say on the matter. Many are hoping the magi will return. They may not be willing to destroy the gates."

"Well, hopefully we can at least secure Uyan," said Aaslo.

Ijen said, "It will be difficult without the assistance of the magi. It takes great power to destroy an evergate."

Aaslo threw his hands in the air. "So not only did they abandon us to our deaths, they left us open and vulnerable to attack? This makes our reason for coming here even more pertinent."

"What does the blight have to do with the evergates?" said the marquess.

After the cheerful reception, Aaslo hated to disappoint the man. He said, "I'm sorry to break it to you, but we didn't come here to cure the blight."

Greylan finally stormed farther into the room from where he had remained by the doorway. "I told you he was useless," he hissed as he stopped beside the marquess. His tense stance and feverish glare radiated fury. "He will drain your coffers and leave our people to perish."

Aaslo met the guard's accusation with defiance. "I didn't come for money. I need power."

"You see?" said Greylan. "He admits it freely. He seeks to use you."

The marquess's expression sobered as he stared at Aaslo with discontent.

"I'm not here for the marquess's power. I need *real* power—power like the magi. The high sorceress told me of someone who might join our cause if given an incentive. According to her, these . . . *people* . . . have power greater even than the magi. They're called the fae. If I can secure their assistance, maybe I can convince them to help you with the blight as well." He looked at the marquess. "You wanted a solution that didn't require burning all your land. This is probably your best bet."

"Then, I again place my bet on *you*, Sir Forester," said the marquess. "What do you need from me?"

"Only information. The prophet says these fae are in Ruriton."

"I think I'd know if they were," said the marquess.

Aaslo pointed to Ijen. "He knows where to find them—sort of."

Ijen stepped forward. "I cannot say specifically. I saw many trees. It looks like a forest on the water—"

With a frown, the marquess said, "Only one place in Ruriton might be called a forest. There is a tract of mangroves along the coast to the west of here. It's in the middle of the blight. If there were any people, they're likely dead or gone by now."

"Even so, we must search for them," said Aaslo. "They may be our only chance for survival."

"I'll go with them," said Greylan.

"That's not necessary," replied Aaslo through gritted teeth.

Greylan said, "I don't trust you to return if you do find this power."

"And I don't trust you not to stab me in the back," said Aaslo.

The marquess interrupted what was sure to become a heated exchange. "I trust that you will return, but I still want Greylan to go with you. You may need another sword arm. Speaking of which"—he nodded toward Aaslo's bandaged arm—"why did the mage not heal your injury?"

Aaslo sighed. "She did. That's why I'm wearing the bandage," he added as he removed the wrap.

Both men recoiled and then looked at Teza. She held up her hands.

"I saved his life! He would have died otherwise. I couldn't fix his arm, so I replaced it."

"With *what*?" said Greylan with a look of horror.

"A dragon's," said Ijen with a grin.

Both men looked at Aaslo's arm again. "I didn't think dragons were real," said Greylan.

"They're not," replied Ijen. "At least, not in *this* realm. It most certainly came from another."

"Sent by our enemy?" said the marquess.

Ijen tapped the book. "I can't say. That part of the story is blank."

Greylan crossed his arms and looked at Aaslo. "*You* slew a dragon? It looks more like he slew you."

"It was a mutual slaying," Aaslo retorted. He tipped his head toward Teza. "Except that I survived because I have her."

The marquess shook himself free of the arm's thrall and said, "I've had rooms prepared for each of you." He tipped his head toward Teza. "You will receive that bath you requested. I expect you may need additional supplies. Master Remmy will be serving Sir Forester and Prophet Ijen. Mistress Keila will be seeing to Fledgling Teza's needs." To Aaslo, he said, "I would like you to join me for a private dinner this evening, Sir Forester, if that is acceptable."

"Of course," said Aaslo, noting Greylan's disgruntled scowl. "Though, as much as I'd enjoy the rest, I plan to leave in the morning. I feel like time is against us."

"Indeed," said the marquess.

"Um, I think we have something to say," said Peck as he hesitantly rose from his chair, with Mory following his lead.

Aaslo and the others turned to him. The marquess said, "Speak, then. What is it?"

"Uh, well, Your H-high Lordship, sir, um . . . we saw the enemy, I think."

"Where?" said Greylan, suddenly alert.

"It was four days ago, north of here, not long after we entered Ruriton."

Greylan crossed his arms and looked down at Peck as if he didn't believe him. "It took you four days to get here?"

"Well," said Peck, "we had to go out of the way to lose them, and Mory can't swim."

"Lose them?" said Aaslo. "Were they following you?"

"I don't know. Maybe not. But I was worried they'd come after us on account of we stole their magic things."

"You did *what*?" shouted Teza.

Peck scowled at her and straightened the velvet jacket he insisted on wearing despite the heat and humidity. "We did it for Aaslo. I don't know what's going on, but we knew it was something important. We figured Aaslo was a part of it. So, when we saw these foreigners with monster guards killing people, we figured it might be useful to steal a bit of their power."

Ijen tilted his head as he studied Peck. "What did you steal?"

"Yes, and what happened," said Aaslo.

"They'd set up camp near us, so we decided to check it out. There were three men, at least one was a magus, and a bunch of horrible-looking monsters. The magus was reading from a book in some other language and waving a stick in the air. I guess he was trying to figure out if any of the prisoners was also a magus because when he found one, the stick started glowing."

Teza said, "That's not a stick, you dimwit. It's a wand."

"All right," he said. "The *wand* started glowing. Anyway, they killed all the prisoners except the magus. They questioned her about the other magi, but she said they'd all gone to another realm. Then, they killed her, too. So, we ran as far as we could."

"I thought you said you stole something," said Greylan.

"We did," said Mory with an excited grin. "We went back."

Peck nodded. "Right. After we caught our breaths, we came up with a plan. Mory was supposed to be lookout, while I snuck into the camp. Only, he thought I'd been caught, so he snuck in too. But I hadn't been caught. Neither of us was caught. Anyway, we stole the bag that held the book and the *wand*." The last he said with a glare at Teza.

Mory proudly exclaimed, "Peck did it. He's really good at stealing things."

"Shhh," said Peck.

"Interesting," muttered Ijen as he scribbled in his book. "What did you do with the stolen items?"

"We hid them when we got to Dovermyer. We weren't sure of the, ah, *reception* we'd receive if we got caught." He glanced at Greylan. "And we got caught."

"Why were you skulking around the estate?" said the marquess.

"Well, if Aaslo weren't here, we doubted anyone would be welcoming the likes of us. That, and we didn't know if you were on Aaslo's side."

The marquess nodded and turned to Aaslo. "It sounds like you have two very loyal men." He then looked to Ijen and Teza. "Of what use might the magical items be to us?"

Teza said, "They won't be of any use to *you*. Most magical items can only be used by magi."

Ijen nodded. "That's true. I would be interested to examine the book. Perhaps we can glean a bit of their language. The wand might be of use. I wouldn't recommend it, though. It leads us down a very dark line of prophecy."

"How is it useful?" said Aaslo, ignoring the prophet's warning.

"Wands are extremely difficult to make, which is why there are so few. Ultimately, though, they are just tools. Each is designed for a specific purpose. It sounds like this one is a scrying wand. It's used to find things—or perhaps more specifically, *people*—of a magical nature."

"So, we could use it to find the fae?" said Aaslo.

"Maybe you can use it to find me."

The prophet tapped his book and pursed his lips tightly, refusing to say more.

"Tell me," said Aaslo. "*I* should be the one to choose my path."

It was obvious Ijen didn't want to say, but he finally relented with a defeated sigh. "It is said the fae are not completely of this world. We don't know the nature of their power, so we cannot attune the wand to it."

"He's holding back."

"You know something more, though, don't you? Otherwise, you wouldn't have hesitated to tell me."

Ijen tapped his book anxiously, then said, "It may be possible to tune a wand so that it understands the difference between the magic of *this* world and the magic of another. In order to do that, though, we would need something that possesses power from another world."

"I'd think the magi would have many magical things from other worlds," said the marquess.

Ijen shook his head. "Not at all. Most magi can only use the evergates to access other gates in *this* world. Only a few have ever been to another, and most of them did not return. It's dangerous. Most realms do not support human life. Additionally, the path to return from another realm is not necessarily the path you traveled to get there. Even if you are lucky enough to find the path to a realm in which you can survive, you probably won't find the way back.

"Another problem with using the wand in this way is that you are looking for something *alive.* That means you would need to have something magical and *living* from another realm. I don't know of anything like that in all of Aldrea."

"Does it have to be the same realm as the fae?" said Aaslo.

"No, just something not of *this* realm."

Aaslo felt a sudden thrill of hope. He reached into the sack tied to his waist, where he had been keeping the things he couldn't afford to lose, in addition to Mathias's head. He pulled out the black seed Magdelay had given him and held it out for Ijen. "Can we use this?"

Ijen's face drained of blood, and he abruptly sat on the floor with his head buried between his knees. He gently struck his forehead against the book and mumbled, "Yes, that will work. I didn't realize we were already on that line. It's not too late, though. We can choose another route."

"What is it?" said the marquess.

"It's a seed from another realm," said Aaslo.

Greylan said, "You just carry those around with you, eh?"

"I carry many strange things," said Aaslo. He turned to the prophet, who was still crouching on the floor. "You tremble before the wind even touches your boughs."

Ijen blinked up at him. He collected himself and stood tall as he said, "The wind has wracked my boughs for decades. You can afford to judge me because it has not yet reached you."

Aaslo glanced at the book in Ijen's hands. "Perhaps you are right, but I cannot believe there is no way to escape the clutches of this prophecy."

"Prophecy is absolute," said Ijen. "One of the lines always comes true."

"Until one doesn't," replied Aaslo. "Maybe it will be this one." He turned to Peck and Mory. "Are the items well hidden?"

"Yeah, boss. Nobody'll find them. Do you want us to go get them?" said Peck.

Aaslo said, "Teza, is it possible to track the items? Can someone use magic to find them?"

"Uh, I don't think so. Not unless they have another scrying wand that's tuned to such items. Why are you asking me? He knows more about it," she said, pointing to Ijen.

"He doesn't trust me," said Ijen.

"Neither do I."

"He thinks I might lie so that I can find the items and destroy them." Ijen looked at Aaslo and tapped the book. "It's okay. You'll eventually realize I'm only trying to help."

"Help you into the grave."

"Help comes in many forms," grumbled Aaslo. "Not all of it good."

"I agree with the forester on this one," said Greylan. Everyone looked at him in surprise. "The items should be remanded into our care."

"You mean *your* care," said Aaslo.

"Naturally," said Greylan. "I'm tasked with the security of the estate."

Aaslo looked back at the two thieves. Peck looked eager to please, but Mory was staring at the air beside Aaslo again. The boy seemed different from the last time Aaslo had seen him, but he supposed being attacked and watching a bunch of people get killed would change a young man. Unfortunately, Peck and Mory were in danger so long as they were the only people who knew where the items were hidden.

He turned to the marquess. "My men and I will get the items. Teza will retain possession of them."

"Me? Why me?" said Teza.

"Because without you, they are useless to us," said Aaslo. "And, Prophet Ijen is right. I don't trust him."

"Harsh, Aaslo. What happened to all that forester wisdom?"

"Should I apologize for being honest?"

"No, that's not necessary," said Ijen. "I completely agree with your decision. I want nothing to do with that wand or book."

Teza glanced toward Ijen with trepidation. "Well, now I don't want them either!"

Aaslo shook his head and motioned toward the thieves. "Come on. Let's go."

CHAPTER 23

MYROPA WOULDN'T KNOW WHO WAS SUMMONING HER UNTIL SHE arrived. Most of the time, the gods' calls felt the same to her. It had been easy when the only one who concerned himself with her was Trostili, but now others expected things of her. When she crossed the veil, she found herself standing in a puddle of water. Drops dripped onto her head and face, and she realized it was raining. She had never seen it rain in Celestria. She turned, looking in every direction, but she saw only the drab grey of rain and wet stone.

The tug at her core told her where to go. She followed it to the mouth of a cave. It was so narrow that she couldn't imagine one of the giant gods fitting through. Still, she had to follow the call. The passage was dark, and she was forced to feel her way along the walls. She finally reached the end of the passage where it opened into a massive chamber. The walls and ceiling glowed with tiny blue specks, but the brightest light was in the center. There, standing on a rounded stalagmite, was a tiny person who stood no taller than half the height of Myropa's shin. The person had a golden glow about her entire body that illuminated the cavern for a dozen yards in every direction. As Myropa neared, she realized the tiny person was Arayallen.

The goddess's attention was on the beetle sitting in front of her. To Myropa, the beetle wasn't worth notice, but to Arayallen it was about the size of a large dog. Arayallen rested her chin on her palm as she tapped her cheek. Then she swiped her hand through the air, and the beetle changed from black to iridescent blue.

Myropa was woken from her mesmerized stupor when the goddess said, "Hello, Reaper. What have you to report?" Myropa would have expected the goddess's voice to be tiny to match her size, but it rather boomed as it echoed around the chamber.

"Um, the forester seeks somebody called the fae. He thinks he can convince them to fight against the prophecy."

Arayallen laughed. "The fae? Oh, little reaper, the fae are never *convinced*. They are bargained with, and there is *always* a price—one that no one would choose to pay if they knew about it before making the deal."

The goddess pinched the air with her fingers and then moved her hands in a sinuous motion. Curved horns sprouted from either side of the beetle's head. Arayallen placed her hands on her hips and tilted her head. She swiped a hand through the air, and the horns disappeared. She snapped her fingers, and they were back again.

The goddess turned and stepped from the stalagmite, growing to her normal size before she even struck the ground. She collected the beetle on one finger and turned to tower over Myropa. Bending forward, she held the beetle out to her. "For you, little reaper."

Myropa looked at the beetle with a mixture of surprise, confusion, disgust, and awe. She hesitantly reached out to take the shiny insect. It crawled onto her shaking palm. "You created this for *me*?"

Arayallen strolled around the cave, seemingly without a care, as she examined a few of her other designs. She said, "I imagine it gets lonely being a reaper. No one who might like you can see you, and no one who can see you likes you. It's a little sad, really. But I suppose that's the point. Either way, it's yours. Don't lose it, now. It's one of a kind."

Myropa had never liked insects and particularly despised the kind that flew into her hair. In fact, her disdain for the little creatures was one of the reasons her life had taken the path it had. This insect, however, had apparently been designed just for her. She didn't imagine Arayallen was trying to make her feel better. She knew the creature had a purpose; but, still, it was hers.

"Thank you," she said. "What is it called?"

Arayallen waved her hand, and a shower of color spread over the moss at her feet. "How should I know? No one has named it yet. Don't you understand how this works? The humans—or other sentient beings—discover and name them."

Myropa held up the beetle where she could see it better in the goddess's light. She was mesmerized by the swirl of dark purples and blues and the way the light sparked off the hard elytra that protected its wings. She said, "Can *I* name it?"

"You're human, are you not?" said Arayallen.

"I was," said Myropa.

Arayallen looked at her sideways. "Do you think that changed because you're dead?"

Myropa looked at her curiously, wondering if Arayallen was trying to tell her something or if she was just being mean. "I don't know," she said.

The goddess waved a dismissive hand. "Be gone, then. And don't lose that . . . ?" Arayallen looked at her questioningly.

"Nebula beetle," said Myropa.

Arayallen tilted her head and smiled. Then Myropa was suddenly back in the living realm. She didn't even remember taking a breath, but she must have, or she could not be there. The beetle was still in her hand. It twitched and then scurried up her arm. Myropa immediately clamped her mouth shut and covered her ears, worried that it would try to crawl inside her. It didn't, though. It stopped on her shoulder, then sat there as if satisfied with its perch.

She slowly uncovered her ears and looked around. She was in a swamp, and unfortunately, her sense of smell worked fine. The swamp was filled with noxious fumes, which mingled with the stomach-churning, putrid, sweet scent of decay. The sounds finally reached her ears, and she spun just as an ugly horse walked right through her. She jumped out of the way and was for once glad that her feet did not truly touch the ground in this world.

Aaslo rode at the head of the line, with Teza beside him holding what was presumably the wand that Peck and Mory had procured from Axus's forces. The prophet and the marquess's guard captain, Greylan, rode second, followed by the two thieves on a single horse, and then eight of the marquess's guardsmen in double file. Mory glanced in her direction as they rode past, and Myropa shivered. For just a moment, she wondered if the boy could see her. Dismissing the ridiculous notion, she turned her attention to Aaslo and smiled. She liked to see Aaslo leading his men. She knew it was pointless to worry. They would all die eventually. She just hoped that Aaslo's death was swift and that she would be there to carry him to the Sea. It was the pain of life she truly worried over. He had already endured so much.

"Careful," said Greylan. "These swamps have claimed many lives. Countless travelers have perished by either getting lost or looking for a shortcut. Well-trained professional harvesters go missing every season. It's even said that during an ancient war, two opposing battalions, each thinking to lure the other into a trap, met their ends here."

"Death seems a meager threat at this point," said Aaslo.

The wand lit with a dull glow as Teza waved it toward her right while muttering words she read from a script in her other hand. Not far ahead was the beginning of the mangrove forest. Myropa followed as they traveled deeper into the muck. The horses' hooves and legs had been wrapped with waxed hide and their muzzles covered with feed bags filled with herbs to help with the vapors. The people wore similar coverings over their faces, and Myropa wished she could do the same.

The horses sank into the mud, which popped as they struggled to pull their hooves free. Their frequent stumbling threatened to spill their riders into the bog, from which they likely would not return. Once they were within the trees, the ground was somewhat sturdier, but the blight-infested roots and branches created more problems than they solved. Myropa wondered if the blight would be the end of them all.

Two tethers suddenly snapped into place at her core, and Myropa's frozen heart sank. One of the horses squealed as its leg caught in a tangle of roots and broke. The beast and its rider both fell into the murky water of the swamp. They wailed and gasped as they became infected with the blight. The others in the party watched in horror, unable to help the man as he flailed. His skin turned blotchy with black spots, and although he and his horse might have lived longer had they been on dry ground, they quickly succumbed to fatigue and drowned in the putrid muck.

"This isn't a natural blight," said Aaslo. "A blight wouldn't do that."

"Do you think the enemy caused this?" said Teza.

Aaslo shook his head. "I don't know. The marquess said these marshes bear useful plants that aren't found anywhere else on Aldrea—plants used for healing. Perhaps the enemy set to destroy them to reduce our chances of survival."

"Seems pointless if they know we are already doomed," said Ijen.

"They didn't know," said Aaslo. "I kept Mathias's death a secret until I told the king. The only other person who knew was the high sorceress. I think this blight started long before then, though. The marquess said he, and his father before him, had been seeking help for many months."

"It's true," said Greylan. "This blight began nearly a year ago."

"So, if this was the work of the enemy, then they began their attack long before they found the chosen one," said Teza.

"Yes," Ijen said. "Given the nature of the prophecy, I think they felt assured of the outcome."

"I have a question," said Teza. "Why is it that prophecies are always in riddles? Do prophets seek to confound us on purpose?"

"Well, yes, actually," replied Ijen. Upon seeing her disgruntled expression, he said, "It's not due to any maleficence. It's a necessity. A prophecy is not completely clear to us. We talk about them like they are a story written out and followed precisely, but that truly is not the case. The visions do not come to us clearly *or* literally. They are specific to the prophet to whom they are delivered. For example, one prophet sees a fox running into a hole and believes that an actual fox will run into a hole; while another may see the fox as a metaphor for the royal house of Pashtigon, whose seal bears a fox. The second prophet may consider holes to mean death and interpret the prophecy to mean that the King of Pashtigon will die. A third prophet might feel that a fox represents a traitor and the hole is his hiding place."

"So, who's right?" said Teza.

"All of them, and none of them," replied Ijen. "It's entirely dependent on the prophet. The first one's interpretation would not apply to the second's vision. Sometimes we do not fully understand the vision and must guess at its meaning. The problem with writing prophecies down as we see them is that the interpretation is lost. *You* may not know what a fox means to the third prophet, so you might make a terrible error in your assumptions. Part of our education as prophets is learning to word a prophecy in such a way that the parts that are clear to us are made clear to everyone else. The riddle is intentionally designed to cause the reader to think critically about the remainder. It prevents people from making hardened, erroneous assumptions. At least, that's what we hope. The *quality* of the prophecy is, again, dependent on the prophet. The Division of Prophecy sees thousands of prophecies thrown out every year because they are not deemed acceptable by their standards."

Aaslo dismounted to lead Dolt through a particularly difficult section of swampy forest, and the others followed his lead. As he did so, he said, "Are any of these discarded prophecies related to the Aldrea Prophecy?"

"I wouldn't know," said Ijen. "As I said before, I didn't tell anyone I was a Prophet of Aldrea, so I wasn't given access to those prophecies. I doubt it, though. I should think that anything written of that prophecy would be taken very seriously."

"Wait!" said Teza. Everyone paused as she waved the wand toward a thick stand of trees. It glowed brighter each time she waved it past the trees. "There," she said, pointing between them.

Aaslo handed his reins to Peck, instructing the soldiers to stay where they were and reminding them to touch nothing. Myropa thought the warning unnecessary after having seen what happened to the guard and horse she had collected. She rarely was called upon to collect animals, so she had been a little surprised when she had received the tether. She hoped it meant that no other reapers were near, and *she* would have the honor of collecting Aaslo and his friends.

She followed Aaslo across the matted lumps of dead and dying wetland foliage. He wore a glove on his good hand and had the dragon arm wrapped as he gripped the tree trunks and branches to balance on their roots. Teza followed, appearing much less sure about her footing. She slipped at one point and was caught by Greylan, who came after her.

"I-I can't do it, Aaslo," said Teza. "I'm sorry. If it was just the swamp, I'd manage, but I'm terrified of the blight."

"You're a *healer*," Greylan said with distaste.

Myropa could see the girl's arms and legs shaking. She was sure that if Teza tried to follow, her soul would end up dangling from Myropa's belt. Teza started to tear up as she waved frantically at Greylan to go back.

"I must go with him," said Greylan, unable to get around Teza to follow Aaslo.

"No, no, no! Let me by. I *need* to go back," shouted Teza, her eyes wild with panic.

"Greylan, take her back," said Aaslo. "She's beginning to lose sense, and you are closest to her. If she falls in, you're likely to go with her."

Greylan fumed as he turned around to lead Teza back to the horses. He called over his shoulder, "How will you find them without her?"

When Aaslo didn't answer, Myropa and the others looked his way in alarm. Aaslo was gone. Myropa quickly focused on her target, and she was suddenly beside him again. The ice at her core cracked and ground against itself as her terror was released through the friction. For the briefest moment, she'd thought he had fallen into the bog, and she'd missed collecting him. She glanced back through the trees and could see his party clearly searching for him. Even though they were looking straight at him, they couldn't see him. Aaslo didn't notice, because he couldn't hear their calls any longer. Myropa knew what had happened. Aaslo had stepped into another realm.

The blight had not reached the tiny haven in the miniature realm between the trees. A large tree unlike the others of the mangrove forest stood before them. The trunk was hollowed with a gaping hole in the center that was nearly as large as a man. Two glowing orbs could be seen in the dark hollow. The orbs winked out, then glowed again, and Myropa realized they were eyes. Aaslo stood perfectly still as the creature slowly slunk into the light, pulling itself from the tree. It started as a bluish-white salamander-like creature. Myropa's knees nearly buckled for its beauty, a reaction that could not have been natural given her general dislike for wildlife. The creature grew and changed shape until it resembled a woman. Her pure white skin glowed with an ethereal light. The silver strands that flowed from her head danced on a nonexistent breeze as they sparkled with the light of stars in the night sky. Long silver lashes fluttered over silver eyes as she blinked at Aaslo demurely. She swayed to a haunting melody as her feet danced gracefully over the muck of the swamp.

"She's a magnificent being, is she not?" said a voice from beside Myropa. Myropa jumped and glanced over to see Arayallen standing next to her. "Not even I have designed something with such perfection."

"How can you be here? I thought the gods couldn't come here."

"Oh, we *can*, but it takes much power." She glanced at the beetle on Myropa's shoulder. Its shimmery wings were spread open. "I hitched a ride with you to save power."

"You were *inside* the beetle?" said Myropa.

"Not exactly," said Arayallen. She nodded toward the scene in front of them. "Be quiet, now. This is getting interesting."

The creature pressed her nude form against Aaslo and brushed a finger across his jaw while he stood entranced. As she looked up at him, her silver eyes darkened to blackish red, and her pout was ruined by the sharp fangs that protruded from between her lips.

"I'm hungry," she said, her voice ringing in harmony to the melody of her song. "Everything here is dying. Will you feed me?"

Aaslo reached up and took her hand from his face. "I'm not here to be your meal," he said.

The creature frowned at him. "You are not enthralled?"

"You are quite the enchantress," he said, "but my need is greater than my desire."

"Not a hapless traveler, then. Pity," she said. "Who are you, and what do you want?"

"I'm Aaslo, Forester of Goldenwood."

"A forester? I don't recall a forester ever coming to my home. Do you taste different from the others?"

"I wouldn't know," Aaslo said.

She stroked a hand down his dragon arm. "Not unchanged, I see. It would be an interesting pairing."

Moving on from the subject of being someone's dinner, he said, "What do I call you?"

She lifted a shoulder. "None who have named me have lived to tell another. Do you care to try?"

"Very well," said Aaslo. "I shall call you Ina. I'm here to ask for your assistance."

"Ina," she repeated as if feeling the taste of it. "Why would I assist you?"

"Because this affects you as well. I know you have heard of the Aldrea Prophecy. The chosen one is dead."

"You lie," said Ina. "He cannot be. The human magi protect him."

Aaslo pulled Mathias's head from the bag, holding it out for her to see. She recoiled and then stepped closer for examination.

"No! You've killed him!"

"*I* didn't kill him. I only brought his head to you as proof of our great need. The prophecy is clear that the enemy will destroy all life on Aldrea. Nothing will live. That includes *you*."

Ina backed away, shifting with agitation as she looked at him skeptically. "What do you desire of me?"

"I intend to fight this. I refuse to believe there is no hope. You and your brethren can fight with us. With your power, we may have a chance."

"No, it is not permitted," she said adamantly. Her gaze flicked to where Myropa and Arayallen stood, then back to Aaslo. "We cannot fight. You must ask for something else. We have much power—power you cannot understand—but we mustn't interfere directly."

"Can she see us?" Myropa said.

"No," replied Arayallen. "She may sense our presence, but she knows not who we are."

"You would rather die than fight?" said Aaslo.

"I didn't say that," said Ina. "I am willing to make you a deal, but I cannot do what you ask."

"Fine," said Aaslo. "If you can't fight directly, then lend me your power."

Ina grinned, her fangs flashing in the glow of her flesh. "Are you sure you want it? Many humans have sought me for power. They satisfied my hunger."

Aaslo said, "I've never sought power. I was content with my life as a forester. But the magi have left this realm and taken all the magic with them. A handful of stragglers is all that's left. The enemy has magi aplenty, and they're strong. We need power if we are to live."

Ina looked around the tiny haven she had managed to protect from the blight. She gazed at her beloved tree, then looked back at Aaslo. She tilted her head. "Are you really a forester?" At his nod, she said, "What you ask will come at a cost."

"I'm willing to pay it," said Aaslo.

"You have not even asked what it is," said Ina.

"What does it matter?" he said. "Without the power, we are all dead."

She grinned and swayed to the music. "There are worse things than death."

"Death does not scare me," said Aaslo. "The end of life does."

"Then, you agree? I will lend you my power, and you will pay the price."

"Yes," said Aaslo.

Ina's glow began to grow. It filled the space between the trees with brilliant white light, then shot from her toward Aaslo. Just before it struck him, Arayallen said, "Oops," and shoved Myropa into the stream. Myropa shrieked as the beam of intense power surged through her, a sound that was echoed by Aaslo when it entered his body. Aaslo fell to the ground, his knees sinking into the muddy water, and Myropa fell next to him.

Ina stood over Aaslo with a severe expression, her voice commanding. "You will rid my land of the blight. That is *my* price. *Your* price will be greater still."

Aaslo struggled to speak over the pain. His throat felt like sandpaper, and everything in his body ached as if it had been crushed beneath a massive fallen evergreen. "I-I don't know how to use it," he wheezed.

Ina leaned over him with a cruel grin and tapped his head. "It's all in there. It'll come to you." Her body began to shift into amorphous forms as light danced around her; then she disappeared into the dark hole in the tree.

Aaslo stayed in the mud on his hands and knees breathing heavily. He looked up and met Myropa's concerned gaze. She knew it was impossible, since he couldn't see her, but he looked straight into her eyes. He said, "Who are you?"

Myropa's shock caused the ice in her veins to crackle like sea ice breaking into slush. "Y-you can see me?" She glanced toward Arayallen, but the goddess was gone. She couldn't believe that Arayallen had tried to destroy her.

Aaslo also started to tremble. He wrapped his arms around his body as he shook. His teeth chattered as he replied. "S-sort of. You're kind of hazy, like you're not all there."

"I'm not," she said, shaking her head.

He reached out to touch her face, but his hand passed right through her. "What are you?"

"I'm a reaper," she said. "I carry the dead to the Afterlife."

Aaslo's brilliant green gaze was full of disappointment. "Am I dead, then?"

"No, I don't think so," she said. "I don't understand. You shouldn't be able to see me. You've never been able to before."

"You've been around for a while?" he said. Her gaze dropped to the sack sitting in the mud still tied to his waist. Aaslo said, "You took him?"

She nodded. "I'm sorry, Aaslo. I didn't want to, but the Fates required it."

Aaslo pulled the bag out of the muck and held Mathias's head to his chest as he continued to tremble.

Myropa said, "You'd best hurry, Aaslo. You don't look well, and your friends are worried. They can't find you because you crossed into Ina's realm. They'll kill themselves looking."

Aaslo looked behind him through the trees to see that his companions were indeed frantic over his disappearance. For some reason, none of them had been able to pass through the gap in the trees, or they could no longer find it. "What's your name?" he said.

"You may call me Myra."

"Myra," he said through chattering teeth. "I'm sorry we couldn't meet under better circumstances."

"Me, too," she said as Aaslo rose on shaky legs. Once he was standing, he didn't move again for several minutes.

"What did she do to me?" he said.

"I don't know," said Myropa.

He finally took a few hesitant steps, then began walking with more confidence. He stumbled through the gap in the trees, then collapsed into the murky blight-infested water on the other side. Teza scrambled over the roots, seemingly without concern for her own safety. She gripped a tree branch with one gloved hand as she reached out to Aaslo with the other. Myropa knelt at Aaslo's side, untouched by the water in the Realm of the Living, and encouraged him to get up. His shivering had gotten worse, but as he stewed in the mud, it slowed. The blight began to seep into his skin, and he stopped struggling as he submerged beneath the water.

"Aaslo!" screamed Teza. "No, Aaslo!"

Myropa's cries were much the same while she peered through the murky water. She searched the one clear ring amid the sooty mess of the blight and noticed the plague was moving toward the spot where Aaslo had sunk. It slipped across the surface and was sucked down into the depths by an unseen undercurrent. Suddenly, Aaslo lurched out of the water, gasping for breath. His chest heaved as he stood in the waist-high water, and he hung his head while he recovered. The blight continued to converge on him, and Teza began screaming again.

"Aaslo, get out of there! It's going to kill you! Come on, take my hand!" called Teza.

Myropa, the thieves, and the guards also yelled, but Aaslo wasn't listening. Myropa wasn't even sure if he could hear them any longer. His mind seemed to be far away. The blight slithered up his body, eating away his thin linen shirt and enveloping him in powdery black slime. Aaslo began muttering to himself, and Myropa wondered if he was talking to Mathias again. When the blight finally reached his neck, it sank into his flesh like water into a drying cloth. As fast as it could cover him, it was consumed, and Aaslo simply stood there muttering. Eventually, he and the entire puddle in which he stood were cleared of the blight. He shook himself and then finally looked up from his daze. He glanced toward Myropa, then blinked at Teza before taking her hand.

Once he was standing atop the mound of muddy dead plants, Aaslo took a deep breath and looked around the swamp. He didn't even acknowledge the others as they continued to ask after his well-being. Without a word, he pulled off his glove and dragged his hand over the blight-riddled trees. Everywhere he touched, the deadly plague absorbed into his skin, leaving behind what looked like claw marks. He looked at the others and said, "You all should go back to where you'll be safer. I need to cure the blight."

"We're not leaving you," said Greylan. "What just happened? You were covered in this black pestilence, yet you are not dead." Aaslo shook his head as he rested his hands on his knees and took deep breaths. Greylan said, "You saw them—these *fae*? Did they agree to help?"

"I saw one," said Aaslo, glancing among the others. Everyone stared at him in earnest except Mory. Aaslo looked back to Greylan. "We made a deal."

"What was the deal?" said Ijen, tapping his book as he sat atop his horse. His expression held only dread.

"She agreed to lend me her power in exchange for curing the blight and . . . something else."

"*Lend* you her power? Those were her words exactly?"

"Yes," said Aaslo.

"What was the *something else*?" said Ijen.

"I don't know. She was a bit cryptic. Come. You all need to get to safety while I look for the source of the blight."

"We came here to help you. Why should we leave now?" said Greylan.

"You came to help me find the fae. We did. Now you can go."

Teza placed her hand on his shoulder. "Are you okay, Aaslo? I thought you were dead . . . *again.*"

Aaslo smirked. "I guess I'm hard to kill."

Myropa wondered about that. Many gods were beginning to toy with him, but ultimately it was up to the Fates.

Aaslo mounted Dolt, who stood still for once, then paused. Turning to Ijen, he said, "I feel different. I feel like . . . like there are forces battling inside me—strange things, *foreign* things." Ijen pursed his lips and anxiously tapped his book as he stared at Aaslo. He offered nothing. Turning to Myropa, Aaslo said, "Are you coming with us?"

Myropa smiled. "Yes, for now."

"That's great!" said Mory. "I thought I saw you before, back in Tyellí, just as I woke up, but I wasn't sure. You were in the marquess's estate, weren't you? It was like I knew someone was there, but I couldn't see you. I'd forgotten what happened, but now I remember clearly. I'm really glad you came back." Then his face paled, and he said, "You're not here to take one of us, are you?"

"No," said Myropa, utterly surprised that Mory could also see her. She glanced at the others, who were watching Aaslo and Mory with concern.

Peck said, "Are you okay, Mory? I think the swamp gas is getting to you. Who are you talking to?"

Mory pointed to Myropa. "The lady that kept me company when I was dead."

Aaslo turned to Mory. "You were dead?"

"For a little while," said Mory. He nodded toward Myropa. "She was supposed to take me. Instead, she waited with me, both of us hoping Peck could save me in time." His grin grew wider, and he slapped Peck on the back. "He did."

Aaslo turned to Myropa. "That's why he can see you?"

She shook her head. "I don't know. Usually only the dead and dying can see me—the ones I take. Maybe it has something to do with the serum the apothecary used."

"What serum?" said Aaslo.

"Hey," said Peck. "How did you know about the serum? And who are you talking to? I'm really starting to worry."

"There's no one there," said Greylan. The other guards nodded, eyeing Aaslo as if he were mad. He imagined their concerns were not far from the truth, and his exposed part-dragon body didn't help matters.

Aaslo looked at Myropa. "They can't see you, but I can. Does that mean I'm dying?"

"*What?*" cried Teza. "You're dying?"

Myropa shook her head. "I don't think so." As Aaslo shook his head at a frantic Teza, Myropa said, "Something happened when Ina was giving you power. I got caught in the stream. I think it changed us. I think maybe you got pulled a little into my realm, and I got pulled a little into yours."

"What makes you think that?" said Aaslo.

"Because I'm not as cold," she said. "And, I can see your eyes. The colors were muted before. I can see their brilliant green, now, like the forest where you were born. They're lovely."

"Aaslo, you're scaring me," said Teza. "First, you're talking to heads, now the air."

"No, he's not," said Mory. "I can see her, too. We're talking to the same person."

Teza looked to Ijen for help. He shrugged and said, "There are no invisible people in the story."

Greylan said to Teza, "You're the healer. Can madness be contagious?"

"No," she said, "but noxious fumes can cause delusions. I've never heard of two people having the *same* delusion, though. I think maybe they really are talking to someone the rest of us can't see."

"How many of these invisible beings are there?" said Greylan, reaching for his weapon.

Aaslo glanced around. "As far as I can tell, only one. Her name is Myra."

"Is she pretty?" said Peck.

Aaslo frowned at him. "We're surrounded by blight. Is that really important?"

Peck grinned. "It's always important."

"Oh, she's very pretty," said Mory. His cheeks turned red when Myropa smiled at him.

"Well, why is she here?" said Teza.

Aaslo said, "She's a reaper. She said she carries the souls of the dead to the Afterlife."

"Are we going to die?" shouted one of the guards. He was a younger man who looked like he would run off into the blighted swamp in a panic.

Aaslo turned to the man, his frustration escaping in his tone. "So what if we are? What do you plan to do about it?" He took a deep breath and more calmly said, "I don't know why she's here. We'll find out later. Right now, we need to get you out of here."

After much argument and discussion, the guards finally turned their horses. Since there was no room to pass, Aaslo and his companions had to bring up the rear. Myropa walked next to Aaslo, snapping ahead with a thought whenever they went too fast, which wasn't often in the bog. As they traveled, she wondered if Arayallen had known what would happen when she pushed Myropa into the power stream. She couldn't figure out if the goddess was friend or foe. Perhaps she was both—or neither, and it only depended on what suited her. That seemed typical behavior for all the gods. Although she didn't understand what had happened, she was thankful and elated that Aaslo could see and talk with her.

Myropa was so happy that she jumped in surprise when several glowing tethers snapped into place at her core. Her gaze followed their lines just in time to witness the attack. Arrows flew out of the scrub on one side of their path, and tiny disks of red light spun at them from the other. Two of the guards were struck down by arrows, one was knocked from his horse into the blight-ridden muck, and two more received terrible injuries to their arms and torsos that would certainly prove fatal if not treated.

Teza launched a ball of bright white light toward the closest magus who had thrown the red disks. He erected a shield before it struck and answered with another slew of disks. Teza and Ijen tossed up invisible barriers along the path, blocking the worst of the magi's attacks. The cost of those that got through was devastating. One of the injured soldiers lost consciousness and fell from his agitated horse. The horse wailed when an arrow struck his hindquarter and began bucking. The other horses startled, trying to move out of the way, and two more guards were overcome by the blight when their mounts lost their footing and began to sink. Myropa busily collected souls, but she knew she was not the only reaper on the field that day, for she did not receive everyone's tether.

AASLO FELT SOMETHING STIR INSIDE HIM, AND SOMEWHERE IN THE back of his mind, knowledge whispered. The thing inside him, the vicious interloper, wanted to fight. The *other* thing, the seductive whisper in his mind, wanted to be remembered. It reminded him of the times when Mathias and he quizzed each other over the ridiculous cultural traditions, rituals, and poems Magdelay had taught them. Then it struck him. The ridiculous things taught to him by the *high sorceress*—were spells.

"Now you're thinking."

"I don't remember," said Aaslo, surveying the chaotic scene as arrows and explosions struck the invisible barriers that Teza and Ijen were straining to maintain.

"Okay, then you can all die. Myra seems nice. She can take your soul like she did mine."

"That's not going to happen," said Aaslo. "I just need more time."

"Do you have a spell for that? Because otherwise you're not going to get it."

"Okay, um—" Aaslo raised his hand and traced a symbol in the air as he whispered the foreign words in concert with Mathias. He didn't know what the spell would do, but it was the first that came to mind. He figured anything was better than nothing, and something inside him whispered that it was right. In his mind, he was standing in the study again with Mathias laughing at him for his terrible pronunciation. Magdelay had walked in on them at the exact moment that it looked like they weren't working.

Just as Aaslo said the last word, one of the intruders that had been stirring in his core jumped to the fore and leapt right out of his body. It surged across the swampland toward the foreign magi, burst through their shield, and collided with the closest magus. The man didn't survive the explosion. Aaslo muttered the next poem on his mental list and performed the associated hand gestures, then thrust his palm toward the saggy-skinned creatures on the other side of the path. Having discarded their bows, they were attempting to attack on foot but

kept bumping against the invisible walls. As the strange power escaped Aaslo, four of the creatures exploded into tiny pieces that, to
everyone's horror, rained down on them over the shields.

The injured guard fell from his horse but managed to stab an attacker through the gut before he expired. Greylan and the remaining
guard continued to engage the monsters attacking from the left, while
Peck used his belt knife to fend off any that came at him and Mory.
When Aaslo turned his attention back toward the enemy magi, he noticed they had moved close enough for him to recognize the eldest. It
was the man named Verus he had met in Mierwyl—the one who had
been searching for Mathias.

With the enemy moving in, Aaslo called to his people to fall back
beyond the trees. He stepped off the path into a pool to make room for
the others, and Greylan's horse fell in after him. The blight began to
consume the horse but then retreated as the plague was absorbed into
Aaslo. He felt something shift inside him as more of the blight filled
him, but there was nothing to be done for it. He was just glad in that
moment that he wasn't dying.

Ijen cast a spell to topple a few trees for use as cover and prevent
the enemy from following. Aaslo, Teza, Ijen, Peck, Mory, Greylan, and
the last guard, a man named Rostus, were all that was left of their
party. Everyone that had been in the front of the line was dead, and
only four horses survived. One of the horses was up to his neck in a
murky pool and another was Dolt, who was an idiot.

Verus called out to Aaslo. "Forester! You lied to me. You said you
did not possess any power."

Aaslo began preparing another attack as he said, "I didn't then. *You*
said you were just a visitor. You made no mention of your plan to destroy the world."

Verus somehow dredged a boulder the size of a horse's head from
the swamp and launched it toward them as if from a catapult. Ijen
swiped it from the air with a spell before the boulder even reached the
shields.

"Not the world," said Verus, looking far too smug. He seemed certain he would prevail. "Just the tainted. How is it you possess power
now?"

"Why would I tell you?" said Aaslo as he tried to remember the last
symbol for the spell he was forming. He had no idea what it would do,

but it was one ritual Magdelay had hesitated to teach Mathias in Aaslo's presence. In an attempt to stall, Aaslo hollered, "Are your people descended of the original fifteen magi?"

"Of course," said Verus as a red light began to surround him. "Did you think none of their descendants left to explore the world?"

Aaslo finally released his mysterious attack. A swarm of black vines rushed toward Verus. The enemy magus responded by flinging the red light toward the vines, forcing them to wrap around themselves and reverse course. Aaslo suddenly felt a burst of strength well up inside him from the *other* thing that squirmed to be released. The scales on his arm, neck, and torso rippled with excitement. His shadowy interloper was pleased to deliver such violence and desired to unleash more. Aaslo shoved the unbridled power at the tangle of vines, launching them back toward Verus. The giant ball struck the foreign magus's shield, causing it to shatter and knocking Verus's young companion off his feet.

Verus hunkered behind a rotting stump and a hastily erected shield, somehow unaffected by the blight. The younger man didn't rise, and Aaslo wondered if he had been killed. Verus said, "You're awfully powerful for a man who says he has no power."

"Today's sapling is tomorrow's mother tree," yelled Aaslo.

"What does that mean?" said Verus. "Your foreign phrase escapes me."

"It escapes us all," yelled Greylan as he jabbed his sword through the tangle of tree limbs to push back one of the grey monster people.

"It means things change," said Aaslo as he tried to think of another spell. He couldn't keep lobbing the same ones, considering none of them had succeeded in vanquishing his enemy. He had to stall. He called, "Where exactly is your home?"

Verus growled at him. "Let's not pretend you'll ever see it, *Forester*. You're going to die here today."

"I don't plan on it," said Aaslo. "Don't you know of the prophecy? Don't you know that your leader plans to destroy *all* life in this world? That includes you and your people, Verus."

Verus said, "I know who the leader is, and I know what he intends. The Deliverer of Grace, His Mighty Light Pithor is blessed by the gods. For our devotion and service, he has promised us a grand luxury in the Realm of the Afterlife."

"How can he promise such a thing?" said Aaslo.

The ground beneath Aaslo began to shake, and the horses squealed as they started to sink. Aaslo thrust his hands into the mud, sucking up the blight in the immediate area. He imagined all of the blight he had absorbed forming a sphere within his core. It built, in his mind, into a massive orb of darkness as large as a wagon. He raised his arms and executed the projectile spell he had used earlier. The massive sphere of blight struck the foreign magus's shield, causing it to disintegrate, then collided with Verus.

The foreign magus was smashed into the ground, and the blight finally began to consume him. Aaslo, Teza, and Ijen ran from their cover toward the downed magus, while Greylan, Rostus, and Peck fended off the remaining grey men.

When Aaslo reached Verus's side, the man was almost finished. Aaslo could see a bright, shining bluish thread linking the magus to Myropa, who lingered behind them. Verus met Aaslo's gaze. His breath wheezing between his bloody teeth, Verus grumbled, "You think you have won, Forester? My death is insignificant. We do not serve a leader of men. We serve the gods, and it is *their* will that the world be cleansed. Axus, God of Death, is our patron. He and his brother, God of War, have blessed this cause. You cannot win. You never could."

"Plant one seed at a time," said Aaslo. "I've defeated you, and this blight will be cured."

Verus's pained laughter was disrupted by a wheezing gurgle. "You think *I* am responsible for the blight? Something much worse awaits you. It's ironic, don't you think? The filth of this plague will rid the world of the true taint."

"What taint is that?" said Aaslo.

Verus grinned as his face turned black, and his lips and nose began to shrivel. "The corruption of *life*." The man finally succumbed to the plague brought on by his own people and shriveled into a desiccated black corpse before sinking into the bog.

"There is something *else*?" said Teza. "Whatever is causing the blight *has* to be worse. He said so."

"He's the enemy," said Aaslo. "He lies."

"At least you have some sense," said Greylan as he approached. Aaslo looked around to see that the grey creatures were all dead, and the three foreign magi had shared the same fate.

"We must get to the epicenter," said Aaslo. "That's where we'll find whoever, or *whatever*, is spreading this plague."

Teza's gaze was far in the distance behind Aaslo. She said, "I don't think that'll be necessary. I think it's coming to us."

Aaslo turned to see something on the horizon. It was a shiny black mass that looked a bit like a tree but with tentacles that slapped the ground and squirmed in the air as it moved. With it came a haunting wail, like the noise that death might make if it were a sound. "What is it?" said Aaslo, glancing at Myra.

She shook her head. "I don't know. I've never seen such a thing. But I need to tell you something. You're not fighting human enemies, Aaslo. I mean, some of them are, but they're just the foot soldiers. Verus wasn't lying. This war really is being waged by the gods. Axus and Trostili want you to fail. I-I'm not really sure what Arayallen, Goddess of the Wilderness, wants. She seems to be helping you at the moment, but the gods are fickle."

Aaslo couldn't believe that the gods—*actual* gods—were involved. "Why are they doing this?" he said. "How can we convince them to stop?"

Myropa shook her head. "Axus gains power through death, and Trostili through war. That's all it is. Axus decided to kill everything on Aldrea to gain more power. I don't think you can change his mind."

"How do we stop it?" said Aaslo.

"I don't know. I don't think you can," said Myropa. "Even the gods' hands are tied by the prophecy. The chosen one, the one Axus and his ilk call the Lightbane, is dead." She nodded toward Ijen. "*All* of the prophets agree that *all* other lines lead to death. Axus *will* win, Aaslo. I'm sorry."

Aaslo grabbed his hair, scratching his scalp with his scales and claws in the process. He said, "You're a reaper. You take people's souls. Can you bring him back? Can you bring Mathias back?"

"No, Aaslo. I would if I could, but he's already been delivered to the Sea of Transcendence. I took him there myself. It's impossible to retrieve a soul once it's in the Sea."

"It's not so bad, brother. We'll be together."

A million thoughts surged through Aaslo's mind as he watched the black creature draw closer. Finally, he said, "It doesn't matter. Worrying over a future fire shouldn't prevent us from tending trees now. They might burn, but they might not. Prophecy or not, gods or no gods, I will tend my forest."

"You're going back to Goldenwood?"

"My forest is Aldrea."

"Are you done?" said Teza.

Aaslo turned to her. Her appearance was hostile, with her crossed arms and angry scowl. "Done what?" he said.

"Talking to phantoms," she said. "I want to know how you already know how to cast spells. It takes years at the academy to learn such things."

Aaslo glanced at Ijen, who looked at him curiously. "Magdelay taught Mathias. I was his study partner. We thought they were just weird poems and cultural traditions. I didn't know what they would do."

"Let me get this straight," she said. "The high sorceress taught you master-level spells that you've been casting without even knowing what they'll do?"

"Uh, yeah," he said.

"You could have killed us all!"

"Since when do you care about the rules?" snapped Aaslo.

"That's not fair," she shouted. "This is completely different. Our *lives* are on the line."

"Our lives are on the line, regardless," said Aaslo. "I told you to go to safety. I'll take care of this."

"Wouldn't that be *so* convenient," Teza said facetiously. "We fall back to safety while you go fight an impossible monster and get yourself killed so that we can die *after* you with no hope."

Aaslo said, "If I *do* die, Teza, that doesn't mean you have to stop fighting."

Teza thrust her nose in his face. "Yes, it does, Aaslo. *You're* the reason we're fighting. *You* are our hope." Her eyes welled with tears as she said, "If you die, I won't have any left."

Aaslo glanced at Peck and Mory, who looked at him sadly. Rostus nodded once, and Greylan scowled at him but didn't disagree. He turned to Ijen, who simply pursed his lips and tapped his book. Then he looked at Myra. She held up a cluster of shining spheres hanging from tethers on her belt. She said, "I lost my hope a long time ago. I am only glad to know you now. *That* was something I thought to be impossible."

Aaslo looked at the monster in the distance that was slowly flailing its way toward them. He looked back at Teza, who was still only inches from his face. "Okay," he said. "What do you suggest?"

She stood back, seeming more relaxed. She said, "You need to figure out what your power is."

"What do you mean? I've been casting spells," he said.

Teza glanced toward the creature on the horizon, and Aaslo followed her gaze. It was still far but closing. She then looked to Ijen expectantly. The prophet sighed and said, "Fine, I will tell you something that might help, but for the record, I really wanted nothing to do with this line of the prophecy.

"A long time ago, there were others who made a deal with the fae. Sixteen people, in fact, asked the fae for power so that they could win a different war. The fae would not give it, but they offered to *lend* it for a price. Each person's price was different, but they all received immense power. Those sixteen people became the first magi, the First Order. One died before he produced any offspring, so his power was never passed on. Most people forget about him. Two of the bloodlines were eventually killed off in the Power War that led to the formation of the council. One line ended a few decades ago from a failure to produce offspring. Only twelve were left—the twelve with which you are familiar. *Your* power will be as great as the first magi, greater than all of the present-day magi combined. *You*, Aaslo, are the seventeenth magus of the First Order—the seventeenth bloodline."

"*Me? I'm* a magus?" said Aaslo.

"Technically, you are what we call an *ancient magus*," said Ijen. "The term was coined for the first magi because, well, they were ancient. Even though you're young, your power is quite possibly equivalent to theirs."

"But, it's just temporary, right?" said Aaslo. "The power was only *lent* to me."

Ijen shook his head. "The fae are pseudo-immortal. They can be killed, in a way, but they otherwise live forever. They live for thousands, perhaps millions, of years. Their concept of time is different from ours. They don't think like us or reproduce like us. They think our offspring, our bloodline, is an extension of each of us as an individual."

"So, to them, I'm just a piece of my father?"

Ijen nodded. "Essentially. That is why the power is passed down the bloodline and why it gets watered down when we breed with seculars. It stays with us until our bloodline dies out. Then, presumably, the power returns to the original fae being. It's no time at all to them. It's just a loan."

Aaslo spied the black monster that had already closed half the distance. He said, "Okay, what does this have to do with fighting this thing that's coming toward us?"

Ijen said, "You can use the spells, although you probably don't need to. It's said the ancients could cast magic without spells. The spells were created to focus our power as each successive generation grew weaker. Anyway, even though you can cast other magic, your strongest magic would be the magic of the fae creature you encountered. Each of the fae creatures possesses a different power. So, what was the power of your benefactor?"

"I don't know," said Aaslo. "She didn't say. She just told me that it'll come to me."

Ijen tapped his book. "Interesting. Perhaps she endowed you with some intrinsic knowledge of how to use it. To the fae, it may be instinctual, like breathing or seeking food or whatever they consume."

"I'm pretty sure this one consumed meat. She seemed awfully eager to eat me," said Aaslo. "Okay, how do I access this instinctual knowledge of my new power?"

"That, I cannot say," said Ijen.

"Can't or won't?" replied Aaslo.

"Can't," said Ijen. "Believe it or not, I don't have all the answers. I never saw your encounter with the fae creature. I only saw where it happened . . . and the aftermath." The man's face paled, and he shivered.

"But you know what the power is," said Aaslo.

"Well, I know what's in the story, but in real life, I haven't discovered that yet. You will definitely be the first to figure that out."

Aaslo felt a gust of hot, moist wind and turned to see that the monster was nearly upon them. He said, "But will I figure it out in time to defeat this thing?"

"In truth," said Ijen, "I wish we had never taken this line of prophecy."

The towering monolith of oily black tendrils had finally reached them. It was less than thirty yards away, and Aaslo had learned nothing useful about his power. "Myra!" he said, distracting her from what-

ever it was she was doing near one of the bodies. He really didn't want
to think about it. He started to call her again, then realized she was
suddenly standing right in front of him. He said, "Can you tell me anything about this monstrosity or how to defeat it?"

Myra looked up at the beastly treelike mass of ick and scrunched
her face in disgust. Its tendrils spewed a powdery blackness over the
land. "I don't know," she said, "but it seems to be spreading this thing
you call the blight." She paused and then said, "Your friends will die
the moment that black powder touches them."

"That's good enough for me," said Mory. "Come on, Peck, let's go."

"What are you talking about?" said Peck as Aaslo turned toward
them. "We're going to help Aaslo."

Aaslo said, "The reaper says you'll all die if you stay. I think that,
somehow, I am unaffected by the blight—"

"That's not true," said Ijen, for once speaking without being
prompted. "It seems to be absorbing *into* you. That is not unaffected.
That is *infected*. We have no idea what it will do to you."

"Well, I'm not dying from it right now, so we'll just have to worry
about that later. In the meantime, you all need to move back."

"I'm not leaving you," said Teza.

Aaslo took her by the arms and met her concerned gaze. "I can't
figure out my powers and worry about you at the same time. Please,
go back—for *my* sake."

She set her jaw stubbornly, but he saw fear in her dark gaze. "Fine,"
she said. "But I'm going to be right over there at the edge of the marshland. You'd best be careful. I'll attach your head to that thing's body if
I must."

Aaslo cringed at the thought, and Teza joined Peck and Mory on the
walk to the edge of the marsh in the distance. Aaslo then turned to
the marquess's guards. Rostus looked anxiously toward Greylan, who
just crossed his arms and made it clear he wouldn't budge. As soon as
he did so, silvery-blue ropes of light zipped from the guardsmen toward
Myra's center. She stared at them and then looked up at Aaslo apolo-
getically.

"What are those?" he said.

She was surprised he'd seen them, since he hadn't said anything
about those from earlier. She wondered if he was beginning to connect
with his power. She said, "I think you know."

He started to warn Greylan but didn't have time. A massive ball of sooty blight collided with the muddy ground between them, casting debris and blight everywhere. Aaslo was showered with muck, and he could no longer see Greylan or Rostus. He picked himself up from the muddy pool and gazed up at the monstrosity before him. It looked like the largest tree he had ever seen except that it was dead and oozing with syrupy pestilence. Its dripping, rubbery branches and roots were the tendrils he had seen in the distance. As he gazed up at the bestial plant, it began to launch seed bombs into the surrounding mire. The giant balls, each larger than a horse, burst apart to sprout hundreds of blight-infested saplings. The saplings moved on tendril-like roots and also spewed black ash from their limbs.

The saplings from the bomb that struck nearest Aaslo surged toward him, lashing out with stinging limbs. Aaslo slashed at the limbs with his sword in one hand and hacked at their trunks with his axe held by his dragon hand. As soon as he felled one sapling, another would sprout from the next seed bomb. He knew there were thousands by that time, and he couldn't possibly fight them all. The oozing mother tree groaned as if it were laughing at him. A decaying root flew at him from the side. Aaslo didn't have time to move out of the way, nor did he have time to think of one of Magdelay's mysterious spells. He didn't have time to consider anything except that he was about to die.

Aaslo was slammed into the murky water. He felt like he was drowning once again, the same sensation he had had after his meeting with the fae creature that had blessed him with seemingly useless power. Unsure which way was up, he opened his eyes. Everywhere looked the same, a vague, ambient light casting shadows over murky rocks coated in slimy algae and moss. Branches clawed at him, and the massive tree root held him pinned to the thick mud of the bottom. He had managed to hold on to his sword and axe, so he hacked at the root with every last ounce of his breath.

When the last bubbles erupted from between his lips, he stopped. He glanced around and saw a shimmering light. It was a sinuous rope, and at the end of it was Myra, watching him sadly. The rope wasn't attached to him, though. It was tied to Greylan, who floated with sightless eyes in the murky water. Rostus wasn't far, and between and around them were others. Corpses, some well-preserved from the anoxic conditions of the bog and others turned to skeletons bearing only wisps of hair. He wondered if these were the wayward travelers or fallen battalions of whom Greylan had spoken.

Aaslo knew that at any second, he would become one of them. He and the other sad souls who had had the misfortune to enter the swamp would dwell together in this quagmire of death until all the world joined them. In that moment, he felt a kinship with them. He was almost glad for their company—just as he now realized he had been glad for Mathias's company these past months since his death. Death was inevitable, but it was not the enemy. Comfort could be found in both its solitude and the embrace of the others who had fallen before him.

With that thought, something inside him stirred. It wasn't the angry, vicious monster that had joined with him through the dragon's arm, and it wasn't a memory of spells that begged for recollection. It was something new—something ancient and powerful, something that reveled in his newfound understanding of death. He felt it grin and stretch within him; then it uncurled to fill his mind with knowledge of who it was—and it was him.

No longer eager for breath, for he had all the time in the world, Aaslo reached out and snatched Greylan by the throat. He spoke in an arcane language—one he'd never known but that came to him as if he'd spoken it all his life.

> Death binds in chain—
> I bear the key.
> Mine living reign—
> Your soul be set free.
> Protector of light,
> By power of Fate,
> I call thee to fight,
> The far Sea can wait.

CHAPTER 24

THE TETHER THAT TIED MYROPA TO GREYLAN WAS SUDDENLY RIPPED from her. It snapped toward Aaslo, then wrapped around his torso and began cinching tighter until the light began to bleed over him. His deep emerald-green eyes began to glow with the luminescence she had only seen in the fae creature and the gods. Then the black plague that had been filling Aaslo since he first fell into the swamp began to leach from his pores and slither down the tether toward Greylan's corpse. As it progressed, it ate at the power that had been the guard's path to the Sea of Transcendence. Once it finally reached his corpse, it soaked into him, sending tendrils of black hyphae sprawling beneath the skin. The hyphae crawled up his neck, which was pasty white in death, and over his face, where his eyes took on the filmy whiteness of death.

Greylan's body began to spasm. His head turned toward Aaslo, and he blinked. The thing that used to be Greylan swam toward Rostus, glancing toward Myropa as he passed. It seemed as if he could see her, despite his cloudy gaze that never settled on anything specific. Greylan grabbed Rostus and dragged him toward Aaslo. Once Aaslo had hold of the second guard, he repeated the ritual, and Rostus's corpse became as drearily animated as that of Greylan. Aaslo then dug his hands into the debris-strewn mud of the mire and released an unconscionable amount of power as he mumbled the foreign words from earlier.

> *Drakvik ji shoudvin—*
> *Houlin kyost.*
> *Kyetrieg priasa—*
> *Pondashá soriak.*
> *Comménua,*

Kwes Meleahn,
Kyfayaso brigatta,
Questissa oure mouduatapen.

Even though she knew not what he said, the words spoke to Myropa. She wanted to go to him. She wanted to accept whatever it was he had to offer. Yet, she knew she could not. Those words were not for her. They never would be. But they *were* for others—for many, many others. The ground throughout the bog began to shift and shake. The water churned with such turbidity that silt and clay rendered it opaque.

Myropa stepped to the surface to glean what was happening. The tree corpse continued to spew its vile curse across the land and into the air, where it was swept afar by air currents. Aaslo's friends, tiny specks on the horizon, must have been watching through bewitched eyes, for they mourned his loss. Teza had collapsed, and Peck and Mory tried to comfort her. Ijen, though, looked terrified, as if he were witnessing his worst nightmare and knew that even greater horrors were to come.

All across the bog, corpses began to breach the surface of the water, some with recognizable faces, others lacking heads altogether. They verged on the monstrous tree and began hacking at the root that held Aaslo with the weapons, now rusted and pitted, that they had held in death. The towering monstrosity gushed oily resin and powder all over the animated corpses, but they did not succumb to the deadly pestilence. The corpses hacked through one of the roots until it began leaking a viscous black liquid. The monstrous entity released an otherworldly shriek, its boughs crackling and whipping in every direction as the root was torn from its trunk. Finally, after what felt like an eternity even to Myropa, Aaslo rose from the water. His skin crawled with black hyphae, and his dragon arm gleamed with black and blue power that radiated from it in wisps of black smoke.

"*Saléhua shoudvin brigattsores!*"

Aaslo's army of the dead responded to his command. They converged on the tree, hacking at its trunk as it ineffectually spewed black powder over them and smacked them through the air with great swings of its tendrils. Some of the corpses battled the cadaverous saplings from the seed bombs. Others fended off flailing limbs and roots. Aaslo charged forward and sank his heavy axe into the trunk. He hacked at it and ripped away chunks with the powerful claw of his dragon arm. When he tired, he stood back and muttered a spell Myropa had seen him cast against Verus. A tangle of black vines shot through the air to dig into the notch he had created. As the notch began to split wider and ooze black sap, Aaslo commanded his monstrous soldiers to focus on the scar he had made.

With the effort of hundreds of dead soldiers and travelers, the tree began to split up the center, and black liquid poured from a bright red heartwood. Aaslo stepped forward and pulled something from his bag. Myropa moved closer so that she could see what he was doing. As his dead minions battled everything the enemy threw at him, Aaslo paused to look at her. She thought she had never seen such depth of pain, clarity, and compassion in one expression. His vivid green gaze was so mesmerizing, she nearly forgot what was happening. He opened his palm to reveal the black seed the high sorceress had given him. He looked at it fondly, then gripped it in his dragon paw and shoved it with all his might into the deepest part of the split in the tree.

Aaslo stepped back and stood there calmly as if the world weren't in chaos around him. A whiplike tree limb swept toward him, but it was intercepted by Greylan and Rostus, who hacked it to pieces without the slightest disturbance toward Aaslo. Myropa watched as a change came over the forester. The black hyphae that squirmed under his skin receded, and the black smoke that fumed from his dragon arm was replaced by a golden glow reminiscent of the gods'.

He placed his hands together in front of him, then thrust them forward, and outward. His right hand drew back, and his first two fingers came to rest on his lips, while his left arm was thrust forward, palm flat, as if imploring someone to stop. Suddenly, that hand clawed at something that wasn't there, and made a ripping motion as the other hand surged forward and upward. Aaslo whispered something unintelligible, and the dreadful tree began to shake. The trunk started to expand, and as it did, the bark split and oozed black liquid over the swamp. The splits became gaps between splinters, and new branches grew out of them. The new branches bore leaves of brilliant green, the color of Aaslo's eyes. Suddenly, the horrid black tree burst apart, sending sharp chunks of wood through the air for hundreds of yards, forcing Aaslo's friends to erect protective shields so they wouldn't be impaled.

In place of the dead monstrosity was a beautiful, living entity that twisted far into the sky. From the ground at its base, Myropa couldn't even see the top. What surprised her most was that it wasn't silent like the rest of the trees on Aldrea. It hummed, the bass loud enough to vibrate through *her* chest, which resided mostly in another realm. Then the tune changed, and it began to sing. Although Myropa could no longer *feel* its song, it brought her warmth.

Aaslo walked up to the tree and placed his hand on the trunk. The tree's song changed again. It elicited such sadness that she felt tortured by her inability to cry, to relieve the pain. Aaslo hummed back to the tree, then sang a strange tune that almost seemed familiar. The tree's tune changed, and Myropa felt hope once again. She glanced around the battlefield. With the death of the dead mother tree, the corpses were able to destroy the last of the cadaver saplings. The bodies of the risen dead, however, remained. They stood eerily still, their milky gazes staring hollowly toward Aaslo.

Aaslo withdrew his hand from the tree, checked the sack at his waist, secured his sword and axe, then began walking toward his companions. Myropa started to follow when she felt the familiar tug. It became more than a tug, and she was suddenly ripped into the realm of Celestria.

Trostili and Axus sat beside Trostili's viewing pool, while Arayallen sat on the divan petting a furry creature from which Myropa probably would have run screaming had she encountered it in the wild.

Axus slammed his fist into the stone that lined the pool, crushing it under the force. He stood and rounded on Myropa. "What happened? How did he defeat the grashtighaton?"

Myropa opened her mouth, but Trostili interrupted. "You just saw what happened, Axus."

"Yes, I saw what happened. I want to know the parts I couldn't see."

Arayallen laughed. "You did choose a *tree* to go up against a forester. It's almost as if you *wanted* him to win."

Axus scowled with fury. "I thought it would be *ironic*. My laughter would have been great if he had died by one of his beloved *trees*. What I want to know is, how did he get that power? Why are the dead rising, and why do they heed his call? How does he know that language?"

Trostili said, "We watched him make the deal with the fae."

Axus turned to him. "The fae creature possesses the power of growth, of invigoration, of reproduction and fertility."

"Well, he *did* invigorate them," said Arayallen.

Axus turned his ire on the goddess. "Ina cannot *invigorate* the dead! They are *mine*!"

Arayallen shrugged. "Then you must have blessed him."

"I did no such thing," he snapped.

Trostili said, "That's an interesting hypothesis, Arayallen." He turned toward Axus. "What game do you play now? Do you intend to make him your general?"

"No! I wanted that forester dead!" said Axus.

"He seems to carry the *power* of the dead," said Arayallen with a smirk. "Is that not good enough?"

"He's carrying *my* power, and I won't have it! He killed that idiot Verus and his team. With Obriday's team dead as well, Pithor will need new generals in the west. I'll have to bestow another blessing." He turned to Trostili. "This is *your* fault. You told me to start with Uyan."

"You forget, Axus, I'm the God of War. Do you not think I know the best strategy? The chosen one—"

"*Lightbane*," said Axus.

"—was in Uyan. Killing him guaranteed the outcome of the prophecy in your favor. Besides, Pithor is *your* chosen one, and you didn't send him to Uyan, did you? No, you did what you wanted as usual."

"Well, there is no reason to stay in Uyan now. I can start sending my forces across Aldrea, and without the magi, the humans will fall without the slightest protest."

Arayallen put the creature on the floor, then strode over to gaze into the pool. She looked up and said, "Why don't you just send a plague across the world? They'll all die quickly."

"Are you willing to give me one?" said Axus. Upon seeing Trostili's furious gaze, he said, "Never mind that. I've promised Trostili a war. It's the only way he supports my endeavor." Looking at Trostili, he said, "Did you have something to do with this loss? Is this your way of prolonging the war so that you get more power out of it?"

Trostili laughed. "I'll not deny that I'll be happy for the war to last forever, but I had nothing to do with the forester's ability to raise the dead. How could I?"

All three gods abruptly looked at Myropa. Trostili said, "You look different—a bit brighter?"

Arayallen huffed and stepped between them. She eyed Myropa as if sizing up livestock at auction. She turned back to Trostili. "Since when have you paid her enough attention to notice a difference?"

"True," he said. Then, to Myropa, he said, "Stay with the forester, and let me know if he causes any other trouble."

Myropa hadn't even gotten a word out, and she was already whipped back into the Realm of the Living.

Teza attacked Aaslo as soon as he reached them. She threw her arms around him, gripping him so tightly he thought she might be trying to strangle him.

"Aaslo, I was so scared. We couldn't see you for so long. I thought that thing had killed you."

"It might have," said Aaslo, pulling her arms from around his neck.

She said, "Where did that army come from, and why are they just standing out there like they're frozen? Who do they belong to? I can't see them well from here."

Aaslo shook his head. "We'll get to that later."

"How did you do it?" said Mory. "How did you defeat the tree monster?"

"I'm not really sure what happened," said Aaslo. "I was drowning, and then I just—*understood*. I knew my power, and I felt connected to it."

"That's wonderful!" said Teza. "You'll be able to help us—help the world. Maybe we really can stop it from dying."

Aaslo looked toward Ijen. The prophet tapped his book slowly and gazed back at Aaslo knowingly. To Teza, Aaslo said, "I'm not sure that I can. I think I made a terrible mistake." Tears welled in his eyes as he considered the horror of his newfound power. "I want to give it back. I *need* to give it back."

"You cannot," said Ijen. "It is your blessing and your curse—and that of your entire bloodline."

"How is this a blessing?" said Aaslo.

"What is it?" said Teza.

"I don't understand," said Peck. "Look at what you did!" He pointed to the tree, which looked to be as high as a mountain from where they stood. Its massive branches appeared as if they could house a city, and its green leaves shone brightly in the sun. It possessed more color and life than anything else for as far as the eye could see. Golden pollen puffed into the air, scattering and covering the blight in dazzling flecks.

Teza said, "It's gorgeous. Just listen to its song. It's so peaceful."

Aaslo shook his head. "I'm sorry. That's not the nature of my power. Yes, I was able to grow the seed, but that's—how do I explain it? It's just not who I am."

Ijen said, "I can cast a shield or knock a boulder out of the way, but I'm a prophet. It's who I am. It's what I must do. Teza can do any number of things, but her primary power is healing. It's her strongest, and it's what she needs to do to feel balanced. Aaslo is a different kind of magus."

"Well," said Mory, "what is it? What kind of power do you wield?"

Aaslo raised his arms and motioned forward. The army behind him began ambling toward them, some dropping into the murky depths to rise again on the other side of the pool. When they were about ten yards away, and Aaslo could see the horror on his friends' faces, he held up a fist for the corpses to stop. He waved two fingers, and Greylan and Rostus stepped forward, coming to stand next to him.

Aaslo said, "I raise the dead."

END OF BOOK ONE

Aaslo will return in
Shroud of Prophecy, Book Two

CAST OF CHARACTERS

Aaslina—Teza's donkey

Aaslo—forester of Goldenwood

Adne—admirer at the feast

Akirini—master of the wardrobe at the palace of Uyan

Anderlus Sefferiah—Marquess of Dovermyer

Arayallen—Goddess of the Wilderness

Arohnu—God of Prophecy

Axus—God of Death

Azeria—Goddess of Women

Balene—Magdelay's horse

Barbach—God of Desire

Baron of Yebury—accused Sir Ciruth of sneaking into his daughter's bedchamber

Bayalin—God of the Sun

Brontus—manservant at palace

Byella—healer

Caris—thief that betrayed Peck and Mory in Tyellí

Catriateza (Teza)—server in the Wooden Spoon Tavern

Sir Ciruth—shot down for drawing his sword in the throne room

Corin—little boy in audience

Dia—assistant (twin) at Silver Sky Inn in Yarding

Disevy—God of Virility

Enani—Goddess of Realms

Wizard Everly—wizard at the palace in Uyan

Fin—palace stable boy

Galobar—caretaker of the Forester's Haven

Master Gerredy—herbalist in Tyellí

Gertridina—former classmate of Teza's

Sorceror Goltry—Magdelay's greatest rival and avid supporter

Mr. Greenly—bookkeeper of Goldenwood

Greylan—personal guard for the Marquess of Dovermyer

Helania—Keeper of the Keys at the palace of Uyan

Ielo—Aaslo's father

Ijen Mascede—prophet Aaslo and Teza meet on the road

Ina—fae creature in Ruriton

Iochtheus—God of Consciousness

Jago—thieves' boss in Tyellí

Jennis—shop assistant

Jessi—young woman in Goldenwood

Kadia—Queen of Uyan

Keila—ladies' maid at Dovermyer

Lena—herbalist's assistant in Tyellí

Lopin—captain of the royal guard in Tyellí

Magdelay Brelle—Mathias's grandmother

Maralee—Galobar's deceased wife

Captain Marius Cromley—captain of the Goldenwood town guard

Mathias—young man from Goldenwood

Mia—assistant (twin) at Silver Sky Inn in Yarding

Mirana—young woman in Goldenwood

Mory—young thief from Tyellí

Wizard Motemer—a wizard at the Citadel of Magi

Myropa—reaper

Wizardess Nomina—a wizardess at the Citadel of Magi

Nova—mistress of the Silver Sky Inn in Yarding

Obriday—wizard who attacked on the road outside Goldenwood

Olios—"Worldmaker"; God of World Creation

Parshia—a historical figure from Lodenon

Peckett "Peck"—thief from Tyellí

Master Pettridge—head groundskeeper at the palace

Pithor—"Deliverer of Grace," "His Mighty Light"

Mr. Poldry—Goldenwood blacksmith

Rakith—King of Uyan

Warlock Rastiv—warlock from Mouvilan

Remmy—manservant at Dovermyer

Reyla—young woman in Goldenwood

Rostus—one of the marquess's guards

Mage Soter—healer in Yardow

Terris—palace stablemaster
Mayor Toca—mayor of Goldenwood
Trostili—God of War
Verus—stranger from a foreign land searching for Mathias
Enchantress Wenthria—Magdelay's longtime friend

PLACES

Aldrea—world
Bellbry—shire in Uyan
Byganth—planet
Cambor Mountains—mountain chain in northeastern Uyan
Celestria—realm
Copedrian—town in Pashtigon
Dempsy—village in Uyan
Efestrian Forest—forest in northern Uyan
Endric Ocean—ocean on southern border of Uyan
Fernvalle—village in Uyan
Fifth Palace—palace in Celestria
Forester's Haven—place of refuge for foresters
Lodenon—country
Mierwyl—town in Uyan
Mouvilan—country
Myrellis—another world
Pashtigon—kingdom to the east of Uyan
Poupilon—another world
Ruriton—country
Sea of Transcendence—pool of souls
Teguei—planet
Tisiguey River—river in eastern Uyan near Yarding
Tyellí—capital
Uyan—country
Yarding—large trading city in eastern Uyan

GLOSSARY

carrackac hats—a type of hat common to Siderian culture

dowdry branches—faint purple lines on the neck and hairline associated with selkesh fever

fiergolen tree—a tree native to the Efestrian Forest that explodes when ignited

fledgling—a student magus

Grave War—massive war in the past

incendia—a leader in the Army of the Deliverer

lellisa—tree with red leaves and pink blossoms

magi—general term (plural) for people who wield magic

magus—general term (singular) for people who wield magic

marmuck root—energizing root used by magi

seculars—people without magic

selkesh fever—an illness that only affects magi

vight—a demon servant of Axus

wanderer—one of the dead

NOTE FROM THE AUTHOR

I hope you enjoyed reading this first book in the Shroud of Prophecy series. Please consider leaving a review or comments so that I can continue to improve and expand upon this ongoing series. Look for Shroud of Prophecy Book Two in 2020!

ABOUT THE AUTHOR

KEL KADE lives in Texas and occasionally serves as an adjunct col-
lege faculty member, inspiring young minds and introducing them to
the fascinating and very real world of geosciences. Thanks to Kade's
enthusiastic readers and the success of the King's Dark Tidings series,
Kade is now able to create universes spanning space and time, develop
criminal empires, plot the downfall of tyrannous rulers, and dive into
fantastical mysteries full-time.

Growing up, Kade lived a military lifestyle of traveling to and living
in new places. These experiences with distinctive cultures and geogra-
phy instilled in Kade a sense of wanderlust and opened a young mind
to the knowledge that the Earth is expansive and wild. A deep interest
in science, ancient history, cultural anthropology, art, music, languages,
and spirituality is evidenced by the diversity and richness of the
places and cultures depicted in Kade's writing.